JEWELWEED

Also by David Rhodes

Driftless
The Easter House
The Last Fair Deal Going Down
Rock Island Line

JEWELWEED

A NOVEL

David Rhodes

milkweed
editions

© 2013, Text by David Rhodes
All rights reserved. Except for brief quotations in critical articles or reviews, no part of this book may be reproduced in any manner without prior written permission from the publisher: Milkweed Editions, 1011 Washington Avenue South, Suite 300, Minneapolis, Minnesota 55415.
(800) 520-6455
www.milkweed.org

Published 2013 by Milkweed Editions
Printed in Canada
Cover design by Christian Fuenfhausen
Cover photos © Shutterstock
Author photo by Edna Rhodes
13 14 15 16 17   5 4 3 2 1
First Edition

Milkweed Editions, an independent nonprofit publisher, gratefully acknowledges sustaining support from the Bush Foundation; the Patrick and Aimee Butler Foundation; the Dougherty Family Foundation; the Jerome Foundation; the Lindquist & Vennum Foundation; the McKnight Foundation; the voters of Minnesota through a Minnesota State Arts Board Operating Support grant, thanks to a legislative appropriation from the arts and cultural heritage fund; the National Endowment for the Arts; the Target Foundation; and other generous contributions from foundations, corporations, and individuals. For a full listing of Milkweed Editions supporters, please visit www.milkweed.org.

Library of Congress Cataloging-in-Publication Data

Rhodes, David, 1946-
    Jewelweed : a novel / David Rhodes. — 1st ed.
      p.   cm.
    ISBN 978-1-57131-100-9 (hardcover : acid-free paper) — ISBN 978-1-57131-106-1
(pbk. : acid-free paper) — ISBN 978-1-57131-883-1 (ebook)
    I. Title.
    PS3568.H55J49 2013
    813'.54—dc23

                                    2012027827

Milkweed Editions is committed to ecological stewardship. We strive to align our book production practices with this principle, and to reduce the impact of our operations in the environment. We are a member of the Green Press Initiative, a nonprofit coalition of publishers, manufacturers, and authors working to protect the world's endangered forests and conserve natural resources. *Jewelweed* was printed on acid-free 100% postconsumer-waste paper by Friesens Corporation.

To my daughters, Alexandra and Emily,
the two lights in the front of my boat.

*When the New Age is at leisure to Pronounce; all will be set right . . .
& the Daughters of Memory shall become the Daughters of Inspiration.*

—William Blake, *Milton: A Poem*

Contents

JEWELWEED

The Taste of Joy

A blinding thunderstorm in central Nebraska thinned traffic along Interstate 80. A few semis moved through the downpour, their dimmed headlights reflecting from the watery road. Rain blew against trailer sides and black wiper blades whipped frantically across windshields, accompanied by the sound of water thrown from tires against wheel wells and the undersides of trailers. In the sky, crackling networks of energy ignited air bombs, exploding the dark open space with brief crinkled light.

Nate Bookchester needed to reach Omaha before daylight. After unloading he'd continue to Des Moines, then on to Moline. Never taking his eyes from the barely visible line between the road surface and the more darkly colored shoulder, he steered the hood of the Kenworth into the storm. Passing time seemed shadowy, suspended in the glow of fog lights.

The rain finally let up, and the CD player in the dashboard ended its story—an audiobook checked out of the Grange Library. He dialed down the speed of the wiper blades. A few wrinkled lines of lightning lit the sky, and the opened space seemed clean and bright. A cowboy with Colorado plates sped by on the left, spraying water, winking top lights, and pulling back into the right-hand lane. Red taillights bled in and out of veins of rainwater. Nate listened for several minutes to drivers jawing about the government, then turned the radio off, shut down the interior lights, and drove on in the dark. A highway patrol car sat in the median turnaround between the eastbound and westbound lanes, red and blue warning lights silently flashing.

Nate's son would soon have a parole hearing, and the thought made the muscles in Nate's neck tighten. This would be Blake's third review, and based on the earlier two, Nate was pessimistic about his chances of getting out. The justice system seemed to resist letting anyone go after it had gotten hold of them. Or at least it seemed that way to Nate. Prisons were made like fishhooks: easy to get in, hard to get out. Without prisoners there would be no need for prisons, and a whole lot of folks—some of them very well paid—would be out of work. So before paroling anyone, the Department of Corrections set up hoops to jump through, and Blake had never been a cooperative jumper.

Nate took the last Omaha exit, stopped at a deserted stoplight on the overpass, and headed north. His worries about Blake had become so familiar that he often did not allow the habitual thoughts to begin their circular march through his mind, refused to let the words congeal, and simply endured the anxious sorrow without accompaniment.

Three loading docks stood empty at the back of the Omaha warehouse; Nate backed into the middle one. The overhead opened and a buzzer sounded as the trailer touched rail. He climbed out of the cab into a warm, drizzling mist. Inside the building, he signed the bottom sheet on the clipboard, unclasped the door irons, and stood aside as the forklift operator navigated inside, guiding the long iron prongs under the pallets.

The bathrooms on the other side of the building were in exceptionally good order. Nate washed, shaved, and changed clothes. He tried to leave the room as clean as he'd found it and shoved his dirty clothes into a bag. Just outside, the candy machine along the wall had cluster bars. He almost bought one, but settled for a paper cup of weak coffee.

After the trailer was unloaded, he asked the operator where he could find a decent place to eat.

"Heading east, not many open this early. If you don't mind driving, there's one maybe five, six miles out of town."

"What's the name?"

"Margo's. It doesn't look like much, but they've got good food."

The sun was just coming up and Nate drove directly into it, ignoring the lower gears and shifting quickly through the upper ones. Designed to pull between sixty and eighty thousand pounds, the diesel hardly worked enough to keep the radiator warm with an empty trailer, and the sides rattled and banged over the road.

Nate found the restaurant painted robin's-egg blue and sitting on the edge of a cornfield, next to an elevator and a grain dryer. He pulled into the mostly deserted lot and climbed out of the cab. As his right foot touched the tarmac and his leg absorbed all of his two hundred pounds, his whole body winced. Circling the tractor several times until he could walk with more dignity, he noticed again that the pavement was dry. This part of the country had not seen any weather at all.

I'm old too soon, he thought.

Inside the small building, an old woman with a pencil poking out of her hair sat near the cash register reading from a newspaper, and a young man in coveralls—maybe a mechanic or a janitor—drank from a thick white mug at the counter. There were four large tables, all empty, and two smaller ones by the front windows. Nate sat at the counter, three stools away from the young man in coveralls. The woman came over and with a wrinkled smile held out a menu. The warmth in her tired eyes seemed genuine, and Nate was grateful for it.

"What's this Breakfast Pie?" he asked.

"Oh, you'll like that," she said. "It's the same as the Dinner Pie—only with two eggs."

"I'll take it."

"Coffee?"

"Do you have hot chocolate?"

"Of course."

"I'll have one."

Nate looked around the little restaurant and could find nothing to fasten his attention to. He tried harder, failed, and the muscles in his neck tightened like knots along a new rope.

Blake was in prison. Over ten years, the last three in that Lockbridge hellhole. They called it a supermax. Couldn't stay out of trouble in the Waupun prison. Said it wasn't his fault. Never is, never was. After his mother left, nothing could be done. She had a way with him and took it with her when she ran off. Blake was only four then. He was a good kid, just impulsive, easily tempted, more easily hurt. Everything was personal, it seemed. As a boy, he brought injured animals home and tried to restore them to health; if he failed he would tear apart his room, a favorite shirt, or something else he cared about. He always made friends with kids who didn't have other friends; later, they were the ones who invariably got into trouble, and out of loyalty he wouldn't give them up. He was good at sports, nice looking, smart enough to get by without trying hard. Loved taking physical risks, but overly timid in other areas. He couldn't just let things happen. When someone pushed him—even if they didn't mean to—he pushed back too hard. And if he was walking next to someone else who got pushed, he pushed back for them. He riled easily, Nate thought, because he was always struggling with the shame of his mother running off, always staring at the door his mother had closed in his mind. And in school, of course, shame was unavoidable. Children were reminded of their place. Older kids picked on younger kids. Lectures in front of class, stand up, sit down, wait here, go there, stay after school, do extra homework, call your parents, tell them to come get you. Blake was in trouble all the time.

And now Blake didn't want Nate to visit him in prison anymore. He said it was humiliating for them both. After coming to see him for over ten years, the only way to talk to him was through letters.

Blake had been in prison so long that when Nate remembered him he pictured him as an infant.

"Careful," the waitress said, setting the cup of hot chocolate in front of him. "It comes hot out of the machine."

Nate sipped the foamy liquid and set it aside. It was too hot.

After high school Blake moved to Red Plain, and after several years there he began running around with that Workhouse girl. She was trouble. Dart, they called her, a bad sign. Bad family. Cute as a brown button, but if Blake had just stayed away from her he wouldn't be in prison now. She was the reason. He was unprepared for anyone like her. Her own father had been in prison for beating her mother; after he died, same story with the stepfather. Drug addicts, both of them. Dart's sister had committed suicide. Bottom-feeders, the whole lot.

Blake and Dart lived together in a hole-in-the-wall too small to turn around in. She was his first. He worked at the foundry, made fair money; she worked in the cement plant. Blake raced motorcycles and she came to watch. She was always with him. He was red-wild about her and defended her even when he didn't need to. He started arguments over nothing, turned the smallest things into big things, and imagined he was being tested by God. Talking to him was like trying to walk through wild blackberry vines without getting stuck. Then he got busted for selling drugs and it was her fault. They called it trafficking.

Nate was rubbing the back of his neck when his Breakfast Pie arrived in a deep blue ceramic dish. Curling blades of steam rose from cracks in the top. He poked his fork in, pried open a piece of crust, and released an eruption of scalding air.

Was everything in this place too hot?

Freeing a small piece from the dish, he held it in midair, watched steam curl around the fork, and slid it between his teeth. Anticipating the heat, he didn't close his lower jaw until his tongue informed him of an acceptable temperature. The taste moved into the corners of his mouth and his feature-detectors identified separate flavors: the crust, as he suspected, was mostly seasoned bread crumbs and mild white cheddar; the mashed-potato base held vegetables and ham, the binding savor owing most of its character to marjoram and thyme.

On the edge of Nate's consciousness a cheerful nostalgia began conversing with the new taste about establishing residency. The rumors of merriment drove out the former resident, worry, leaving in its place lighter, almost-buoyant thoughts.

He took a drink of cocoa. All too soon, the cheerful nostalgia faded, and the former resident moved back in.

He ate another forkful. Chopped scallions, sharp cheddar cheese, peppers, and diced tomato were added to the list of identifiable ingredients. He was now in egg territory, and the yolk formed a mutual partnership with marjoram. His mouth became saturated with the taste.

Once again, a pleasant mood settled inside him.

After another bite the restaurant seemed a friendly, almost-familiar place. His thoughts seemed to glow, as if blushing from inner contentment.

Such easily won peace rarely visited Nate, and he tried to prolong it, draw it out, attach it to more-permanent things so it would linger. The knots in his neck loosened as though unseen fingers had solved the mystery of physical stress and freed him from its grip. His breathing came easily. His shoulders, elbows, wrists, and fingers moved in a painless fluid manner.

The Breakfast Pie was nearly gone.

"More hot chocolate?" asked the old woman.

"Nope," said Nate, and grinned as if she were an old friend.

"How's the pie?"

"First-rate," he said.

"Good," she said, and the lines around her eyes narrowed into tributaries leading through the rest of her face. In response, Nate's face expanded its welcome further. He knew her, it seemed. Morning light beamed through the front windows in broad bold shafts, and he took a deep breath. Memories of his childhood opened in his mind and he pored over them, looking for some explanation of how the taste had acquired such appealing and vigorous associations.

Not wanting to leave, he ordered a cup of coffee. He slowly sipped the hot liquid to the bottom of the white mug, though it had neither the strength nor the character he desired in coffee. He knew a man in Missouri who roasted his own beans, and even the thought of returning there and buying some filled Nate with an unexpected and delighted expectancy.

He checked the clock on the wall, left a tip, and paid for the meal at the register.

In the lot, he walked around the truck several times, inspecting the tires for loose treads. There was a drip line on the asphalt where the last of the Nebraska rainwater had run down the sides of the trailer. The geometric straightness of the water-mark seemed extraordinary. He climbed into the cab, pulled the door closed, and relaxed for several more minutes inside the fading remnant of the taste. His hand moved to start the engine, changed its mind, and he climbed down to the asphalt, remembering to let his weight onto his left leg.

Inside the restaurant, he reseated himself at the counter, smiled self-consciously at the waitress, and ordered another Breakfast Pie. She scribbled several words onto her pad and carried it back to the cook. When she returned, her glance lingered on Nate longer than usual, and he explained, "The taste reminded me of something I can't quite remember. It must be from my childhood."

Listening in, the young man in coveralls said, "You should rinse out your mouth with something. That way the next taste of it will be fresh. The first taste counts the most."

Nate remembered that twenty or thirty years ago people in small restaurants, taverns, and grocery stores thought nothing of making a stranger's business their own. If you wandered into their area you were open game. That didn't happen much anymore, at least not near major highways. People usually kept to themselves now, hid behind their clothes and faces.

"Maybe it's something he shouldn't remember," said the woman.

"Don't think so," said the man in coveralls, who appeared to be about Blake's age. "He wants another one."

Nate grimaced self-consciously.

"I know, drink some whiskey first," the young man said. "Clear your taste buds."

"We don't have a liquor license," said the woman. "But we might have some cooking wine in back. Would that work?"

"Lemon sherbet would be better," said Nate.

The woman went back into the kitchen and returned with the cook—a thin leathery man wearing a brown apron over a clean white shirt and black denim pants. Nate thought he looked as if he might be married to the woman, or if he wasn't, should be. He set a small dish of lemon sherbet on the counter.

"Swallow it slow," he said in a suggestive way.

Nate did.

"Is it working?" asked the cook.

"I think so."

"What did you drink with your meals as a child?" asked the woman. "It could make a difference."

"The folks gave us milk. I didn't like it and neither did my sister, but the folks thought it was good for us."

"You'd better have a glass of milk, then."

"Did your parents drink milk?" asked the cook.

"No. They just wanted us to."

"My parents were the same way."

"Where you from?" asked the young man.

"Southwest Wisconsin," said Nate.

"The Ocooch?"

"Right in the middle of it," said Nate. "You been there?"

"Used to have family there. It's a unique area. Hill country with a lot of open timber, different from everything else around it. Good fly fishing. They call it the Driftless Region."

"I think I can smell it," said the waitress.

"I'll see if the pie's ready," said the cook.

"It's not that important," said Nate, embarrassed about the attention.

"There aren't many good feelings left in this world," said the young man.

"He's right," said the woman. "We don't want the good Lord to think we're not paying attention."

"Here we are," said the cook, carrying a steaming red dish. He set it in front of Nate.

"Wait," said the old woman, "let me get you that glass of milk."

Nate picked up a fork. The other three moved away, as if to allow more privacy to maneuver around in his remembrances.

Nate took a bite, waited as his tongue explored the texture. And then, at the place where the marjoram announced its distinctive presence, he drank from the glass of milk.

Triumph glowed in his face.

"I have it," he said, setting down the fork.

"Tell us," said the young man, and they came in closer.

"I saw this spot of yellow-gold light and it led me to a shade of green. The colors came together and then I could see a pattern. It was the carpet in my grandparents' house in Slippery Slopes, Wisconsin—in the room just before you stepped into the kitchen. But that's not the memory. It's just related to it."

"What is it?"

"Beulah."

"That's an old-fashioned name. Who is she?"

"My cousin, Beulah Pinebrook. We called her Bee. Sometimes when the folks would go out at night Bee would come over and stay with my sister and me. She often brought a meat pie with her, made with mashed potatoes and sharp cheddar cheese, the way our grandmother always made them. If she didn't bring one, she'd make it. They tasted something like this."

"It's an old recipe," said the cook.

"I thought the world of her. She was four years older than me. After we ate, she'd turn off the television and tune in one of those old radio programs, the ones with dark voices and easy-to-imagine stories. Radio dramas, she called them. My sister and I would turn out all the lights and sometimes I'd sit so close to Bee I could smell her. I was never as happy as when I was with her. And I never understood this before now, but that's the reason I listen to audiobooks in the truck."

"Where is she now?"

"She lives in Red Plain, I think, ever since her mother's stroke. At least that's what I heard."

"How long since you've seen her?"

"Twenty years, probably more."

"You haven't seen your cousin in twenty years?"

"No, I haven't."

"Families are what we have to fall back on in hard times," said the woman.

"Some, maybe," said Nate. "My family was the kind you fell away from."

"You've got to go see her," said the cook. "That's what this means."

"Of course," said the young man. "You must go see her."

At that moment the front door opened and four people came in and sat down at one of the tables.

Nate left money on the counter and returned to his truck.

Inside the cab, he started the diesel and thought about Bee. Though his recollections of her were shamefully dated, their vitality remained astonishingly vigorous. He could picture her standing before him, and his heart beat with enthusiasm. Among his other memories, she stood out like a single red flag in a yard of drying army blankets.

There was a bang on the cab door and Nate opened it. Below, standing on the asphalt in her white and gray uniform, the old woman looked up at him.

"Did I forget something?" he asked.

"No," she said, and turned away from him several degrees. "I probably shouldn't say this, but I don't think you should look for your cousin Beulah."

"Why not?"

"Leave the past alone."

Opportunities

Cripes, still in the fifth grade.

Ivan couldn't get over it, no matter how many times he tried. The shame burrowed into him from wherever he looked, from inside every thought. It was true and nothing could change it. They'd kept him back. Everyone agreed—his teacher, Mrs. Beamchamp the guidance counselor, Ms. Spindle, and the director of special education. "Hold him back," they all said, as if they wanted to grab his shoulders and waist to keep him from running off.

Of course they had their reasons. And they explained them before the Grange School Board, after his mother's repeated demands for what she called a "fair trial."

"Ivan doesn't know his numbers."

"He can't spell."

"He's incapable of following the simplest directions."

"This was a probationary year for Ivan because he failed to meet the performance and proficiency standards as determined by the state at the end of fourth grade."

"His test scores barely reach the bottom lip of the bell curve."

"Oh sure, he has adequate language dexterity, but those skills don't outweigh his impaired abilities."

"He has delayed social functioning and immature decision-making."

"He can't concentrate or sit still."

"Ivan has no apparent aptitude for conceptualizing integers or manipulating numerical tokens of quantity."

"He's unsuited for the more demanding curriculum of sixth grade."

"He doesn't try."

His mother stood her ground. A defiant stare burned from beneath her Brewers baseball hat, and at the bottom of her faded jeans her feet were planted inside new white running shoes, fished out of the bargain bin the day before. She folded her arms in front of her and from time to time tugged on the bill of her hat—a quick, nervous movement that seemed to Ivan as if she were batting away the words being thrown from the authorities sitting behind the tables.

As far as Ivan was concerned, she was the fiercest defender anyone could ever hope for. If the enemy hadn't outnumbered her ten to one she surely would have prevailed. She cut through even the most tightly bunched arguments with comments like "He isn't like that at home. So how come he acts like that here? Whose fault is that?"

"Those records don't prove anything."

"He's as smart as all get out when he's interested in something."

"Is passing out tests all you people do? I thought you were supposed to actually teach something here."

"You're wrong about that."

"I don't believe it."

"You're lying."

As the night wore on and the slippery yellow files of evidence mounted into a pile, a few stray ends of her curly black hair came jutting out through the metal eyelets in her hat, like burned tufts of grass through holes in concrete. It seemed like a bad sign to Ivan, and he got a sick feeling. At around seven thirty, just as the light began to die in the windows in the conference room, she lost her temper and called Mrs. Beamchamp a rotten excuse for a woman and said Ms. Spindle didn't have sense enough to come in out of the rain. Then she threatened to hit the director of special education if he didn't stop looking at look at her the way he was.

Ivan thought he should have warned her. It never paid to get excited in school. The whole place was crouched down and ready to pounce on the slightest twitch of real feeling. Anyone who smuggled the tiniest smidgen of emotion into those airless halls had better beware. There was no limit to the forces that could be set loose on someone who didn't talk quietly, stand still in line, and wear the fake smile demanded inside that building.

Frankly, Ivan was a little alarmed she didn't understand that. She must have gone to school herself, and how could you possibly ever forget? They practically beat you to death with boredom; he couldn't imagine anyone ever getting over it.

But there were many mysteries about his mother's past that he hadn't solved yet.

After her outburst, all Mrs. Beamchamp had to do was put the files down on the table and cast a long sad look from his mother to the committee, making it clear that a vote for passing Danielle Workhouse's son into the sixth grade was a vote for parent terrorism.

"We approve the decision to hold him back," said the head of the school board.

Riding home in their Bronco, his mother gripped the steering wheel with white knuckles and explained in a worried voice that Ivan shouldn't worry. Everything would turn out all right. Plenty of successful people had repeated fifth grade and many others would have been successful if they had only had the opportunity to repeat fifth grade. Abraham Lincoln, she was pretty sure, had repeated fifth grade, following in the honored footsteps of Benjamin Franklin and Saint Paul. All of them had repeated fifth grade and gone on to marry attractive women, own fancy houses, and earn the respect of all their neighbors. Besides, she pointed out, Ivan was a little small for his age, and this would give him a chance to catch up.

Unfortunately, this seemed a lot like the problems he always had with math. How was he supposed to catch up to the size of others when they kept growing too? As soon as he got to where they were now, they'd be bigger. Shouldn't he go ahead in size instead of being held back? Wasn't that what had gone wrong with his size in the first place? The whole thing seemed a lot like second-grade subtraction.

"See, Ivan, here, look at the board, look: you have twelve and you take away three," Mrs. Wallington would say.

"Take three away where?"

"It doesn't matter. You just take three away. Look up at the board here, Ivan. Look up here. You start out with twelve, and—"

"Twelve what?"

"It doesn't matter, Ivan. Twelve anything."

"Could it be twelve cats?"

"Yes, twelve cats. Then you take three away. Look at the board."

"How do I do that?"

"We subtract. This is called subtraction, Ivan."

"How do you take away three cats? Where do you put them? Who's going to feed them?"

"It doesn't matter where you put them. You just take them away. Ivan, look here, look up at the board. We start with twelve."

"Who starts with twelve cats? That's a lot of cats."

"The problem starts with twelve."

"Where'd they come from?"

His mother went on to explain how repeating fifth grade would teach him patience, and because of it he would be offered many important opportunities for achievement. People would trust him because they would see he would not run off before the job was finished. When he got bigger, everyone would see how much he had to offer—all because he had repeated fifth grade. He would become a great man.

"Was my father small?" he asked. "I mean, was he small like me?"

His mother was silent as she leafed through her memory and measured the height of his father. "No," she said.

"Then why am I small?"

"You get it from your father's mother, your paternal grandmother."

"Is she small?"

"She was."

"Is she small now?"

"No, she died."

"Did they die together?"

"No."

"How did my father die?"

"I already told you, Ivan."

"You said he died in a car accident, but you also said he died in the hospital."

"He was in an accident, and he died later in a hospital."

"How did he get to the hospital? Did he walk? What happened to the car?"

"I told you, Ivan, it's just you and me now. We're together, we'll always be together, and that's all that matters. Just forget about your father."

"You can't forget someone you never met."

"Stop thinking about him."

"Trying to stop thinking about him just makes me think about him even more."

"Stop it."

"But I don't see why you can't just—"

"I said stop it and I mean it." She gripped the steering wheel in a way that began to worry Ivan.

"It's not fair that—"

"There are many things in this world that aren't fair, Ivan. And I know one young man who is about to get the whipping of his life if he doesn't respect his mother enough to do as he's told."

Ivan looked out the window then and thought about his friend August, who was probably the only good thing about repeating fifth grade. Now they'd be together all the time.

August was a little different, Ivan knew. There was no doubt about that. He was a lot different, really. He thought things and did things and said things that no one else would, like the time he said, "You know, Ivan, your mother is unnaturally quick to violence."

It was because August was homeschooled before coming to Grange Elementary, and his mother mostly taught him from religious books on account of her being the pastor for the Words Friends of Jesus Church. August said she never wanted him to go to a public school at all until he began spending so much time alone, roaming through the woods and fields around their house. Then, after August got a pet bat and named him Milton and started talking to him, his parents began whispering after they thought he was asleep. His father said it didn't matter if August was a little different from other people. But his mother wasn't so sure. She said if he got any more comfortable out of doors he'd never be comfortable in human society. She feared he'd have trouble when he got older—turn out too much like she was. Anyway, his mother won the whispering contest and they put August in Grange Elementary so he could be around kids like Ivan and learn to be normal.

They were best friends. August and Ivan didn't get along very well with most other people, but together they got along fine. For the same reason most other kids didn't like August, Ivan liked him and he liked Ivan. August's mom once said they were good company because they understood each other, but Ivan didn't think that was right enough. There was a difference between understanding and liking, and liking was bigger.

"Look, Ivan, I've got to make a quick visit up here," said his mother, turning down a long rutted drive. Because of the bumping, several balled-up candy bar wrappers and a bent plastic straw jiggled over to the rust hole in the floor and fell through. At the end of the drive was a shack with a tin roof on one side and some regular shingles on the other. "This won't take long. After I come back we can go home and I'll fix you something to eat."

"Okay," Ivan said, and watched as the rottweiler living in the abandoned automobile in the front yard came over, barking. His mother took off her baseball cap and arranged her black hair with her hands while looking in the rearview mirror. Then she found her name pin inside the bag of cleaning supplies and stuck it to her shirt. She stepped outside, ignored the dog as if it had no teeth, threw the bag over her shoulder, and walked to the front door.

Ivan had done a lot of waiting in the truck while his mother visited. About a year ago she started working for Ace Cleaning. She cleaned people's homes and did other jobs. Some people simply hired Ace to clean while they were at work, but others called when they got sick or needed help of some kind.

The rottweiler went back to the abandoned car, but before climbing through the back door it noticed Ivan in the Bronco. It came over and started barking again until the window fogged up on the outside. Ivan felt empty inside, as if the dog knew he'd flunked fifth grade. He almost started crying, but instead he made his hands into fists and squeezed until they hurt. Then the anger came and he felt a bit better.

When his mother walked out of the house, she guided a bent-over woman with her robe dragging on the ground. They wobbled all the way to the truck and opened the door.

"Ivan, scoot over. We're taking Mrs. Goodenow to the hospital. I think she has a urinary tract infection. There now, in we go."

The old lady mumbled something in an unknown language.

"Yes, dear, we have your things, don't worry," said his mother. "Here, let's keep your legs wrapped up. There, that's better."

The truck filled with oldness and Ivan sat as far away from it as he could get without becoming part of his mother.

At the entrance to the three-story brick hospital in Grange, he again stayed in the truck and watched as his mother wobbled Mrs. Goodenow through the doors. Inside the glove compartment was a roll of Life Savers with only three or four missing. He peeled back the paper and pulled off the top one. Cherry. The taste reminded him of one time when August and he had gone to see a movie. August said to keep it secret because he didn't want his mom to know on account of some swearing in the movie. In the lobby they looked at the candy inside the glass case and that's when Ivan found out they made packages of all-cherry Life Savers.

A while later the doors to the front of the hospital opened again and his mother stood in the opening and shouted something he couldn't quite hear. Then she went back inside to shout some more, and finally came back to the truck.

"Those idiots wanted to send her home," she said, turning the key and stomping on the gas pedal. "Can you believe that, Ivan? An eighty-six-year-old woman who lives alone and can't drive and can hardly see and they wanted to send her home with a temperature of a hundred and three. Someone ought to shoot those worthless fools in the head."

By the time they got home it had started to rain and water from the downspout around the corner ran across the sidewalk in front of the meat locker. They splashed through. Inside their apartment the roof leaked in the corner of the kitchen, where it had before. His mother got the pail to catch the drips and put in a piece of wood so the splashing wasn't so loud.

They ate carrots and macaroni and cheese. Then his mother fixed him a cup of hot chocolate while she drank her coffee. He had the last half of an ice cream sandwich before brushing his teeth and going to bed.

After Ivan lay down he listened to the dripping in the other room and cars pulling in and out of the parking lot behind Smokey's. That lonely crying feeling got inside him again and he stayed still and just hated school for a while. Then he could hear his mother cleaning up, and each time she walked past the doorway her shadow streaked all the way to the wall. She went toward her bed and all the lights went out except the bathroom glimmer. Then the glimmer went out and orange from the lamp beside her bed came into the kitchen. She was under the covers, probably reading her catalogs, he thought.

His mother had catalogs—stacks of them—with pictures of houses and rooms with furniture, clothes, kitchen utensils, automobiles, shoes, curtains, bedspreads, jewelry, watches, televisions, cameras, computers, camping equipment, snowmobiles, books, magazines, fans, coats, garages, lawn ornaments, flower seeds, mirrors, and framed pictures to hang on walls. As soon as they paid off the money borrowed to buy the Bronco, she always said, they'd start getting some of the things other people had.

"When we get our own place we're going to have folks over and entertain," she said.

Ivan tried to imagine who those folks might be, because no one ever came to their apartment except his grandmother, and she almost never came. She and his mother couldn't talk about anything without shouting at each other. Grandma would cry, say she did the best she could, and leave. Then later she would call back and they would shout at each other over the phone.

In the morning they ate cold cereal. His mother poured all the remaining milk in Ivan's bowl. She said she didn't want any anyway.

Because it was Saturday they had to go into Ace Cleaning to hand in reports. It was not far away, so they walked. The sidewalk and roads were still wet with soaked trash along the curb. Everything had a watery smell.

Inside the building Ivan sat on one of the chairs Ace kept for visitors, next to the hoses. His mother told him to keep his hands to himself and then she went and talked with her supervisor, Mrs. Borkel, behind the counter. The two of them didn't seem to belong together, his mother as hard and brown as a Slim Jim and Mrs. Borkel all blotched and bulging like an uncooked bratwurst. She was upset his mother had not called the office before driving Mrs. Goodenow to the hospital. It was not proper procedure, she said.

"Dart, you can be an efficient and competent worker, but you must pay attention to the rules. You were written up for something like this a month ago, and it's a black mark in your file."

His mother tugged at her cap. Ivan was afraid she was going to say something, but she kept quiet.

People who had known his mother a long time, including Grandma, often called her Dart instead of Danielle. She was apparently such a different person before he was born that she'd even had a different name.

Mrs. Borkel slid some papers across the counter and his mother read them without looking up.

"Something like this doesn't come along often," Mrs. Borkel said. "It's a chance for you. You've had a rocky beginning, but if you work hard even you can make something of yourself. Do you know the Roebucks?"

"I know who they are," said his mother.

"Good, then you know what it would mean to work for them. They're looking for a live-in to cook and clean and help the nurses take care of their son. As you'll see in the evaluation forms, managing Kevin falls within some of the training you received last year. The position doesn't start until summer, but I want you to consider it. This could be good for you and Ivan. Roebuck Construction employs many people, and succeeding at this job would mean a great deal to your future with Ace."

His mother stared into the papers on the counter. "Would I be working for Ace or for Buck and Amy?" she asked.

"You'd be working for Ace, but you'd be living at the Roebucks' twenty-four-seven. Like I said, you don't need to decide right now, Dart, but how does this opportunity sound to you?"

"I'll think about it."

"You'll need to make a formal application and go over for an interview. I'd suggest doing it this week. I mean, I'm looking out for you here, Dart. I'm trying, but there are also others to consider."

"Thank you, Mrs. Borkel."

His mother adjusted her baseball cap, and Ivan stood up and stepped toward the door.

"Dart," said Mrs. Borkel, "did you hear that Blake Bookchester is up for parole?"

"Who says?" asked his mother without turning around.

"Blake's father said if he can find a sponsor they'll release him from prison."

"That has nothing to do with me," said his mother, and they walked out.

Evolution

Buck Roebuck lived four miles from town with his wife, Amy, their fourteen-year-old son, Kevin, Buck's father, and Amy's grandmother. Behind their three-story home, a pond lay wide and deep. A dock made of wood planking extended over the water to a painted gazebo. Nearby, a tethered boat floated, its oars slanting out of the oar-locks like the back legs of a cricket. Though the surface of the water seemed as smooth as glass in the dim morning light, an unseen current beat one of the oar-shafts against the side of the boat in a slow, hollow drumming.

Buck paid little attention to the hypnotic noise or the extraordinary tranquility of the morning. There was a creature living in the pond that he needed to get rid of, and for this reason he was pacing back and forth along the dock, waiting for the conservation agent from the Wisconsin Department of Natural Resources. Wispy strands of fog clung to the water's surface, and the sound of his boots pounded through it. He didn't like it when people were late, and being an unusually large man, with thighs as big around as his wife's waist, his impatience could be understood from a long way away.

Buck had dug the pond four years ago, and a great variety of living things immediately appropriated it for their own use. Innumerable tunnels, paths, and flyways led to the water's edge, and what at one time had belonged only to his wife's vision of the future now belonged to more creatures than anyone could fully fathom. At least eight kinds of fish now thrived somewhere beneath the surface. Buck had caught a three-pound bass himself, and no one would ever call him a fisherman; with a construction company to run, he simply didn't have the time.

His seventy-eight-year-old father, Wallace, had once caught an enormous orange carp, and no one would call Wally a fisherman either.

Since no one had stocked the pond, Buck sometimes wondered how the fish arrived there. Did the feeder-spring connect to a larger body of water? And could full-grown watery creatures actually move through the underground passage like refugees from another world? Frankly, Buck didn't really care, but thinking about the astonishing fecundity of the pond sometimes gave him a fleeting pleasure. Nature had apparently focused its green eye upon it.

It had been his wife's idea to turn the swampy ground behind their house into a pond. Amy said their son, Kevin, would find reason to leave the confinement of his room. It would encourage him to rise above the disabilities that usually prevented his participation in outdoor activities. So Buck agreed to complete it.

Problems had mounted quickly. Before issuing a permit, the DNR required a costly study of the watershed's drainage grid and an assessment of the environmental footprint of impounding three hundred thousand gallons of water with an anticipated flow rate of ten thousand gallons per day. Buck hired a consultant to work with the department, draw up a land-use plan, and complete the legal forms.

When the permit finally came through, Buck began pumping water out of the swamp and pushing dirt with his dozer, filling trucks and hauling the dirt, clay, and rocks to a construction site on the other side of Grange, where it could be used in later projects.

By the time he dug down six feet, the spring dried up. The DNR sent people out to look and Buck's consultant agreed with them: the weight and vibration of the machinery had temporarily sealed the channels in the rock and clay. But everyone was sure that the spring was still down there and further digging would open it up.

Buck brought in his excavator and went down another ten feet, enlarging the diameter of the hole as he went.

"This is bigger than we planned," said Amy, standing with her husband on the deck off the back of the house, her hands clasped behind her back. She was a tall woman with wide shoulders, and her upright posture argued against the worried expression on her face, creating an image of optimistic anxiety. Beneath them, the excavator loaded rock and dirt into trucks parked on a second tier of ground. The dozer carved out another ramp into the pit. Smoke belched from the engines.

At twenty feet there was still no water.

Buck signaled his operator to go deeper.

At thirty feet the spring opened up.

"Oh good," said Amy, watching water rise around the tracks of the excavator. Farther away, the dozer tried to climb up the muddy incline and slid backward.

Buck scrambled down from the deck and ran forward, shouting at his men standing along the sides of the pit.

By the time the equipment was pulled out, water had seeped into compartments, shorted circuit boards, fouled switches, filled intakes with gritty water, and damaged the pumps. Repairs cost over eight thousand dollars, even with his own men doing most of the work.

But no one had been hurt and the DNR didn't complain too long or too loudly when the size of the pond turned out to be three times the one originally proposed. It now extended from the edge of the deck on the back of the house all the way to the windbreak along the gravel road.

The following summer, the grass on the earth dam sprouted thick and green. The dock and gazebo were completed on schedule, at a thousand dollars below the estimated cost. With warmer weather, Amy coaxed Kevin out of his room, away from his video games, computers, and magazines. The boy inched across the redwood deck in his slippers and placed his thin hands on the railing. He looked over the pond. A squadron of mallards flew overhead. Four of them broke formation and dropped out of the sky. At about twenty feet above the pond, wing and tail feathers fanned open, necks arched, green heads rose; the ducks appeared to be standing up in the air, sinking slowly. Then their wide orange feet skidded across the glazed surface, spraying water. Seconds later, they folded into compact oval shapes, bobbing up and down contentedly in the undulating wake of their own landing.

A smile spread across the boy's face. With the help of his mother and nurse, Kevin climbed onto the lowest terrace of the deck. From there they ventured onto the dock, Amy steadying his progress and the gray-haired nurse pulling the oxygen tank and keeping the tubing from tangling in the wheels of the cart.

Beneath the dock, lazy liquid slapped against oak posts, and water bugs skittered madly in and out of rolling shadows. The hoarse croaking of a bullfrog sounded like an ancient door pried open, thick ribbons of iridescent green slime grew underwater, and the smell of moist heat, earth, and damp wood rose into the air. These sensations dove to the bottom of Kevin's mind, where they were set to work in the mines of his young imagination.

Amy later recalled this moment to her husband as they ate dinner at the kitchen table. "I wish you could have seen his smile, Buck. It was like he finally—" She stopped, set her cup of coffee down, and listened.

"Finally what?" asked Buck.

Before she could answer, Kevin began coughing and Amy hurried down the hallway toward his bedroom, leaving Buck to eat the last of the salad from the wooden serving bowl. At the other end of the table, Buck's father rose, centered his weight on both legs, adjusted the suspenders holding up his pants, and walked out of the kitchen, closing the door.

Unfinished sentences had become a way of life, thought Buck. He was still hungry, but resolved to eat nothing more. He listened to his father climbing the stairs to his bedroom on the second floor. Buck had offered to move his furniture into available rooms downstairs, but Wally preferred to stay upstairs. In the morning he could look out and see farther, he said.

Though he did not like to acknowledge it, Buck often felt abandoned, first by his wife and later by his father. The feeling shamed him, made him seem weak, childish, and ungrateful for the many privileges that he enjoyed.

For thirty-five years he and Wally had worked side by side, building Roebuck Construction from a father-and-son team with a pickup, cement mixer, ladder, and two wheelbarrows, to the largest construction company in the area. They'd constructed so many retaining walls, parking lots, sheds, garages, shops, additions, houses, and commercial buildings that Buck had recently walked into a store, finished what he'd come in for, and left without remembering that he and his father had built it.

Together, they had borrowed money, bought more equipment, bid on jobs, and hired workers. The company grew until they could no longer handle the paperwork. Two new employees helped with that—a younger woman with a lively telephone personality and secretarial skills, and an older bookkeeper. A new office building in Grange provided them with a place to answer the phone, make payroll, deal with vendors, send out bills, pay insurance, apply for permits, and file contracts.

During this time Buck married Amy Fisher, which seemed especially appropriate to everyone who thought about it. Because of Amy's six-foot-three-inch height they made an almost-normal-looking couple, and people often said how fortunate they were to have found each other. Someone as big as Buck married to an average-sized person would look like a giant married to a child, and seeing such a mismatch would be uncomfortable for everyone. They also seemed to have temperaments that fit nicely together: Buck was reserved yet amiable, and Amy was amiable yet reserved.

Amy's mother ran the Cut & Curl in Grange, and her father had traveled through a large area of Wisconsin, Minnesota, Illinois, and Iowa, selling farm machinery. She had one younger brother, named Lucky, and although the two siblings were often together they never formed a close relationship. From an early age they nurtured separate agendas. Lucky wanted to be admired and Amy wanted to belong, and the paths leading to these respective fulfillments headed in different directions.

Amy and Buck both liked hiking and camping, and whenever they got a chance, they walked into wilderness areas with packs on their backs and compasses in their pockets. They canoed the Boundary Waters and in winter went cross-country skiing. One year they hiked much of the Glacial Trail.

Amy liked to make love inside tents, Buck discovered. Something unraveled inside her when the wind blew the canvas sides in and out, and even when it didn't there was something exciting about the thin walls and pointed, membrane-like ceiling.

Buck also discovered that Amy loved her grandparents' house outside Grange more than anywhere else in the world. Much of this had to do with her grandparents, of course, to whom Amy felt a deep and relaxed affinity—a fond attraction stronger even than her feelings for her parents, in whose presence she always felt disapproval hiding behind measured acceptance, a silent nagging insistence for her to become someone more accomplished and petite.

Amy experienced unmetered acceptance from her grandparents and spent as much time as she possibly could with them. They were like her, laughed at her jokes, understood her quiet ways, and appreciated her without her needing to do something flamboyant or cute. Her grandfather taught philosophy at the university in La Crosse until he retired, and their big old country home possessed all the seclusion and grand enchantment that her parents' home in town lacked. There were three full floors, ten-foot ceilings, leaded windows, walnut baseboards, and a library on the third floor for all her grandfather's books. On the outside were wooden sides painted in gray, ceramic roofs, gutters, and downspouts. Her grandmother, Florence, kept a flower garden and orchard that extended the quaint features of the house a short ways into nature. Everything about the property seemed to exist in an earlier era, a different time to which Amy felt perfectly in tune.

As they aged, her grandparents became increasingly unable to conduct war against the omnipresent forces that seek to erode the unique charm of any particular place and time, to hide its attractions and obscure its beauty, and the place fell into disrepair. When her grandfather died, Florence put the house up for sale. Amy couldn't bear to have anyone else own it, so she talked to Florence and implored her to allow Buck and her to move in. Flo agreed, and Amy at once began the deliberate process of turning back the clock and restoring the house and gardens to their former condition. She attempted to enlist her grandmother as an adviser in the restoration, but found her oddly uninterested in the furnishings and condition of her surroundings. Having already lived through the period of history that Amy longed to re-create, Florence had no desire to see it resurrected, and preferred to pass the years and hours left to her making rosaries, or in silent contemplation.

Then Amy got pregnant inside a tent on a windy night, and after he was born the baby seemed fine for a week or two. He looked normal, but over the next month he failed to thrive, which was how the hospital staff referred to it. Something was wrong, and after kissing the infant's forehead one morning, Amy noticed that her lips were salty. Tests were run and discoveries made: Kevin's DNA made errors in translating its coded material into proteins. His heart and lungs were weak. Amy and Buck were told that these impairments would certainly increase with age, and might later prevent his proper growth. He would most likely need some type of care for the rest of his life.

"Nature's way of experimenting," said the counselor who had been recommended by the hospital.

"No," said Amy, "it's not. It's the opposite."

The counselor folded his hands over his stomach. "Evolution," he said, "progresses through little mistakes. Some are beneficial and over time become refined into species-wide adaptive traits. Unfortunately, others are not beneficial at all. These cases of cystic fibrosis are well documented, and with modern drugs much of the discomfort can be alleviated. A palliative treatment routine can be readily administered within a proper facility."

"Will he live? What kind of help is available in the home? What could we have done to prevent this?"

"Look, Mrs. Roebuck, let's not make ourselves out to be victims here. In my experience there's nothing more difficult than people who see themselves as victims. You need to stop thinking of this as some kind of cosmic injustice. Your first obligation is to your own mental wellness. If you don't feel adequately prepared to care for this child, there are alternatives that may prove—"

Buck leaned forward in his chair, picked up the compact carved maple desk between them, and held it several feet off the floor. Then he put it down and everything, including the phone, pens, and papers, remained in place. Afterward, the counselor adopted a different, more sympathetic approach.

"I wish you wouldn't do things like that, Buck," said Amy afterward.

"I'm sorry."

Over the years, caring for Kevin brought Buck and Amy closer together in many ways, though this seemed somewhat paradoxical because they had little time to themselves. They were silently united in rejecting all social norms that prescribed failure for their son. Kevin would have a good life and they would see to it. They encouraged each other, supported each other, and even pressured each other to never give up. When problems arose, they could be fixed. And when they couldn't be fixed, they could be lived through. People could be happy in a different kind of way, and they were.

In the meantime, however, Buck lost the larger portion of his wife.

There was little of Amy leftover and he accepted that. She was too busy with Kevin and Florence. But it didn't matter. He and his father had a construction company to run and he threw himself into his work with missionary zeal, always aware of the rising cost of his son's medical needs.

Buck liked construction and even suspected that his father had started the business to provide him with the incessant physical activity he had required as a young person—pushing wheelbarrows of wet concrete, shoveling gravel, and climbing ladders with pallets of shingles and brick. They had a mutual love of the work, and even many years later, when all the other workers had gone home, Buck and Wally remained at the job site, tying up loose ends and planning out the following day.

Then Buck's mother died and Wally's interest in the company died with her. He continued another couple years and just gave up.

"You take it, Buck. I'm through," he said one morning, looking out the window in the office in Grange.

"Never thought you'd say that, Dad. What will you do? You ought to think about it a little longer."

"Buck, I can't do it any longer."

And so Wally left the construction business and entered into what seemed to Buck and Amy like an uninterrupted two-year-long drinking binge. After wrecking his pickup twice, setting fire to his kitchen, falling asleep on his front lawn in winter, buying and selling a tavern in the same week, tearing up the road in front of his house with the construction company's biggest dozer, urinating in front of the police station, and otherwise proving to everyone concerned that he could not live alone, he sold his house and moved in with Buck and Amy. He preferred one of the rooms on the second floor, he said.

Amy agreed to it. She wanted him there. Wally would stop drinking, she said, as soon as he was living with family. And he did.

As Amy had also foreseen, the pond ignited Kevin's enthusiasm for the out of doors. He spent many of his summer afternoons inside the gazebo, where he could lie down and plug any needed equipment into the outlets. Stacks of magazines spread across the table, accompanied by computer cords, video game controls, and sketching tablets, onto which he drew images of the pond and the creatures that came there. Once, when his resistance to infection, mildew, and dampness in general seemed especially strong, he even slept overnight in the gazebo, overruling the disapproval of his nurse. He felt connected to nature there, in touch with a wider experience.

Then one night in early autumn, Wally couldn't sleep. He carried a tackle box and a fishing pole out to the end of the dock, baited a hook, and caught a fish. It weighed over five pounds and was followed by six others, ranging between two and four pounds. He put them all on a stringer, tied the stringer to the end of the dock, and went back to bed. While falling asleep he thought about batter-frying the smaller ones and taking the biggest to a man who smoked fish inside a metal drum behind his garage. But after he went to sleep Wally dreamed of an elegant woman with a sensuous smile and a bulbous eye on each side of her head.

Since his wife's death, Wally had become increasingly sensitive to any signals from the next world—a sensitivity he consciously nurtured. He wanted to be ready to calmly greet whatever waited for him after his death, and he tried to live accordingly. Because of his dream, Wally decided to free the fish on the dock. But first he wondered if his grandson Kevin might want to see them.

"I caught some nice fish last night," he announced Sunday morning while he, Buck, Florence, and Amy ate scrambled eggs and buttered toast. "I'm going to turn them loose, but I wondered if the boy would like to see them first."

"I'm sure he would, Wally," said Amy, setting down her fork. "I'll ask him."

When Kevin was dressed they all went outdoors together. Buck carried his son, the nurse followed with the oxygen tank, and Amy and Wally helped Florence, who brought a camera.

"Put me down, Dad," said the fourteen-year-old, and Buck set him on the bench beside the gazebo. The boy's eyes followed the stringer over the dock and into the water. Wally stepped forward and drew it up. Six ragged heads dangled in midair, their bodies missing. The nurse muffled a shriek with a gasp. Kevin drew back in horror. Unable to interrupt her intended movements quickly enough, Florence took a picture.

Wally dropped the stringer.

Kevin's face darkened.

"Turtles do that," said Wally, trying to sound comforting in an informative way. "A turtle leaves heads."

"He ate them while they were alive?" asked Kevin.

"Well, yes, in a manner of speaking."

"I want to go back inside now," said Kevin.

"Sorry, Amy," said Wally as they walked up to the house.

"It will be all right," said Amy. "I know it will."

At first it seemed as if Amy's resolute optimism might prevail. After several weeks, Kevin again was drawn to the water, and once again ventured out to the gazebo.

Migrating geese stopped that autumn, sometimes a hundred at a time. They dove beneath the surface looking for food, slept on the water, and talked to each other in wild squawking tones.

As Kevin watched them, he tried to imagine being a goose, having feathers, and floating half in and half out of the water, webbed feet dangling. He wondered what it would feel like to be surrounded by an enormous extended family of geese, to fall asleep with your head lying on your back, the naked sun overhead and the cool water beneath—a seamless connection to the rest of the world.

That's what I want, thought Kevin, a seamless connection—every stir stirring through me.

Several days later, Kevin sat in his chair in the gazebo and an unusually large flock of geese circled the pond and landed. The noise was deafening in a good way. Kevin stood up and gripped the railing.

"We should throw out pieces of bread," he said to the nurse. "Go get some."

"I'll be right back," she said, putting her book aside and slipping her shoes on.

After checking the tubing and settling Kevin back into his chair, she walked down the dock, up onto the deck, and into the house.

Kevin watched the geese. They covered nearly all of the surface. Then they rose at once in a cacophony of beating wings and loud fearful cries. Kevin sat forward. Within seconds, they were flapping over the top of the windbreak—all but one, who appeared to be having some trouble taking off from the surface of the pond. The lone goose slapped its wings against the water, lurched upward, and continued to bleat as it sank deeper into the pond. Finally, only its neck and head remained, and then these also disappeared and quiet ripples radiated from the place it had gone under.

The pond became absolutely silent.

When the nurse returned Kevin said he wanted to go back inside the house.

"Where'd all the birds go?" asked the nurse.

"I told you I want to be back inside."

"We have to wait for your mother to come back from town."

"I don't want to wait."

"I'll go in and get your grandfather. He can help."

"Hurry, I don't want to be out here any longer."

The nurse went back inside. Kevin listened to the deafening silence of the pond and felt alone. He stood up and walked out onto the dock. Staring into the blue-green water, he thought he saw something. The color of the water seemed to coalesce beneath the surface, drawing together, taking on form.

It seemed as if the old nurse was taking forever to come back, and Kevin grew increasingly anxious. As his anxiety grew, his breathing became more labored. His chest hurt and he stared into the water again.

The greenish-blue form had turned more yellow since he last looked, and it had a definite shape now. It looked like a boulder three or four feet in diameter, lying at the bottom.

Then it slowly rose and a dark bony shell broke through the surface, wet and slick. Finally the turtle's knurled head and neck emerged. Its bright reptilian eyes contemplated him, and Kevin could not at first understand—beyond the sickly horror he was experiencing—what manner of stare it was. The neck swelled out from beneath the shell, serpent-like. The head drew closer and the mouth opened, revealing the full width of its bite. Kevin felt the animal's dark intelligence, as if all its ten million ancestors were scoffing at Kevin, laughing at evolution's latest doomed experiment. Long after Kevin had taken his last labored breath, the turtle would still be here, living beneath the surface.

Satisfied with its communication, the giant turtle then closed its mouth, drew its neck in, and slowly sank until it disappeared completely.

From then on, Kevin refused to have anything to do with the pond.

"It's the turtle, Buck," said Amy. "You've got to get that thing out of there."

"How am I supposed to do that?"

"Wally said he saw it once. He poked it with a stick and it bit off a piece of the wood."

"Seeing it and getting rid of it are two different things."

When the DNR agent finally arrived later that morning, they stood together on the dock and Buck explained what he intended to do.

"Oh no, you can't drain the pond, Mr. Roebuck."

"I have all the pumps I need."

"I'm sorry, Mr. Roebuck. We can't let you drain the pond."

"I want that turtle out of there."

"We talked about this turtle, Mr. Roebuck. I discussed it with our fish and game people and none of them think there's a snapper like the one you described anywhere in Wisconsin. They're certain, in fact, that there isn't."

"I don't care a whole lot what your people think," said Buck. "My father saw it. My son saw it. I'm going to drain the pond."

"We can't let you do that. It's disruptive to the ecosystem. You already ceded this. It was part of the agreement you signed before impounding the water."

Buck knotted his hands together.

"We can bring in a seining crew," said the field agent. "It would be expensive, but we could drag the pond and pull up whatever you have down there."

"With nets?"

"Nylon nets. Nothing escapes the nets, especially something as large as you think you have here. We'll bring it up and remove it."

"What if it comes back?"

"It won't. You want me to put in a requisition for a crew? Remember, Buck, it's expensive."

"Do it, as soon as possible."

Loyalty in Lockbridge

Reverend Winifred Helm had been thinking about visiting Blake Bookchester for a long time. Ever since her husband, Jacob, told her that Blake had been transferred from Waupun to the prison in Lockbridge, it seemed like something she should do. Lockbridge wasn't all that far away, and Blake's father, Nate, was a frequent customer at Jacob's repair shop in Words. But visiting an inmate was a good distance beyond Winnie's comfort zone.

As a younger woman she would not have hesitated. At the beginning of her ministry, Winnie efficiently converted the first twinge of moral impulse into an imperative for action. If the urge she experienced seemed sufficiently demanding, self-denying, and righteous, she at once assumed the source of the prompting to be divine—a Voice commanding her obedience. As she grew older she learned to more patiently examine the complex routes by which moral urges arrived in her conscious mind. All too often, she discovered, impulses of a self-serving and reward-seeking nature cleverly disguised their ignoble ends, professed virtues they did not have, and mimicked the Voice. With astonishing ingenuity, her desire for attention, praise, and achievement found ways of pretending to be something else, something bigger, something noble, and the ruse could be sifted out only by repeatedly testing her urges over a period of time. Consequently, though she often thought about visiting Blake Bookchester in the Lockbridge prison, she didn't go.

Then one night Winnie had an especially frightening dream of demonic creatures with purple throats, rooms with long sloping hallways, no exits, and red floors.

"Are you all right?" asked Jacob, stirred awake by the sudden turbulence in bed.

"I had a nightmare," said Winnie, sitting up.

"You shouted something."

"I'm sorry."

"Can I get you some tea?"

"No. Go back to sleep. You'll wake up August."

Their eleven-year-old son was in the room down the hall. His overly active mind had an enormous appetite for raw experience, and leaped to life at the slightest provocation. Jacob lowered his voice.

"Tell me about your dream."

"I have to think about it first. Go back to sleep."

Jacob worked long hours in his repair shop, so going back to sleep came easily to him after he understood there was nothing better to do. He was a good man in that and many other ways, and deep rhythmic breathing soon emanated from the other side of the bed. As the sounds grew more sonorous and underwater-like, she turned toward the nearby window and was greeted by a cool, lazy breeze.

Only a few stars were visible beyond the thickly growing pines in the backyard, blinking on and off with the movement of feathered limbs in the wind. The sporadic flickering made the distant lights seem less like objects in space and more like airborne fireflies igniting unpredictably as they flew. She smiled. The living world contained so many merry minor moments that sometimes it seemed as if fresh entertainment waited behind every turn of her head.

Yet the dream troubled her. It indicated a serious rift at the base of her psyche. There were clearly vital parts of herself she did not recognize and had not confronted. They wanted in and had assumed the terrifying shapes needed to draw her attention.

Following a successful effort to forgive her father for leaving her mother and other cruelties committed during her childhood, Winnie had been free of nightmares for several years. This was mostly thanks to her paternal uncle, Russell Smith, whose harsh and reactionary manner had slowly informed her—from the safe distance of living in another house—how someone in her own family could hurt those around him without consciously intending to. Uncle Russell responded to everything that made him uncomfortable with a habitual blind urgency. For reasons known only at an intuitive level, he simply lacked the capacity to understand himself or his surroundings any better. Those who loved him, including his wife, Maxine, had learned to accept this in exchange for his more-agreeable qualities, like reliability and the absence of guile.

Winnie had been lulled into thinking her deep challenges were over. She assumed that taking care of her son, husband, and church family would continue to round out her life in the same hectic yet mostly satisfactory manner. The future would bring only more of the same. The trials of childhood, insecurities of adolescence, and other extra-hormonal adventures had thankfully concluded and she was now safely grounded in the staid-fastness of middle age.

But the dream indicated otherwise, and now Winnie watched stars appear and disappear through the giant pine tree, thinking about how she might know herself better. Soon, the prisoner returned to her thoughts. As she continued staring out the window, she realized that some of the blinking stars really were fireflies, and this greatly amused her. When proven to be a fool, dance, she thought, and quickly stifled a giggle.

Before committing to visit someone in prison, however, Winnie explored the idea further by preaching a sermon on the subject the following Sunday. It was a fairly good homily, she thought, seasoned throughout with biblical references. Jesus asked his disciples if they ever visited him in prison, and when the disciples dodged the question and asked, "When were you ever in prison?," Jesus said anyone hungry, needing clothes, or in prison should be seen in the same light as himself. The Prince of Peace had made it clear: the faithful should visit prisoners.

Her congregation that day—some twenty-five people out of a total membership of somewhere between forty and two hundred, depending on how membership was defined—listened attentively, sang two hymns, prayed, and went into the basement to eat a potluck meal with hamburger casserole, cheese, green beans, spaghetti squash, Jell-O salad, peanut butter bars, and triple-chocolate cake. The conversation was quite lively, but no one mentioned visiting prisoners.

When the idea still would not go away, she took it to the Faith and Spiritual Oversight Committee, a group of two men and six women who met monthly to deliberate with her about church programs and her pastoral duties in general.

"Whatever do you mean?" asked Violet Brasso, a stalwart woman in her eighties who, after decades of devoted service to the community, had risen to an unofficial position of authority.

"I mean," said Winnie, enunciating clearly for the benefit of her mostly hard-of-hearing committee, "do you think it would be appropriate for your pastor to visit an incarcerated individual?"

"Incarnated?"

"No, incarcerated—a prisoner, someone locked up in prison."

"Yes, of course, of course, visit with prisoners all you like, but try not to run the phone bill up. With the small Sunday offerings we've been collecting lately we have to cut back on nearly everything. These are hard times."

"I don't think you can call them on the phone," said Winnie. "You have to go there."

"Go where?" asked Florence Fitch, sitting to Winnie's left.

"To the prison."

"Where?" asked Ardith Stanley, sitting to her right.

"To the place where prisoners live."

"Do you know someone there?" asked Ardith.

"Not yet."

"I should hope not. Why would you ever go into a prison?"

"To talk to a prisoner," said Winnie.

"My sister, Olivia's, husband, Wade, was in prison once," said Violet.

"He was never in prison," corrected Florence Fitch. "He was in jail. Olivia says there's a big difference. Jail is not nearly so serious. People end up there almost by accident. Or at least that's what I heard."

"I think that's right," said Earl Forester, choosing his words with great care. "There's a difference between jail and prison."

Winnie looked around the sanctuary, from one committee member to the next. Their faces were in many ways better known to her than her own. Afternoon light streamed through the windows and glowed around them, bringing to life the familiar smell of aging carpeting and pew upholstery. The long history of their togetherness seemed almost overwhelming, as if anything unfastened to that history would be absorbed like a ripple into a pond—the new made old.

Sometimes Winnie could hardly remember who she had been before she came here. They had welcomed her straight out of seminary—a fragile, confused young woman—into their small circle. She owed them, especially Violet, more than she could ever imagine repaying.

Violet had repeatedly encouraged Winnie to accept life as it presented itself, to stop letting her religious ideals get in the way of her happiness, to trust herself and marry Jacob. Violet had stood in the very front at their wedding. Later, after it became uncomfortably apparent that the pastor's first child was going to be born a couple of months early, it was Violet who told everyone, "Most children are born to a man and woman in about nine months, except the first one. That one can come at most any time. It's the Lord's way."

By now Winnie had been preaching in Words for over sixteen years. She and Violet and the rest of her church family had sailed in the same boat for such a long time that Winnie seldom needed to think beyond their mutual shoreline.

That's why the things going on inside her—the nightmare and the impulse to visit Blake Bookchester in prison—were so disquieting. They lay deeper than belonging, possibly deep enough to upset everything.

She gently pressed her committee. "As you will recall from the sermon several weeks ago, Jesus commanded his disciples to visit those in prison."

Long pause.

Earl Forester spoke deliberately out of his white beard. "It was needed in those days."

"We live in a Christian nation now," said Delores.

"Our laws are God's laws," said Violet.

Once again, Winnie found herself standing against them in her mind. She rearranged her thin legs in the pew, folded her hands, and said: "Yes, Violet, but in your heart don't you sometimes think that very little has changed since John the Baptist and the Lamb of God were executed? Herod's Army still lusts for power and continues to sharpen its long swords. Injustices are commonplace and ordinary people are often crushed by civilization."

"I don't think that at all," replied Violet. "The founding fathers and mothers of this country were devout Christians. It's written into the Constitution. The leaders of the United States of America serve with God's blessing, though occasionally they may fall a little short of what is expected of them, as we all do. We're only human."

"Besides," said Delores, "there is so much work to be done here, among your church family."

"That's right," said Ardith. "The need is great right here at home."

Winnie felt a sinking fatigue; her wish for everything to remain the same was dying inside her. She closed her eyes. She didn't understand what was happening.

The next Monday—her official day off—she headed out to the prison in Lockbridge. In the hope of quieting her apprehension before she arrived, she took the long way, driving sixty miles of back roads along the sprawling beaches of the lower Wisconsin River, where eagles posed in trees and turkey vultures unfolded their black wings above the moving water.

The prison wasn't hard to find. Set off from the highway and isolated from the rest of town by a thick stockade of black pines, the low-lying complex squatted squarely in the middle of a desolate field. A long horseshoe drive led up to the main building.

Inscrutable, the brick exterior seemed to willfully obscure the purpose of its cavernous interior, as if the designers had wanted the building to resemble nothing in particular. Four empty exercise cages extended around the northwest corner, chalky-white concrete slabs with high cyclone fencing and loops of razor wire.

An iron sign bolted to a brick-and-mortar stand in the parking lot stated: Wisconsin Secure Program Facility. The shapeless name suggested a warehouse of locked file cabinets, and Winnie had reason once again to wonder at the deathless ingenuity of government language.

She parked in the visitors' lot, walked toward the front door, and checked her watch. Ten minutes early. She stopped walking. A length of discarded red thread hurried over the asphalt, chased by a lively wind, and she went back to her car to wait. She didn't want to be early. After deliberating for a moment, she sat on the car's yellow hood.

The smooth sloping metal felt good underneath her, surprisingly comfortable, and yet she worried the video guards might think she was a vain woman in her forties who wished to appear younger by sitting on the hood of her car. She nurtured this unflattering thought as long as she could keep it alive, then gradually felt even better about sitting where she was. A late-morning sun crept shyly across the southern sky and lit up the left side of her face as she reviewed everything she knew about the prison. It had been imagined, planned, built, and sold to the State of Wisconsin to lock people inside with the least expenditure of effort—509 windowless, single-occupancy cells, doors that opened and closed from a centrally located electronic panel, iron slots (chuck holes) through which to shove food trays in and out, lights that never turned off, wall-mounted metal toilets, concrete-slab beds, and small cameras to search into the most forlorn crevices without leaving the surveillance room. An innovation in population management, the Wisconsin Secure Program Facility was one of the newer additions to the state's ever-expanding penal infrastructure. It was intended for prisoners too dangerous for even maximum security, or too psychotic to be around ordinary prisoners. When it opened, the governor called it a place for "the worst of the worst."

This phrase bothered her most. How could there be over five hundred worst-of-worst? Shouldn't that number boil down to only two or three? And on top of that, who determined which criminals belonged in these categories? Wouldn't those people need to be the best of the best?

"You take things too seriously," Jacob often told her. August mostly agreed with him, and maybe they were right. Some people had come up with an idea for making money and built a prison. They hired lobbyists to market it to the appropriate government bodies, the complex was purchased, government speech writers made up some exaggerated things to say about the need to spend the money, and the overcrowded prisons in the rest of the state began shipping inmates they didn't particularly like to Lockbridge.

It was time to go in.

A uniformed guard pushed a button, allowing the front door to open. Winnie stepped into a glassed-off entry booth and placed her driver's license in the metal drawer. Another guard, stationed in an adjacent glass booth, pulled the drawer inside his fortified space, inspected her card, looked up her name on his computer, returned the card, and then pushed another button, allowing a second door to open.

Behind a curved counter, a guard asked which prisoner she'd come to see, and checked a second computer file to verify that her name appeared on a list of approved visitors. He watched as Winnie put her handbag on the conveyor leading to the X-ray machine and walked through the detector arch. She signed her name and printed the date and time on an official form. The guard handed her a key to open one of the nearby lockers, where she put her handbag and car keys and everything else that she wasn't allowed to take with her. Then he picked up a telephone and called for another guard to escort her deeper into the prison.

She followed the pressed uniform down a long corridor and into a narrow room unlocked by remote control. Inside the windowless enclosure stood a single chair and a small monitor mounted on the wall, a video camera above it. Prisoners housed at Blake's level of security were not allowed face-to-face visitors, even preachers. They were kept in a separate building. She sat in the molded plastic chair and waited for the image of Blake Bookchester to appear.

When the monitor came on she saw a young man wearing a flat green V-neck pullover shirt without buttons. He looked at least ten years younger than her, his skin unnaturally pale.

"Who are you?" he asked. Winnie could hardly hear him, and she wondered if the volume had been turned down on the electronic apparatus between them. He seemed to be looking at the floor, but every so often his eyes darted up, studying his own monitor in furtive glimpses.

"My name is Winifred Helm," she answered, as calmly as she could. "I live in Words with my husband and son. I'm the pastor of the Words Friends of Jesus Church."

"Why are you here?" he asked, rubbing his hand quickly through his short ragged hair. The chain from his wrist shackles clattered like loose change. Though she couldn't be certain, he looked no taller than five-nine, muscular but not heavy.

"To be honest, I'm not sure why I came here. Your father told my husband you'd been transferred, and he told me. I made an appointment to come."

"Why are you here?" he repeated. The chains rattled again. As if he was annoyed by the sound, he jerked his shoulders and looked down to where the wrist chains connected to a larger loop of chain around his waist.

Winnie spoke again, unsure of what to say. "Not far from the church, my husband owns a shop for repairing mechanical things. He knows your father and sometimes works on his truck, or at least that's my understanding. About five years ago I think he put in a new clutch."

"I remember the place," Blake said, cocking his head like a gun and staring straight ahead for a brief moment. "Look, lady, why did you come here?"

"I told you," said Winnie, her temper flaring up unexpectedly from its shallow trench in her anxiety. "I don't know why I came here and I don't appreciate being called lady. I don't believe there are any of those left anymore, and the way you're using the term is insulting. I thought you might appreciate someone to talk to."

He glared back at her, his eyes hard. "Whatever you have to sell, I'm not buying. And I'm not going to pretend that your religion or whatever you think—"

"I should hope you wouldn't pretend anything," interrupted Winnie, crossing her long skinny legs inside her ankle-length dress and folding her arms on her lap.

"Then what do you expect us to talk about? You're a preacher. Isn't it your job to convert me?"

"I gave that up a long time ago. I've had to edit my beliefs so many times it wouldn't make sense to insist that someone else subscribe to them."

"You're a preacher, aren't you?"

"Yes, but stop making assumptions about me from that. I've tried very hard not to make any about you."

"I didn't ask you to come here," he snarled.

Winnie found herself on the edge of an abyss. What a colossal mistake, coming here. But rather than backing up, she threw herself over the edge and waited for something to catch her.

"Let me try to explain," she said, exhaling. "See, after I learned you'd been transferred here it occurred to me that I should visit. At first I ignored it. Then I started having nightmares, indicating to me that I needed to push myself into uncomfortable psychological areas. Either that or live the rest of my life wallowing around in past realizations."

Blake starred out of the monitor at her.

"Go on," he said.

"To explain this next step you need to understand something I believe. It's fine if you don't believe it yourself, but to understand why I came here you need to understand something about what I believe. Can I tell you?"

"Go on," he said.

"Thank you. I believe that who I am is made up of many loyalties. I feel loyal to preserving my physical body, to surviving. I feel loyal to my husband, Jacob, and to my son, August. I'm loyal to my congregation. I'm loyal to my community and to preserving my good standing within it.

I'm loyal to many other things, too, like being honest with myself, or at least trying to be. I feel loyal toward many cherished memories, like my mother and my loyalty toward—"

"And these loyalties," Blake interrupted, "they connect to each other, don't they?"

"Yes," said Winnie. "If you could feel the tugging of all my loyalties at once you would know what it feels like to be me at any particular moment. And the very best moments occur when all my loyalties are in harmony—when the loyalty to my church, for instance, does not conflict with the loyalty I feel toward my husband, and the loyalty I feel toward my husband does not inhibit the loyalty I feel to my son, and so forth."

"But sometimes they do," said Blake cautiously. "Sometimes they surely do."

"Yes, sometimes they do, and that's when everything gets mixed up. That's when holding myself together becomes more difficult, when it becomes—"

"Then you have to choose," Blake interrupted.

"Exactly. All loyalties are not the same, and sometimes a few of them must be forsaken, set aside for a short time. But there are some I dare never ignore because they lie at the root of me, and if I turn my back on them, well, that's—"

"That's apostasy!" said Blake, the veins in his neck bulging, his body shaking and the chains clattering. "That's the unforgivable sin, the curse against the Holy Spirit. You can't do that! There'd be nothing left of you, Mrs. Helm. All the others depend on that one."

"Yes, Blake, and the deepest loyalty I feel is also the hardest to explain, because it's not just me at that level. It's me and—"

"Something else!" yelled Blake. "It's you and something else, something that can never be defined or casually talked about, or anticipated or even understood. It's a feeling at the ground zero of consciousness, but it's not just a feeling and it's not totally your feeling either, it's also an experience and—"

Winnie interrupted, "It's me and something sacred."

"I understand," said Blake.

"Thank you."

"Please, tell me something else about you, Mrs. Helm. You're actually talking about things that matter, real things. I never expected that. For three days I thought about a visitor coming to see me, because they told me someone was coming, and I thought about it in every way I could, but I never expected this."

"I guess I don't know what else to say."

"Say anything. God, you can't imagine how wonderful this is, talking with someone about something real."

"How old are you, Blake?"

"I don't know. I've forgotten."

"That's impossible."

"You're right, it is. I'll be thirty-two in six weeks."

"I'm forty-five. Do you think that's too old to sit on the hood of a car?"

"What?"

"Do you think I'm too old to sit on the hood of my car? I was doing that in the parking lot. I didn't want to come in earlier than our scheduled visit and I was trying to prepare myself. I was sitting on the hood of my car and feeling insecure about being too old. So what's your opinion?"

"What good is freedom, Mrs. Helm, if you never do anything unusual or odd? That's what freedom means—doing whatever you need to do so long as nobody else is hurt by it. That's what you were talking about before, doing things that conflict with your sense of yourself in other rooms of your mind. You have to be able to do that or you're not really alive."

"So there's nothing wrong with a middle-aged woman like me sitting on the hood of my car?"

"Of course there isn't. Sit wherever you want and if anyone criticizes you, tell 'em to come see me."

Winnie laughed. "Good. I wasn't sure what someone else would think."

"Did you say you knew my father? How is he?"

"I'm afraid I don't know him very well, Blake. My husband is better acquainted with him from his repair shop. I think he currently works for that shipping company north of Grange, delivering heavy products in his truck. As far as I know he is in good health. Does he come to see you?"

"I talked him out of that. He's emotional and there's nothing the guards here like better than for relatives of prisoners to cry. It makes them feel proud of a job well done."

"Surely that's not true."

"Of course you don't believe it, Mrs. Helm. No reasonable person should. It's just one of those little humiliating horrors brought to you by the human garbage pit. Right now—did you know this?—someone is listening to us. Someone is actually being paid to press a tiny wire to their ear and listen to us. It's insane. Yes, I told my father to stop coming here. Having a son should not include the kind of snickering abuse that runs wild in here. He doesn't deserve to feel the way he feels when he's here, and I don't want him to. If you lived in a garbage dump, would you want your father to visit?"

"My father is deceased, but he wouldn't have visited me no matter where I lived."

"Why not?"

"That's simply the way he was."

"Frankly, I can't imagine that. My father is a saint and I sometimes hate him for it."

"Why?"

"I could never live up to it."

"Does he expect you to?"

"No, of course not. He's a saint."

"Can I ask another question?" asked Winnie.

"Sure."

"Have you been able to find some small measure of peace here?"

"Not really."

"I always hoped that prisons were in some way having a positive influence on the people inside them."

"I'm afraid you couldn't be more wrong, Mrs. Helm. Does that offend you?"

"No."

"You have no idea, I'm afraid, what it feels like to try to understand how a single thoughtless action should result in years and years of living in a cage while fools with tiny brains poke you with sharpened sticks."

"You're right," said Winnie. "I have no idea."

"What can I say? I feel small about the resentment I feel. Some guys who get sent to prison, they know as soon as the door closes behind them that they'll be treated like lizards. It's fools like me who imagine that some degree of respect and dignity should still govern the way people relate to each other, even in here. I can't get over it. Why, for instance, do they search visitors when they don't even end up in the same building with the person they're visiting? It's unnecessary, but they do it anyway. Why do they search our rooms and throw things all over when nothing comes in that has not been inspected? They have rules for everything, but no one can tell you why using the telephone here costs ten times what everyone else pays. Why is that? Go ahead, ask them. They don't know. There are countless things like that, and it makes me angry. I can't help it."

"Anger is never constructive," said Winnie, "though I often can't avoid it either."

"Anger proves I'm still alive," said Blake.

Winnie looked at the wristwatch strapped loosely around her thin wrist. "I'm afraid my time is almost up. I'll be back though. I promise to visit you again. You have my word."

"Look, Mrs. Helm," he said. "I mean, you did it once and I appreciate it, but you don't need to come again. It's against nature. This is a human garbage pit. Don't come back."

"I'm coming back," said Winnie.

"Good," said Blake.

"Is there anything you would like me to bring next time? I'm sure there are many things, but please limit yourself to things that are inexpensive, not difficult to obtain, and meet the narrow requirements of the prison. Let's say three things."

"Three things?"

"Yes, three things."

"Books, books, and books. I'll pay you back someday."

"Do you like to read?"

"You have no idea."

"Am I allowed to bring books in here?"

"They'll make it as difficult as they possibly can, believe me. They can't help themselves, but please, please bring me some books."

"What kind of books?" she asked.

"Any books are better than none, of course, even books written without much thought—flavorless fantasies relying on clichés and stereotypes. I'll read those too, but what I really want are thick books with fine print, difficult sentences, long words, and enormous ideas, books written in a feverish hand by writers who hate the world yet can't keep from loving it, whose feelings so demand to be understood that if they didn't write them down they would go blind. Bring me books by women who have fallen out of step with society and refuse to march and sing the old songs. Books by men who through terrifying sacrifice overcome all the challenges set before them but one. Find me books by sensualists who drink their cups dry every time and yet never figure out why they're so thirsty, and books by pious men and women who continue to believe that being good will save them. Bring me books about people in love, people so passionate about each other they will stand against family, community, country, fortune, and fame in order to be together, and books about people who don't have a chance in hell yet somehow find one. Bring me books about the fear of God and the depths of nature, books about history, philosophy, psychology, science, and motorcycles."

"I will," said Winnie. "I promise."

"And say hello to my father. Tell him that—"

At that instant, from somewhere in the prison, the screen was turned off.

The Wild Boy

Ivan asked and asked, until finally his mother arranged for him to spend a weekend with his friend August. "I'll drive you over in the morning," she said.

After hearing this, a tyrannical anticipation governed his actions and thoughts, driving him from one frenzy of expectation to the next. He packed twice before going to bed, slept fitfully, got up at first light, dressed in his lucky green shirt and favorite jeans, and waited silently for his mother to get out of bed.

When they climbed into the Bronco at last, the drive over seemed unbearably long. They had to stop dead and wait at every one of Grange's six stoplights. Adding embarrassment to frustration, his mother blasted the horn at a driver who pulled out of the hardware store parking lot and cut her off. "Get off the road, idiot!" she yelled.

Then, after a couple of miles on the highway, they heard a sound like a helicopter. Dart pulled over, got out, walked around the Bronco, and found a flat tire.

They were in the middle of nowhere—weeds and sky everywhere, no cars, no buildings, no signs, no nothing—and Ivan's sense of urgency bloomed into horror over the likelihood that his time with August had been jinxed.

"No worry, this is a piece of cake," said his mother, yanking the jack out of the back. "Come on, Ivan, give me a hand here."

They got the old wheel off, but when the wrench slipped, his mother cut her hand. She wrapped a rag around it to stop the bleeding. After the spare was on it looked about half as big as the other tires. His mother said it would be fine. All spares were like that, she said.

Just as they finished, an Amish buggy came around the corner. The two horses pulling it were big and brown, with black manes and tails, and breathing hard. The buggy and its wheels were also black. Inside were maybe eight faces, old and young, a nest of humans. They all waved. Ivan started to wave back, then checked the movement in reference to his mother's expression. "Hill people," she said, and spit into the weeds.

They got back into the Bronco and continued up the steep winding road, to the top of the ridge. Ivan looked down into the valleys extending to the right and the left. Then they had to stop at the four-way intersection that August called Creepy Corners. Someone had put a white cross about as tall as Ivan in the ditch nearby, along with some plastic flowers. After several years, black mold had grown over the flowers and covered most of the cross.

They turned right and headed down, curving first one way and then the next, heading toward the road to August's house. If they didn't turn on his road and kept going straight they would end up in the town of Words, which was so darn small there were no stores other than the Words Repair Shop, where August's father fixed things.

"We can take the flat tire over to August's dad," Ivan told his mother.

"I'll take it somewhere later," she said. "I'm sure he's busy today."

That was probably true, but Ivan knew the real reason his mother didn't want to take the tire in. She never wanted anyone to know when something went wrong. "Never complain and don't bother people with your troubles," she always said.

August told Ivan his father had so much work to do at the shop that some nights he never came home. Sometimes August's mom would get up in the middle of the night and drive into Words and yell at his dad. Whatever you're doing can wait, she said. She said she'd rather be a wrinkled old maid in a tin hut on a cold mountaintop than have a husband who didn't come home. And at that point his father always came home—because, August said, his mother was hard to refuse when she got worked up. Most people called her Pastor Winifred, some called her Preacher or Reverend, and some called her Winnie. But Ivan's mother said he was only to call her Mrs. Helm.

August also said his father had to work so hard on account of the government in Washington, DC, moving so many of the good jobs over to foreign countries. And to make matters worse the government started gambling with all the money inside the banks. They kept gambling until just a few gamblers won everything, took their loot, and moved to an expensive island resort. And that's why the economy went bad, such that no one around here could afford to buy new things. Everyone had to take their old things to August's father for repair.

The Words Repair Shop had a pop machine next to a hunchback lathe, where curls of shiny metal piled up on the oily concrete. There was also an old woman who sold kitchen crafts in an adjacent room. But that was it. The rest of the town was nothing but houses, garages, sheds, and the church where August's mom preached. There was nowhere to buy food in Words, and you could walk all the way around it in less time than it took August to get through one of his shorter explanations of why things were the way they were. In fact, he and August had walked around it many times while waiting for August's father to stop working.

Sometimes Ivan had to remind himself that August came from such a tiny place. He had no idea what went on in important places like Grange, where there were a lot of stores and cars and lights and noise, and several thousand people living close together. Ivan never made fun of him, though. It wasn't August's fault that he was born in deep ferny woods in the middle of the Ocooch hills. Besides, he had Ivan to ask about the rest of the world, and they shared everything.

Dart turned down the dead-end road leading to August's driveway, and Ivan checked again to make sure he still had his suitcase with his stuff. It was actually an old blue plastic typewriter case, which his mother called a suitcase. The typewriter had been taken away, but it still smelled like ink inside. It made a fine place for clothes, though, with a little compartment for special things and a hard plastic handle for carrying.

Ivan liked going to August's. He lived in a log house with big rooms. There was always something to do, even though August's mom wouldn't let him watch most television shows or play video games. They burned wood for heat and his dad had a homemade wind generator for electricity. On days when the blades didn't turn, the lights sometimes went off. Coyotes screamed at night, owls hooted, and you never knew what to expect.

He and August knew everything for miles around. They found animal trails snaking along the rims of valleys, and holes as big as barrels in trees.

They made bridges over the creek so they could cross without getting wet, they found places where they could swing over on a rope and places where they could jump all the way across. In the middle of a ravine they built a fort with long spiky poles, windows, and a roof. They knew where rattlesnakes lived by the hundreds in Sun Rock Cliff, and the Secret Night Gate, where the militia went into the Heartland Reserve to do its martial arts training and plan to overthrow the government. There was almost nothing they didn't know about in the area.

Still, whenever Ivan stayed away from home for very long he wondered about his mother—what she did when he wasn't there. He knew she had lived in Red Plain after she moved out of her mother's house in Luster and before she moved to Grange, and he wondered if she went back. He didn't know what she did when she lived in Red Plain, and he'd never been there himself. But somehow the name of the town seemed dangerous, filled with blood.

"What are you doing this weekend?" Ivan asked as they neared the end of the dead-end road, where August's driveway went off into the trees.

"I've got errands to run and some cleaning jobs."

"Is anyone coming over?"

"Not that I know of. Ivan, are you worried about something?"

"No. I just wondered what you would be doing."

"Same thing I always do," she said. "Work."

As they turned off the road, his mother put the Bronco into four-wheel drive, and they bumped over the narrow dirt lane through the trees. August's pet bat heard them coming, flew around in front of the windshield, and sped off into the woods. About a year ago August had found Milton lying on the floor of his bedroom. He brought him back to life with drops of warm milk with insects mixed in it. During the winter Milton was gone for a while—back to the cave beneath Sun Rock Cliff, where August thought bats hibernated. But in the spring Milton came back and stayed with August most of the time, except when August was in school.

"Just look at that," his mother said, scowling. "A bat in the middle of the day. Horrid, filthy things."

Ivan didn't reply. Adults and flying mammals never got along, and talking about them usually just made for trouble. Even August's mom sometimes had a problem with him, and she had feelings for animals and bugs that were unnatural in a grown-up.

August said Milton was a long-eared bat. They were pretty rare, with ears that were larger than those of an average bat. August thought he looked quite distinguished, which was sort of true.

As they came closer to the house, Ivan noticed that his mother's face got a pinched look from all the old engines and four-wheelers and snow-mobiles and everything else August's dad had stacked around and was going to fix up someday.

"A nice home like this, with two incomes. It's a crime, Ivan. When we have a place of our own it's going be different. It's going to be nice."

Ivan guessed that August's mom felt the same way. Women were especially alert to things looking good. Mrs. Helm's response to the situation was to make her own little place away from the house. It had thousands of flowers and bushes, a fountain with running water, fancy fish, and colored rocks, and it was almost done. All that was left was for August's great-uncle Russell, whom people called "Rusty," to build some chairs and benches.

Mrs. Helm said she needed a park for her peace of mind, which is something August said adults didn't have a lot of, at least not around here. August said his mom thought a peaceful place was needed because something very bad was beginning to happen to the whole world. Ivan kept trying to get August to tell him what this was, but he hadn't figured it out yet. He just knew it was real bad.

When Ivan and his mother walked up and knocked on the front door, no one answered. They climbed between several four-wheelers and ride-on lawnmowers without wheels, but they still couldn't see anyone back there. There were trees everywhere.

"Hey, August!" Ivan called, but his mother said not to shout, because only people with no class talked without keeping their voices down.

From about a hundred yards away August's mom yelled back, telling them to come on ahead. For some reason Ivan's mother didn't find anything wrong with August's mother shouting, and they hurried through the backyard and down the path leading through Shrubbery Jungle. Then they walked through the tunneling vines of flat-headed red and orange flowers to where Mrs. Helm had set some small sandwiches and lemonade on a wooden table. A tiny smile crept over his mother's face. She clearly agreed with August's mom that eating triangular cucumber-and-lettuce sandwiches with napkins next to a fountain was a very good thing to do. But it was also true that she liked her a lot more than she liked most people. When they got up close she even allowed Mrs. Helm to hug her, though she didn't hug her back.

There weren't any chairs to sit on, so the two women carried their lunch over to the colored rocks beside the fountain. After August's mom said a few words of prayer, they each picked up a sandwich and nibbled on it, wiping their mouths with red napkins after every bite. Ivan said he wasn't hungry and just watched. His mother rarely talked to anyone. She said most talking went nowhere fast. But now the two women chattered away like a couple of finches, pecking at their brown-bread sandwiches and sipping from plastic cups, perched on rocks with their knees together. Several times Ivan's mother laughed, then quickly covered her mouth with a napkin, prompting Mrs. Helm to smile and say, "Oh, Danielle, you're such a treasure."

His mother even told Mrs. Helm that she was thinking about applying for a live-in job with the owners of the construction company.

"Oh, I hope you do," said Mrs. Helm. "I've met them and they're nice."

"I don't see how they could be," said his mother. "They're rich."

At that point Mrs. Helm looked at Ivan and said that August was somewhere down by the creek. Ivan left his suitcase on the table and walked into the woods. It was cooler there. Before long Milton found him and flew around his head several times while he crawled through a hole in the fence. Ivan followed him across the Long Stretch, where it was hot without the shelter of the trees. Pretty soon they were back into the cooler woods again.

August was a short distance down the creek, sitting with his back against a tree and staring into the water. Ivan could tell—even from that far away—that August was trapped in one of his moods again. He was odd that way. Ivan knew him so well that he could almost see his thoughts. Sometimes August worried about his great uncle and aunt because they were so old, other times he thought something would happen to his father when he worked without safety equipment, and then often he just worried about why people were always thinking up ways to hurt each other. There was almost nothing he couldn't worry about.

Ivan didn't really understand why August got so upset by things. Compared to him, August had everything. His dad and mom were the best parents, and August's mom was so kind and warm that sometimes Ivan could hardly keep from going up and asking her to hold him. That was stupid, he knew, because he was almost twelve, but she was like that. As for his dad, when he looked at August, Ivan could tell how much he liked him. And then August's bedroom was nearly as big as Ivan's whole apartment. He had a computer and he took music lessons, Science for the Gifted, and Latin. He seemed to have everything, but he still couldn't stop worrying. Ivan told him he was too nervy, but it was like telling someone they were too small. It was just the way August was.

As August stared into the moving water, Milton dove in circles around him, catching mosquitoes, biting flies, gnats, picnic bugs, mayflies, and no-see-ums. After he cleared the air of everything he could eat, he landed on the tree trunk several feet above August's head, folded his pointed wings, and disappeared into the knurled bark.

When he saw Ivan he jumped up and came over.

August seemed to change more than anyone Ivan knew. Every time he saw him he was different. Sometimes he moved different and other times he just looked different. This afternoon his hair looked long, shaggy, and very light brown, almost blond. He also seemed bigger, almost as if his arms and legs had grown. His jeans were wet all the way up to the pockets, and water oozed out of his shoes.

"Hi, Ivan," he said, smiling. "Did you just arrive?"

This seemed too dumb to answer, so Ivan didn't respond. August was so used to being alone that sometimes the first things he said were kind of stupid.

"What are you doing?" Ivan asked.

"Making a dam," August replied. "We can do it together, or we can do something else. Your choice."

"I like making dams good enough," Ivan said, and August showed him what he'd already done.

The dam was about half-built.

"We're going to need some bigger rocks," said Ivan.

"I know," replied August.

"How long you been out here?" Ivan asked.

"I don't have a watch."

"I have one, see. My mother got it for me at the dollar store. Oh, by the way, your mom says to come back and get something to eat if you're hungry."

"I'm not."

"Me neither. Besides, I brought a couple candy bars. Want one?"

"Maybe later."

"Yeah, maybe later."

Milton flew around them several times, devouring the latest crop of flying insects, then went back to the trunk of the tree, where he again disappeared into the bark.

They set to work and before long found a rock in the shape of a rhinoceros head with the horn busted off. It took both of them to carry it, and when they put it down August called it "the buttress."

Then they found an even-heavier rock—boulder-sized, weighing maybe two thousand pounds. "It would be nice to have that one," Ivan said, "but there's no one in the world can lift that rock."

"Not anymore," said August.

"There never was."

"There was someone, but he's gone now. My dad said there was nobody like him."

"Who?"

"I told you about him before. His name was July Montgomery and he had the strength of three or four men, maybe more."

"How come?"

"No one knows how he got that way. He and my dad were best friends."

"Where is he now?"

"He died before I was born. Most people believe the government killed him. When they discovered his body everything looked highly suspicious, like some government agency had murdered him and tried to make it look like they hadn't."

"How did they do it?"

"They used a tractor."

"And he was a friend of your dad's?"

"Yes. My dad was a close friend of his, maybe the only one, and they went places together all the time. Dad won't talk much about those old days now because of how much it hurts to think of his best friend being murdered. And my mom won't either. She was well acquainted with him too. I think my dad was the only person July Montgomery trusted, because as a rule he didn't have much time for other people. He was a loner."

"Like we are when we're not together," added Ivan.

"Correct."

They went back to building the dam, finding rocks and stacking them up. When water began to seep around the sides, they went after sticks and leaves, chunks of sod and clay. The air filled with insects again, and Milton came out to get them. Then the water started coming over the top and they hunted for a long curved rock. But as they worked Ivan could feel August worrying, until finally he couldn't take it anymore.

"Okay, I'm not working on this one minute more until you tell me why we're doing it."

"We're doing this—" August began, then paused. "Because making a dam is fun."

"You're not telling me something," Ivan said. He went over and stood next to the tree that Milton had disappeared into. "You never do anything just because it's fun, August. You've been in one of your moods ever since I got here. What is it? Don't forget, we've got a code between us. And I can tell you're breaking it."

"I'm not in a mood," replied August distantly.

"Yes you are."

"I saw him again, Ivan—the Wild Boy."

"The ghost boy?"

"I told you, he is not a ghost. Don't call him that."

"But you are the only one who ever sees him."

August's face turned white. "I know it, and I've seen him before too."

"You told me, three times. You saw him twice sitting in the trees behind your house after dark, and once you saw him following you, jumping in and out of the bushes while you walked along Winding Ridge. But I've never seen him."

"He was standing right over there," August said, and pointed to the bank on the other side of the stream. "He was crouched down looking into the water, studying it, but when he saw me he leaped up and ran off."

"What did he look like?"

"I couldn't see him very well, but I think he smiled before he took off."

"What was he doing?"

"I told you, he was looking into the water, here where it's deeper. Maybe he likes looking into deep water. So I thought if we made the water even deeper he might come back. And then you could see him too, and maybe we could even talk to him."

"When did you see him?"

"Last night after dark."

"You came out here?"

"I woke up and had this feeling."

"What feeling?"

"A feeling I get sometimes before I see him. It's a real sad feeling, like everything is far away."

"So you came out here?"

"Yep, and I saw him looking into the water."

"Did you tell your parents?"

"No."

"Why not?"

"The Wild Boy has to be kept a secret. I've researched feral children on the Internet, and read a few books about them. Every time adults get involved it turns out bad."

"What's 'feral'?"

"It means wild. Feral children return to a more natural way of living. Some are raised by wolves, some by coyotes, others are just instinctively more primitive. When adults find them they always try to change them. But in most cases they never adjust to being away from nature, and they die young. So we have to keep him a secret."

"Where do you think he sleeps?"

"Most likely in caves where he can still see the sky."

"Do you think he sleeps during the day and then comes out at night?"

"Maybe," said August. "He's probably like other wild animals and sleeps no more than an hour or two at a stretch—never very soundly, always partly awake."

"So let me get this straight, August: you caught a look at this wild boy again. He was staring into the water, right here. And we're building a dam to make the water deeper, so that when he comes back we can see him and talk to him. Is that right?"

"Pretty much."

"Then why are we just standing around? Let's get to work. We can have this finished before dark, and I guarantee you it's going to be really, really deep when we're done."

"Perhaps we should have one of your candy bars first," August suggested.

"Good idea."

They split one, but before they were finished chewing, August's mom hollered. They couldn't understand her, but August said the way she hollered meant she wanted them to come back.

After they'd gone a little ways, August made a low whistle and Milton crawled out of the tree bark, flew over, and dove into his shirt pocket. He stayed in there a lot, Ivan knew, especially when grown-ups were around.

When they got back to the park Mrs. Helm and Ivan's mother were carrying a wooden chair through Shrubbery Jungle. Ivan's mother held the heavy end, and Mrs. Helm held on to the other.

Ivan was surprised and glad his mother hadn't left yet.

"What have you two been up to?" she asked, tugging down her baseball cap to just above her eyes. "You're all wet."

"Nothing," replied Ivan.

"Don't get smart with me. On God's green earth there isn't a living thing that has been doing nothing for the last hour. Now you boys go help Preacher Winifred's uncle carry the rest of the chairs and benches. And be right quick about it, Ivan, because he's an old man."

They ran off and found Uncle Rusty at the back of his pickup, parked next to the house. He had a wrinkled look and moved slowly.

"These chairs are too heavy for you boys," he explained. "I'll take 'em myself."

"Not too heavy for us," they said, and Ivan jumped into the back.

"Here, Uncle Rusty," said August, leading the old man toward the house. "Mom's got something she wants you to look at inside."

"What you got in there, boy?" Uncle Rusty asked gruffly, limping along like a cricket.

"The spring on the screen door doesn't close right."

"I've got to carry those benches out, boy."

"Ivan and I will carry them. We enjoy carrying heavy objects."

"You still got those blasted bats in your house?" asked Uncle Rusty, walking inside.

"They're mostly gone now."

"You let me know next time you see one. I'll come over and blast 'em. Does your dad still keep his tools in the middle drawer?"

"Yep, and mom says there's a sandwich for you in the refrigerator."

"I didn't ask her to cook me nothin'."

"I'm only reporting what she said."

"She's got better things to do than cook for me."

"I'll just leave it here on the table and be right back," said August. Then he ran to help Ivan haul the furniture out to the park.

"He's really a grouch," Ivan said.

"Mom says he's that way without actually meaning to be."

"Maybe so, but that is the way of a grouch."

After they moved all the chairs and benches, Ivan's mother and Mrs. Helm walked from one place to another, looking at the park from as many angles as they could. When they wanted a bench moved to another place, August and Ivan would carry it over.

"No, a little farther away."

"Wait, not so far."

"There, now bring the other one closer."

"How about moving the table and chairs over there?" Ivan's mother asked Mrs. Helm.

"Excellent idea, Danielle."

"No, not that far, Ivan. You listen to what I'm telling you, now. There, face it in toward the fountain a little. Wait, no, back this way."

The boys were about to scream when Ivan's mother finally said, "There, stop, don't move it any farther. Right there. That's perfect." Then the two women stepped back, tilted their heads to the side, and smiled in a sleepy way.

"Now, that's nice," said Ivan's mother, taking off her baseball cap and putting it back on.

"You have a genius for this, Danielle," said Mrs. Helm. "I'm so glad you were here to help."

By this time Uncle Rusty had hobbled out. He sat down on one of the benches next to the fountain, leaned forward, and splashed some water on his wrinkled leather face.

"Please don't drink that water, Uncle Russell," said Mrs. Helm. "We haven't had it tested yet."

"This all you're needing now?" he asked, water dripping off his chin.

"Yes, and just look at those beautiful chairs and benches. Thank you so much."

"I'm going home."

"You should stay for supper."

"Maxine's got things she wants done at home," he said, starting to get up.

"Here, Uncle Rusty, let me help," said August, rushing over.

"Get away from me, boy," he snapped, and hobbled off toward his pickup.

After he was gone, August looked hurt, and his mom said, "He doesn't mean it."

"Oh, he means it," said Ivan's mother. "You just can't let him get to you, August. My family is full of people like that—folks who wouldn't know something nice if it came up and bit them."

"Russell's had a hard life, but he's certainly been good to me," said August's mom.

"I shouldn't have stayed so long," said Ivan's mother. "Thanks for lunch, Preacher."

"Call me Winnie, you goose."

"Someday Ivan and I are going to have something nice like this here," she said, looking at the park one last time. Then she turned and told Ivan to do everything Mrs. Helm said or when he got home she'd get out the strap and take off some skin, and she walked away without looking back.

Serving Time

Blake Bookchester watched the caged bulb in the ceiling grow dim, causing his cell to appear even smaller. But it did not go out. Lights in Lockbridge prison never went out. Darkness was a security breach.

He'd been lying on his bunk most of the day, reading Spinoza. As his eyes grew tired, individual words grew hair. Sentences floated off the page and tangled into semantic fur balls. Ideas jiggled against each other inside his brain. Spinoza believed that all attributes, qualities, and thoughts were of God. This belief stood in direct opposition to that of Moses Maimonides, who had announced centuries earlier that God had no attributes at all. Both men had been raised within similar Hebraic traditions, yet after thinking their whole lives about the same problems, they had reached opposite conclusions.

Closing the book, Blake sighed briefly, quietly expressing the momentary exhaustion of the ever-thinking mind. Faced with diametrically opposed conclusions, his reasoning faculty surrendered.

Chances of going to sleep seemed pretty good, and he turned toward the wind-up clock on the concrete slab jutting out from the cell wall. The impudent white face pointed to eleven thirty, its incessant ticking sharpened by the humidity. Blake got up, moved the clock a short distance on the shelf, and lay down again. Now the knob on top of the alarm lined up with the pipe running down to the metal sink. That's where it was *supposed* to be.

No one needed a clock in here. His father had brought it for him, and Blake couldn't tell him he didn't want it. In a place where every day unraveled in exactly the same way, it was impossible not to know the time. Lights always dimmed at eleven thirty. And eleven thirty always sounded, looked, and smelled the same.

Two televisions jingled at the end of the corridor, adding to the rhythmic murmur of bodies sleeping on either side of the walls. The stale sigh of the air vent, cooler in the evening, exhaled with characteristic eleven-thirty candor.

There was no escaping time in prison. Gone were the days of getting lost within a temporal labyrinth, suddenly realizing, I have absolutely no idea what time it is.

None of that here. No absent moments. No forgetting about civilization's central method of control—scheduled awareness. Here on the front lines of the forced march of time, each measured step performed an existential insult, and with each insult another drip-drip-dripping away of life's precious energy.

Blake grimaced, hoping that outwardly condemning the current trend of his inner thoughts would be sufficient to change their direction.

But it didn't work, and his disquiet actually grew more determined, drawing strength from his efforts to derail it.

Then Blake thought of how absurd he must look to the guards on the viewing end of the security cameras—grimacing on his bed while his precious life dripped away from him. And the more he thought about this, the angrier he became.

Dog whistles blew in every corridor in his brain. Anger had to be controlled. Nothing posed a greater threat. Fear and anger had to be caged. They could feast too readily in here.

Calm down, Blake thought to himself, you're all right. Calm down. The concrete ceiling looked back at him, the familiar irregularities of the surface illuminated by the overhead light.

He got off the bunk and did seventy push-ups. Then he paced back and forth from the metal toilet to the steel door, rolling his shoulders to keep from stiffening up. Three steps one way, three steps back.

"Hey, Blake, you still awake?"—the forced whisper of the sixty-year-old across the hall, a lifer. He'd probably heard him pacing.

No, he didn't want to talk. Definitely not.

"Thanks, Jones," he said in the same practiced whisper, a voice appropriate for use only after eleven thirty. "I've got to get some sleep."

"You sure?"

"Not now, Jones."

Dexter Worthington Jones stayed quiet after that. He was a decent fellow, Blake thought, but he liked talking too much.

Still, Jones was one of the better guys, and Blake didn't want to offend him.

Contrary to the popular notion of prison, including Blake's before he found himself inside one, it was filled not only with meth-soaked gangbangers, though some of those could be found in here too. Prison society was about as diverse as any other, though the etiquette was more strictly enforced. Keeping on good terms with men who wanted to be locked up with you about as much as they wanted to be dragged behind a car required an almost-Victorian attention to power structures, personalities, and social nuances. Even in a prison like this one, where inmates couldn't usually see the person they were talking to, social pressures were enormous. Falling out with someone in a neighboring cell could poison a whole week for everyone. Not a place you wanted to be unpopular in. Speaking to other inmates was sensitive business. That said, outside the community of fellow inmates, Blake knew his chances of remaining whole shrank to almost nothing. All he could expect was whatever ragged shred of humanity could be stitched between cells. And if he didn't or couldn't participate, he was finished. The human garbage pit would have completed its work on him and he'd be done, bled out, fried.

The decent ones were priceless—the cognizant ones, the guys whose minds hadn't rotted. Never forget that, he reminded himself. Hold to them, because just beyond the companionship they offered waited a thriving emptiness with no hope at all. There, prison shoveled you like compost inside oblivion's garden.

Blake crossed over to the iron slots in his door and whispered, "Hey, Jones, you okay? Jones?"

"I'm okay, Blake. You okay?"

"I'm okay. Thanks for asking."

"Good night, man."

"Good night."

Feeling better, Blake did fifty more push-ups and about as many sit-ups, then returned to lying on his bunk. The two guys with televisions at the end of the range turned them off and one of them flushed his toilet. From the other direction came the indistinct jabbering of guards in the center hold, talking while they drank coffee. Down another corridor a crank yelled several times, fell quiet, and yelled again. Cranks were head cases who never should have been put in prison in the first place—and never would have been if the government had another place to put them. Prison was for the unneeded human labor that didn't stay inside the lines. Some of them yelled all the time, usually biblical stuff mixed with obscene sexual and racial profanities, evincing that the language of both the saved and of the lost was sourced from the same material.

Thankfully, most cranks were kept on Range C. Being locked up with them would undo even the best-trained minds. Blake had seen it happen to several guys. It took about three weeks. They started by yelling back at them to shut up. After this failed they simply yelled all the time, like barking dogs answering each other.

Blake felt secretly grateful for the range he'd recently been assigned to, filled with Level Two inmates, who in the opinion of the guards demonstrated better attitudes and behavior than those on Level One. Levels Four and Five were the highest, of course, and supposedly entailed privileges like computers. But descriptions of Level Three remained vague, and no one seemed to know anyone who had ever been on Level Four or Five. And needless to say, asking a guard about it could get you bounced down to Level One.

My father would be proud of me, Blake thought, if he knew. He didn't, though, because about a year before, Blake had told him never to visit again. Still, it made Blake feel good to think of his father being proud of him, even if it wasn't true.

He wondered what Nate might be doing. His ancient Kenworth might be broken down somewhere in Montana, with him sitting beside it along the road. Or he might be at home, eating chicken and biscuits.

Blake smiled at the latter thought. No one loved good food more than his father, and he spared no effort in obtaining it. Blake's memories eagerly crowded together—accompanying his father to remote farms, knocking on doors, asking, "Excuse me, but I heard you have some red peppers for sale, grown without pesticides. . . . Is it true you have air-cured beef? . . . My son and I would certainly appreciate your letting us know when these muskmelons are ripe. . . . Did you say corn-fed, walk-around-the-yard chickens without antibiotics? Brown eggs? No, we don't give a flying grommet whether you're inspected or not. . . . Yes, we would be very interested in goat cheese if you had any to spare. Do you know of anyone who raises shallots or mills their own wheat? . . . Sorry for the intrusion, but I recently had a cup of cider made from windfall and cherries; is there any chance that cider came from around here? . . . Someone told me you smoke carp. Is that true? . . . Say, are those freshly woven garlic braids?"

11:46 p.m. Blake decided he should pray before falling asleep, rolled out of his bunk, and knelt on the concrete.

This posture always felt a little undignified to Blake, especially under the omnipresent eye of the security camera. It was the position the guards made you get into before putting on the shackles—one of the reasons most inmates refused the once-a-day court-mandated optional exercise period in an outdoor cage. Yet almost everyone who claimed to have made some contact with God insisted upon it, Muslims especially.

Blake had at first complained (to himself) that a particular posture had nothing to do with how genuine his prayers were, and refused to kneel. If the legitimacy of prayers depended upon the physical arrangement of the body from which they were released, then the delivery system was more important than what it delivered, the law more valuable than the spirit. No, he wasn't going to do it. If God couldn't recognize true humility from the inside, then God wasn't God.

But eventually Blake noticed that his arguments against kneeling always seemed to come from an especially unreliable corner of his mind, where a well-known choir of dissidents greeted most things with scoffing contempt. A company of old boys, they automatically condemned anything new. And this more than anything else convinced him to discredit their voices. Who knew? A certain posture might play some role in praying. Perhaps it would help. Who could say? He'd try anything and needed whatever help he could get, however he could get it. And after he became accustomed to kneeling he was quick to ridicule any attempts to pray in another manner. The unreliable choir of dissidents took up the kneeling practice, as committed to protecting one habit as another.

The other problem Blake faced concerned the nature of the god he prayed to. All day long he'd been mostly agreeing with Spinoza, who did not believe the deity was a prayer-listener or prayer-grantor. Moment by moment, Spinoza's god created the universe and everything in it by revealing himself through all emerging phenomena. He couldn't listen in on his creation any more than the law of gravity could fall through space.

And though Blake mostly agreed with Spinoza, his need for a god of a different nature—a listening, sympathetic, humanlike god—temporarily vetoed this particular teaching. Born out of desperation, Blake's god was greater than reason, greater than Spinoza, greater than Blake. He could be both a listening god and a god who couldn't listen. There were no limits to his ability to manifest himself in whatever form his creatures needed him in.

Blake first began praying for his father. This was fairly effortless. He could easily imagine ways to improve his father's circumstances, including a better son, a better truck, and a girlfriend. Unsure of the appropriateness of the latter request, however, he decided not to allow that particular imagined good fortune to enter into his communication with the divine, and kept his well-wishing more generalized. He simply thought of his father with a distant fondness, and fervently desired the best for him.

Next, he prayed for Reverend Winifred Helm. Whatever events the Creator envisioned in his ongoing manifestation of unfolding glory, Winifred Helm deserved to be at the very center of them. Blake was sure of that.

These two were easy. His father and Winifred Helm already had one foot in heaven as far as Blake was concerned. They were perhaps the last virtuous ones—those whose luminous presence on the earth kept the rest of humanity from cosmic condemnation and eradication. Praying for them felt as natural as praying for peace.

Then Danielle Workhouse walked into his mind, and Blake's prayers for her—like those for his mother, whom he hadn't seen since he was four and could hardly remember—were far more complicated. He loved Danielle Workhouse in an especially soul-devouring way, and because of this he could not honestly pray for her without including himself inside the prayer as a stowaway to her dark ecstatic presence. And it was impossible to imagine God approving of anything that included Blake and Danielle. The two of them together almost ensured the absence of everything a person should pray for. According to Spinoza, God manifested them both, of course, yet it seemed impossible to believe they were divinely intended to be anywhere near each other.

Danielle. Her name bullied around in his mind, knocking over everything else and shoving it beyond his awareness. He asked her to leave, but she stayed. The more he insisted, the stronger she became. She wanted his full attention. She wanted him to remember how her body smelled in the morning, with baked steaminess from the night's rest.

Soon, Blake found himself still on his knees, but not praying at all. She'd banished his reverential mood. Feeling like a failure, he got off the floor and sat on the bunk. Then, needing a new view, he walked over two steps and sat on the floor with his back against the steel door, staring at eye level with the flusher mounted above the toilet on the other side of the cell.

Women presented enormous difficulties for Blake, especially in here, where there were none. The distress he suffered through them had a history long before Danielle Workhouse came to embody everything he most wanted and feared from them. He could remember envying other children who lived with their mothers. He'd watched them longingly, wanted to be close to them, marveled at their shapes, the way they moved, the clothes they wore, the sound of their voices, their hair, the way their arms poked out of their sleeves and their feet slid into shoes. Everything about them seemed in contrast to the spartan world he and his father lived in. The smell of perfume filled him with a wonder too delicate to explore. What kind of creatures would wear that scent?

What was going on with females, anyway? What made them different? Could their difference be unmade? How did one go about talking to them? Everything about them seemed terrifyingly attractive yet alien. He couldn't imagine any appropriate way of approaching them, and when he saw others performing this utterly impossible feat, he couldn't imagine himself imitating them.

On one particular occasion in his adolescence, he had succeeded in making eye contact with someone he felt deeply attracted to, and immediately burst into tears. Needing to protect himself from further occasions that could provoke this shameful vulnerability, he energetically applied himself to excelling in activities designed by males for avoiding this vulnerability altogether: sports, roughhousing, and risk-taking.

After high school Blake began working in the foundry. He bought an old pickup and several motorcycles to race on weekends. He moved out of his father's house and into a room in Red Plain. Several years went by, and while he was living there he met, or rather saw, Danielle Workhouse.

She rented a tiny apartment above a secondhand store, and six days a week walked to and from the cement plant on the edge of town.

The way she walked drew his attention. It was almost as if one leg might be slightly shorter than the other. The tiny imperfection caused her hips to swivel a little farther around on one side, though not enough to unbalance her stride. The visual result was a subtle clicking into place, a repeated cocking motion. Most people would not have noticed, but Blake had always been interested in how people moved forward. Each step entailed a conscious act of falling into the future, and even though the act had become habituated to where there was little conscious effort involved, it still revealed something essential, an infantile attitude toward the unknown. No one moved forward in the same way, even in the same family. Danielle Workhouse was determined to get where she was going—an adventure looking for a suitable place to unfurl. There were no extra movements, no swinging arms; there was no looking to either side, changing speeds, or adjusting clothes—just a straight-ahead-leaning, brisk, and thrusting movement.

She walked from her thighs.

She also looked as if she might cut her own hair. The sides of her black curly mane appeared better thought-out, more even than the back, and Blake didn't think there were styles in which the back was supposed to be crooked. It looked a little like his own hair, which he cut himself.

She seemed to have three outfits: a blue skirt with a white top, a brown dress, and black slacks with a ruffled orange blouse. And she appeared to have just two pairs of shoes, brown and black. She wore a thigh-length gray sweater with widely-spaced buttons up the front in even the coldest weather.

At exactly seven o'clock each morning, she stepped out of her building, locked the door leading up the narrow staircase, and walked the ten blocks to the cement plant. Her return times apparently depended on how busy they were at the plant. Some nights she didn't get home until Blake had left for the night shift in the foundry.

Once, when leaving the plant, she stepped out of the stone building and crossed the street between two cement mixers. Blake was on his way to work. He turned around in the gravel lot, drove back, and asked if she wanted a ride. He'd never been this close to her before. Without stopping, she glared at him through the pickup window, her eyes bright black inside a tightly stretched brown face, an angry yet slightly fearful expression. Scrubbed clean, no makeup, no jewelry, no frills. Her black hair had the color of a burned field, her lips straight across and full. She reminded him of a drawn bow.

From this distance, Blake noticed that her shorter leg made more of a difference than he'd thought originally; each time her weight shifted and her hips made the small but perceptible cocking motion to the side, her body gave a little jerk, readying for another stride. As soon as he noticed this, he felt a corresponding lurch inside him and an ache opened up in his throat. Her sexuality seemed to be exercising inside him.

He drove beside her for several blocks, but she never looked at him again. Finally he turned off at the gas station and took the back road to the foundry.

Then one night she stood on the sidewalk in front of her building. An older man, maybe fifty, prevented her from going inside. When she turned away from him, he swung her around roughly to face him. She spit on the pavement and he shouted something and grabbed both her arms. She knocked his hands away and stepped farther down the sidewalk. When he lunged at her, she ducked to avoid him and shoved him to the side, where he stumbled into the street. Her movements seemed almost practiced. He came after her again and she easily outmaneuvered him again.

By this time Blake was out of his pickup and could hear them.

"You're drunk," she said, avoiding him now with mocking ease. "There's no use you ever coming over here. Don't do it again. Go home, idiot."

As Blake crossed the street he wondered what part he intended to play in this. When he reached the other side the older man saw him and shrank back, muttered something, and hurried away, heading toward the nearest tavern.

"Are you all right?" asked Blake.

Her black eyes glowed fiercely and she took a step away from him. "Beat it, fool. Nobody asked you to crawl over here. Get the hell away from me before I tie your dick in a knot."

She opened the door leading up to her apartment and slammed it closed behind her.

Blake was unprepared for such a wide splattering of words, as if some well-established history of malevolence already existed between them. He was so unprepared for it that by the time he got back into his truck and drove away, he wasn't sure exactly what had happened.

That night at the foundry he broke hot castings from molding frames and ground off the sharp ragged burrs. And as he worked he kept thinking about her.

By the time he got off in the morning, he could hardly remember anything she'd said—only the vitriolic manner in which she spoke, as if a relationship somehow existed between them.

She must like me a little, he thought. It was the only way to explain the connection he felt to her.

11:56. Down the corridor, the electronic lock on the central hold snapped and the range door banged open, followed by a quick succession of echoes. Third night check. A guard stepped into the hallway, his movements announced by the dragging shuffle of his feet and the rattle of the keys hanging from his belt. Shuffle, rattle, shuffle, shuffle, rattle, shuffle, rattle.

Blake climbed back onto his bunk, felt his stomach turn over as he recognized the slow, 250-pound amble. Bud Jenks didn't usually work the night shift. Shuffle, rattle, shuffle.

Maybe Bud Jenks hadn't always been the way he was now, thought Blake, trying to talk himself into a better frame of mind. Maybe he was just an ordinary guy living in a small town and looking for a job, when he heard the Lockbridge prison needed more corrections officers. After his initial training, he got a uniform and for the first time noticed a curious mixture of hatred and fear in prisoners' eyes when they looked at him. And he liked it.

It might not have been the first taste of power that changed him. Perhaps it took several years. Blake wanted to think so. He was desperately trying to believe in something larger than himself, something at the foundation of the world that could not be held responsible for making Bud Jenks. Bud Jenks alone should be blamed for Bud Jenks.

The shuffle stopped outside Blake's cell, followed by a long reign of silence. Then a heavy boot kicked the bottom of the steel door and the cell exploded with sound. "Hey, Bookfucker, you asleep in there?"

Blake said nothing.

"You, Bookfucker, I'm talking to you. I asked if you were asleep."

Another kick and the room again exploded in sound.

"Hey, you insubordinate asshole, you better answer me when I ask you a question."

"I'm awake," said Blake.

"I thought so, because, see, I'm concerned maybe you don't have the right sleeping habits. So every hour tonight I'm going to check to make sure you're sleeping. Is that okay with you, Bookfucker?"

"Leave him alone," said Jones across the hall.

"What was that?"

"Leave him alone."

Following a long silence, Jenks spoke. "Did you just swear at me, Jones?"

"No."

"I think you goddamn did, Jones. You swore at me, and that's a violation. And look here, what's this piece of crud on the floor? You threw this at me through the vents in your door."

"No I didn't."

"Too bad, Jones. You've been over here on Level Two for quite a while now, haven't you? Nice place. It's quiet here most of the time. A couple of you guys got televisions over here and you get to see all those nice visitors from time to time. You get to make phone calls once a week, and for some reason the food here doesn't get all mixed together and taste like someone pissed in it. Too bad, Jones."

"What are you talking about?"

"See, there just happens to be a cell open over on Range C. You know where Range C is, Jones? I've got an uncle who delivers the food over there. You know where Range C is, Jones?"

"Yes sir."

"Of course you do. Range C is way over on the other side of the building. And guess what cell just happens to be empty right now? I'll tell you. It's the one just across from Raymond Cawl. You know Old Ray, don't you, Jones? He's the great big guy missing most of his teeth, the gentleman who never showers and screams all night and throws his feces into the hall. I'm sure you remember him. Well, tomorrow your door is going to be right across from his, and you're going to be behind it for a long, long time. Oh yes, I forgot to tell you, Jones—and you'll love this part—just beside that empty cell is Bernie Hortell. I'm sure you remember him. As you probably already know, Mr. Hortel sings while he beats on his walls. And the food over there, well, you remember what it's like. You were over there once, remember?"

"No call for you to do this, sir. I never swore at you or threw anything."

"Rules are rules. I don't make 'em, you know. I just enforce 'em. It's my job and you wouldn't want me to not do my job, would you, Jones?"

Silence.

"Of course, you got the right to file a complaint. That's also the rule, Jones. You can do that. Once you're over on Range C you can file a grievance report. You can tell them how you came to the aid of this punk here, who beat up a police officer and later assaulted a guard. You can tell them. First thing tomorrow morning you'll be moved."

Shuffle, shuffle. Silence. Then another boot against the door of Blake's cell.

"Sleep tight, Bookfucker. I'll be back."

Shuffle, shuffle, rattle.

Blake lay on his bed staring at the dim light above him, his anger mounting. He knotted his hands into fists, closed his eyes, and fought with himself. It was Jones's own fault. He'd brought it on himself, broke the cardinal rule: don't get involved in any injustices other than your own. Mind your own business.

It didn't work. The anger was still there. Shaking with impotent rage, Blake rolled out of the bunk and onto his knees again, praying for help, for strength, for mercy, for anything. How could so much wrong be allowed to continue? God save me. I can't do this any longer.

Without getting up, he crawled over to the door and whispered through the grate. "Jones, hey, Jones. Are you all right? Jones?"

Silence.

"Jones? Hey, man, I'll make the complaint tomorrow to the review committee. We'll tell them the truth . . . Jones? . . . I know this time they'll listen. They will . . . Jones?"

Silence.

Suddenly Blake felt something inside him split open and spill out, a rupture deeper than he could reach. He lay flat on the concrete floor, looked at the ceiling, and did something he'd done only two other times in his life—once, at four, when he understood his mother was never coming back, and once when he'd first entered prison. He found the part of him that was not.

It was very small, hard to find, impossible to understand. It did not think, feel, imagine, or remember. It did not know Jones or anything about prison, had never heard of Spinoza, did not know Bud Jenks or Winifred Helm, or his father or Danielle Workhouse. It was the part of him neither attracted to nor repelled by anything else, the space-within-space and time-within-time that did not recognize the survival of Blake Bookchester as a valid concept. It was the part of him that was not. It contained only a cold flickering awareness of nothing in particular. And to that dark flickering he wholly committed himself.

Standing in the Middle

Heading into Chicago on Interstate 94, transparent waves of heat rose from the pavement and curled off the long hood of the Kenworth. The air trembled and glowed, luminous with baked humidity. Nate turned to merge onto I-294 and the taillights in front of him lit up in a stream of angry red. The traffic stopped, started, slowed, and then came to a standstill. Nate thought he could remember when—if you avoided certain times of the day—you could stay out of this. But Chicago traffic could snarl at any time now.

The station wagon directly in front of him moved ahead eight feet and he took up the slack. Over the next forty-five minutes he repeated this stop-gap movement three times, but he was still on the merging ramp.

He brought his logbook up to date, filled in several additional columns, and thought about nothing in particular. The temperature outside continued to climb, and he noticed with some concern that the heat gauge on the dashboard had inched up as well. He successfully assured himself this was only natural, given the situation. When it rose higher he turned off the air conditioner to take a little stress off the diesel and rolled down the window.

Then the engine began to idle unevenly and the color of the exhaust turned a shade darker. Again, he refused to worry. The injectors needed cleaning—he already knew that. The engine had over six hundred thousand miles on it. Still, there was maybe a cushion of fifty thousand or so before things really started going south.

The air seeping through the opened window felt like breath from a large mouth.

Taking a drink of water, he drew his spiral-bound notebook from the dash compartment and read over a letter he'd started to his son. Unable to think of anything to add, he put the notebook back.

The heat gauge climbed higher, accompanied by a barely audible whine. Then the whine grew more persistent, and the fan belt broke, snapping against the inside hood with a crack. Warning lights lit up on the dash, matching the color of the brake lights outside.

Nate pulled onto the shoulder, crowded close to the embankment wall, turned off the engine, and phoned the dispatch operator in Wisconsin.

"Water pump seized up—I'm broke down."

"Where are you?"

"Outside Chicago, just off I-94, on the entrance ramp to 294."

"Full or empty?"

"Full."

"There's a Mack shop not far from you. I'll give you the number."

Nate called and the service person said they could bring the tractor in and fix it tomorrow, but they couldn't tow a loaded trailer. "You've got to lose the trailer. Call me back. I can have someone there in forty-five minutes."

"Not in this traffic," said Nate, and called dispatch again.

"Okay, Nate. Hold on, let me check." Click. Silence. Click. "Here's one. Bob Miller is about an hour from you and he's got a load he can put up for a while."

Nate turned on his warning lights and climbed out. Blistering heat and blinding light gave him the impression of stepping onto the surface of the sun. He placed warning markers along the shoulder and thought about calling highway patrol. The metal was hot. He lowered the jacks on the front of the trailer and broke open the hitch. Then he moved the tractor forward enough for someone else to hook up.

In the hot shade of the embankment wall, Nate watched the traffic slowly lurch forward again, gaining speed. Most of the other truck drivers waved as they went by, or at least smiled. The others glanced at him with a mixture of anxiety and disapproval—a premonition of their own breakdown.

Two hours later, a Peterbilt pulled onto the off-strip and backed into the waiting trailer hitch, the traffic speeding by only several feet away.

The driver climbed down onto the pavement—mid-forties, unshaven, open white shirt, sleeves torn off, jeans, and untied shoes.

"It's a hot one." He spoke rapidly and without looking up. "Where do these electric motors have to go?"

"South Side." Nate gave him the paperwork.

"Been here long?"

"Long enough. Thanks for coming."

"Wrecker on the way?"

Nate nodded.

Above him a small face appeared fleetingly in the window of the Peterbilt—a girl, maybe fifteen or sixteen, disheveled, dirty hair, pretending to look indifferent.

"You got someone with you," Nate observed.

"Not for long," he said, glancing briefly up at the cab. "Look, you need anything?"

"I'm good to go."

"We're done here, then," the man said, opening the door and climbing up. Nate made quick eye contact again with the teenager inside, then looked away.

It wasn't that long ago, it seemed, when truck stops and public lots did not have as many people selling themselves to drivers. There had always been some of that, of course, but with the crippled economy it was now so bad that some parts of the country put security fences around parking areas and charged fees for the privilege of avoiding the prostitutes, dealers, pornography vendors, and other lot lizards.

I must be getting old, Nate thought. These things didn't used to bother me.

The shadow running along the embankment wall was thicker now, more luxuriously dark. He returned to sitting in it, and a small breeze found him.

All things considered, trucking was a good way to make a living, though there was no doubt that it had contributed to his wife running off. He'd left her alone with the baby too much. He should have known that, or rather, what he did know should have meant more to him than it had.

Afterward, he told everyone—especially those in his family, his aunts, uncles, cousins—that he hadn't seen it coming. Her leaving had no warning, out of the blue. Here one day, gone the next.

But it wasn't true. Her escape had been building for years. She'd carried it in her hands, worn it on her face. Her eyes couldn't stop planning it. He knew, or should have known, from the way she moved, sitting on the bed in the middle of the night, holding the baby, slumped over and staring out the window.

Ignorance was the problem, he knew. Some people were just too damn stupid to see what was going on right in front of them. And ignorance wasn't simply a failure to register facts and understand them. No, Nate's kind of ignorance had been more like a force. It persisted vigorously in knowing that all women were natural mothers. He'd known that with absolute certainty. Having children fulfilled women, all of them. They needed babies to take care of as surely as plants needed water. Difficulties might arise, sure, but those were to be expected. And even if they weren't expected, a mother would never reconsider motherhood. Such an idea was beyond possibility's outer wall. And as for a mother leaving her child, well, that was unthinkable. Did apple trees produce oranges? It would never happen.

Nate often wondered where his false confidence had come from, how the notion became planted in him that no matter how difficult caregiving seemed, all women actually enjoyed it. Did someone teach it to him? If so, he didn't remember the instruction. Somehow he'd swallowed the corrupted seed on his own.

Nate could still see her frantically signaling to him with a thousand silent pleas. He could feel her broken hope, failing courage, and frightened despair. I can't do this any longer, Nate.

He should have known the truth, and the truth should have changed him. Instead, he ignored her, left her alone, month after month after month.

Oh Christ, he thought, looking into the heat rising from the concrete. His kinship to himself sometimes felt unbearable.

He saw a tractor coming toward him with a piggyback fifth wheel. It pulled out of the traffic and backed up behind the Kenworth.

"I'll take you into the shop," said the driver.

After he locked down Nate's truck, they climbed onto the seat together, then drove up the ramp and onto 294.

"How long you been out here?"

"Couple hours."

"Hot day."

"Yep."

"You got a place to stay?"

"Not yet."

"There's a little motel not far from the shop—pretty cheap. I can drop you off."

"Thanks."

They hit a chuck hole and it moved through them.

"These roads are getting bad," said the driver.

"My boy's in prison."

"Sorry to hear that. Nothing serious, I hope."

"Drugs."

"What kind?

"The kind you go to prison for."

"Sorry to hear that."

"You said that already."

"I know. I couldn't think of anything else."

"He doesn't want me to visit, says it's humiliating."

The driver said nothing.

That night at the motel, Nate lay on the bed and hurried through television channels. He found a western, but he had already seen it. Then he took a shower and fell into a fitful sleep.

The following afternoon he called the Mack shop and talked to one of the mechanics.

"We've got the pump out and will have a new one in by four o'clock."

"I'll be over."

"Your engine needs an overhaul. Bearings are loose, pistons slapping in the cylinders."

"I know it."

Then he reported in to the dispatch operator.

"Nate, are you running?"

"I'll be up tomorrow."

"There's a load of plastic wrap and freezer paper in North Chicago. It needs to go out tomorrow to Wormwood, Iowa, to arrive before nightfall."

A small town in southeastern Iowa, Wormwood was Nate's least favorite place to go. On the edge of town was a slaughterhouse bigger than the rest of Wormwood. The packing plant there butchered hogs and cattle. You could smell it for miles. There was a security fence surrounding the plant, separating it from a rambling slum of trailers, rusting motor homes, and tin and tar-paper shacks, where mostly Spanish-speaking people lived.

The Wormwood workers were nervous, and the security guards and management were surly. The loading station was around behind the hog pens, chutes, and offal rendering. There were about a dozen docks, and all the good slots were always taken. To maneuver into position you had to turn so sharply that the end of your trailer disappeared in the mirror. Some of the younger drivers would try for hours to get lined up. It was a nightmare. No one wanted to try it after dark. When you finally got in, there often wasn't anyone around to open the doors or who understood English. They sometimes wanted the drivers to unload the trailers themselves, because most of the workers couldn't, or wouldn't, operate the forklift.

"Can't make that one," said Nate. "The repairs won't be done in time. Do you have a later one?"

A long pause reminded Nate of the management's grudging acceptance of drivers who owned their own trucks. "Maybe I can make it," he added. "I'll push them at the shop."

"We'll get someone else. Wormwood Packing locks up early and we've had trucks stuck in there overnight. Can't find anyone to sign off on the papers or even open the damned front gates. They don't speak English. I don't know what goes on there, but . . . forget it. I don't give a rip what they do there."

Nate didn't want to imagine what went on there either. It was an ugly place. One time he'd delivered a load of refrigeration units and another truck backed into the dock next to him—a rusted out cab-over Freightliner. Everyone seemed in a hurry to open the trailer, and inside it smelled like something he didn't want to identify. It was filled with packing crates and corrugated boxes on pallets, each about four feet square—big enough for washers and dryers, maybe.

"What are those?" he asked the man he'd just handed his invoice papers to.

"I don't know," the man answered, and walked away.

While they were unloading, one of the boxes fell over and two people rolled out—a man and a boy, frightened, dirty, and emaciated. Several large men told Nate to leave.

"Like I said, I can try to get the shop to—"

"Forget it. I've got a load for you in North Chicago. Take it to the shipping plant in Mason City, Iowa. There's another load waiting for you there."

"Where's that one headed?"

"New York."

"Thanks," said Nate, and the dispatcher hung up.

At the machine shop, the bill came to over eight hundred dollars.

"Is that a problem?" asked the woman who had just passed the slip of paper to him through the little window in the glass booth.

"No," he answered, and wrote out a check. When he got back to the motel he called his bank to see if his account would cover it.

In the middle of the next afternoon, somewhere in northern Iowa, Nate's mood began to darken again. The recently cultivated cornfields around the moving truck spread out flat in all directions—horizon to horizon in uniform lines of sprouting green on a black-earth background. Planted along a grid, each corn plant currently stood at a uniform height of about twelve inches. Nate could feel his mind growing numb. All these plants in perfect rows, maturing at exactly the same rate, racing toward the grain harvest and into the mouth end of livestock digestive tracts, creating more civilization, more government, more laws, more prisons. On and on, as far as the eye could see, the raw material of man. Agribusiness was the ultimate expression of the times, making skyscrapers, universities, computers, and particle colliders irrelevant by comparison. Mile after mile inched by and the surrounding green rows never changed.

His mood darkened further when he remembered that there was a weigh station about a half hour ahead. Though his truck was well under the eighty thousand-pound maximum, the Department of Transportation sometimes had its inspection agents there as well, and heavy fines were levied for things like out-of-date fire extinguishers, expired transit permits, and the small crack in his windshield that could easily be seen from the inside.

He radioed eastbound drivers. "The station, are they open?"

"You bet. Light's on and they're hauling 'em in."

"See any DOT?"

"The Suburbans are there and brown uniforms everywhere."

"Can you get around? Do you know this area?"

"Go twenty miles or more before you cut back. DOT's got another trap set in a wide place in the road about ten miles west."

"Thanks, friend."

"Back at you."

Nate turned onto a country road heading south, deeper into the young cornfields. A cloud of dust rose up behind the trailer, filling his mirrors.

Most country roads in Iowa are laid out in square miles, but for some reason this one continued for miles without intersecting another. When he found one he turned right onto patched macadam, where the shoveled-in and stamped-down repairs were lumpy and darker than the rest of the faded surface.

In the far distance, Nate saw a little rise of land. His attention clamped onto this blip on the horizon. He turned at the next intersection to draw closer, and after several miles he could see it more clearly. On top of the little hill was a tree, and it rose up against the sky like a lone plant growing in the middle of an empty lot. When he imagined sitting beneath it, he felt better.

He turned the Kenworth onto a smaller, narrower road. Later, Nate turned again, this time onto a dirt surface, where he hoped he would not meet another vehicle, because there was barely enough room.

After another mile, the hill and tree came clearly into view, separated from a weathered house and a small garage by a broad section of corn.

A poorly maintained drive connected the house to the road.

Nate did not pull in. Instead, he parked the Kenworth as far into the ditch as he dared go. After turning off the engine, he walked down the lane, with rows of corn on both sides.

A small garden grew between the garage and the house, connected by a worn path. The inside door was open to allow air from the screen door to enter, and faint music could be heard inside, the kind often played on afternoon public radio programs. Nate knocked and waited as the music stopped and other sounds arranged themselves inside, then gathered and came toward him.

"Come in," said a man who appeared to be ancient. He was wearing a pair of faded gray sweatpants and a paint-speckled blue work shirt with an orange patch sewn onto the right shoulder. An impressive growth of fine white hair grew out of his face, but the top of his head appeared to have retired from growing anything a long time ago. His eyes were gray and surprisingly expressive, beneath two white thickets of brow.

"I'm sorry to bother you," said Nate, "but I was wondering if I could walk over to the little hill behind your house and sit under the tree for a while."

"You're not bothering me at all," the man said, reaching for the door-frame to steady himself. "You can sit under that tree as long as you want, young fella."

"Thank you," said Nate, amused to suddenly feel a bit younger. "I was driving by and I just thought, well, a little more elevation would be welcome . . . anyway, thank you."

"Go right ahead. That's what the tree's there for."

Nate did not want to prolong the old man's standing, which seemed to require a great deal of effort.

"Thank you again, then," he said, backing away from the door.

To reach the hill Nate first had to walk through a hundred yards of cornfield, and the young leaves scratched against the sides of his pants. The black dirt was soft under his boots, still holding moisture.

When the ground began to rise, he walked out of the cornrow and into grass. The soft stems brushed his shoes as he climbed.

The giant silver maple at the top of the hill had a trunk nearly as wide as a garage door. He looked up into it and saw massive limbs flowing outward and upward, supporting an array of branches and stems and a plantation of leaves that quivered audibly in the breeze. The undersides of the leaves, lighter in color, glittered when the leaves moved.

It was twenty degrees cooler here in the shade, and Nate immediately felt his body relaxing. He sat down and leaned against the trunk, then looked out across the ocean of cornrows below. On and on the green plants grew, pulling nutrients from the ground and turning them into corn.

The darkness that had afflicted him earlier evaporated. From up here he could see all the way into the next county. He imagined the roots of the tree entering the hill beneath him, tunneling down, extending tendril threads into the roots of the corn plants, passing from one to another, following the rows, moving in all directions through the ocean of plants, on to the ends of the earth.

The tree had presided over generations of crops, stretching back a hundred years or more. When the maple first began to grow, there was probably a collection of small farms and homesteads beneath it, hundreds and hundreds of them with different crops, different roads, different colors, different smells, different sounds, different people. All were gone now. Nate let his mind flow into the tree, wanting to feel the sky in the tree's way of feeling.

He lost track of how long he had been sitting there, but as the sun fell farther west and the air softened, he thought he could hear a new sound. The sound continued, and when he turned toward it he saw the old man walking out of the cornfield at the bottom of the hill and begin climbing. His movements were slow and halting, and every so often he leaned against his cane to center his equilibrium and nurture his remaining strength. His shadow followed him step for step. A cloth bag hung from his shoulder, and Nate considered going down to help him, but something convinced him to remain sitting.

When the older man reached the shade of the tree, Nate stood up and said hello.

"Hope I'm not disturbing you, young fella."

"You're not."

"I hoped I wouldn't be. I thought you might enjoy something to drink. And I brought along a little something for us to eat together, if you wouldn't mind sharing a meal with an old man who doesn't see many people anymore."

"I'm honored," said Nate. He helped the old man pull the cloth bag from around his shoulder and eased him onto the grass around the base of the tree.

His thin wrinkled hands pulled two metal cans of beer from the pack. Next came two red plastic food containers of the kind Nate remembered everyone having forty years ago, when plastic was hard, thick, and brightly colored.

They opened the cans and drank. The old man handed one of the plastic containers to Nate along with a four-pronged fork. Nate pulled off the lid and a drift of steam came up from what looked like stew.

"I heated it before I came," the old man said. "It tastes better than it looks."

Nate stuck his fork in and took a bite. A moment later he set the dish down, rose to his feet, and backed away. "Where did you get this?" he demanded.

"What?"

"This mashed-potato pie. It's the exact one. Where did you get it?"

"I made it myself," he said, looking at Nate with studied bewilderment.

Nate sat back down. "I'm sorry. It seemed for a moment like someone was playing a trick on me. Excuse me. This was very kind of you, bringing food up here."

"Don't mention it. Like I said, I don't get many visitors. And come to think of it, I learned how to make this pie from someone whose car broke down near here about a year ago. As I remember, she had an accent something like yours when she talked. She seldom did, though—a quiet, lovely person."

"No kidding. Where was she from?"

"Somewhere in Wisconsin."

"Who was she?"

"I don't know who she was, but the timing chain broke in her car and she couldn't get it fixed for several days. Because I had an extra room, I offered to put her up. While she was here she made one of these pies for us to eat. I liked it so much she later sent me the recipe. I make it about once a month."

"I don't suppose you remember her name."

"Of course I do. Her name was Beulah, but she said most people called her Bee. It's an unusual name, and I remember it partly because of that."

Nate stood up again. "No," he said. "She's my cousin."

"Well, that accounts for the accent, I guess."

"Tell me about her," said Nate.

"If she's your cousin you ought to know already."

"I do, or did. I haven't seen her in many years. Did Bee come up here?" asked Nate.

"At least twice a day—usually early in the morning and then later at night. She often stood right where you're standing now."

Nate looked out over the ocean of young corn and thought about this. The green leaf-blades yielding to the variable wind seemed to be dancing from their own power, and he understood something that he hadn't known before: time moved both ways. He felt it pushing him out of his past and pulling him into the future. Before this moment he'd known only the pushed-from-behind part, away from events in the past. But now, standing under the soft maple, he felt the unfinished at work. He and Bee were being drawn together into an as-yet-unrealized actuality. He felt like an infant floating downstream in a basket, and at that moment he shivered.

The Interview

Ace Cleaning scheduled a morning interview for Danielle Workhouse. Before the streetlight went out in front of the meat locker, Danielle was up. As usual, she sat at the table for a while, and as Ivan crawled out of bed he could hear the pages turning in her catalogs. Then she took a shower, and when she came out of the bathroom she had on a pair of new jeans, a gray shirt, and sneakers.

Ivan wore his best brown pants and a white shirt with the store creases still in it. His mother drank a cup of cold coffee to settle her nerves, and Ivan ate a bowl of oatmeal with brown sugar sprinkled on it.

Outside, the sun had just come up and the air felt misty-cool. Most of the cars still had their lights on. The Bronco didn't start, because the battery was shot, but Danielle had another one from the Buick her mother had wrecked last winter. She lugged it down from the apartment, clamped on the jumpers, and the motor started on the second try.

The Roebuck home was not very far from town, set a good distance back from the road. The long driveway leading up the hill was made of poured concrete. Turning onto it, his mother said something in a scornful manner about how wastefully expensive so much concrete must have been. Looking out the window, Ivan thought about this, and privately decided that if someone owned a construction company and a cement plant, they could probably have as much as they wanted. Somehow the idea of wasting didn't seem to fit with unlimited supply.

Trees grew on both sides of the drive. A flatbed truck loaded with cement blocks was parked to the right, and farther up, a crawler with wide steel tracks. There were dumpers, graders, front-end loaders, double-cab pickups, and a cab-roller. And all of them said Roebuck Construction.

There was a parking lot at the top of the hill, with a large pole shed in the middle of it and doors tall enough for eighteen-wheelers. His mother parked in front of the building. Men in work clothes walked in and out of the service door on the side. They watched Ivan's mother climb out of the Bronco as if she were the last glazed doughnut on the shelf, but they didn't come over or yell or whistle or anything. Ivan felt relieved. His mother stuffed some papers under her arm, and together they walked up the sidewalk leading to what Ivan thought must surely qualify as a mansion. The men watched all the way.

Up close, the house looked like a castle. It was tall, with conical roofs, and even the chalky-gray paint looked castle-colored. A covered porch reached all the way around the ground floor. There were porches on the other floors too, but they didn't go all the way around. Some were just big enough to step outside, turn around, and go back inside.

They climbed the seven steps to the porch, and were met by a wide wooden door with no window. Danielle rapped with her knuckles, but it didn't make much noise. Even pounding with the side of her fist didn't have much effect. Then she noticed the plastic button.

When the door swung open a woman towered on the other side, dressed sort of like an office worker. Amy Roebuck seemed older than his mother, Ivan thought, but it was hard to tell with grown-ups. And she talked the way women do when they have too much to do.

His mother handed over the papers she'd brought from Ace. Mrs. Roebuck flipped through the documents quickly, then handed them back.

"I've already seen these," she said. "Come in. Do you like to be called Danielle?"

"You can call me Dart."

"Like the game?"

"Just like it. This is my son, Ivan."

"Hello, Ivan," Mrs. Roebuck said, looking down at him.

"Hi," said Ivan.

"Very well, Dart. Thank you for coming. I apologize for all the equipment in the yard. Buck had to vacate a job site in Red Plain on quick notice, and it was easiest to bring it all here. He promised to move it soon, but you know how that goes."

Danielle and Ivan didn't know anything about how that went, but they stepped inside anyway.

"Take your shoes off, Ivan," snapped his mother.

"That's not necessary," said Mrs. Roebuck, smiling in a painful way.

"Yes it is," said Danielle, and sloughed off her own low-cut sneakers by digging into the heels with the ends of her toes and stepping out of them. On the shiny wood floor her bare feet stood next to a humungous pair of shoes that looked to Ivan more like brown leather infant car seats than shoes. They were so large that both his mother's shoes could have been dropped down inside one of them. "No sense messing up someone's hard work."

Ivan took off his shoes. The floor felt smooth, hard, and very flat under his white socks.

They followed Mrs. Roebuck into the first room, which she called the formal dining room. "We almost never use it," she said, and for some reason this made her look sad. Then they went down the hall.

There was a big table in the kitchen, with fat wide chairs. A white-whiskered man in suspenders, loose tan pants, and a long-john top sat on a stool at the counter, eating cold cereal. Mrs. Roebuck introduced Wallace Roebuck, explaining that he was her father-in-law and lived on the second floor. He didn't seem very sociable, at least not this early in the morning, and after scowling at Ivan's mother he slurped up the rest of his cornflakes and left the kitchen, carrying his cup of coffee.

Danielle looked through the cupboards and pantry. Every time she opened a cabinet, Mrs. Roebuck shifted her posture, stood straighter, flinched, took a quick breath, or gave some other sign that she wasn't used to having other people in her kitchen. When Danielle slid a pantry shelf out to look in the back, Mrs. Roebuck leaped forward to catch a falling jar of pickles. But Danielle caught it, prompting a pained smile from Mrs. Roebuck. "That always tips over," she said, taking the jar from Danielle and setting it back in its place.

"We're not real big breakfast eaters," Mrs. Roebuck explained as she carried the old man's bowl and spoon over to the sink. "Buck is usually gone before I'm up. It's unpredictable when Wally gets up, because he's trying to get ready for the afterlife. He pays a lot of attention to his dreams, and his schedule varies from one day to the next. He prefers to find something himself rather than eat what you put in front of him—except for coffee, which he drinks all day long. He'll even come down in the middle of the night looking for caffeine. I try to always keep a pot on."

"I know folks like that," said Danielle, and Ivan wondered who they were, because he didn't know any. He also had never heard of someone getting ready for the afterlife and wondered what would be involved other than dying. August would probably know, he thought, and he made a mental note to ask him.

"We should go up now and meet Grandmother Florence. She lives on the third floor."

"Your grandmother?" repeated Danielle, as if she'd never heard of such a thing.

"Yes. Florence is one hundred and eight years old and doesn't require much help. One meal is all, and she eats the same thing every day."

"What's that?" asked Danielle, as they followed Mrs. Roebuck down the hallway and up the wide wooden staircase. There were enough rooms, Ivan noticed, for five or six families.

"Sardines and raisin toast."

"That's it?"

"We argued for years over her diet, but after she reached one hundred the doctors said we should let her eat whatever she wants. They said she'd outlived what medical science could make sense of."

"Is she always in bed?"

"Oh no. She gets up every morning at seven thirty, takes a bath, dresses, lays out her clothes for the following day, and then sits in her chair by the window. She usually stays there most of the day, making her rosaries."

"Her what?"

"Her prayer beads. She's made over a thousand. The church takes them to less-fortunate countries for people to pray with."

Ivan couldn't think of anything more wacko than praying with beads.

"A thousand?" repeated his mother.

"She enjoys it."

"She doesn't need anything else—just sardines and toast?"

"Not usually. She's happy as long as she has her supply of beads, crosses, and the special thread to string them. If she needs anything else, she'll tell you."

"She can talk?"

"Of course."

"Where do you get her supplies?"

"The church sends them after the priest blesses the thread."

By this time they'd reached the third floor. Danielle and Ivan followed Mrs. Roebuck down a long hallway, at the end of which she gently tapped on a door.

From the other side Ivan heard, "Come in, Amy."

"She always knows it's me," Mrs. Roebuck explained as they entered the room.

"You always knock the same way, dear," said a wrinkled old woman only slightly larger than Ivan. She was sitting in front of an arched window with stained glass around the sides. There was enough room for another person to sit on each side of her in the overstuffed chair, and her black shoes hovered several inches above the floor. She speared a bead with a long needle and worked the red crystal all the way down the thread to a waiting line of other beads.

"Oh, visitors," she added, noticing Ivan and his mother. She set the wooden bowl of beads beside her on the chair.

"Florence, this is Ms. Workhouse and her son, Ivan."

"Dart," said his mother.

"Welcome, Dart and Ivan, to my little room," said the miniature woman, whom Ivan now thought of as Bead Lady.

Her voice came out thin, weak, and her speech was very slow. Waiting for her to finish a sentence was like watching the very last drop of syrup grow, stretch, and plop from the bottle.

"I hope you didn't find the climb up the stairs too difficult."

"We didn't," said Dart.

"How about you, young man?" she asked Ivan, her eyes dancing with pale fire.

"He didn't, either," said his mother.

The Bead Lady winked at Ivan, taking about the same amount of time as it would to close and open a window. "My mother was just like yours," she said and smiled.

This didn't seem possible to Ivan, and he asked, "How old is your mother now?"

"Ivan!" shouted his mother, gripping his shoulder with a five-pincer crab claw. "I apologize, Mrs. Roebuck. It's because of the rotten school he's in that he thinks he can ask questions like that. They taught it to him."

Florence laughed and another drop of syrup came out. "I'm afraid my mother doesn't have any age now, Ivan."

Ivan was all ready to say that everyone had an age, but the look on his mother's face kept that thought inside him.

Just then a ruckus kicked up outside, and footsteps climbed the stairs and came down the hall. Wallace Roebuck stuck his head into the room. Now he was wearing a pair of faded blue overalls and knee-high rubber boots. "They're pulling in the net," he said.

"We better go down," said Mrs. Roebuck. She went on to explain that a team of people from the Department of Natural Resources was seining the pond behind the house. "They want to be able to see all the creatures living in the water."

Wallace helped Florence, and Mrs. Roebuck led the way down the stairs to the first floor and out onto the back deck.

A huge pond spread out beyond the house. About thirty or forty yards away from the deck, several utility trucks with winches on the front were parked uphill from the pond. They were cranking in steel cables from the water. Three men watched the cables winding up into the winch drums. One of them might have been a woman, but Ivan wasn't sure. Four men were standing in the water wearing waders and holding long poles with nets on the end. One man in green coveralls had a pole with a spiked hook. The drums turned slowly and the six cables made crunching sounds as they wrapped up.

"Can I go down there?" Ivan asked his mother.

"No."

"We're looking for a big turtle," explained Mrs. Roebuck. "They're going to catch it and take it away."

"Why?" Ivan asked, and again felt the crab on his shoulder.

"He's too big for this pond, Ivan," said Mrs. Roebuck. "The fish don't like him."

Ivan wanted to ask how a turtle could be too big for a pond, or how anyone knew what fish thought, but he kept quiet.

"They tried to catch him yesterday with smaller nets," said Mrs. Roebuck.

"So today they brought in the heavier equipment, to make sure they're reaching the bottom."

Wallace left Florence standing next to Ivan and started down the deck stairs toward the pond. Mrs. Roebuck warned him about keeping his balance, but he waved his hand at her as if he were shooing away a mosquito.

"Wallace, be careful," said Florence.

The door opened behind Ivan and he felt the deck boards sink. When he looked around, a giant had come out of the house, wearing the infant car seats on his feet. Ivan came up to his waist. Each of his legs was bigger around than Ivan at his widest. His hands looked to be carved from tree stumps.

"Careful there, Dad," the giant said, and hurried down the steps after Wallace. "Some of those young government guys aren't familiar with the machinery they're using."

With each monster step the deck shuddered, and Ivan wondered if a five-gallon bucket would fit over the giant's head. His hair was tar-black and buzzed short. He caught up to Wallace and extended a hand to steady him. Wallace waved it away.

"I've been around machinery and young people my whole life," he said, and headed toward the turning drums. The giant was right behind him.

"I'll introduce you later," explained Mrs. Roebuck apologetically. "Buck is protective of his father."

"Is he real?" Ivan asked.

"Ivan, shame on you!" shrieked his mother. "It's that rotten school, I swear, Mrs. Roebuck. You have no idea what idiots them teachers are."

When Amy stopped laughing she said, "Buck's real, Ivan, though he takes some getting used to."

Standing beside Ivan, Florence spoke, her tiny hands on the porch rail.

"It comes from his mother's side of the family, Ivan. One of them worked in a circus. I'm still not used to him."

Ivan was beginning to like her a lot, though she spoke unbearably slowly. The pale fire in her eyes never went out.

"Can I go down there?" he asked his mother.

"No."

The edges of the net were coming out of the pond and the men in the water moved in closer.

"Careful there!" shouted Wallace, wading into the water. "Don't hurt those fish. Work through them slowly. Easy does it."

"Dad, get out of the water."

"I had another one of those dreams last night, and I don't want any more fish weighing on my conscience," said Wallace. "You there, toss that grappling hook out onto the grass. That's a weapon, not a tool."

"Look, Buck, you better take your father back into the house," said a man standing next to the turning drums. He had a badge on the front of his jacket and a mustard-colored mustache. "This isn't the place for him. There's a lot of tension on these cables."

"This is where he lives and he goes wherever he pleases," said Buck. Then he turned to his father. "Dad, get out of the water."

"No one could ever tell Wallace anything," said Florence.

More of the net came out of the pond, and as it did, fish began to break through the surface of the water, flopping, gulping, and jumping in the air. Diesel exhaust poured out of the trucks.

"Can I go down there?"

"No."

The door opened behind them and a woman came out onto the deck. She crept over, walking as if all the good people in the world would die if her shoes made any noise. "Excuse me, Mrs. Roebuck." She sighed. "I'm sorry to bother you. I apologize. Excuse me."

"Oh, Grace, let me introduce you to Ms. Workhouse and her son," said Mrs. Roebuck.

After they all said hello, Quiet Shoes—who was a nurse dressed up to not look like a nurse—said Kevin wanted to come out. She wondered if that would be all right. And if it was all right, she needed help bringing him.

"Yes, of course he can," said Mrs. Roebuck. She and Quiet Shoes went back into the house, and when they returned there was a boy between them. Kevin was older than Ivan, pretty tall, real skinny, and the color of a peeled onion. He wore pajamas and a plastic tube was stuck up his nose, attached to a tank on wheels, which Quiet Shoes pulled behind her.

When Kevin was introduced he looked at Ivan as if he knew Ivan had failed fifth grade. Then he turned away.

More of the net came out of the water, dragging a load of shiny, wriggling fish—black, gold, blue, orange, green, brown, purple, and red. It looked as if the plug at the bottom of the world had been pried open and all the things living down there had come up. Wallace waded out farther, giving orders to the men with poles as they lifted the fish over the side of the net and put them back into the pond.

"Easy there, go easy."

Some fish were so big it took two men to get them out of the net.

Snakes slithered over and under the fish, escaping back into the water. Every once in a while the men would find a brown, green, or yellowish turtle—including some big ones—but not the one they were after. These turtles, too, were tossed back into the pond. Crayfish and salamanders climbed over the fish. Frogs hopped among the decaying waterweeds. Slimy things writhed around, churning up the slimy water.

Some fish were making noises, quietly screaming, and when their gills opened they were red inside. One of them had a hog's face and another had human eyes, only yellow. The government men were standing waist-deep in them, hurling them over the cable-net back into the pond, looking for the giant turtle.

The truck engines smoked, the drums turned, and the cables squealed and howled as they wound onto them.

"Let up on those winches!" shouted Buck. "You're dragging dead-weight uphill. The lines will break. Dad, get out of there!"

One of the trucks stalled. Another backfired and a black belch of smoke came out.

"Lampreys!" one of the men yelled, and held up a fish with a dozen bloodsuckers hanging like attached hoses from its sides. It looked sucked dry. "Lampreys!" someone else yelled. All the fish with suckers on them were thrown out onto the bank.

"Can I go down there?" asked Ivan again.

"No," replied his mother.

"They'll never get him," said Kevin.

"Why not?" asked Mrs. Roebuck.

"Because he's the devil, that's why."

"Of course he isn't, Kevin. He's just an old turtle."

"He's the devil. They'll never get him."

The air smelled like fish, rotten plants, mud, and exhaust. Flies swarmed around the net and settled on the exposed fish and muck and everything else. Then birds came out of the trees and started squawking and gobbling up the flies. Other birds were pecking at the lampreys and the fish that had been thrown out onto the bank. Turkey vultures floated overhead, wishing they could get at the fish. Dogs came to the edge of the pond and one of them carried off a fish.

"Get out of here, you!" yelled Wallace, waving his hands in the air.

"I wish I'd brought a rosary," said Florence, and took hold of Ivan's hand. He smiled at her and her eyes smiled back.

"Come out of the water, Dad!" shouted Buck.

Suddenly one of the cables snapped with a whistling crack from the drum and whipped over the water. Two men ducked and just barely missed having their heads cut off. "Jesus!" one of the men yelled. A corner of the net fell away and fish poured through it back into the pond. Another net was brought in to cover the open area and keep the fish from escaping before they were examined.

"Careful with those fish!" shouted Wallace, just before losing his balance and falling sideways into the pond. Somehow he kept his head above the water until Buck plucked him out and carried him up to the dock at the bottom of the deck stairs. "Stay here, Dad," he said. "Please stay here." Mrs. Roebuck climbed down and sat with him while Buck hurried toward the trucks.

The men in the water were still throwing fish back into the pond while they fought off the birds and the flies. On the bank, two dogs fought over a fish. They tore it open and its insides fell out. Then other dogs came over and they all started fighting.

"Take me down there," said Kevin. "Right now."

Quiet Shoes sighed and said that perhaps going down to the water wasn't the very best thing for them to do. Kevin cut her off.

"You get paid to do what I want and I want to go down there."

After another deep sigh, Quiet Shoes called down, "Excuse me, Mrs. Roebuck. Excuse me, I don't mean to interrupt, but Kevin says—"

"Yes, Grace. Of course he can. I'll come help. Wally, you stay here."

Mrs. Roebuck climbed up. Wally poured water out of his rubber boots, put them on, and headed back toward the fish.

When Kevin, Quiet Shoes, and Mrs. Roebuck were halfway down the steps, Buck called for Mrs. Roebuck to come get Wally.

"I'll be right there," she said and smiled her pained smile.

"Now!" shouted Buck.

"Hold on, I'm coming," she said. "Ms. Workhouse, do you suppose you—"

Ivan's mother was already moving. "Call me Dart," she said, and scrambled down the stairs as quick as spit.

"I'm coming too," added Ivan.

"Oh no you're not," snapped his mother, turning back and giving him a look. "You stay right where you are and I mean it."

Then she hurried ahead, took Kevin's arm, and they continued along the edge of the pond, walking through the grass.

Florence and Ivan were the only ones left on the deck. Another fish was found with lampreys hanging all over it. The men threw it onto the bank right in front of his mother, Kevin, and Quiet Shoes. Ivan thought it looked from that distance like a picture in August's Greek mythology book—the head of Medusa with snakes growing out of it.

Kevin took one look at it and demanded to go back to his room. He whirled around so fast he almost got away from Dart. The tubing came out of his nose and Quiet Shoes jumped to bring the tank closer. In no time at all they were back on the deck and Quiet Shoes was breathing hard from lugging the tank up the stairs.

"Don't stop yet," Kevin barked at Quiet Shoes. "I want to go back to my room."

Dart opened the door and helped him inside. Ivan came too.

"What kind of name is Dart?" asked Kevin.

"The best kind," she said, leading him down the hall.

"Two doors down," said Quiet Shoes, sighing, and they veered off to the left.

Kevin sat down on his bed and rearranged the tubing. Ivan looked around at all the video games. A cabinet filled with DVDs ran across one wall. There were two separate television screens hanging down from the ceiling and several cabinets of medical supplies next to a recliner.

"Get me a Coke," said Kevin to Dart while Quiet Shoes was feeling his pulse and staring down at the second hand on her watch. "With ice."

Dart didn't say anything and Kevin repeated it. "Get me a Coke."

When she understood that Kevin was talking to her, her eyes narrowed.

"Listen, Kevin," she said. "Your attitude needs to change real quick. There are plenty of cute young girls out there just waiting for you to get yourself together, and I mean really cute ones—the kind with perfect, firm round fannies like mine. They're waiting for you to grow up, so no ordering me around, okay? I mean, some folks may be waiting for you to die, but you aren't dead yet."

Kevin looked like he'd just been slapped for the first time in his life. Quiet Shoes opened her mouth and rushed out of the room to get Mrs. Roebuck.

Kevin just stared at Dart, looking hurt.

Ivan was afraid something like this would happen. Sometimes it only took a little heat to light his mother up.

Out the window, Ivan could see Quiet Shoes talking with Mrs. Roebuck. Then they both came hurrying back into the house.

"Come on, Mother," Ivan said. "Let's get out of here."

Dart hesitated, then the two of them rushed out of the room and down the hall. They ran out to the parking lot carrying their shoes.

The Bronco didn't start right away, so Dart was getting the other battery out of the back when Mrs. Roebuck came bursting out the front door.

"Dart, wait," she said, catching up to them.

"Don't get your expensive panties in a twist," said Dart. "I'm leaving."

"This interview isn't over," said Mrs. Roebuck in a stern manner. "I haven't shown you where you and Ivan would be staying if you decide to take the job."

"Oh," said Dart, setting the jumper cables down next to her sneakers. "I guess you didn't."

"And I'm not wearing any underwear," Mrs. Roebuck added. "I couldn't find a clean pair this morning. I can't keep up with all the work and I need your help."

"Why me?"

"You clearly have something the others didn't," she said and smiled.

Ivan could feel his mother getting ready to smile, but she held back. "Yes, well, I suppose we could see if your accommodations are suitable," she said.

Suitable wasn't the word to describe them.

Down from Kevin's room there was a furnished apartment on the other side of the hall. The door swung open easily, leading into three separate rooms, not counting the bathroom. Each of these rooms was bigger than their whole apartment in Grange, with tall wide windows. There were comfy chairs, a sofa, beds, and closets big enough for cows or horses to stand in, along with doors with working springs in the knobs. The floors were level, the walls straight up and down. There were ceiling fans, a refrigerator, a sink, a stove, and counters. Clean water whooshed out of the faucets.

"Much of this could be moved out to make room for what you have," said Mrs. Roebuck.

"I see," said Dart, stepping into one of the closets.

Somehow Ivan knew she was going to refuse. He'd seen it before. And sure enough, when she came out of the closet her face had hardened.

"I don't want this job," she said.

"Why not?" asked Mrs. Roebuck.

"Mother," began Ivan, but she stopped him with an angry look.

"I wish you'd reconsider," said Mrs. Roebuck.

Dart was quiet for a moment, and then she told Mrs. Roebuck that she had something to say. "To everyone."

"All right," said Mrs. Roebuck. "You and Ivan go down to the kitchen and we'll all meet you there in a couple minutes."

Ivan and his mother went down to the kitchen and waited. It wasn't long before Mrs. Roebuck came in with Florence and Wally, followed by Kevin and Quiet Shoes. The five of them sat at the table. Several minutes later Buck came in. He walked over to the refrigerator, opened the door, and took out a can of grape soda. It looked like a Dixie cup in his hand. "We didn't find the turtle," he said.

Just like Kevin said, thought Ivan.

"You want one of these, Ivan?" he asked.

Ivan's mother frowned and he shook his head.

"Anyone else?" asked Buck.

There were no takers so he closed the refrigerator, then drained the can in one swig.

"So, what's the deal?" he asked, sitting carefully on one of the stools by the counter and looking over at Dart.

"I've got something to say," she said.

"Okay, let's hear it," said Buck.

"I'll work here and I'll work hard, but no one is ever going to hurt my son. Ivan's going to amount to something and nothing is ever going to happen that would make him feel cheap or unclean. No one is going to touch him, ever. And that goes for you too, big guy. If any of you ever harm him in any way, I promise you'll be sorry. I'll make you wish you were never born."

She stood there with her eyes blazing, hands pressed to her sides, shoulders hunched forward, and elbows cocked out. Ivan sighed. It was hopeless. Once again his mother had ruined everything.

Buck looked over at his wife. Mrs. Roebuck looked at him, and Florence smiled at Ivan. Buck stepped away from the stool. "Sounds fair to me," he said. "Is that okay with the rest of you?"

Five heads nodded around the table.

"Good, then we have a deal. When can you start?"

"Today," said Ivan.

"We can be here within a week," said his mother, and relaxed her arms.

"Is that okay with you, Amy?" asked Buck.

"The sooner the better," said Mrs. Roebuck.

"Are we done here?" asked Buck. "The permit came through and they want us back at the job site in Red Plain."

"I'm going upstairs to think about my dream some more," said Wally, filling a cup of coffee.

Mrs. Roebuck stood up from the table. "Buck, wait. Dart's car won't start."

"The battery's shot," added Ivan.

Buck walked over to the phone on the wall, picked up the receiver, dialed a number, and talked into it. "Carl, there's a Bronco out front. Put a battery in it. If it doesn't start, fix it."

Intimate Imperatives

Outside the Words Repair Shop, Winnie nosed her little car between a piece of unidentifiable farm machinery and a heap of twisted metal. Her husband's work generated an astonishing amount of refuse, and she often thought of the little shop as a cement-block creature feeding on oil and electricity and eliminating ferrous waste through its windows and doors. She climbed out of the car and smoothed her clothes over her body, flattening a few wrinkles.

Inside, the shop was furnished with a haphazard arrangement of chain saws, lawnmowers, garden tractors, pumps, generators, tillers, three- and four-wheelers, and farm implements needing repair. Surrounded by his well-worn shop manuals, machines, tools, testing equipment, grease guns, and other things that Winnie could not readily identify, Jacob stood on the other side of the building, hunched over the howling bench grinder. He hadn't heard her come in. A bright stream of yellow sparks erupted from the piece of metal he was pressing against the abrasion wheel. Directly above the workbench, grayish-white clumps of smoke clung to the ceiling. The shop smelled like a shorted-out toaster. Choosing her path carefully, Winnie slowly made her way over to him.

Jacob turned off the grinder and removed his goggles. "Winifred! What a surprise." His face, neck, forearms, and hands were black except where the goggles had been, and his smile seemed unusually white. Fragments of burned metal were embedded in his forehead. He put down the bar of steel he'd been grinding.

"Hello, Jacob," she said.

Eye contact made them real to each other again. Animal warmth hurried out of him, attached to her, and woke up their shared history of unrehearsed movements, unplanned utterances, natural smells, and comforting connubial habits. She smiled and Jacob came closer. More layers of their public selves peeled away, replaced by the latent excitement that normally characterized their nearness to each other.

Winnie cherished Jacob's need for passion from her, and sometimes imagined that his consciousness consisted primarily of an awareness of his own sexual instinct—his only gateway to rapture. Thankfully God had created this vital opportunity for bliss, yet Winnie remained convinced there were many more avenues that could be followed to divine pleasure. People could become hyperconscious in countless ways. It was possible. The sight of a hummingbird—along with the sound of its thrumming wings—once revealed to her how she had long ago lived with tiny black feet and a nectar-searching tongue. Her shoulders remembered the thrilled rhythms. On another occasion, the taste of a strawberry related its entire history of self-propelled spirit into matter. All human sensations could, she believed, provide paths to the same state of ecstatic worship.

The principalities of civilization had hidden most of these gateways to heightened awareness, however, and for most people now, the only way back to the blessed original state involved a spectacular sexual event. And while Winnie rejoiced as much as anyone else in extraordinary sexual events, she sometimes feared that keeping the species alive had nearly replaced being alive, as if the entire galaxy of spontaneous felt-unity threatened to become perversely focused on one narrow impulse.

But as soon as she entertained this thought, Jacob picked up an orange oil rag and began wiping his thick hands in a vigorous and methodical manner. The simple gesture was artfully performed, and it implied a level of satisfaction with his work. Perhaps he knew of many other avenues to heightened awareness as well. The thought greatly amused her.

"Jacob, we need to talk," said Winnie.

"Good," he said. "Can I get you something to drink?"

"No, thank you."

"What do we need to talk about?" He sat beside her on the ripped seat of a four-wheeler, his teeth still gleaming from the surrounding darkness of his sooty face. She looked for somewhere clean to sit, and stayed standing.

"You have far more work here than you can do yourself. It keeps you from sleeping well and it steals from the time you spend with August and me. And there's absolutely no reason for it."

"I thought you said I had more work than I could do," he said playfully. His smile suggested he might not be taking her seriously.

"You could have someone else working with you. Another person could do all the things you can't do yourself in a reasonable workday. You could hire someone."

"We can't afford that," said Jacob.

"Yes we can," said Winnie. "In fact, it's necessary."

"No we can't. Besides, you already make more money than I do, and if I have to pay someone else I'll be even further behind."

"That's ridiculous, Jacob. You don't make more money, because many of your customers don't pay, or don't pay enough, and you let them get away with it."

"The economy's gone south and people pay what they think they can."

A truck pulled into the lot just then, and after several clanking, scraping, and banging sounds, an older man came in with a weed eater.

"Good afternoon, Pastor Winifred," he said.

"Hello, Mr. Roebuck."

Jacob nodded imperceptibly in greeting. Wally nodded back.

Leaving them alone, Winnie went into the craft room and spoke briefly with the woman behind the counter. She was knitting a red sweater from a muskmelon-sized ball of yarn that was lying on the floor. Winnie looked through some of the items on display. One black-and-green pot holder had been made to look like a face, and it continued to haunt her even after she stopped looking at it. Something about the sewn mouth made her think about pure evil, which was surprising because the concept no longer held a respected place in her collection of thinking utensils. Its sudden appearance in her mind seemed a little like coming upon a long-forgotten article of clothing in the attic, and she made a mental note to later contemplate how discarded pieces of herself could still be so handily attached, ready for service.

When she rejoined Jacob in the shop, he was alone again. Sunlight fell through the open double doors, making it seem as if there were two separate areas, one light and one dark. Dust motes filled the bright area.

"So, who do you want me to hire?" asked Jacob.

"I'm sure there are many highly skilled and reliable workers who would be pleased to share your responsibilities," said Winnie.

"For some reason I think you have someone in mind," he replied, picking a piece of metal out of his forehead.

"Why do you think that?"

"Just a guess," and he smiled again in a way that suggested he might be thinking about sex in addition to not taking her seriously.

Her voice assumed a slightly angry tone. "I think you should hire the Bookchester boy."

"Isn't he in prison?"

"Yes."

"He's not a boy and I don't want to hire him."

"He's almost fifteen years younger than you. Why not?"

"He's been in prison over a decade, Winifred."

"That's all the more reason. Without a sponsor he might not be released this summer, if ever. You have no idea what an unholy place that prison is. I try to get you to visit, but you won't. That building is a monument to the ignorant cruelty that characterizes much of our civilization. The damage it does is unspeakable. Our nation has more people in prison than any other country on earth. It's an abomination and it mocks the civic ideals we profess to believe in. It's essential that we get him out of there as soon as possible."

"He's in the supermax because he's uncooperative and violent," said Jacob, rearranging the position of a socket set on the workbench.

"It should be beneath you, Jacob, to repeat the same stories the government uses to frighten people. Men are sent to maximum-security prisons for such small infractions as not looking straight ahead when the guards bolt shackles onto them. Blake Bookchester is not overly violent, and even if he was a little impulsive a long time ago, he's changed. He reads books and thinks deeply about them. I've been visiting him and I know."

"You know the part he wants you to see."

"That's unfair, Jacob. Everyone shows their best side."

"True, but Blake has more he's not showing than most of us. He was arrested for carrying over two pounds of black tar heroin and convicted for drug trafficking."

"He wasn't the only one. There were other arrests around the same time. There was a man working at the foundry outside Red Plain with connections to a Mexican drug cartel. He had a number of young people delivering drugs for him. Four or five others were caught as well."

"Yes, but unlike the others, Blake put the officer who arrested him in the hospital. Eight years later he was sent to Lockbridge because he hit a guard at the Waupun prison. His father told me."

"I know all about that," said Winnie. "Blake understands that those were mistakes."

"Mistakes?"

"All of us fall short of the people we'd like to be, but we keep trying and so does Blake. He knows about machinery and how to fix things. He's worked as a mechanic before."

"He's not working here."

Winnie took a deep breath, slowly blew it out, and threw her head back. A cat crept cautiously in the open garage door, hurried into a darkened corner, and disappeared underneath a shelf of oilcans and a coil of chain.

"Jacob, we have a predatory criminal justice system in this country, operated by people who in one way or another make money from its operation. They try to keep inmates from getting out, because profits accrue from keeping them in. Whenever there's a possibility for meaningful penal reform the prison lobby advertises the few really horrible crimes, and everyone gets frightened and keeps as quiet as rabbits. Meanwhile, people who never should have been locked up in the first place die on the floors of their cells because they can't get the medication they need, and others simply go crazy. Imagine, Jacob, what it would be like to live in a cement room all year long, eating food shoved through an iron grate, never seeing people you love except during rare visiting hours, and then through wire and glass, monitored the whole time. That hell-house in Lockbridge is nothing more than a human garbage pit."

"Stop making speeches, Winifred."

"Everything I say is true."

"I want no part of prisons or people who have been inside them," said Jacob. "Living without you and August would reduce me to a reptile in a couple weeks. I don't know how those guys survive. I couldn't. I try to imagine it and watch myself melting from the inside."

"Good, then you'll hire him."

"No I won't."

"You said I was right, Jacob."

"Someone as damaged as Blake Bookchester probably can't be set free among people who aren't trained to deal with him. Brutalized people brutalize others."

"The injustice must be addressed. It's a moral imperative."

"There's no telling what he might do. I'm sorry for what's happened to him, I am. But he's not coming here. Sometimes the harm done can't be fixed. Maybe Blake never should have been sent to prison in the first place, but that doesn't change the fact that it's the only life for him now."

"You're afraid of him, Jacob."

"I am not. All right, I am. He's unpredictable. His own father is afraid of him."

"Those who see the injustices in our society are obliged to do something about them. How can you live with yourself, Jacob?"

"The way most people do, with difficulty."

"I knew you'd be like this," said Winnie.

"And I knew this was coming."

"What was coming?"

"This discussion."

"No you didn't."

"You talk in your sleep, Winifred. You've been worrying about this for months."

"Jacob, you can't bring up something intimate between us and expect to win the day. You won't. I'm right about this and you know it. And I don't talk in my sleep."

"You do."

"Then you shouldn't be listening."

"You say the same things over and over."

"Besides, I've already told them you'd sponsor Blake."

"Told who?"

"The prison authorities asked for the name of two sponsors and I wrote down yours and mine. It's done now and nothing can change it. He's going to live with his father and work here."

"Winifred, that better not be true."

"It is," she said.

"I'll undo it."

"Jacob, please. I thought you'd understand. When I started visiting him he seemed to be like all the others. But he isn't. I care about him. Deep inside me, in that quiet place, he's now among that small group of people. I tried and tried to keep him out, but he got in somehow. What could I do? I don't control who gets in, and now I'll never forgive myself if we don't try to help him."

"At least now you're talking about something real," said Jacob.

"I'm sorry," said Winnie. "I should have started here in the first place, but I didn't know how to begin. It seemed too much to ask, I mean, on my account."

"Why can't he work for someone else?"

"No one else will have him."

"Okay, he can work here. To be completely honest, I decided two days ago it probably wouldn't hurt to have him here."

Winnie stepped back. "No, you didn't," she said, throwing her head back.

"I did—two nights ago, when you woke me up again. I just wanted to see if it was possible to talk you out of it. I mean, I think it's a bad idea, Winifred, but I know you well enough to know that if I win the argument you'll only get stronger from losing, and then several days later you'll be back more determined."

"So you'll let him work here?"

"Yes."

"And you're not angry with me?" Winnie shifted her stance and leaned against a short wooden stepladder that looked fairly clean.

"No."

Winnie frowned. "You were just pretending to listen, weren't you? You weren't taking anything I said seriously."

"Deep inside me," said Jacob, "there are only two other people, you and August. I've tried to let more in, but like you say, we're not in control. There's just you two, and whatever you say or do will never change that."

"Only two? That's kind of sad, Jacob."

"I know. Well, there's one other, but he doesn't count."

"Why not?"

"He's dead."

"You mean July?"

"Yes."

"The dead can be in there too," said Winnie. "No one can keep them out."

"And I was trying to take you seriously, Winifred, I really was. I just couldn't stop thinking about how soft your skin feels behind your ears."

"I hate you," said Winnie, leaning forward to kiss him. When she drew away, her lips, cheeks, and the tip of her nose were black.

Jewelweed

The night sky dumped warm rain on southwestern Wisconsin—a dark violet vertical downpour—as Nate Bookchester turned onto the blacktop road in front of his house. His headlights lit up thirty feet of boiling, dancing liquid runoff tumbling over the gravel shoulders. As the Kenworth slowed down, oceans of fatigue moved through him.

He inched beyond the driveway and backed the tractor-trailer down the drive, between the house and his pickup. The motion detectors on the side of the porch failed to turn on the lights. They'd quit working last winter.

Nate turned the ignition key back toward him and the diesel's rattling vibration died; the wipers collapsed at the bottom of the windshield. With competition from the engine gone, the rain beat more boldly, washing away memories of intersections, flashing lights, merging lanes of traffic, exit signs, blasting horns, public restrooms, and loading docks. The liquid drumming coaxed his muscles toward a yearned-for resignation. The trunks of the trees in the yard trembled in the storm; their limbs flailed.

On the front of his house a waterfall rolled off the sagging, leaf-clogged gutters, and he thought about marching into the deluge, unlocking the door, clambering inside, and dripping all over the floor—greeted by walls, doorways, and pictures that always seemed to resent late-night intrusions, and to hold grudges every time he was gone this long.

Nate shut off the running lights and the rain beat even louder in the surrounding darkness. Somewhere overhead, lightning split open the sky, gulped a lungful of wet air, and roared. The decision was made: he liked sleeping in the truck during thunderstorms. He liked it even more than the promise of a hot shower and clean sheets.

In the bunk in back, Nate listened contentedly to the rain and the popping sounds of the engine shrinking under the hood in the cooling air. With each crack of lightning and clap of thunder, crooked veins of water flashed against the window. Sleep came closer, stalking his imagination, coaxing his attention toward descending spirals of fainting pleasure.

Tomorrow, Nate knew, the preacher woman and her husband were going to the prison to talk about Blake's work release. Also tomorrow, Nate was going to the cement plant in Red Plain to see his cousin Bee. As he imagined the reunion, excitement collided with fear, and to free himself from the anxiety he concentrated again on the sound of rain. He thought about his rain-loving garden behind the house, sprouted from rain-loving seeds—tomatoes, zucchini, eggplant, peppers, arched-neck squash, pumpkins, potatoes, and sweet corn. He imagined picking a ripe tomato sometime later in the summer, presenting it to Bee—her hands reaching, curling, tightening, lifting it to her mouth, biting through the skin, her tongue in the juice—and fell into a watery sleep.

New light and quarreling squirrels woke him early. It had stopped raining. Several small birds hopped with scratching sounds on the roof of the cab, bathing in a six-year-old dent filled with rainwater—a present from a couple of kids in Kentucky who'd dropped a brick from an overpass.

Trying not to disturb the morning, Nate quietly opened the door, lowered his bad leg out of the cab, and stepped onto the soaked, squishing lawn. A shallow fog roamed knee-high over the ground, the air above crystal clear. From beneath the horizon, the sun burnished the rounded edges of several low-lying clouds, and the early light found drops of water hanging from grape leaves along the trellis, tiny stars gold-burning inside them. A slanting strand of spider-silk drifted silently across the front yard, a cast-off ladder to another realm.

The drawn-out lament of a mourning dove stretched the dawn further and Nate thought about his son. Would Blake have forgotten mornings like these? Would forgetting make them harder to find?

No, Nate assured himself. Mornings like these would rise through the deepest forgetting. They needed no introduction, no endorsement; they simply announced themselves. You had to find yourself inside one, watch your thoughts effortlessly rising into radiance, and join the celebration.

Behind the house, his garden glistened in wet light. The mulched rows oozed when walked on, exuding a damp, rich, fecund smell. Small green tomatoes had already set on—beefsteak and heirloom. They dangled haphazardly from their vines like ornaments waiting for Christmas. The zucchini—true to their nature—had puffed up to many times their size since he'd last seen them, and were now too bold, too proud to hide beneath the green leaves.

The mourning dove called again and Nate's eyes followed the sound east, past his beehives and across his neighbor's small pasture, where two Angus steers loitered next to an old water tank. On an outcropping of sandstone at the edge of the treeline, a lone boy stood. He watched Nate silently from beside a stand of scrub oak and birch. His weathered face and hands looked as brown as branches.

Nate instinctively recognized the Wild Boy. They looked at each other and the shared exchange seemed to Nate like that of two men who had long ago learned to be wary of others, communicating cautious goodwill through separate solitudes. Nate couldn't tell for sure what the boy was wearing, but his watchful expectancy seemed to be from a different time and place.

Without looking away, Nate crouched and plucked an early cabbage—a prize, without blemish. Holding it dripping and cool in front of him, he walked slowly through his backyard. The boy continued to watch him from the other side of the pasture. Nate set the cabbage on a wood post at the corner of the fence and backed away. The boy's gaze followed.

Nate tried to hold the cherished sight of the boy before him without any distracting thoughts, to fix the image clearly in his mind. Several years ago he'd seen—or at least imagined he saw—this boy running through a forest closely bordering the road. It was only a fleeting glimpse, and at dusk, but the memory immediately rose to a prominent position in his mind. Then about a year later, while climbing into his truck outside a restaurant on the edge of the reserve, he saw a quick, darting movement, something child-shaped sprinting into the cover of foliage along the edge of a field. The solitary movement was as different from other children's as the movement of a coyote from that of a house pet.

When Nate told his son about seeing a wild boy, Blake's face lit up like candle. It was the first time Nate had seen him smile since he was sent to prison. Later, when Nate told him about the second time he'd seen the boy running along the edge of a field, Blake laughed. "No kidding? Do you really think that's what you saw, Dad? Really?"

Nate asked about the Wild Boy throughout the Ocooch, even in places where the Driftless Region sprawled over into Minnesota and Iowa. "Have you ever heard of a wild boy living somewhere around here? Do you know anyone who has seen him?"

Mostly, no one had heard of him. Some said they'd seen footprints and other signs, but hadn't thought much about them. Others said they wouldn't be at all surprised if a wild child was living somewhere in the Driftless. Connected tracts of forest, abundant freshwater, and deep pockets of human poverty seemed conducive to such a phenomenon. Some local historians he talked to were reminded of years ago, when "hidden in the Ocooch" had been a common phrase referring to members of the Ho-chunk Nation (People of the Big Voice), who had escaped their desolate reservation in South Dakota and illegally returned to the lush land they had been driven from.

But no, they hadn't seen a wild boy, and neither had anyone else he met. Only Lester Mortal, a recluse living in a melon field miles from town—he'd seen him, Nate heard. Yes, Lester had seen him. Three people were sure of that.

Nate once talked to a woman working in a Luster grocery store who had heard from her neighbor about a couple of men in Chicago who owned four hundred acres of recreational land. They auctioned off deer-hunting rights to the highest bidders, and to advertise the sporting opportunity they collected pictures of trophy bucks taken by video cameras placed on their property. One of the motion-activated camcorders had captured a brief woodland scene of a deer with a boy standing next to it. The quality was poor, but the image clearly showed a boy and a deer standing next to each other, then moving together out of the frame. Several weeks later, all their cameras disappeared.

Because their property bordered Lester's along one valley, they carried the video over to the recluse and showed it to him. They asked if he knew anything about their missing camcorders. After looking at the image of the boy with the deer, Lester reportedly stood up from the table in his hut, walked over to a nearby cabinet, pulled a double-barreled shotgun from the rack, broke it open, shoved two shells in, locked it closed, cocked both hammers, and set the gun on the table. "Jesus said for his disciples to shake the dust off their sandals," he said, "and I think you'd better leave now." Fully satisfied that the old veteran belonged in an institution with barred windows, they left.

After hearing this story, Nate followed the narrow path littered with cans and bottles to where Lester lived. Before Nate reached the sod hut, however, the veteran came out and stood in front of the open door. "Leave me alone, goddamn you!" he screamed, his voice cracking-shrill, hair leaping from his face and head like black flames. "Leave me alone, Nathaniel Bookchester, leave me alone." An ancient Browning automatic rifle rested in the crook of an arm and he yelled again. "The angels of heaven sing and the chorus is always the same. Go to hell, Bookchester."

Nate returned without talking to him. Then he went to the Words Repair Shop to see Jacob Helm. People said Jacob knew more about Lester Mortal than anyone else, and apparently he had helped the returning veteran buy the piece of land he lived on. Jacob had even taken some time off when Lester needed help building his house, and, some said, loaned him tools, equipment, and money. And on several occasions when the old veteran had issues with his neighbors or county zoning agents, Jacob had smoothed things over.

But when Nate asked Jacob about Lester, he said very little. And when he asked about the Wild Boy, Jacob just shook his head and said, "I don't know anything about that."

"As near as I can tell," Nate said, "that child showed up at about the same time that Lester came back here."

"Like I said," replied Jacob, "I don't know anything about that."

"But you're not saying there isn't a wild child out there somewhere?"

"I don't know anything about it," said Jacob.

Two other people had been listening to their conversation: Jacob's son, August, and a tourist from Minneapolis who was lost and had stopped for directions, his wife's grayish-blue shadow waiting behind the tinted glass in the passenger-side window. August studied his father without saying anything, but the man from Minneapolis thought the idea of a wild boy was preposterous. And when Nate explained that he'd seen him, the man became almost apoplectic, as if Nate had insulted him personally.

This wasn't the first time Nate had run into this attitude. Some people, he'd discovered, simply did not want to believe that the Wild Boy existed. In fact, they scoffed at the very idea of wildness. Just thinking about it made them angry. For these people, well-ordered, efficient, and productive habits were mandatory. Children could not live without help and supervision. They had to be protected from nature's realities. Civilization made childhood possible, and while groups of feral children might exist from time to time around unfenced urban dumps in third-world countries, they could not exist in nature.

Nate easily dismissed these people. They were usually the same folks who owned heated garages. Something about keeping their cars warm seemed to kill a vital agency inside them. First, a false realization of their own importance had dulled their natural senses until they no longer heard geese flying at night. Next, they walked without stopping past jewelweed in late-summer bloom, having no time for ditch beauty. And then, finally, heated garages finished them off. Of course they didn't believe in a boy sleeping in caves and roaming through untended fields, his eyes filled with an ancient shameless wonder. If there were such a child, his untaught contentment would mock everything they had traded their souls for.

Yet here he was—wild as life. Put that in your garage and heat it, Nate thought, though by the time he emerged from his reflections the boy was gone.

Nate hurried inside the house and stuffed a canvas bag with a blanket, two pairs of wool socks, an old coat, several bars of soap, scissors, thread, a package of needles, a bottle of aspirin, a loaf of bread, peanut butter, and blackberry jam. He carried it outside and hung it from the post under the cabbage. Just in case the boy was still watching from an unseen location, he waved, turned, and walked away, his steps lighter than before, his leg not hurting at all.

Inside again, Nate showered, shaved, brushed his teeth, and slept through the rest of the morning, naked between smooth, line-dried sheets.

That afternoon, he sorted through the mail, paid several bills, cleaned out the eaves and downspouts, carried in clothes from the truck, started a load of laundry, and prepared for his visit to Red Plain. He took a crate of Georgia peaches from the trailer and set them in the kitchen. Next to these he put six pints of Michigan raspberries in balsam-and-wire baskets.

The phone rang and Nate answered it.

"Hello, Mr. Bookchester, it's me, Winnie."

"Hello, Reverend Helm," said Nate, forcing himself to breathe normally.

"Jacob and I met with the officials at the prison."

"How did it go?"

"It was difficult, but in the end everything was agreed. The papers were signed."

"What's the next step?"

"We wait. Your son will come home in two weeks. He'll be working for Jacob and living with you. His release agent will deliver him from the prison. It's all been approved."

"Two weeks," repeated Nate, forcing himself to stop holding the telephone like a hatchet.

"Yes. Blake will be out in two weeks. There will be restrictions—way too many, in my opinion—and his release officer will be most exacting in their enforcement. The slightest infraction will trigger a revocation of his release and he'll be sent back to prison."

The preacher continued, her voice hurried, rising, "But I'm sure there'll be no trouble. Everything will be fine. You'll see, Mr. Bookchester. Blake's finally getting out of that horrid place. The cruelty he's experienced will soon seem like a bad dream. Everything will be fine."

"Call me Nate, Reverend Helm."

After hanging up, Nate sat in his living room and looked at his hands. A secret sense of well-being sprang to life inside him and he fought against it. Such brave delight should not be set loose without some assurance, and Nate didn't have sufficient authority to assure himself of anything. The felicity burgeoning inside him seemed so reckless, so groundlessly naive, so desperately wished for. It wasn't right. And on top of that, Nate didn't trust people who called him Mr. Bookchester. It meant they didn't know him, didn't understand that most things he'd desperately wanted hadn't worked out very well.

An hour later, he was still there, grappling with hope and staring at his hands.

Finding Bee

Nate's drive to Red Plain took a little over an hour, an interminably long time for his heightened expectations. Yet when the road curved around the last outcropping before continuing into the haphazard assortment of nine hundred homes and commercial buildings, he didn't feel sufficiently prepared. Familiar sights on both sides of the street presented a gauntlet of memories, impeding his movement. After Blake's mother took off, he found a short-distance hauling job with regular hours, and often delivered beer and other supplies to the taverns here. The rooming house where Blake lived when he first moved away from home now had a Room for Rent sign hanging out front. In the old downtown area, one of Nate's uncles owned a secondhand store, and the side of the building still read Antiques & Treasures in his aunt's bold red-and-green lettering.

The cement plant's sign had been repainted recently. He parked underneath it and entered the office with a quart of raspberries. Pictures of patios and tile samples hung on the wall, and a sagging line of seventy-pound mortar bags led away from the door. A woman was seated behind the counter. She was wearing a tan short-sleeve blouse, buttoned up the front. Her fingers frolicked over a computer keyboard as she stared into the monitor. She glanced quickly at Nate. "Be right with you." Then she stood up and carried several papers into a back room, her skirt falling behind her calves, her shoes somewhere between brown, tan, and maroon. An unseen fax machine hummed, dialed, whistled, and beeped. When she came back, the telephone rang and she picked up the receiver. Nate slid the basket of raspberries onto the counter and shifted his weight from his right leg.

"Sorry to keep you waiting," she said, hanging up. "Everyone wants things done yesterday. How can I help you?"

"Bee, I'm Nathaniel, your cousin."

She lowered her glasses along the ridge of her nose and looked over them. "No you're not."

"I'm pretty sure I am."

They looked at each other more carefully.

Unable to discover the Bee he remembered, Nate panicked. He tried to match his memory's picture with the person in front of him, but it didn't fit. Taking a deep breath, he tried again to rediscover her, and with each failure he encountered inner weakness. He followed the curves in her face and studied her neck, the tiny earrings, and the streaks of gray in her short brown hair. All these features led to her eyes, blue-green-and-brown irises with lively, almost-black centers. Holding these glistening planets in front of him, he tried again to fit his memory's stubborn image to her living form. Again he failed, and his soul withered inside him, like someone returned from war to discover that the sacred place of his childhood was gone.

Then a dimple caved into her chin as she smiled, and his joy launched. Bee lived, and from this glad discovery came feelings he feared he'd outgrown. Visions of youth seeped into his mind, recollections of more wonderful things than he had time to recall—tumbling scenes peopled with beauty and enchantment, and standing in the middle of them, the person before him.

"Bee," he uttered softly.

"You're older, Natie," she said.

"I brought some raspberries."

Again the dimple winked from her chin, engaging an even more satisfying level of familiarity—Bee's extra portion. As a girl, this characteristic had seemed like a protective coating, a genetic guarantee that her knees would never be knobby. But in its present form it was clearly not that at all. Rather, something better-than, an infectious merriment, a double helping. Something that could never be defined in her overflowed in him and filled his conscious container to the brim with clear and untroubled ambitions. In her company he felt good about himself, better than anywhere else. She licensed him, loaned him the rightful authority to be himself. With Bee, the memories of his family became memories of their shared family, and they were no longer hard to carry. Her presence taught him where to find the right dramas and how to discard the rest. Through her dimpled smile he could stare into the future without blinking.

"When can you leave here?" he asked. "Is your car outside? I have some fruit for you. It's so good to see you, Bee. I have so much to tell you. Where are you living? Do you remember a man in Iowa near Mason City—an older fellow with a beard? You'll never believe this, but I was there. I stood under the tree. Can you believe it? And the old man, he walked through the rows of corn carrying a meal you'd taught him to make when the timing chain blew in your car. You sent the recipe. I was there. I ate the lunch. See, I pulled off the road because the corn grew so flat and uniform and straight for miles and miles. It seemed like it would never end, and I couldn't remember ever being young and I thought—"

"Slow down, Natie."

"It's so good to see you, Bee. Do you remember me?"

"Of course I do, dummy. What do you think?"

"When can you get out of here?"

"I've got another ten minutes before I close up."

"Is your car outside?"

"I don't need to drive. I've got feet, you know." As evidence, she lifted one behind her and looked over her shoulder at it. Again the dimple winked at him, an almost-flirtatious beckoning, the come-hither nod of a gatekeeper opening the door, the effortless charm his older cousin had always wielded, subduing him without effort, comforting him with the protective wing of her approval.

Nate couldn't look away. He rediscovered the old Bee in every part of her, rushing from one view to the next like someone returning to the place they had once lived and hurrying from room to room. Yes, I see what you've done with it, and I also remember when the table used to sit against the wall over there, and the back door rattled when the wind blew. . . .

"Then I'll drive."

"I can't go anywhere, Natie. I've got to get supper for Mom."

"Yes, of course, of course you do. How is Aunt Nadine?"

"About the same as she's been for several years—since her stroke. If I don't sit with her she won't eat."

"She lives with you?"

"Of course she does, Natie. What did you think? Mom had a stroke."

"I thought Rufus might be looking after her."

Bee horse-snorted at this suggestion, puffing air out of her nostrils in a time-honored, species-jumping expression of scorn. "Rufus can't take care of his electric bill, let alone anyone else."

Bee had always illustrated her feelings with physical expressions borrowed from the animal world. When Nate was young, he was a little frightened by this uncanny ability, but he had learned to accept it. Now he cherished it. For some reason creaturely mannerisms seemed to be more available to her than they were to most other people, and he felt a glimmer of childlike awe in the presence of her clearly superior skills.

"I'll come with you."

"No you won't. Mom gets mixed up about when she's living—now or then. Having you there would tip her off-center. I'll need a lot of time to prepare her."

"I'm in no hurry," he lied, and Bee knew it.

"Look, Natie, go outside. I'll come as soon as I finish a few things."

Then she put a berry in her mouth, bit into it, chewed thoughtfully, and took another.

"Hmmmm. Where did you get these?"

"Michigan."

She took a third and handed the basket to Nate. "Take these with you," she said, looking out of the corners of her eyes in comic mimicry of a wary animal. "If Gladys comes in there won't be any left. You can't find good raspberries anymore. Go on now. Go on."

Nate walked out. Too pleased with himself to get into the pickup, he walked around the parking lot and inspected a cement mixer in need of a registration sticker, then considered a green refuse bin next to the warehouse. A shallow pool of water lay between, an oil-film rainbow greasing one end. Nate walked around it three times and went back to his truck.

When Bee came out, she sat next to him in his pickup. While she ate raspberries, he drove the eight blocks to her gray bungalow with green trim and parked on the road in front. The small house was patrolled on all sides by an army of lawn ornaments, and Nate remembered how his aunt Nadine's yard had always looked like that. She was a collector, and everywhere she went she found something to go nicely with something she already had. She never tired of stopping and looking, and as a result no one ever wanted to go anywhere with her.

He glanced quickly at his cousin. A fondly remembered shame threatened to make him blush. "Take the berries," he said. "I'll go over to the tavern and come back after an hour or so. Could we go somewhere together then?"

"Which tavern?"

"The closest one. Can I at least carry the peaches up to the porch for you?"

"No. Mom might see you. She usually goes to bed right after supper. You can bring them then, though I'm not sure what I'm going to do with all of them. They don't last very long, Natie. What were you thinking? A whole case?" Again the dimple winked at him from her chin.

Nate watched Bee get out of the truck. She hurried through the lawn ornaments and he observed the way she walked—a unique uplift in her step, a midstride bounce, almost a gambol. Everything about her possessed an unanticipated exuberance.

At the mostly empty tavern, Nate drank a dark beer and contemplated his own eagerness for time to pass. Fifteen minutes later he bought another beer, and the man behind the counter asked, "Is your last name Bookchester?"

Nate nodded.

"I thought I remembered you."

Nate said nothing, so the man continued. "You made deliveries years back. And you've got a son named Blake—"

"He's in prison," said Nate, completing the thought for him.

"Bad luck, that. Good kid. He used to live around here—he and the Workhouse girl."

"I guess he did at that."

Nate carried his beer to a booth by the window, where he sat down and watched the evening cast shadows along the street. When Bee walked by, he went out to meet her. She'd changed into a sweatshirt, faded jeans, and tennis shoes.

"That didn't take long," he said.

"I already had supper made, just heated it up. Mom ate a couple bites, then went to bed and fell asleep. It's one of the things she does well, dear thing. Look, Natie, maybe you could help me put up those peaches. I worry about leaving Mom home alone at night. We'll have to be quiet, but the jars are already clean and I have all the lids we need."

"Nothing I'd rather do," said Nate, grinning like a jack-o'-lantern.

They walked back to the bungalow, and Nate carried the fruit through the menagerie of ceramic gnomes, dwarves, cherubs, bears, rabbits, squirrels, wizards, giant mice, and red rhinoceroses. "I didn't want all these dumb things in my yard," said Bee. "But they came anyway."

Inside, Bee reminded Nate that they had to be very quiet in order to keep from waking her mother. Then she rustled through the cupboards, looking for pans: an old black-and-white-speckled canning kettle with thin sides, a smaller midnight-blue baked-enamel dual-handled pot for blanching, a stainless-steel pot with a long handle for the sugar syrup and lemon juice, and a saucepan for the jar lids. Climbing onto the counter to reach above the cabinets, she handed down twelve blue-sealers, quart-sized. Nate set them on the counter and they cluttered together in antique conformity, shining, bulging, their round mouths gaping open.

Nate sharpened paring knives on the stone. Bee said they didn't need sharp knives for peaches. Dull ones worked better. Much better. Nate shook his head, disagreeing.

They half-filled the speckled canning kettle with tap water, centered it over the hottest back burner, and put the lid on. Nate slid a stack of yellow-gold canning lids with red rubber rings into several inches of water in the saucepan, and put it on the other small back burner. Bee took down a sack of sugar from the cupboard, and Nate found a fresh lemon in the refrigerator. He cut it in half, testing the edge of the knife. Bee mashed the pulp against the ribbed nose cone in a glass juicer. Like a struck match, the pungent citrus smell came alive in the air between them. She poured the juice into a measuring cup.

"You don't need to measure it," whispered Nate. "It's just to keep the color."

"I'm older than you and I know what it's for," whispered Bee. "And I always measure."

They poured four inches of water into the smaller pot and set it on the front burner. Nate set the crate of peaches on the counter and they inspected them for rot and bruises. Their skins were fuzzy, firm, and fragrant—a little larger than tennis balls. Bee bit into one and a stream of peach juice ran down her chin. She stopped the drip with the back of her hand and handed the peach to Nate. He bit into it, felt his teeth scrape against the pit, and his mouth filled with flavor. He bit off another piece and fed the last dripping piece to Bee.

Then they rinsed off their hands under the faucet and went back to inspecting the rest of the peaches in the crate.

They talked in muted voices about relatives and places in their memories, circling each other in ever-narrowing spirals until they found the courage to speak of the real things near the bottom of the reservoir, moth-souls circling the Holy Flame.

"After your wife ran off, you stopped coming around, Natie. No one ever heard from you," said Bee, peering into the scalding water.

"I know it."

"Why did you do that?"

"I don't know," said Nate. He stepped onto the back porch to open a noisy tray of ice and dump the cubes, clattering, into a red plastic bowl. Looking through the screen, he noticed the squadron of lawn ornaments again. A barred owl cried wildly from a nearby tree, adding more insanity to the scene.

"Did you think I gave a hell-hello whether your marriage worked out?" asked Bee when he came back inside.

"I hoped not, but you didn't come to the wedding."

"I know it," said Bee, turning away from him.

"Why didn't you?"

"I just didn't." Silence. "All I could ever think about was you out there driving in that old truck of yours. I never knew where you were or how you were doing," she said.

"The water's ready," said Nate, staring into the scalding pan. He had read somewhere that when water came to a boil there was a transitional state between liquid and gas in which the binding energy of water molecules was released in the form of light, causing the steam just above the water to appear slightly luminescent. Since then he'd always watched for it, and tonight in Bee's kitchen he was sure he could see it. He tried to get his cousin to see it as well.

"Red rubbish," she whispered. "If that were true, I would have noticed it a long time ago."

They lowered two peaches into the boiling water, where they jiggled around on the bottom of the pot, bumping into each other. Streams of air bubbles rose around them. After one minute they scooped the peaches out with a slotted spoon and placed them in the bowl of ice water. Then they peeled the skins off, leaving the peach meat round and slippery. The kitchen filled with a humid fruity smell.

In the saucepan on the back burner, the yellow-gold lids rattled like a confined earthquake.

The kitchen grew warmer and warmer. Nate and Bee took off their sweatshirts. Bee's arms were round and firm, pale near the shoulder. Perspiration dotted her forehead. Nate could smell her and a cherished shame darkened inside him again. His heart beat so fast it began to cloud his vision. He came up behind her and stood close. He knew he shouldn't, but he placed his hands on either side of her waist.

His fingers and palms fit against her as if they had been sculpted from the same material. A compelling hollow space between her hips and spine made him feel as if he were grafted onto her. Every contour beckoned him to follow. He drew her back toward him and pressed his face into her neck. The taste of her skin leaped up inside him. She gently pulled his hands away and they stood for a moment like birds drying their wings.

"If we open that door now there's no telling what might come out," said Bee. She stepped to the sink and placed her hands in the soapy water.

"I'm sorry," said Nate, her taste still living inside him.

"Don't be."

Nate stepped closer. His passion made it hard to think, hard to be sure he understood what she meant, hard to know what she wanted, and impossible to know what he should do. He'd carried this same desire inside him most of his life. And now he was unsure if he really wanted to act on it. He feared falling out of balance with himself, of losing the Bee he knew. He wanted more of her, yes, but there was danger in that as well. He also felt somehow complete in his yearning, grateful for the moment, loyal to the present scene, needing nothing yet filled to bursting with his dark longing.

"People say Blake is getting out of prison soon," she said without turning around.

"He'll be out in two weeks," said Nate, moving to the counter and cutting up the peeled peaches. "But I'll believe it when I see it. So far, they've done everything they can to keep him inside."

"Where's he going to live?"

"With me."

"How do you feel about that?"

"Good. I feel good about that."

"I can only imagine what this has been like for you, Natie."

"Everything will work out, as long as he stays away from that Workhouse girl."

"Dart?"

"If it wasn't for her he never would have been in trouble, and he wouldn't be in prison."

"How do you know that?"

"She's from a rotten family. It was her fault."

"You might be wrong about her, Natie. I worked with her for several years at the plant."

"I'm not wrong," said Nate. "I know I'm not. God, I missed you, Bee."

"Slice those thinner, Natie. What are you thinking?"

"Why didn't you get married, Bee?"

"I guess no one ever asked," she laughed, drawing two more peaches out of the scalding water with the slotted spoon and placing them in the ice water.

"I don't believe that."

"Well, those who did weren't the right ones. I always knew I'd never marry."

"Why?"

"I'm just strange." As if to demonstrate, Bee stepped out of one of her shoes and danced, pivoting around on her left foot, kicking up her right leg behind her.

Nate joined in, dancing in the opposite direction, twirling his paring knife in the air. To his surprise, he knew the steps, understood the dance. Then they stopped, laughing self-consciously, looking into each other's eyes like two suns in the same solar system.

"We'd better get those jars cooking," said Nate.

"Here," said Bee, "measure out the sugar. And try not to spill. I despise ants."

"I never spill," said Nate.

"Right," scoffed Bee. "You used to spread your peanut butter with a fork."

One by one, she lowered the canning jars into the boiling pot on the stove.

"What's going on out here, Beulah?" asked her mother, following her aluminum walker into the kitchen.

"Mom, I thought you were asleep."

"I heard someone," she said, scowling, staring at Bee's bare foot. "Natie, what are you doing here? Does your mother know you're over here? You're always hanging around Beulah. It's late and she has work to do. Go home now."

Nate turned toward a shriveled face he'd recognize anywhere. She looked like his father before he died.

"He's helping me can peaches, Mom."

"Stop making excuses for him, Beulah. No one said anything about this to me. I'll call his mother. You two are always up to something."

"Here, let's get you back to bed."

"As soon as I turn my back you two start up something. What a mess this kitchen is. Your father will be furious when he gets home."

"Not too likely, Mom."

"What's Natie going to do when that wife of his takes off? Because she will, I can feel it. She's not the sticking-around kind. Her whole family is cut from the wrong cloth."

"Mother."

"And it wouldn't surprise me if that boy of Nate's ends up in the slammer, either. Not the way he's going. That boy's going bad, I tell you."

"Mom, this is embarrassing."

"I'll show you embarrassing, young lady. Where's your other shoe? Put it on right now."

"Mom!"

"Natie, what are you doing over here? Do you know what time it is?"

"I'll be going soon, Aunt Nadine," said Nate.

"Well, the sooner the better," said Nadine, as Bee led her into the other room.

By the time Bee came back, Nate had filled the sterilized jars with sliced peaches. They poured in the sugar-honey-lemon syrup, wiped the mouths down, and fastened on lids. Then they lowered the jars back into the cooker.

"Sorry about that," said Bee. "She doesn't know what she's saying."

"She reminds me so much of Dad in his last years—an old guard dog keeping the moon out of the yard."

Finally, they ate all the peaches and syrup that wouldn't fit into jars, with ice cream. Nate watched Bee guiding her spoon into her mouth, listened to the purled sound of her swallowing. When the timer went off, they took the sealers out of the cooker and set them on the counter.

After the first lid snapped, Nate stood up and said he should leave.

"It's early," said Bee, letting a childlike sorrow glide through her voice.

"I'd better be going."

Bee turned on the porch light. When she turned around, Nate was right behind her. They brushed together, and he smelled her again.

"Bee," he said, but couldn't find a way to continue.

"I know, Natie. I know. It's just—well, never mind."

"Can I call you again?"

"Why would you ask?"

"I wanted to be sure."

"Here, take one of these," she said, and shoved a hot jar of peaches into his hands. Then she pushed him out the door, closing it behind him.

The evening was clear, all the way to the stars, the moon half-cocked. Nate walked through the lawn ornaments and stood beside his pickup on the empty street. He felt a hollow place open up inside him, waiting for Bee's return, closed his eyes, and remembered the sensation of his right arm brushing against her. Her smell was still inside him, and he tried to herd it into a room of his memory, where he could easily find it again.

He bought a cold six-pack to go at a tavern on the edge of town.

Along the road pairs of animal eyes lit up in the headlights, raccoons mostly, along with a few cats and a deer. The drive seemed to take no time at all, filled as it was with his thankfulness for the several hours he'd spent with Bee. He felt decades younger, and he was determined to do nothing—to will nothing—that would burden their renewed friendship.

At home, there was a message on his answering machine from the dispatcher—a load in Milwaukee to pick up and deliver to Columbus, Ohio. Tomorrow morning.

He folded the laundry and packed some clothes.

When he went outside again, the moon hovered just above the dark horizon, casting silver light across the backyard. The grass was still wet from the previous night's rain. At the wooden post on the corner of the back fence, both the cabbage and the canvas bag were gone.

Not knowing exactly why, he pushed down the top strand of barbed wire and crossed over it. He walked through the pasture and climbed the rock outcropping where the Wild Boy had stood that morning. The birch trees seemed thin and spectral in the moonlight, the bark stretched as tight as snakeskin over the trunks. He remained a long time, listening. Once, he felt sure someone was nearby, but then he lost confidence in the feeling. In the distance, the windows of his house cast yellow into the yard, and he imagined what it might be like to look at his house while he was inside it. The stars reminded him of Bee and his son and the future's gravitational pull.

He climbed back down and walked across the pasture, keeping close to the fence. He crossed into his yard and once again checked the wooden post. This time, three smooth stones about the size of quarters rested on top. As he picked them up, he looked in all directions, but could see nothing. In his palm, the stones felt warm, almost alive. Nate put them in his pocket.

Returning to the house, Nate found the jar of peaches, carried it outside, and put it on top of the post.

Moving Out, Moving In, Moving On

The prison van arrived on a warm evening in June. The vehicle moved heavily along the narrow roads, mashing gravel. As if prepared for the visit, the moist air in Words marshaled its fragrances into separate zones.

Blake Bookchester sat stiffly in the passenger seat, breathing carefully and wearing a new plaid shirt, creased denim pants, and shiny brown medium-duty work shoes.

Long-forgotten smells entered the open window: clover, litter, and duff from the woods, river mud, late purple lilac, compost, burning brush, road tar, honeysuckle, two-cycle exhaust, and freshly mowed grass. As he reclaimed each sensation, an alarm of sad familiarity rang inside him, a dark beckoning to return to someone he could no longer be.

Blake hadn't expected this much difficulty reentering the free world, but to stay alive in prison he'd allowed his spirit to drink from the shallow well of the future, and now all the joys of the unfolding moment were gone, treasured earlier in a thousand imagined scenes of returning. Anticipation had drained the lifeblood of the present. I don't regret it, he assured himself. I don't. Otherwise, some nights never would have ended.

As the dark van came to a groaning rest before the Words Repair Shop, the odor of oil, grease, and diesel fuel established provisional sovereignty around it.

Perhaps because the town had no public buildings, the shop also served as a community center of sorts. And after its double garage doors were thrown open, people could drift in and out without feeling as if they had to spend money or explain why they were there. Like birds in a bush, this summer gathering spot came without charge.

When the van arrived, seven men and three women loitered in the gravel parking lot among pieces of machinery, lured from their homes by the evening sky's multiple lanes of horse-tail clouds and long shadows spreading on the ground. Dressed in whatever had come readily to hand after getting out of bed that morning, they presented a colorful yet faded collection of individuals. Most were unemployed or retired. Two held coffee mugs; one drank from an aluminum soda can; two smoked; one chewed. They talked without hurry, their attention occasionally wandering into wider circles around the neighborhood. With winter so recently departed, they revered warm evenings, a deference later withheld from the evenings of July and August.

Most of those gathered in the parking lot had known each other a long time, and a long time before that had learned from watching their parents and grandparents how to talk with neighbors. Like riding a bicycle or tying a shoe, these informal, out-of-doors interactions came without conscious effort. They listened, spoke, nodded heads, shuffled feet, changed expressions, stuffed hands in and out of pockets, and assumed different positions in response to an inaudible rhythm.

Yet as Blake stared out of the van, he realized he'd forgotten how to relate in this way. Nothing seemed recognizable in the gathering twilight, like an unknown tribal ritual. While he'd been away, real life had been replaced by a foreign film about real life. He had no idea what they could be thinking. What did people care about out here? What did they talk about? These people in Words seemed to exist in a parallel world, similar to but different from his. The fact that he had once lived here himself only heightened his sense of alienation, and hardened the certainty that if placed among them he would fail.

"Stay close to me," ordered the driver, a man of forty-five, smaller than Blake and wearing a leather jacket. He shut off the engine and pocketed the keys. "I'll do the talking."

Blake and his release agent climbed out of the van. Simply being outdoors overwhelmed Blake initially—the immensity of everything. An infinite variety of visual avenues extended away from him. Every object had objects behind it.

Mrs. Helm stepped from the repair shop and into orange-tinted sunlight. She looked earnestly at Blake's discolored and swollen face. Her dismay ripened rapidly into anger and she came stridently toward them.

Blake could feel the man next to him gather himself, bristling. His discomfort amused Blake, and he cautiously experimented with smiling. It hurt.

When she reached them, Mrs. Helm appeared determined to hug him, as if to demonstrate some moral principle to his agent. To prevent this, Blake drew back in time for her to disguise the intention. She folded her arms in front of her.

"What happened to him?" she demanded.

"He got hit a few times."

"Who beat him?"

"Other prisoners, mostly an inmate named Jones. He'll get over it."

"Why are you government people incapable of protecting those placed in your care? Isn't that your job?"

"I don't work in the prison."

"Yes, but you're deeply associated with those who do."

"Not that deeply."

The informal group in the parking lot had stopped talking, turned, and stared. To avoid meeting their eyes, Blake watched them through his peripheral vision, a skill learned in prison, where eye contact was often interpreted as an act of aggression by guards and inmates alike.

A man walked toward them from inside the building, taller and heavier than Blake and maybe fifteen years older. His shadow followed him along the ground.

The agent continued: "I'm here to introduce Blake to his new place of employment. Then I'll drive him over to his father's house. He'll start in the morning."

"You won't get away with this reckless negligence," said Mrs. Helm. "I intend to bring attention to this abuse, and to everyone who should have prevented it. People will know and you'll be sorry."

"Go ahead. Nothing will come of it."

"Hello, I'm Jacob Helm. Blake, good to see you."

Jacob offered his hand. Blake shook it—too vigorously, he suddenly feared. He withdrew his hand, put it back in his pocket, and looked at the ground. He didn't recognize his own feet inside the new shoes. "You must be his agent," said Jacob.

"Jack Station."

"Thank you for stopping by. Let's go inside. I'll show you around."

"We won't stay long," said Station.

They walked across the lot, around pieces of machinery and people, and into the cooler air of the building. The smell of oil and grease was even stronger inside. Bugs clustered in the corners of windowsills, on the edge of the light.

The gathered neighbors looked at each other and privately imagined scenes to explain Blake's severely beaten face. They tried to balance these imagined events on the scale of their earlier conversations, the warm evening and intricately laced sky, then gave up and dispersed like a flock of birds at an imperceptible signal.

Inside, Jacob gestured to dozens of waiting saws, mowers, four-wheelers, and service engines. "This is a busy time of year. That's why we're open so late tonight."

"Didn't know you had a lathe," mumbled Blake, walking into the northeast corner.

"Are you familiar with machining?" asked Jacob.

"Of course he is," said Mrs. Helm. "Aren't you?"

Blake moved his left hand over the four-jaw chuck and sealed gearbox, followed the carriage to the tailstock, and turned a little chrome crank. "Feeder screws seem pretty tight for an old one," he mumbled.

"It holds to about three-thousandths," said Jacob.

Blake knew he needed to say something else, something confident, reassuring, and friendly. Everyone waited. But at that moment he saw through the smudged window an old woman with white hair and wearing a brown dress carry a red bowl out of a beige house and set it in the green grass. Three white cats hurried over and stuck their heads into it, and the vivid complexity of the event erased everything else in his mind. There simply wasn't enough time to figure out what these things meant, how they related to him. He felt trapped on the other side of the smudged window. Did the cats belong to the woman or was she just feeding them? Did someone ask her to? Why were they all white? What were they eating? Did this happen every day or had it never happened before? He tried to return to the shop and the conversation he was supposed to be participating in, but too much of him stayed with the old woman. He couldn't keep up, and his frustration knotted into a bitter rose.

"Should be close enough," he mumbled.

"What?" asked Jacob.

"Three-thousandths should be close enough."

"Nothing's ever close enough," said Jacob.

It seemed like a rebuke, but Blake wasn't sure. Something in Jacob's voice defied interpretation. Blake thought he might be hiding some resentment, but it would take time to learn.

Blake thought he should smile, but before he did, the time for smiling ended. He couldn't keep up.

He wondered if everything out here was going to happen at this speed—lurching unpredictably from one instant to the next—and while he wondered about this, Mrs. Helm said something he didn't quite hear. Then the old woman out the window walked away from the bowl, stopped, and looked directly at him. His release agent moved farther away from Mrs. Helm, his head half-disappearing inside a shadow. A Buick with an open trunk moved along the road in front of the shop. And a boy of about twelve appeared out of nowhere, stood next to Jacob, and stared at him with a worried look. Blake assumed this must be August, Jacob's son. The boy had many of his father's features, but his expression mirrored his mother's serious concern.

"Mr. and Mrs. Helm, this is a copy of Blake's release conditions, just so everyone understands." Station handed a folded piece of paper past Winnie to Jacob. "Read through them. You will also find a description of your obligations as sponsors of a convicted felon. If he violates a single rule—for whatever reason—he goes back to prison. Do you understand that, Blake? Your release continues only as long as you remain within the restrictions explained on this sheet of paper."

The old woman stared at him through the window, a dull blue bewilderment taking shape in her eyes.

"Blake, do you understand? Blake?"

"Yes, sir."

"What time do you open your shop in the morning, Mr. Helm?"

"Eight."

"I'll see that he's here. Let's go, Blake."

"Excuse me, Mr. Station," said Jacob, looking up from the papers. "I know Blake will do well here, but how often, in your own experience, are parolees returned to prison?"

"Three of four are back within the first month."

"Why is that?" asked Jacob.

"They can't stay out of trouble."

Station turned and walked away, dust rising around the dark cuffs of his pants.

"If we had a lawyer, you'd be hearing from her," said Mrs. Helm, more to herself than anyone else. Every time she looked at Blake's swollen face, she promised herself not to look at it again, then immediately broke the promise. It seemed as if there should be someone to file a grievance with, to redress the inhumanity of human civilization. If men could walk on the moon and compute probabilities based on the random emission of particles from the nucleus of a decaying atom, was it asking too much for those with power to behave decently?

Mrs. Helm, August, and Jacob watched them climb back into the van.

Before leaving Words, Blake again saw the old woman behind her house. But now she had something else in her hands—something unidentifiably dark and strange. He tried to get a better look at it, but then the van moved beyond the yard, beyond the village, out into the country.

Already, more had happened here in Words than what he often experienced over a whole month inside the supermax.

The thirty-minute ride to rural Grange passed too quickly, Blake thought. He tried to prepare himself, but as soon as he'd collected all the memories he needed to redeem before reacquainting himself with the domestic architecture of his childhood, a cloud shaped like Finland drifted south and hurled a great shadow onto the nearby field, turning a sea of green, gold, red, and yellow to brown, blue, and gray. His thoughts scattered like fleeing ants. He'd forgotten clouds did that and he didn't like it. Nothing should have that much influence. How could anyone succeed in a place like this?

I'm going to fail, he thought, and then panicked as he recognized the road in front of his home. Fifteen miles had vanished since the shadowed field. He tried again to collect his memories. Too late. They were outside him now. Beyond the windshield a jungle of entangled intimacy reached into and beyond even his most infantile feelings. He knew every inch of this place. More imperatively, it knew him. His conscious life had been built, sensation-by-impulse-by-feeling-by-dream-by-thought, upon the horizon seen from this road.

"Stop," he said.

"Why?" asked Station without slowing down.

Blake knew why, but he feared showing weakness more than he cared for honesty.

"Forget it."

They continued past significantly weedy lawns, leaning mailboxes, and ditches filled with daylily spears, headless dandelion stalks, mullein, quack grass, burdock, and thistle. Then he could see the house, and its color and shape seemed too much the same to be believed, as if someone had recently built it on a smaller scale to resemble his memory. The roof still sagged, making it impossible to enter or exit by the front door when it rained; the trees were larger yet the same; the eighteen-wheeler was parked next to the shed and the dip in the driveway was filled with water.

The shallow pool drew his attention. Water had always gathered there after a rain. Some of Blake's earliest upright steps had wobbled unsteadily toward it. He'd stared into it, waded, stomped, run through it, dropped stones, sailed leaf boats, and ridden his tricycle through it. At night, the moon reflected like a shining eyeball from its surface. Birds drank from it and clouds floated on it. That water ran deeper than the earth itself.

The front door opened and his father stepped outside, wearing faded jeans and a work jacket. The door closed behind him, and though Blake could not hear it, the sound moved through him. The glass rattled in the frame as the wood banged. His hands trembled.

His father stood for a moment, then took several steps toward them as the van pulled into the driveway. There was a little gray in his hair, and something else was different too. He favored one leg. His shoulders were thinner, slightly stooped.

Blake silently cursed and gritted his teeth until it hurt too much. He'd often thought about his father getting older, but he never imagined it would look quite like this.

There was so much he intended to make right. But how could anything be made right if the person he'd let down had gone on and become someone else—a man with a new set of concerns, closer to the end of his life? This older father standing in the driveway, the hurt was part of him. Blake could see it and it would never go away. Making amends would be of little consequence.

Nate took another couple of steps toward them, limping again. His aging seemed to Blake like a scar inflicted by the time he'd been away—caused by Blake's absence. If someone was loved in the right way, they didn't get old. With the mallet of neglect, he'd beaten his own father.

"Are you coming?" asked Station, standing outside the van.

Blake stepped out.

"Hello, Dad."

"Good to have you home, Blake."

His father walked forward, his gentle eyes stopping at the sight of Blake's swollen face. He reached to embrace him.

"Forget it, Dad. It's nothing," said Blake, backing away, trying to interrupt the sudden journey of tears toward his eyes. "It's nothing."

"Come inside. Thank you for bringing him, Mr. Station."

Blake looked away, pained by the kindness his father had shown to this worthless bastard.

Nate held the door open and Blake went into the house. Station followed. The smell of warm food in the kitchen made Blake want to go back outside. It seemed sacrilegious to savor these smells with Station in the house.

"We'd like you to stay for supper, Mr. Station."

No, we wouldn't, thought Blake.

Station looked around the room.

"There's plenty," said Nate.

"I'm only here to make a few things clear."

Once again, Blake's conditions of release came out of an inner pocket in the leather coat. "I know you've seen this before, Mr. Bookchester, but I'm required to personally hand you a copy. Did you get rid of the firearms?"

"I took my twenty-two to my cousin's, and please call me Nate."

"Alcohol?"

"She has that too."

"There can be no firearms or alcohol here. As you already know, Mr. Bookchester, we have the right to search without notice. If drugs, firearms, or alcohol are found—"

"I know that," said Nate.

"For the first week I'll have someone pick Blake up in the morning, take him to work, and bring him home. When he gets his license, he'll be restricted to commuting to and from work for the first month. He will keep to a twelve-hour curfew, seven days a week. If I ever come here or call after seven-thirty at night and I don't talk directly to Blake, he goes back to prison. He's not allowed inside a tavern, or to associate with any other felons. He can't leave the state of Wisconsin for any reason without prior written permission. Because his crime was drug-related, he can be called anytime for drug tests, and he must report within seven hours of notification. Not showing up, showing up late, or failing the test will send him back to prison. Do either of you have any questions?"

Nate shook his head.

"Mr. Bookchester, you have a legal obligation to notify us about anything related to your son that may compromise the terms of his release. Failure to do so makes you complicit in any wrongdoing. Is that clear?"

Nate nodded.

"You're responsible for your son, and he's responsible to me. Is that understood by you both?"

"Yes," said Nate.

Blake stared around the living room.

"Blake, is that understood?"

"Yes, sir."

"Good, then we're done here." Station walked outside, stopped, turned around, and spoke through the open door. "You have a comfortable home here, Mr. Bookchester. It reminds me of where I grew up in Iowa. There were four of us, counting my parents. It was the best place I ever lived, but we lost it. Do you know why?"

"I don't," said Nate.

"My sister got sick. While she was in the hospital my father was laid off from the factory. When he found out he was responsible for the monthly insurance payments, he drove the premium to the company in Des Moines and handed it to them in person. They said it was late—three days late. And they refused to cover the hospital bills for my sister. The following year we lost the house and moved to Davenport."

"Your sister?" asked Nate.

"She died a couple years later."

"I'm sorry."

"My father should not have been late," said Station. "Those were the rules and he should have known them."

And with that he turned and walked to the van. Blake watched him until Nate walked over and closed the door.

"Our supper is getting cold," said Nate.

Blake sat at the yellow Formica-top table. Nate set a plate of batter-fried chicken in front on him, along with garlic mashed potatoes, homemade egg noodles and gravy, baked beans sweetened with maple syrup, a garden salad, a dish of peeled scallions, homemade cornbread, butter and honey, a giant glass of cold milk, and a mug of steaming hot coffee with cream.

Blake took a bite out of a drumstick and ignored the taste. It had been so long since he'd eaten anything good that he feared being unglued by the sensations. When he chewed, the left side of his head lurched with pain.

"Is everything all right?" asked his father.

"Everything's fine, Dad. No one could have made a better meal—all my favorites."

"I found a farm that raises the best chickens. The family takes good care of them. No chemicals and not too expensive, either. And I found a place to buy open-pollinated corn, ground just right for cornbread. Can you taste the hint of cinnamon?"

"Yes, of course—cinnamon. Noticed it right off."

"Are you ready to tell me what happened to your face?"

"It doesn't matter, forget it."

"How'd it happen?"

Blake felt his five-year-old self walk down the hall, leap inside him, take command: Dad wants you to explain. You can't tell him everything. He's kind, unsuited for the world you know. You can handle this, you've done it before.

Using all the psychic strength in his possession, Blake cast aside his younger self, determined to start over on firmer ground. He took a deep breath and said, "They've got rules."

Then for several moments Blake couldn't continue. He couldn't talk and hold his fork at the same time, and he set it down. "The Department of Corrections won't release anyone straight from maximum security. They're afraid you won't be ready for the outside, not socialized enough, so they assign you to a month of GP before they let you out."

"I don't know what GP is," said Nate.

"General Population is a lesser security classification. Instead of staying locked in your own cell, you share one, watch TV in the common room, and eat in the cafeteria. Everyone in GP knows who's getting out, and the lifers—guys who will never get out—sometimes pick fights. They've got nothing to lose. Having their sentences extended means nothing. If you fight back, no matter who starts it, you are sent to Maximum or Administrative Segregation, and no one is ever released from there."

"These men actually try to keep you from getting out?"

"Some of them."

"What kind of twisted men would do that?"

"The same kind you or I would be if we had no hope of ever getting out."

"What good does it do them? What do they get out of it?"

"Dad, you don't have to understand. Don't try."

"If we're going to get through this together, everything has to be out in the open. I need to know what happened and why."

Blake looked up from the table, but he could not meet his father's eyes. He feared that a channel would open for the knowledge of prison to flow through. Some things didn't need to be understood. Originating in the lowest levels of spinal function, they should be kept there. The only way Blake could survive in prison was by not thinking about what he knew, the way a lizard knows snakes. Some of the guards taught you cruelty, and from many of the inmates you learned malice. Those spirits lived, but they did not merit understanding.

And yet the bond between him and his father went even deeper, and he had to answer.

"Guys serving life sentences have status. It diminishes when someone gets out."

"I don't understand."

"You don't need to."

"I want to."

Blake picked up his fork and began tapping it rapidly against the Formica tabletop. "You learn to respect the guys doing more time than you. That's just the way it works. You think about how much time you've got left and imagine what it would be like to have more. The lifers get the most respect. They're looked up to. In some cases they use their status in decent ways, to teach younger guys how to get along. But it throws everything off when someone actually gets out. It disturbs the order."

The fork-tapping grew in pace and intensity, until Nate reached across the table and touched Blake's hand.

"Why don't the guards prevent fighting?" he asked.

"The guards don't prevent anything. Most of those guys are in there because of the guards. Prison reduces everyone inside, and there's less left of some guards than there is of the inmates. It's just the way it works when people are divided up like that. You couldn't possibly understand it."

"Not all guards can be bad."

"You're right. They aren't. But they're still guards."

"So you let them hit you?"

"I wanted out," said Blake, trying to keep his voice from rising.

"It must be hard not to defend yourself."

"I wanted out."

"Why aren't you eating?"

"I'm not hungry."

"Can I get you something else?"

"No."

"Is something wrong?"

"Everything's fine, Dad, perfect. I just can't eat right now."

Nate took a sip of coffee, then another. "I'm not hungry, either," he said. "Too bad Jack Station didn't stay. Maybe he was hungry."

"Why did you invite him to stay?"

"It seemed right."

"You don't have to respect people like that, Dad. It's wasted on them."

"I don't want to believe that," said Nate.

Blake's anger flared briefly inside him—a burst of lightning that thankfully stayed within the rain cloud. He started to say something else, thought better of it, and took a drink of coffee. Then he looked straight at his father. "You seem good, Dad. How are you, really?"

"I'm fine. I tried to arrange a couple days off, but I've got a run tomorrow and won't be back for four days. The company is pushing us pretty hard lately, especially the independents. It's the busted economy, they say. I'm sorry—I wanted to be here."

"What time do you have to leave?"

"Before sunrise."

"Better get some sleep then. I'll clean this up and pack lunches for tomorrow."

"I can do it, son. You just got home."

"I want to. It will keep me busy."

"Your room's made up, and there are some old clothes in there. Should be everything you need. A pair of my boots—we used to wear the same size. There's plenty of food for the week in the refrigerator, and some cash in the cabinet above the sink if you need something while I'm gone."

"Thanks. Say, who's this cousin with your rifle and beer?"

"Bee," said Nate. "My cousin Bee. She lives in Red Plain. I'm seeing her."

Blake didn't know what to make of "seeing her." It both tried to communicate something and didn't.

Packing away the food proved unusually satisfying, as did washing, drying, and stacking the dishes. As Blake worked, the last of the light drained out of the sky, leaving the outside world muted all the way to the glowing horizon.

He put two sack lunches in the refrigerator, side by side, then wiped off the table and counter. He stayed calm as long as he kept moving.

There was still an inch of coffee left in his mug. He drank it at the table, listening. June bugs and moths thumped numbly against the screen, eager for the humming fluorescent light above him. A catbird tried to sing himself to sleep somewhere nearby. Toads creaked like winding wooden clocks behind the house. Water ran through a basement pipe and the door to his father's bedroom closed, followed by muffled footsteps, a sliding wooden drawer. Blake heard a car passing on the road, and he went to the window and watched red taillights moving off slowly.

The house felt insubstantial—a veneer, almost. Even the moths seemed to know they could eventually break through. Blake felt exposed.

Then he stood up, ran his hand over the wall, found the light switch, and closed his eyes. Feeling his way forward, he sat back down at the table and waited, drawing out the moment. The sounds around the house became concentrated. The suspense became delicious, exciting. When the bugs stopped beating against the screen, Blake opened his eyes.

Darkness—soothing, feathery, drowning softness. He inhaled the black radiance. It had been so long since he experienced darkness. A peal of laughter coiled up inside him, an ungovernable howl of relief. It rose up so fast to his vocal chords that when he actually laughed it sounded almost like a scream.

He laughed and laughed, sitting in the dark kitchen. It felt good, even with his face hurting. When it passed, his father was standing in the doorway to the living room.

"You all right, Blake?"

"I'm fine. Sorry I woke you."

"I wasn't asleep. You sure you're all right?"

"It's just good to be home."

Nate turned and walked back down the hall.

He probably thinks I'm crazy, thought Blake. He wondered what someone who was completely sane would do in his situation. How different could it be?

The darkened living room entertained him for half an hour, presenting one time tunnel after another. Then he went back to his bedroom, opened the door, turned on the light, and shuddered. Nothing had changed—the same bed, walls, bureau, and closet. It was as if he had never left home. His father had even kept his wrestling and motorcycle-racing trophies on the shelf next to the window.

I'm different now, he thought. There are new layers this room knows nothing of.

He turned off the overhead light and lay down on the bed. Again, darkness enveloped him and he immersed himself in it until a deeper need bloomed in another part of the room, stronger than the touch of darkness. He turned his head. Dim greenish light entered from outside and glimmered in a patch on the floor—a fluorescent lure dangled from the sky, coaxing him out of bed, nurturing his movement across the room to the window. Beyond, the backyard waited.

The sash moved in the casing without a sound. He unfastened the screen effortlessly and lifted it away from the aluminum frame.

Blake climbed into the night air. The ground felt unnaturally soft. He took his shoes and socks off to feel the wet grass. His father had left an upright wheelbarrow next to the garden—half-filled now with rainwater. When he looked into it, a miniature heaven of stars looked back at him. Then the beautiful sadness forced him to look away. Putting his shoes back on, he moved silently through the yard, past the beehives, until he stood at the back fence along the neighbor's pasture.

This probably isn't a good idea, he thought, but the argument had no appeal compared to the welcoming outline of trees in the distance. The smell of living vegetation joined the sound of frogs, insects, and whippoorwills in nocturnal intoxication. After a brief glance at the dark house behind him, Blake squeezed between two barbed wires and moved toward the rock outcropping. He found the remembered path up the incline, each handhold engaging a memory retained more by muscle and bone than mind.

At the higher elevation a new horizon opened. A moonlit path led deeper into the woods. He remembered that by following the trees southwest he'd enter a larger forest, without roads, homes, or people. With each step his soul expanded. He heard an owl. Prison and the civilization that had built it slipped farther away.

As his eyes adjusted to the light, he moved more quickly, following animal trails with a pleasure known only to him. Damp leaves cushioned his steps and the underbrush allowed him to pass without hindrance. In the open spaces, the great reeling constellations pursued him. He crossed a deserted highway, plunging deeper into rocky, uninhabited forest. The smell of humus climbed into his mind. I'm alone, he thought, and this realization was even better than darkness, better than anything else he could imagine. No one could hear, see, smell, or touch him. Nothing he did or thought could affect another person, and nothing anyone else did or thought could affect him.

He sat on the ground, leaned back on his arms, looked up at unspooling generations of stars, and wondered what would happen to him next.

Settling In

In one afternoon Ivan and his mother moved all their belongings from the apartment above the meat locker in Grange into their much bigger accomodations at the Roebucks'. All their old things fit nicely among the new furnishings, and Amy Roebuck gave them a television from an upstairs storage room. Dart advertised the old one on craigslist, and when it didn't sell, she threw it into the dumpster behind the machine shed.

Mrs. Roebuck also gave Ivan some clothes that used to belong to Kevin. Most of them were almost brand new, which Ivan assumed was probably on account of Kevin not moving around more than a wooden hanger in a closet. His legs sometimes got tired just walking to the kitchen. One of the shirts smelled like the medicine fog they sprayed in Kevin's room in order to help him breathe. But Dart said it would wash out no problem.

Ivan liked his new home, and when people asked his mother what she thought of working for Buck and Amy Roebuck, she often joked, "The commute's not hard."

His mother hardly ever kidded around, and it always made Ivan laugh when she said it. Dart was mostly serious. She liked to be busy, and she often told Ivan that the world was full of lazy people, shirkers, slackers, sluggards, sloths, laggards, loafers, lollygaggers, lounge lizards, idlers, day-dreamers, do-littles, do-nothings, and folks who liked to sleep in. "Don't ever let someone catch you napping" was one of her dire warnings.

When the rest of the Roebucks' big house was still sleeping, Dart's light would snap on and the pages in her catalogs began to rustle. Then she showered and dressed, and by the time the birds started yakking outside she was banging around in the big kitchen. Every morning, the first thing she did was make breakfast- and lunch-boxes, along with two thermoses of coffee, and set them on the corner of the counter.

Buck was usually the second one up, and after sleepwalking into some clothes he would stumble down the stairs like a drunken horse, shaking the whole house. He was usually too tired to say anything to Ivan's mother on his way through the kitchen, so he would just grab the food boxes and coffee and continue down the hall. After getting his shoes on and closing the front door, he would clomp down the porch steps and onto his truck. Ivan often looked out of the window in his bedroom and saw Buck's taillights descend to the bottom of the drive, then turn up the highway toward Thinker's Ridge.

When Buck's engine started it almost always woke up Florence on the third floor, and by the time she had bathed, dressed, and settled into her chair, her thick glasses perched on the end of her nose, Dart was there with breakfast and chamomile tea. When Dart and Ivan first arrived, Florence had eaten only sardines and raisin toast, but Dart told her that simply wouldn't do. "Not on my watch," she said.

Dart ate breakfast with Florence. She sat beside her, with just a small folding table between them. No one else was to come into Florence's room while they were having breakfast.

In fact, nobody cared. Everyone else was either sleeping or trying to sleep. And their breakfast lasted only about fifteen minutes, anyway. After that, Dart came back down to the kitchen and set out fruit, yogurt, granola, oatmeal, toast, low-fat butter, coffee, and more tea. Only on Sunday morning were there eggs, pancakes, ham, and fried potatoes, or something else.

Amy Roebuck usually got up next. She ate breakfast in the kitchen while talking to Dart about work that day. If Kevin was too tired to get out of bed, she ate with Kevin and the nurse. But Kevin usually came to the kitchen to frown and watch Ivan's mother out of the corner of his eyes.

Wally and Ivan were usually up last. They sat at the kitchen counter. Wally drank black coffee and told Ivan what he'd dreamed about, if he could remember. Ivan ate cereal with jam, honey, or sugar. Meanwhile, Kevin slumped at the table next to the window, where he could pick at his fruit and yogurt and get a good view of the sink.

At that point Dart would begin doing the dishes, but she was still usually available for conversation. And breakfast time was often good for conversation. Lately, Quiet Shoes wanted to talk about the prisoner who worked for August's dad. She remembered him from before. He was crazy reckless, she said, and hard to get along with. She imagined being in prison had probably made him worse. "It's best to stay away from him," she said.

"People catch diseases in prison," Kevin added. "It's second only to hospitals in spreading infections."

Amy said everyone deserved a second chance, but Dart disagreed. Prisoners should never be released, she said. Once they proved they couldn't be trusted, they should be left in the clink.

Quiet Shoes said the prisoner was out on account of August's mom. Everyone knew it was her doing, she added, and the people in her church weren't happy about it.

Wally said churchgoers were never happy about anything. That's why they were in church. He knew August's mom and liked her. "Pastor Winnie just thinks people could be better than they are. There's nothing wrong with that."

"Look, I'm not against trying to do good," said Dart. "But people who do good should stay out of other people's business."

Quiet Shoes asked Dart if she had known Blake before he went to prison. Dart said she didn't remember meeting him. But later, when Quiet Shoes said he had reddish hair, Dart corrected her. "No, he didn't," she said. "It was black." And then she quickly added, "Or at least that's what I heard."

Wally remembered that Nathaniel Bookchester, the prisoner's father, had driven trucks for Roebuck Construction a long time ago. Then he took a different job after his wife ran off and he needed to be home more. Quiet Shoes said he wasn't home enough, even so, but Wally replied that it was hard when you had to make a living and take care of a child on your own. He remembered that Blake had later worked in the foundry and raced motorcycles. "The kid had grit," he said.

"Blake's bike was quicker than spit, and nobody ever outran him except Skeeter Skelton," said Dart. "And nobody ever beat Skeeter Skelton. I mean, that's what I heard."

Everyone agreed. Skeeter Skelton must have been born on a motorcycle. For many years he did tricks in the foundry parking lot at lunch, and the workers—even the office workers—came out and watched. He could ride standing on the tank, do wheelies all the way across the lot, tilt the bike up on the front tire and pivot around, cut figure eights in the asphalt, and get off the bike while it was still moving, then catch up to it ten or twenty yards later and get back on. After he was done, they would put dollar bills in his helmet. He once rode ten miles of railroad—a single rail between Grange and Luster. Nobody ever beat Skeeter. He had so many trophies he began giving them back to the clubs so they could use them again. Around Grange, Red Plain, and Luster, Skeeter was a legend, said Dart.

Ivan liked breakfast time, especially when they had waffles with strawberries, syrup, and whipped cream. There was even maple syrup at the Roebucks'—the real stuff. Wally had made it several winters ago and put up jars and jars of it in the pantry. He showed Ivan the trees he bored. That's what he called it—boring, with a big drill. Ivan could stick his fingers right into the old holes. It didn't hurt the trees one bit, Wally said. They sealed up good as new.

After he bored the trees, Wally put in spiels and the sap dripped out into buckets. It ran faster, he said, when there was a hard freeze the night before, followed by clear skies. That's when the buds on the branches sucked hardest, filling the trunk and limbs with sap. He told Ivan he could sometimes collect a whole bucket from one tree in a single day. It ran out clear. Then he poured the buckets of sap into a long, flat pan sitting on concrete blocks with a fire underneath. The clear sap boiled down until it was brown and thick.

You had to be real careful, he said, not to boil the liquid down so far that the bottom of the pan showed through. Then it would burn and you had to throw the whole batch away. So you kept adding more sap to the boiling pan. It took a long time to do it right, and a lot of firewood. He said Ivan could help him make syrup next winter.

Wally told Ivan about a night years ago. He and his wife stayed up all night boiling out sap in the sugar bush. As morning came on, the thickening syrup was getting just about right. They added another log to the fire and more sap to the pan, then watched real close to make sure the sugar didn't burn. That's when a black bear walked up a path out of the woods and came right over and looked at them. Wally told Ivan that meeting a bear taught him everything he ever needed to know about humility. He bowed and backed away slowly. "Easy now, easy," he said. But his wife wouldn't leave. She stayed with the boiling sap. "No old bear is getting this," she said. When the bear rose up on his back legs, she waved the long spoon she'd been stirring with in his face. Then the bear got down on all fours, growled, and went away.

"Is that story true?" Ivan asked.

"Yes," he said, and went on to explain that something had happened between the bear, the spoon, and his wife—something that might never be repeated. He said life was full of things like that, but most people chose not to think that way. They liked everything standard.

After the breakfast dishes were done, Dart usually started making some kind of soup for lunch. Unlike other foods, she said, soup filled up all the little empty cracks. Then she would get a load of laundry going and begin cleaning. And if it was a shopping day, she would set out early, so she could be back in time to finish making lunch. Ivan would go with her if he wasn't doing something else.

Amy Roebuck wanted the house to look just the way it did when she was a girl. All the furniture was old-fashioned, and everything had to look just so—the floors, ceiling, walls, even the lights and light switches.

Ivan's mother helped her and sometimes Ivan did too. It was really boring work, especially scraping and sanding some crusty old bureau or chest. There was also gardening to do, because Mrs. Roebuck wanted peonies and irises to grow along the sidewalk. Her grandmother had had peonies and irises and she wanted rows of them just the same.

One afternoon, Amy and Dart were putting up wallpaper in the dining room. They called it "hanging" but there was nothing hung that Ivan could see. They used paste to stick it to the wall. While they were working on a long piece along the doorway, Dart slipped on the ladder and a big blob of paste fell into Amy's hair. "Oh crap," Dart said, and climbed down from the ladder. For some reason this got them both to laughing so hard they couldn't stop. Then they went after each other, throwing paste.

"Get away from me!" yelled Dart.

"Don't you dare!" howled Amy.

"Stop," said Dart, giggling. "You stop."

"Dart, put that down right now." Amy laughed. "Let go of me."

"Look what I've got for you, Mrs. Roebuck."

"If you call me Mrs. Roebuck again—okay, now you're really going to get it."

They were running around, tossing paste and paper, and shoving each other and hollering like wild monkeys in the jungle. The ladder fell over and Ivan's mother jumped over it. When Kevin came in to see what was going on, the two women were lying on the floor next to each other, laughing uncontrollably. The room looked as if a Tasmanian devil had just gone through it.

When Dart saw Kevin she turned white, jumped up, peeled a piece of the wallpaper off the front of her shirt, and began to clean up. Amy stayed on the floor laughing, spread out as if she were floating in water.

Then Kevin spoke up in his jittery old-person voice. "Mom, what are you doing? Mom?"

"It's all right, Kevin," she replied. "You don't need to worry."

"What do you think you're doing?" he demanded.

"I guess we weren't thinking," she said. "We were just doing."

"I don't like it," said Kevin. He was talking to his mother, but looking at Dart.

Amy climbed slowly to her feet and wiped some paste from her cheek. "Well, Kevin," she said, "this isn't something you need to like." And then her laughing face disappeared into her normal expression.

At that point Quiet Shoes came in, sighed loudly, and joined the other women in cleaning up.

Kevin scowled at Ivan, and Ivan felt more embarrassed than he could ever remember. His mother had never done anything like that before, and from that moment on, every time he saw Amy Roebuck he remembered her laughing and lying there on the floor.

Everyone wanted Ivan to be friends with Kevin, but it wasn't easy. Kevin was crabby. It was as if someone had kicked the kid out of a fourteen-year-old and put a jittery old man inside. He hardly ever left home except to visit doctors, and he knew way too much about hospitals, infections, pills, and disease—at least according to Dart. Nobody that young should know that much about unpleasant things, she said.

Kevin loved video games, and sometimes he let Ivan play them with him. Kevin was much better, but Ivan still liked to play, and sometimes they played together until Kevin got too tired and went back to bed.

As the days continued and he felt more and more at home at the Roebucks', Ivan found himself spending more of his free time with Wally. Being with him was often easier than being with anyone else, depending on what everyone was doing.

Wally carried a pocket notebook in whatever drooping shirt he was wearing, and from time to time he scribbled in it. He was making a list of all the things he'd miss after he was gone—two lists, really, one short, one long. The long list included items like lightning bugs, early light, the smell of grease in the alley behind a restaurant, water running from roofs, barred owls, holding a shovel, clear skies, listening to a crowded swimming pool on a hot afternoon, leaves, wavy windows, snow piled on limbs, coffee, putting on a clean undershirt fresh from the dryer, moss on stumps, the sound of a well-hit nail, paths in the woods, women talking far away, spiderwebs with dew, the moon, and fish.

The short list had things like Buck, Flo, and night air.

"Night air?" asked Ivan.

"Night air is just what it says," replied Wally. "It's the way it feels when you step outdoors at night."

"Sure," said Ivan, "but that isn't air, it's the dark."

"Night air means dark and it also means cool. And it means anything can happen."

Then Ivan told Wally what August said once: "Words don't always say what they mean." Ivan went on to explain who August was, and Wally said he must be a good friend, to say something like that and for Ivan to remember it.

A couple of days after they'd moved in, Florence explained to him what part of Jesus's life each bead in a rosary stood for. Then she paused and asked, at the speed of ice melting on the North Pole, "Are you satisfied with your new accommodations, Ivan?"

Ivan said he was, and to illustrate the point he described a few of the very worst things about their old apartment above the meat locker. He also told her how he and his mother had once lived in the Bronco for six months, after they got kicked out of an even worse apartment. At that moment his mother came in, looking as if she'd just been stabbed with a dull knife, and said that in fact they had never lived in the Bronco.

That wasn't true, of course, and Florence didn't believe it either. She understood that Dart was really saying something like "I feel ugly when people know we lived in the Bronco, and I'd like to kill my son for telling you about it."

Florence smiled, slid her glasses down her nose until only the very tip bumped out, and tugged a red bead along the string to its place above the plastic cross. "I see."

Buck was almost always gone during the day, and when he was home the phone rang all the time. Some nights after dinner he had to go out again, and when he did, Ivan often asked Buck if he could go with him.

These requests usually prompted Buck to ask Dart. "Excuse me, Ms. Workhouse," he would say, "I have to go back to the office for a couple minutes. Would it be all right with you if Ivan came along? You have my word that we won't be longer than an hour."

At first Dart said no, there was work for Ivan to do.

The second time he asked, she was standing barefoot in the hallway, holding an armload of laundry in front of her. "Okay," she said, then turned around and walked away. Buck watched her until she turned into the laundry room.

"Let's go," he said. When he opened the front door for Ivan, a herd of moths flapped inside. Buck's hand shot out and caught one.

"How'd you do that?" Ivan asked, trying six times and missing.

"Practice," he said, and *blammo* he caught another one.

"It helps to have a catcher's mitt on the end of both arms," Ivan said.

"That too," said Buck, and laughed in a way that felt good to both of them.

On the way down the sidewalk, Ivan asked if Buck had ever known someone called July Montgomery. Buck said he had, but not very well.

Ivan told him what August said about July Montgomery being stronger than anyone else, and asked if Buck thought that was true.

"Strength is an odd thing," Buck said. "The strongest men sometimes have no strength at all, and even those with hardly any strength will sometimes surprise you."

"What's that supposed to mean?" asked Ivan.

"It means a man might be strong one day, but not the next. So it's hard to say who is and who isn't. It changes."

"Is it true that July Montgomery was murdered in cold blood?"

"I don't know, Ivan. I hope not."

Buck's red pickup had a step-up super cab and suicide doors. It was hard to find a place to sit inside because of all the wiring, hard hats, tool cases, chains, electrical boxes, clipboards, and other things that Ivan didn't recognize. Buck had an even more difficult time, and scrunched up behind the wheel like a rabbit too big for his cage.

On the road, the cab seats rode a lot higher up than in the Bronco. Ivan asked if Buck had ever thought about getting monster tires. Buck said, "No, not really."

When they got to the office in Grange and parked in front of the brick building, Buck climbed out and said he'd be just a couple minutes. Then he went inside and Ivan could see him through the window talking to an older woman behind the counter. They passed some papers back and forth. Buck wrote something on a couple of them, then she handed him a telephone. He talked into it and then hung up. More papers.

Ivan went in and sat in one of the chairs. Buck introduced him to the woman, his bookkeeper, and she smiled a tired, worn-out smile.

"This may take a couple minutes longer than I thought," said Buck. He tugged his billfold out of his back pocket, which remained fastened to him with a chain, and handed Ivan a five-dollar bill. It looked like Monopoly money in his hand.

"Here, Ivan, go across the street and get some ice cream."

Ivan went out. There was a Deep Freeze on the corner. The sign with a grinning ice cream cone had been turned off, but it was still open. When the guy in the window asked what Ivan wanted he ordered three Chunky Shakes and slid the five dollars over the counter.

The man with the paper hat said that wasn't enough, and Ivan said it was for Mr. Roebuck, across the street.

The man looked out, saw Buck's truck, and gave Ivan three Chunky Shakes for free.

When Ivan carried them into the office Buck looked surprised to see him for some reason. The bookkeeper didn't. She looked tired and hungry.

"What is this?" Buck asked, taking a bite of his.

"A Chunky," said Ivan.

"What's in it?"

"Ice cream and chopped-up cookies."

Ivan handed the five dollars back to Buck and explained how the man had given them the shakes.

"Really?" said Buck. "Who was it?"

"I don't know."

"Who works over there?" Buck asked the bookkeeper.

"Williams from Lake Street."

"Oh, Bob," he said, as if that explained everything.

Buck looked over three papers and signed them as the bookkeeper gulped down her Chunky, scraping the bottom with the green plastic spoon like a mouse in a wall.

"I didn't know they had these things," said Buck, taking another bite.

"They've had 'em forever," Ivan said.

"Do you want to send back the load of trusses?" asked the bookkeeper.

"No," said Buck. "Send it over to the cement company. Let them sort it out over there."

"Beulah won't be happy about that," said the bookkeeper, throwing the empty cup in the trash and wiping her mouth with the back of her hand. She smiled at Ivan.

"Probably not, but they've got storage. Have her call me."

"Here, initial this before you leave."

"What did you call this, Ivan?" asked Buck, taking another bite.

"A Chunky."

"They're something new?"

"They're not new at all. They've been selling 'em since the Stone Age."

"You think your mother would like one?"

"She doesn't eat ice cream. She says it's not a smart use of money."

"Good point. Is that all, Rebecca?"

"What do you want to tell Harvey about the drainage chase?"

"Don't tell him anything for now. Have him talk to Bernie next week and tell Bernie we're not doing business with that company anymore."

"Okay."

"Let's all go home," said Buck. "It's late. Thanks for everything, Rebecca. I don't know what we'd do without you."

"No trouble, Buck."

On their way back, Buck took a side road below the water tower, and while they finished the shakes he pointed to a house. He said he'd grown up there. Six blocks later was the house where Mrs. Roebuck had lived when she was a girl.

"You could put both those houses inside the one you've got now," Ivan said.

"I know," said Buck. "But back then you didn't need much to be happy."

"What do you need now?"

"I don't know, Ivan. If you find out, tell me."

"Okay. And if you find out, you tell me."

When they got back, there was a car with tinted windows and wide tires parked beside the machine shed.

"Who's that?" Ivan asked.

"Amy's brother," said Buck in a flat voice.

Just inside the door sat a tall, well-dressed man with watery blue eyes. A slim black briefcase rested beside him on the chair. His shoes were polished black and he had long clean fingers.

"It's after nine," said Buck.

The man laughed as if he'd just heard a very old joke. "Business never sleeps," he said. "I thought you'd be glad to see me. Who's the boy?"

"Ivan, this is my brother-in-law, Lucky."

Ivan looked puzzled.

"That's right," said the man. "You know—like, it's better to be lucky than good." And he laughed again in a not-funny way.

"Go on, now," Buck said. "Make sure your mother knows we got back on time."

They went into the little office and closed the door.

Ivan found his mother in the laundry room, folding clothes.

"We're back," he said.

"Where did you go?' she asked.

"To the office, like Buck said."

"Anywhere else?"

"No."

"That's good. I'm almost finished here and it's getting late. Go clean up your room."

Ivan went down the hall, but he did not go right to his room. Outside the door to the office he crouched down and listened.

Buck spoke first. "I don't like giving money to people who work for the government, especially when business is slow."

Lucky replied, "But you have to spend to make any money these days.

State contracts have been good to you before, and they will be again. They're the only way to do well in bad times."

"We can bid like everyone else," said Buck.

"Sure," said Lucky, "but if certain people don't know you, nothing will come of it. You have to develop a relationship. Then they remember you."

"We did that two years ago."

"And now the relationship has to be renewed. If we get started before the end of the month, the chairman will float the early bids and we can lowball."

"There's too much paperwork with government jobs," said Buck.

"Hire someone to do it for you." Lucky laughed. "These jobs are plums. Delays, cost overruns, substandard material, subcontractors, it doesn't matter. The only people minding the store are the ones you have a relationship with."

"I hate this," said Buck.

"These people make the laws, Buck. Get over it. It's the way the country's going. Put up or shut down. Get ahead or get behind. Your equipment will be bought out from under you by those new outfits with Mexican labor. You'll be out of business."

"My father's still the head of the company, and he has the last word."

"Say, who was the quick trick in the hall?" asked Lucky. "When Amy answered the door there was a caramel number behind her, standing there like a piece of licking candy. You ever think about squeezing into that, Buck?"

"Watch the way you talk, Lucky."

"No offense." Lucky laughed. "Just pointing out the obvious."

August

August was worried about Milton. A mysterious fungal disease called White Nose Syndrome had been killing bats across the country. He'd been reading about it on the Internet. The scientific name of the fungus was *Geomyces destructans,* and some fatality estimates ran higher than one million. In some areas of the country nearly all the hibernating insectivorous species had been wiped out. Many of the carcasses were still in sleeping mode when they were discovered, but most fell to the ground and piled up on each other. They appeared to be spotted with frost. There were no living bats for hundreds of miles around the fungal extermination zones, and August was horrified by the thought of such barren places. How lonely those night skies must be, he thought.

Apparently no one knew exactly how the fungus killed its victims, but most scientists thought something in the fungus caused the unsuspecting bats to end their hibernation early and go hunting in the middle of winter. Bats were extremely sensitive to low temperatures, and they often died from exposure. Others just stopped breathing while they slept.

August sensed that his mother was tired of him talking about it, but she also said it was an important topic, and suggested he make a presentation about it at the next science fair, which was two weeks away. He immediately began preparing his report, intending to warn everyone in attendance that most scientists expected WNS to soon arrive in Wisconsin. And once it got here, the contagion would spread through direct contact with other bats, which was especially problematic for a highly social species.

August thought it reasonable to assume that Milton was not as vulnerable as other bats because he spent most of his time with him. But Milton's family was surely in grave danger, and August was convinced that Milton knew this. After all, Milton knew things people couldn't even begin to think about. And he'd also been anxious lately. When he hunted he often came back early, hours before sunrise. His body weight had gone down a half ounce in the last month.

August wondered if he could find where Milton's family lived. He ordered a bat detector on the Internet and his dad helped him solder it together in the shop. It could detect the ultrasound emitted by bats during echolocation. The instruction manual said he could "listen to the night skies and identify whether the bats were hunting, talking to each other, or singing." It seemed wonderfully strange to think of bats singing in a medium inaccessible to the sensory capacity of humans.

Whenever August thought about the bat world his imagination was set on fire. He had just learned from a library book that when Milton or any other insect-eating bat identified a flying insect, the signal bouncing back informed him of its species—say, a mature lacewing—how far away it was, the angle of its flight, and how fast it was flying. He also discovered that as soon as the bat made contact with the lacewing, the lacewing would also know about Milton. The insect had the same sensory equipment, which meant the night skies were filled with a kind of knowledge that humans could only dream about accessing.

August's detector really worked too. He could dial in Milton when he was flying. The signals were especially clear as he caught bugs under the light pole in the yard. With the pocket-sized device positioned on the ledge just outside his bedroom window, August could hear Milton far in the distance—up to one hundred meters away. He could listen to him coming across the valley and into the room.

Blake Bookchester had helped with making the detector, too, though August's dad had to redo some of his soldering. And he'd offered excellent suggestions about how to position all the components within the small plastic carrying case.

At first, August had kept his distance from the ex-prisoner, but August spent a lot of time at the shop during the summer, and after a couple of weeks Blake seemed less threatening. He got along all right with his father most of the time, and even seemed to go out of his way to be pleasant to customers.

Still, there was plenty of talk about him around Words, and August's parents' voices got low, slow, and careful whenever they mentioned him. Everyone seemed to know he worked at the shop, and some of the people at church were upset about it. One Sunday a couple of old folks had talked to his mom after the service about how she never should have visited the prison in the first place. It was just plain wrong, they said, and now people in other churches were talking about it. His mom said she appreciated how they were willing to share their feelings, and then after they went home she sat by herself for a long time in her garden.

Uncle Rusty was even more wound up about it, and he came into the shop almost every day to hobble around and stare at Blake through the dark plastic goggles that protected his cataracts. And whenever he got the chance he yelled at August's mom, saying she had no understanding of the darker side of human nature, and needed to live in the real world.

August didn't think his dad particularly liked Blake working in the shop, either, and it wasn't just because Uncle Rusty came around a lot more often. Blake repaired some things almost as well as his father did, but he didn't seem to understand chain saws, and on some days he seemed too tired to do anything but stare out the windows and throw wrenches around when he lost his temper. He complained that he couldn't sleep at night.

Still, whenever August's mom asked about Blake, his dad always said he was improving. Even when Blake yelled at customers, his dad would say, "It will work out, Winifred. Don't worry. Things take time. Blake finished the stalk-chopper today."

But when Winnie asked Jacob to bring Blake home for supper after work, Jacob said Blake wasn't ready yet.

"Why won't he come?" August asked.

"He's waiting," said Jacob.

"Waiting for what?"

"For something inside him to change."

Blake never went anywhere, even though he had a license now and drove his father's old pickup. He just came to the shop in the morning and went home at night. He never went anywhere else, even on weekends. August heard him talking to his dad once about needing to stop at the library to check out some books, but the next day, when Jacob asked him if he'd gone, he said he hadn't.

A week later August went to the library himself, looking for more information about White Nose Syndrome from Mrs. Landwagon. She was a friend of his mom's and worked behind the desk. He asked if Blake Bookchester had been there. No, she said, he hadn't. She wondered aloud if prisoners were still permitted in public libraries. She thought maybe they were, but she wasn't sure. The new governor was said to be tough on crime.

When August was leaving, she called him back. "Here," she said. "You might as well take these. Your father ordered them last week." She put eight books in a plastic bag and handed them to him. They were schoolbooks, and August wondered why his father had ordered them. Later, Jacob explained that they were for someone from church. Then he put them away.

Blake had been out of prison for only about three weeks, and he'd already been called in for three drug tests. His parole agent came to the shop pretty often to make sure he wasn't drinking beer or carrying guns, or talking to other men who had been in prison. That was one of the rules—no talking to felons who'd committed major crimes. Jack Station also made surprise visits to Blake's house at night, just to make certain he was there. One time Station showed up in a van loaded with police officers and they searched Blake's house from top to bottom, looking for alcohol, drugs, and guns.

Blake was really mad the next morning at the shop, and Jacob spoke firmly with him for a long time over by the drill press. Blake said Station hadn't found anything, but he'd still torn up the house looking. Apparently Station even went through his father's bedroom and yanked all the clothes out of the drawers. Jacob told him to calm down, but Blake didn't seem to know how to do that. His rights had been violated. They had disrespected his father, he said, and then he talked for a long time about the government.

On the ride home after work, Jacob told August not to say anything to his mother about what had happened at the shop that day. She thought Station was trying to push Blake into doing something, so he could send him back to prison. So August didn't say anything.

Three nights later, just as August was falling asleep, he heard a scraping sound, followed by a thud. He went to the window. The moon lit up the yard and he could see the limbs in the big pine trees all the way to the sky. And then he saw the Wild Boy. He was sitting on the first limb up, his feet hanging down about six feet from the ground.

When August saw him the Wild Boy rocked back and forth, swinging his legs. Then he jumped down without making a sound.

They stood there for a moment, August on the inside and the Wild Boy on the outside, looking at each other. The Wild Boy was wearing a shirt and pair of shorts that looked to be too large. August waved and the boy smiled, his teeth white. Then he ran off.

August tried to keep him in sight, but he disappeared into the woods. Then August saw a jar on the window ledge, and he brought it inside. After looking at it he carried it down to the kitchen, where his dad was sitting at the table, eating an egg salad sandwich.

August showed him the jar and he set his sandwich down, unscrewed the top, and pulled off the lid, making a little *psssst* sound. After smelling the contents, he stuck in a spoon and pulled out a piece of fruit.

"It's good," he said. "Peaches. Where'd you get this?"

"It's a secret," said August.

"Can't you tell me?"

August thought about it for a moment and decided that he could tell. The peach delivery seemed to place everything on a higher level. "The Wild Boy."

His dad looked worried, but it didn't last long. "I see," he said, and stood up to get two bowls.

"I've got to find him, Dad."

"Why?"

"I have to. He has a scar on his face and I have to find him. I have to."

"That's not a good idea, August."

"It is to me."

They ate in silence, and after Jacob finished he looked out the window and said, "July Montgomery would have liked this."

"Why?" asked August, alert to any information about his father's friend.

"He liked anything homemade."

"Why?"

"That's just the way he was."

"Did July Montgomery grow up around here?" August asked.

"No."

"Where did he live before?"

"I don't know," said Jacob, and then he looked sad. "I should have known him better. He was my friend and I should have known him better."

But then Jacob smiled. "Say, those were great peaches. Really great."

"Why?" asked August. "Why did the Wild Boy leave the jar here?"

"He wanted you to have it."

"But he might not have enough to eat himself."

"If he didn't, he wouldn't share with you. I promise, August, there's nothing to worry about."

"I have to find where he lives."

Jacob took their bowls and spoons and washed them, then he turned back to August. "Look, I can't tell you where he lives, but if you give me a couple days I think I can tell you someone to talk to. In the meantime, I'd like you to keep this between the two of us. Do you think you can do that?"

"I can."

When August went back to his room he sat at the window for a while, looking outside. The moon was covered by clouds, and the leaves shook in the wind.

Searching for the Wild Boy

After supper a few days later, August quietly went out of the back door of his home, walked through the yard, and headed up the ridge. Three full hours of daylight remained.

The overhead clouds bunched tightly together in a central area of the sky, like a handful of marshmallows in the bottom of a big blue bowl. The grasses had grown taller than knee-high, and the leaves had changed from spring's light green to the first phase of summer's darkening glossy green.

August followed trails that he and Ivan had found, and Milton flew on ahead, clearing bugs and checking out noise from the sky. They continued climbing Old Baldy, and from the top of it August could see into three valleys. Then he took a drink of water and began walking downhill.

At the bottom of the first valley he found the swampy path with empty bottles and cans strewn along it. About a half mile later he came to the melon field, which stretched out flat, open, and wide before him. On the other side, where the second valley began its rocky climb, stood the dirt house.

August remained in the cover of trees and bushes, hesitant to walk into the open field. He watched Milton fly over it. His father had said he could visit Lester Mortal and ask him questions about the Wild Boy. But he'd also told him to be particularly respectful of the old veteran and not stay very long, and August wondered about the meaning of these added precautions. Was his father attempting to warn him of some potential danger, or did he caution him simply because of his own discomfort in talking to him? After thinking about this for some time, August decided he could not resolve either question without more information, and so he started into the field.

He walked slowly, watching for signs of movement and trying to keep from trampling on watermelons, muskmelons, and pumpkins, which were everywhere, most of them a little smaller than softballs. After what seemed to August like a long time, he reached the middle of the field, where he felt exposed on all sides.

Milton saw the hermit first, standing in front of the hut. Then August saw him cross his arms in front of his chest and stand motionless. Milton swooped down and dove into August's shirt pocket.

"Stop right there, stranger!" shouted the hermit. "Stop right there."

His voice seemed bigger than life, August thought, but he didn't look overly large. His dark hair and beard were his most arresting features. Both flared out beyond his face in an explosion of untamed growth. People at the shop said he hadn't shaved or cut his hair since he got out of the military. His mouth didn't seem to move when he talked, and he was dressed in camouflage fatigues with black combat boots. Even from this distance, his shirt and pants appeared shiny—the way clothes look when they haven't been washed in a long while. His eyes glowed like hot coals.

"Who are you and what do you want?" he asked in an angry tone.

"My name is August and I want to know about the Wild Boy."

"Are you friend or foe?"

"Friend."

"What have you got in your pocket?"

August wondered briefly how the hermit knew there was anything in his pocket, then fished out the camp knife he'd brought to give to the Wild Boy.

"Not that pocket. Your chest pocket."

"Milton's in there."

"Who's Milton?"

"He's my bat."

"What do you mean?"

"He belongs to me. He's a long-eared bat. And he's mine."

"I don't believe you. Take him out."

"No."

"Why not?"

"He doesn't want to come out."

"Take him out so I can see him."

"No. He's afraid of people he doesn't know."

"I'll give you twenty dollars if you take him out."

"Absolutely not."

"You're that preacher's kid," the hermit said. "The woman preacher."

"That's correct," replied August. "And I'm proud of it."

"I guess I can trust you, then. Come on ahead."

As August walked forward, he asked, "Why did you decide to trust me, Mr. Mortal?"

"If you'd protect a bat, you'll honor the truth."

He talked odd like that. August didn't understand exactly why, but he wasn't afraid of the hermit. He looked frightening enough, with all that hair and those red, glowing eyes, and he'd heard a lot of bad things about him at the shop. But his dad had let August come, and though he was uncomfortable he wasn't afraid.

"That was a long walk," the hermit said. "Can I get you a glass of water?"

"No, thank you. I brought along my thermos."

August couldn't take his eyes off the hermit's hut.

"I guess you've never seen a home like this before," the hermit said, watching him.

"I guess not."

The shack looked like a large mound or a small hill with steep sides. There were two large windows in front, but they were covered by vines and couldn't be seen from a distance. Even the front door was covered with moss. And when the hermit reached out and opened it, there was a tearing sound, like when a piece of sod is ripped out of the ground by its roots.

"Come inside," he said.

"How did you get the dirt to stay up like that?" asked August, feeling the wall with his hand as he went through the doorway.

"This isn't really a sod house," he said. "It just looks like one. The basic structure is made of straw bales covered with wire and mud."

From what August could see there were only three rooms. It was dark inside, with several kerosene lamps glowing orange and yellow. The first room, the biggest, had a rack of guns along one wall—maybe thirty rifles of different sizes, and an open case of a dozen or so pistols. Boxes and boxes of ammunition were stacked alongside the weapons. Along another wall stood shelves of canned and dried foods, but there wasn't enough light to recognize the different kinds.

August stared at the guns until the hermit asked, "Do you like guns, August?"

"I know little about them," he said. "But my mom is against them."

"How does your father feel?"

"Dad's feelings don't usually come out from under Mom's."

"You mean he doesn't say anything that disagrees with her?"

"Right."

"So you probably won't tell them about these."

"Probably not."

The floor appeared to be covered with several inches of mulch. In the middle of the first room stood a woodstove made from an oil barrel. There were also two painted statues made of wood. They were large, and at first August thought they might be giant cigar-store Indians. He'd seen several of those on a vacation in North Dakota last year, but these seemed different. He couldn't see them very well, but there didn't appear to be any feathers, tomahawks, or cigars sticking out.

One of the statues hadn't been completely painted yet, and around it were paint cans on top of the wood chips. The hermit sat down on a stool next to them. He dipped a brush and started painting. August wondered how he could see well enough in the dim light.

There was a room off to the left as well. August could make out the corner of a table and some boxes in there. And then off to the right was another room, but the door was closed.

"So, what is it you want, August?" the hermit asked.

"The Wild Boy," August said. "He put a jar of peaches on the window outside my room and I saw him up close."

"The child left peaches?"

"That's correct," said August. "A jar of canned peaches with a smidgeon of honey."

"I wonder where those came from," said the hermit. "How were they?"

"My dad liked them more than me, but they were good. If you could please tell me where he lives, I'd like to talk to him."

"I can't do that," said the hermit. He changed brushes and started painting with a different paint.

"Why not?"

"For one thing, the child doesn't talk."

"Why?"

"Just doesn't."

"Never?"

"Nope."

"Everybody can talk."

"Not that child."

"Have you ever seen him?"

"Sure, many times—the child stayed here several nights last winter."

"Here?"

"Slept in that room," said the hermit, jabbing his brush in the direction of the closed door.

"He came inside?"

"It was cold out there."

"He slept here?"

"A couple nights at least."

The hermit changed paintbrushes and began working in yellow.

August looked more closely at the statue. He could make out a leg and a foot and the outline of a head.

"What did the two of you do when he was here?"

"We slept, got up, ate something, carried in firewood, watched the snow fall, and boiled water for bergamot tea—things like that. And then one night we put a pine knot I'd been saving in the fire, and watched it burn. It was a pleasant evening. Have you ever seen a pine knot burn, August?"

"No, I haven't."

"Then you've got something to look forward to. The colors are better than anything you can imagine. It's like watching the soul's fire."

"He watched the colors?"

"We both did, for hours."

"He drinks tea?"

"Yes."

"What's he like?"

"A lot like you, August. A lot like you."

"Is he stupid?"

"Not at all."

"But he can't talk."

"That child is smarter than most people I know."

"But he can't talk."

Milton climbed out of August's pocket, climbed up on his shoulder, opened his leather wings, and flew around, exploring. He seemed to enjoy the interior of the shack.

"There's your bat," said the hermit.

"I hope you don't mind him flying around."

"I don't. He can't hurt anything."

"Good," said August. "Most people don't seem to like him."

"That's probably because they think Milton's stupid."

"He's not stupid," August said, stiffening.

"But he can't talk, can he?"

August thought a moment and then said, "Okay, okay, I see what you mean. When was the last time you saw him—the Wild Boy?"

"Oh, let's see." He stopped painting, leaned back, and looked at the ceiling, which was made of round timbers with mud plastered between. "Not that long ago."

"Where?" asked August, sitting down on the wood shavings.

"A mile or two north of here."

"What did he say? Oh yeah, I'm sorry, I forgot he can't talk."

"It's a hard thing to wrap your head around, isn't it, August?"

"Someone should teach him how."

"Why?"

"Because he needs to learn."

As August's eyes adjusted to the dim light, he recognized first one part of the statue, then another, and then he finally saw the whole thing together. He'd never seen anything so horrible. It was a man screaming. One of his eyes had been burned out and there were deep cuts on his face and neck. His stomach was sliced open and you could see his insides. His penis and testicles had been cut off, and there were pieces of rope around his ankles and wrists.

"Is something wrong?" asked the hermit.

"What is that?" asked August, backing away. "What is that?"

"In the war we caught this enemy soldier—pulled him out of a dug-in. We tortured him for most of an afternoon, and as near as I can remember he looked just like that before he died. It's one of the things I can't forget. It haunts me. So in my spare time I carve my memories, paint them as realistically as I can, and burn them on a stone altar in the woods. It helps free me from them."

Milton flew back into August's pocket.

August turned his attention to the other carving, the finished one. It was a man with muscles like thick cables in his neck and arms, blue eyes, a square jaw, and a faraway, heroic expression.

"You want to know about him too?" asked the hermit.

August nodded.

"He was the leader of one of our units—bravest man I ever met. He risked his life again and again to save those under his command. Many men owe their lives to him, and I'm one of them. He was dedicated to serving his country, loyal to his superiors, and he did everything expected of him."

"You're going to burn him too?" August asked.

"Yes."

"Why?"

"I wanted to be like him."

"What's wrong with that?"

The hermit set the brush in the can and put his head in his hands. Then he looked up at August. "I shouldn't have let you see these carvings," he said. "I'm sorry. It was a mistake. In many countries boys your age are forced into armies, trained like other soldiers, and expected to swim in the same bloody slime as the older men. But that doesn't excuse it. I shouldn't have shown you."

"Tell me why you're burning the figure of the man you admired."

"You won't understand."

"I don't like people saying that to me, Mr. Mortal. Just tell me why you want to burn him and let me worry about understanding it."

"These two memories—these two human truths—are the same. This one," he said, pointing at the hero, "contains the other one. When you have one, you get the other. To be rid of one, you must also get rid of the other."

"I don't understand," said August.

"I told you."

August turned away and his face hardened. "Most people think you're crazy," he said.

"That's useful."

"How?"

"It keeps people away."

"Can I come over when you burn that one?" August asked, pointing at the carving of the screaming man.

"Why?"

"I'm afraid it will haunt me too, and I would like to see it burn."

"You're welcome to come, but I'm burning both of them at the same time. So if you don't want to see the other one burn, don't come."

"I'll come," August said. "Can I bring my friend Ivan?"

"How old is he?"

"He's about my age. What difference does it make?"

"I can't get along with adults for very long," he said. "If they've never experienced combat I despise them for what they don't know. And if they were in combat I resent them for what we know together. For some reason younger people like you escape my prejudices."

"So Ivan can come?" asked August, unable to look away from the carving.

"Can you vouch for him, August?"

"I can," he replied. "When should we come?"

"In three weeks—on the next full moon."

"What time?"

"Ten o'clock. Can you get out that late?"

"I will."

"Then I'll wait for you."

"Excuse me, Mr. Mortal, but did the Wild Boy see these carvings?"

"Yes. The child walked over and touched them."

"He touched them?"

"Put a hand on them."

"What else did he do?"

"The child backed away and looked at the statue again—just like you did. Then touched it again, with both hands."

"Which statue?"

"This one."

"How about the other carving?"

"No, not the other one."

"And you think he understands them?" asked August.

"In truth, I do. I've been carving and burning these war memories for many years, and these are the last of them. Every time, the child has come and watched."

"You mean the Wild Boy will be there?"

"I expect so."

Then the hermit jerked up his hand in a warning manner. He turned his head to the side and listened, his eyes flashing in the lamplight.

"Someone's coming," he whispered, and passed quickly to the window. A rifle leaned against the wall beside it.

"Who is it?" asked August.

"*Shhhhhhhh.*" The hermit stared out the window, his right hand on the rifle. Then he left the rifle leaning against the wall, crept quickly back to August, and whispered, "Look, I don't want anyone to know you're here. Go into that room there, stay out of sight. Can you do that?"

August hurried through a thick doorway and into what he assumed was the room where the hermit slept.

It was really dark inside, and filled with many things. There were shelves of drying herbs, wooden boxes, a bureau, trunks, and leather. He pressed against the wall to the side of the doorway.

The front door opened with a root-ripping sound, and the hermit stepped outside.

After a short time August began to relax.

Beside the bed stood a little table—another wooden box with two sides cut out. On top of it were five or six dried wildflowers, with a purple thread tied around the stems. He picked them up. They still had green in the stalks.

August tried to be patient, but a desire to explore the rest of the hut soon overcame him. He wanted to look inside the other room, where the Wild Boy had slept, and he walked carefully away from the bed and toward the closed door, going the long way around the screaming statue. And then through the window he saw his father standing in the melon field beside the hermit, talking. They seemed to know each other, and a few times it even looked as if they were laughing. The exchange concluded with Jacob handing him a plastic bag, then shaking his hand and leaving.

August headed back to the bedroom.

"Sorry for the interruption," the hermit said, coming inside. "It's odd, August. Several months go by when no one visits. Then today, one right after the other. Are you sure I can't get you something to drink? Are you hungry?"

"No, thank you, Mr. Mortal. I should be getting home. Is it still all right for Ivan and me to come back on the twenty-second of July?"

"The twenty-second?"

"That's the next full moon," August said, showing him his pocket calendar.

"I'll be looking for you."

August started for the door, stopped, and walked back into the room.

"Forget something?" the hermit asked.

He went over to the smaller carving, which seemed even more horrible up close, almost alive. The places where the new paint had been applied reflected the lamplight. August forced himself to reach out with both hands and touch the statue. An awful shiver moved up his back, but he held his hands against the painted wood for at least two full breaths, and then went outside.

"Good-bye, August," said the hermit.

Inching Into the Present

Before very long Blake could see through both eyes, hear out of both ears, chew without discomfort, and shave without avoiding sensitive areas. The discoloration took a little longer to fade, but the darker calico splotches eventually blended into the surrounding skin tones.

His psychic wounds presented a more complicated challenge. Something was needed in addition to the autonomic remedies provided by dreams, shaking, weeping, hollering, sweating, and vomiting. For true recovery—involution—Blake required satisfactory relations with other creatures over extended periods of time, and lots and lots of rest. And therein lay the problem.

Blake didn't sleep well and his brooding desire for companionship refused to provide any clues about how to find companions. He harbored no insights into how to dress up his need in an acceptable manner. Not out here.

In prison, shared fears, animosities, and frustrations had often provided the assumptions necessary for shared identity. He had friends there, even if they were temporary. There were guys to talk to, other inmates with whom he could complain about the food, make fun of the guards, talk about old times, and imagine what absolutely perfect women might be like.

But out here, assumptions about things in common seemed wildly presumptuous. He simply couldn't allow himself to think he shared anything with anyone else. Too much of what he had come to understand about the compelling ignorance of hatred—and the distress entailed by coming to understand it—had to be kept hidden.

Invariably, when Blake recognized someone he remembered from before, the last eleven years opened up between them like an unbridgeable ravine. After making eye contact he usually looked away, acknowledging that whatever they might have held in common at one time was now private property.

His father was always there for him, of course. And because of Nate, Blake could sometimes imagine what a reasonably balanced state of mind would be like. He could almost picture a less-haunted edition of himself, sense an inheritance that might come due someday. Because of his father, he had a chance of succeeding in a better world. He knew this because he could feel his father knowing it.

But fathers didn't count as friends.

There were also Winnie and Jacob, of course. They had found a way to bridge the ravine, or at least they were willing to try. They were maybe, theoretically, hypothetically, possibly, perhaps potential friends. But as much as Blake liked Winnie—and he liked her enormously—he had to stay away from her. No better world that he could imagine would ever allow Reverend Winifred Smith Helm and him to be friends. It simply would not happen, and Blake was determined never to act on his impulse to resume the friendship they'd struck up during her visits to the prison. He owed her too much for that. He had vowed that she would never regret those visits, and the only way to ensure this was to stay away from her. He was not going to muck up her life with his own.

And as for Jacob, he was both Blake's employer and married to Winnie. Bosses could sometimes be friendly, Blake thought, but they could never be friends. And single men couldn't really be tight with married men. Different rules applied to married men. Everyone knew that.

Also, Blake occasionally detected a hint of charity in the way Jacob and Winnie related to him. It slipped out unintentionally, in nearly imperceptible expressions of patronizing indulgence. And this type of fond patience differed from the reflective good humor that sometimes characterized how older people related to younger people—the amused detachment of remembering earlier years while witnessing someone else living through them. And Blake could tell the difference.

His hostility to charity had been polished to a dazzling glare. At an early age he could tell from clear across the room if someone saw him as a victim of maternal absence. And by the second grade he had little tolerance for kindheartedness of any sort.

With the first money he made at the shop, Blake repaid Winnie for all the books she'd brought to him—with interest. He still felt morally indebted for the world of refuge the books had provided, but at least he'd dispensed with the monetary obligation.

Thanks to her, Blake's passion for reading had grown exponentially. With books, there weren't the difficulties of up-close relations. All the immediate, personal barriers were gone. Through the ladder of language he could climb into the minds of others.

He reread all the books Winnie had brought him in prison, especially those by Baruch Spinoza. Though separated from him by some four centuries, Blake identified with the solitary lens-grinder. Spinoza had been excommunicated in his early twenties. A branded outcast whose unconventional ideas were widely known, he lived a careful, examined life. When a zealot viciously attacked him once, Spinoza barely escaped with his life. And rather than repairing the hole left in his jacket by the attacker's knife, he wore it that way in order to remind himself that no endeavor was more dangerous than expressing new thoughts. Supported by a few anonymous individuals, he continued to puzzle out the problem of God's everlasting goodness and the enduring presence of evil, until he died from inhaling glass dust.

Sometimes at night, beneath the only burning light in his father's house, Blake's loneliness often gave way to such thought. He walked beside Spinoza along narrow trails of speculation, into the wilderness of thought, searching for that precious living concept that would allow the mute and unconscious wonder of nature to escape the captivity of inert matter and leap into pure conscious bliss. Each night they ventured a little further, as far as Blake could go, and the path grew increasingly hard to follow.

In order to keep moving forward, Blake needed more books. But when he went to the library in Grange to look for them one day on his lunch break, he immediately recognized the woman behind the front desk. She had worked as a secretary in his high school, and he could tell that she remembered him too. They looked at each other briefly and Blake quickly left. He tried to make himself go back, but he didn't know what to say. Though he hadn't really known her, he didn't know how to talk to her, how to sound casual, normal, unlike someone who had just been released from prison. He finally convinced himself there wasn't time, anyway. Jacob needed him back at the shop.

When Blake returned home that evening, he parked the pickup next to the house, carried in the mail, checked the answering machine for messages, and ate a piece of bread with peanut butter in an attempt to counteract a nauseous fatigue. His father was supposed to be back by now.

He reread a section from Spinoza's *Short Treatise on God,* mowed the lawn, carried out the garbage, and went out back behind the house to pick a small armload of vegetables. Standing in the garden, he watched his release officer's blue Mercury drive slowly along the blacktop and turn into the driveway.

Jack Station sat in the car with the motor running. He did not get out.

Bastard even uses his own car for harassment, thought Blake.

He checked his watch. Curfew in a half hour. The week before, a parolee Blake had known in Waupun was returned to prison for walking out of his Milwaukee apartment after curfew to bring in a package from UPS. Jack Station made sure Blake heard about it. "Rules are rules," he said.

Blake freed another cucumber from the vine and stepped from behind the house. Cursing himself, he waved, smiled, and walked down the driveway. As he approached the rolled-up window, Station backed out and drove away.

Blake went inside, washed off the vegetables, and set them in neat rows on the Formica counter. Then he went back outside and stood for ten minutes. The air was heavy, hot, and hazy along the horizon, a single contrail dividing the sky. A flock of blackbirds landed in a nearby field, scattering onto the ground like a handful of tossed raisins. Somewhere down the road, a horn honked. He walked across the driveway into the side yard, pried the shed door open a little ways, and squirmed inside.

The shed housed everything his father hadn't yet talked himself into throwing away. As the stored objects waited to be used again, sold, or taken to the landfill, small mammals had made homes among them. Cobwebs and dust rounded off the sharp edges. The cramped space smelled of shed mold, sweet rot, and rodent urine. Gritty light struggled through a nearly opaque window, the sill dotted with dead insects. Four large cardboard boxes sagged into themselves, filled with kitchen utensils, truck parts, gardening tools, dried-up cans of turpentine, paint, car wax, and winter clothes. An old washer and dryer stood in the corner beside a ride-on lawn-mower without a seat or mowing deck. Bicycles hung from the overheads, along with an old horse harness, pruning shears, a cross-cut saw, a clock, pole lamps, and an iron bed frame.

Then he saw some heavy spokes beneath a canvas tarp and pile of scrap lumber. His father had kept his motorcycle. The smaller dirt bikes were gone—Nate had never liked him dirt racing—but for some reason he had kept the road bike. "Thank you," Blake whispered.

Clearing a path through the shed, he waded in and removed the lumber.

The tarp was stiff and had to be lifted up like a lid. Beneath it, the motor-cycle lay on its side. Mice had chewed off the gas lines, burrowed into the seat. A hole had been gnawed into the corner of the air box. The mufflers were rusted through, the headlamp was broken, and a grainy green chemical reaction foamed out of the battery compartment.

With some effort, Blake pulled the motorcycle upright, brushed off the seat, and straddled it. The shocks squeaked. Reaching forward, he attempted to twist the throttle—the cable was rusted tight—and looked down at the dusty tank.

This is pathetic, he thought, staring into the dirty gauges.

And then something stirred inside him, vibrating out of a nameless silence.

Over the years, the shed door had sunk into the grass, and to open it all the way he yanked up pieces of sod until he could force the opening, carving a dirt arc with the bottom of the door. He frantically cleared a path through the shed, throwing things out.

By the time Nate backed his rig into the drive, the side yard was filled with items from his past, heavily stacked around the shed door, thinning toward the house. Nate noticed a two-by-six plank ramped up the front steps.

The tractor and trailer came to rest in their accustomed place, the diesel turned off.

From inside the house, Blake heard talking and laughter outside. His father had someone with him. He could hear her voice as they climbed out of the cab.

Beulah and Nate came inside. They both wore baggy shorts and red T-shirts and were carrying groceries and bags of crushed ice, jostling against each other. Their chatter was soon silenced by the sight of the motorcycle in the middle of the living room, wrenches and disassembled parts spreading across the floor, on furniture, leaning against walls. Blake sat on the wood floor, without a shirt, scrubbing a piece of metal with a wire brush held over a can of oil.

"Son," said Nate, withering disappointment dripping from his words. "Why didn't you at least put down some plastic, a tarp or something?"

Blake looked around and at once recognized the problem, which he'd glimpsed before only indistinctly. Suddenly, all reasons for using the living room as a motorcycle emergency room that had seemed so compelling now seemed woefully inadequate.

"Shit, I'm sorry," he said, pulling on his shirt.

"You just don't think," said Nate.

"I know it. I'll go out and get something."

"Better not. There's a dark blue Mercury parked down the road and it's after eight."

"Bastard," growled Blake.

His father's face flinched. "Do you remember my cousin Bee?"

They were both looking at him with such eager anticipation that it didn't feel right to disappoint them. "Of course," Blake said, even though he didn't.

Bee smiled and Blake felt a flurry of exploration flashing between the three of them. He regretted swearing, but her eyes forgave him. He'd never seen his father in shorts before. When had he started wearing them? Something about Bee seemed familiar. His father seemed different, almost cavalier. Bee had a dimple when she smiled, and when it appeared something seemed to change in Nate. She knew it and she smiled a lot. Bee glanced at the motorcycle. Nate set two bags of ice on the floor. Bee seemed unnaturally at home in her shorts and T-shirt, as if she'd grown up inside them. His father wanted Blake to like her. Bee liked his father, and wanted Blake to like her too. Nate felt similarly, and Blake did like Bee, at least initially. But for some reason they were also frightened of each other, embarrassed. Bee didn't know what to think about Blake. She was glad he'd put on his shirt. Nate glanced out the window. Blake wasn't sure he'd ever seen his father's knees before. They looked tragically inadequate, especially when compared to Bee's. There was something playful yet sturdy about her. It made Blake uneasy. The way she stood seemed more familial than Blake thought it should. Nate was still upset about the motorcycle in the living room, and he didn't like the swearing. Bee was worried about Blake. Everything was happening too fast.

"Yes, I think I do," Blake added, and smiled to help make this seem true.

"Look what we got here," said his father. "We drove up to Uncle Bill's old place. No one lives there now, but strawberries were still growing beyond the orchard. We picked them. Then we bought farm cream and eggs, and stopped at the station for ice. We're going to make frozen custard if the ice cream machine is still in the basement, with lemon verbena and extra eggs."

"Sure, good idea," said Blake.

They disassembled the sacks in the kitchen. Bee explained to Nate with some enthusiasm what she remembered about the house from years ago. Nate inspected and then reordered the row of vegetables on the counter. Bee came over to look. Nate bumped into her, and once again Blake noticed how painfully cautious they were with each other, alarmed by the slightest closeness, as if both of them were charged full of static electricity that discharged through even the most casual physical contact.

A tiny merriment leaped inside Blake before rushing back into hiding, a fondness seeking cover.

Nate went into the basement to look for his ice cream machine.

Bee rushed into the living room.

"Tell me where I can find something to put under your bike before your dad comes back up." Her voice was surprisingly sympathetic and it caught Blake off guard. She did not appear to be the least bit afraid of the stranger in him, and he cautiously allowed himself to continue to like her.

"In the shed," he said, studying her. "There's a tarp, or tear apart one of the boxes."

Bee hurried outside, returning a short time later with a large, disorderly piece of cardboard. Working together, they cleared a space and pressed it flat against the wooden floor.

Nate rummaged in the basement.

Then Blake remembered her for sure.

"You used to work for the cement company in Red Plain," he said.

"Still do," she said. "Different owners now, though."

"You worked with Danielle Workhouse. She liked you."

"I liked her too. Still do."

"Is she still working there?"

"No."

"Does she still live in Red Plain?"

"No."

"Do you know where she is?"

"She's working for Buck and Amy Roebuck, out at their home."

"Doing what?"

"Cooking, cleaning, everything."

"Do you still see her? Do you know how she is?"

"I haven't talked to her for a while. What do you mean?"

"Is she with someone?"

"Not that I know."

"We used to—"

"I know," said Bee. "I remember."

"She's okay, though? She's all right?"

"As far as I know."

"Is she still the same?"

"Same as what?"

"The same as she was?"

Bee didn't know how to answer. "I guess it depends on what that means to you."

Nate's footsteps climbed the basement stairs.

"Dad never liked her," whispered Blake, backing the motorcycle onto the cardboard and setting the stand.

"I know," said Bee. "And I'm afraid he hasn't changed on that."

"You probably shouldn't tell him I asked about her."

Bee went back into the kitchen and Blake moved the tools and parts onto the cardboard.

Carrying the ice cream maker, Nate glanced into the living room.

The sugar dissolved into the milk and the lemon verbena, sweet cream, and crushed strawberries were added and poured into the metal cylinder. Nate lowered the covered cylinder into the wooden tub and poured ice along the sides. Bee moved the chips around with one hand while shaking salt over them with the other, until the space between the tub and the cylinder was full. Blake came in from the living room and said he'd crank. At intervals, more ice and salt were added.

Nate made coffee. The smell of roasted beans overpowered the petroleum odor and soon subdued the air around them. Outside the kitchen window, the sun dove beneath the horizon, leaving behind a sheet of glowing light. The blue Mercury moved slowly down the road, around the corner.

When the cranking grew difficult, Blake pried open the cylinder to see if the custard had hardened sufficiently.

It had, and Bee got out spoons and bowls. Nate said they should wait an hour while the custard cured in the freezer, but he was silently overruled by a quick flurry of scooping and bowl-filling activity.

"Let's go out on the back porch," said Nate, picking up a CD player from the countertop. Bee carried the custard. Blake took the coffee and cups.

"I remember this porch," said Bee fondly, bouncing up and down lightly as if her athletic feet needed exercise. "Uncle Bill and Aunt Ellen were out here one summer. Bill played his harmonica. It was the saddest sound I'd ever heard. There were watermelons—yellow and red. Grandma wore her dress with the wide blue collar. She told us about listening to geese when she was a little girl, thinking they carried horns. Do you remember, Natie? Uncle Joe tried to sing along with the harmonica. You and I were running through the wet grass, hiding from the others. No one could find us. We were laughing. There were cicadas and crickets. It was warm and dark. There was magic everywhere."

Bee and Nate sat on the leather truck seat, watching the evening light falling asleep in the backyard. They listened to a 1950s radio drama. Every few minutes a phrase harmonized with memories from their childhood, and their postures relaxed slightly, or they made short, whispered comments. Lulled by strawberries, long shadows, and mnemonic effervescence into a heightened state of position-shifting, they cautiously leaned into each other, then immediately separated.

Blake sat on the steps and sipped his coffee. The antique radio drama limped along in such a primitive manner that his attention drifted away from it. The scene behind him on the truck seat, however, was interesting. There was something new in the tone of his father's voice, something playful and intelligent. But because it seemed impolite to actually hear what they were saying, he just listened to the sounds their voices made, which led him into an oddly pleasant reverie—the most peace he'd experienced in a long time. His thoughts wandered through the backyard and beyond. He pictured his father running in the dark grass, chasing his older cousin through a much simpler time, hiding behind the shed, along the grapevines. The image of the two children darting from shadow to shadow was so clear, so astonishingly tranquil, that Blake discovered he was smiling. Danielle was still in the area. He took another sip of coffee and wondered how to be appropriately thankful for this rescued joy. Then he simply closed his eyes and gave himself over to a sense of gratitude.

Blake vaguely remembered reading about Jean-Paul Sartre's notion that there was a God-shaped hole in the human psyche longing to be filled. He wondered about his own empty shape. How much of it would remain if his mother suddenly reappeared? Where was she now? Was she still alive? It had taken his father some thirty years to overcome her departure. How long would it take for Blake to stop wondering about her?

When his father was chasing Bee around in the dark grass, his mother had been somewhere too, existing in that same simpler time. And right now she could be anywhere, possibly even listening to a faint sound that reminded her of years ago as well. In remembering, Blake wondered, does she think of me? Does she have any unfilled shapes? Would she recognize me if we were to walk by each other on the street?

When the radio mystery ended, Blake decided to go back inside. He wanted to read Spinoza and think about Danielle.

"Thanks for the ice cream and coffee," he said, standing up. "Nice to see you again, Bee."

"I can make more coffee," said his father. "I have some beans from a guy who roasts his own in Doe Run, Missouri."

"No thanks. By the way, I forgot to mention that the dispatcher called. They want you back on the road tomorrow morning."

"Surely not," said Nate.

"The message is still on the answering machine."

"They're pushing too hard," said Nate.

"I know it," said Blake. "And on top of that they want you to take a load to Wormwood."

"That's really bad."

"I know it. You always hated going there."

"Oh well," said Nate. "I guess I don't have a choice. Did you bring in the mail?"

"It's on top of the refrigerator."

"Thanks for mowing the yard."

"No problem. Good night."

"I enjoyed sharing the evening with you," said Bee, flashing her dimple. "And don't forget that you owe me a ride on your motorcycle."

Blake went into the living room and tried to make the motorcycle a little less noticeable by putting couch pillows on the tank and handlebars. Then he went into his bedroom and found the place where he'd left off in Spinoza.

Several minutes later, Nate drove Bee back home.

Expectancies

Toward evening, Buck walked through the muddy construction site in Red Plain, up the teetering metal steps, and into the trailer. His foreman wasn't there. He shut the window, closed a file cabinet, sat on the desk, and called his engineer. No answer. An avalanche of papers and envelopes spilled onto the floor next to the copy machine. On the wall, the calendar had been written on so many times with different pens that it no longer resembled a calendar.

There were several other people he needed to phone, but the impulse to get out of the trailer as quickly as possible seemed more urgent. Last week, Kevin had come down with pneumonia. After five days in the hospital—three on a respirator—he came home attached to intravenous electrolytes, six-carbon monosaccharide, and three recently synthesized antibiotics. Since then, Buck's mood had been erratic. His son's misery festered in his heart, and inside the cramped trailer the worry worked its way into his thoughts about deadlines, meetings with the city administrator, back-orders, bills, permits, taxes, stalled equipment, substandard lumber, cost estimates, plumb lines, loans, insurance adjusters, and bank accounts.

Stepping outside, Buck took a deep breath, locked the trailer door, and cautiously leaned against the metal railing on the makeshift landing. He wanted a cigarette—an unfiltered one, ideally—and the resurrection of this long-buried urge felt strangely welcome. He hadn't smoked since Amy became pregnant, over fifteen years ago, and the desire transported him briefly back to that less encumbered time. But he resisted giving himself over to the recollection.

For some reason Buck's memories often seemed to feature someone slightly other than himself, someone related but not identical to him, whose inner life was only half lit by the same psychic flame. He assumed this phenomenon resembled what happened when Amy's grandmother Flo remembered things in her childhood, but could not recall if they had happened to her or to someone else in her family.

A hundred yards away, four construction workers climbed into Dylan Johnson's brown Ford. The vehicle didn't move for several minutes. Then it emitted a short puff of exhaust and inched north across the site, around the Caterpillar, and onto the highway, spraying mud.

A half dozen cliff swallows were catching gnats above a shallow pool of collected rainwater, flying low, turning, and coming back around. Just beyond the new foundation and scaffolding, an old dog lay on a piece of plywood, thinking about the weedy field that had been there a month ago.

Behind him, Buck heard the sound of a vehicle moving across the grocery store lot, along the street, and into the construction site. A gray Explorer parked beside the trailer. His father climbed out, adjusted the waistline of his trousers, found the right place for his red suspenders over the black T-shirt, and walked up beside him.

"Hey, Dad," said Buck.

"Thought I'd check on everything," said Wally.

"Thanks for coming," said Buck. "I don't get to see enough of you."

"Couple hours of daylight left," said Wally, looking from the sky to his watch. "Where's the crew?"

"Men won't work the way they used to. Women neither."

Wally sat carefully on the steps. "People don't do anything the way they used to. What is this, anyway—a retirement home?"

"Health resort."

"I guess that sounds better. How many units?"

"Eighteen."

"Whose is it?"

"Some investment group out of La Crosse. Bill Larch put it together."

"Who's he?"

"You remember the guy who owned that equipment dealership?"

"In Luster?"

"That's him."

"No kidding! There was a time when all Billy Larch could do was find his own house keys, and he couldn't even do that very often."

"I know, but things change."

"What's that smell?"

"Portable sewage collector under the trailer isn't as tight as it should be."

"Good, I was afraid it was me. Say, let's drive over to the steak house and get something to eat."

"Right now?"

"It's after seven."

"There's probably something waiting for us at home."

"No, there isn't. That new gal you hired is making vegetarian pizza."

"Amy and Kevin should be happy about that."

"I'm sure they are. So is Flo. She's getting goat cheese on hers, and except for her rosaries there's nothing she likes better than goat cheese." Wally found a toothpick in his right hand and put it in his mouth. "Look at that old dog. I'll bet he knows a thing or two."

Taking a small notebook and pen out of his pocket, Wally added "old dogs" to the list of things he was going to miss after he died.

"You never liked pizza, did you, Dad?"

"Never did, that's a fact," he said.

"I don't remember Flo liking goat cheese before."

"That's because she never did. But beginning today there is nothing she ever liked better. It's that new gal you hired."

"I'm not dressed for a restaurant," said Buck.

"Me either. We can ask them to give us a table in the dark."

"I better call Amy and tell her."

"No need. I already told her."

"What was she doing?"

"She and Ivan are watching a movie with Kevin—in his room."

"Is he any better today?"

"Not as far as I can tell. He never got out of bed."

"What's Danielle doing?"

"I told you. She's making pizza."

"Oh, right."

"And Lucky's helping her. He came over. That's another reason I thought I better get out of the house. I never liked your brother-in-law much, and I want to avoid getting in an argument. It's not good policy at my age. It makes it harder to travel in the dreamworld, where it's best to be free of attachments and ready to move wherever you need to."

"Lucky isn't that bad of a guy."

"He isn't that good of one either. He's been coming over a lot lately, hanging around that new gal you hired."

"Her name's Danielle, Dad."

"She's still 'that new gal' to me."

"You ought to call her by her name."

"She grew up tough, Buck. There's nothing that gal wouldn't do if she thought she had to. Can't you see that?"

"People don't get to choose how they grow up."

"True enough. I like Ivan, though—like him a lot. We're going four-wheelin' next week."

"Where?"

"Along the river."

"Has he ever been on one before?"

"I don't know. He's got a knack for machines, though, sort of like you used to. He's a little rough around the edges, but he's a good kid. And he grows on you. Or at least he grows on me. We're going to make maple syrup together next winter."

"Kevin can go with you too. He'd enjoy that."

"No, he wouldn't, Buck. You know that. Poor kid lives inside himself. He knows more about hospital equipment and video games than he does about his front yard."

"I know it. I wish he and Ivan got along a little better."

"Kevin has all he can do just to stay with us. Your mother got like that too, before she left."

"The doctors don't expect Kevin to live much longer," said Buck, walking down the steps and over to the Explorer.

"I didn't know that," said Wally.

"A year, maybe less. They don't say it right out, but you can tell."

"It's not always what people say, it's the way they talk."

"Right."

"The kid never really had a chance," said Wally, standing up. "Nothing anyone could do, Buck. And if there was anything, Amy and you already did it. Kevin's lived longer than anyone thought he would. If a blade of grass in a swamp in China would have helped him even a little, Amy would have found it. Nothing anyone could do, Buck."

"Maybe so, but somehow that never seems to help."

"I know it," said Wally. "I know it."

Along the horizon a cloud opened up, draining a shaft of light.

"What does Lucky know about making pizza anyway?" asked Buck.

"Quite a lot, according to him. Where's your truck?"

"Over on the other side."

"We can swing back on the way home. Here, you drive." Wally tossed Buck the keys. "I like to look out the windows."

"If it's all right with you, I'm going to stop at the station and buy some cigarettes."

"Fine with me," said Wally.

Lucky

Lucky sat on a stool at the kitchen island, the heels of his polished shoes locked behind the leg rungs. His forearms—inside the ironed sleeves of a silver shirt—rested on the green-gray soapstone surface, his hands playing idly with his wristwatch. On the other side, Dart flattened a lump of whole-wheat dough onto a dusted board, transferring her weight down her arms and into her palms in a quick rhythmic plunging. Lucky studied her with both attraction and alarm. The front of her apron, upper arms, chin, and cheekbones were brushed with flour. The crust widened, releasing a thick yeasty smell.

"Now, you take Chicago," said Lucky. "There you'll find world-class pizza. They've got deep dish supreme deluxe that twirls onto your fork like sticky silk, or, if you prefer, cracker-thin, wafer-delicate crusts, served on heated ceramic plates, premium cheeses, spices, and condiments, smoking hot from brick ovens. Fancy places too, with live jazz and blues, just down from the big hotels, where half the cars are limos and crossing the street feels like walking onstage. On hot summer nights like this one the moist lake air moves in and gives the streetlights a special glow, and there's a crackle of anticipation everywhere. You know what I mean?"

"Ivan and I once had a pizza in Madison," said Dart, flipping the dough over once more before pressing it thinner. "It was good value."

Lucky scoffed. "Madison doesn't even compare. In Chicago people line up in front of the parlors before the clubs open, waiting to get in. You can smell the pizza for blocks around. Hey, I'll admit it's pricey, but it's worth it. All the women are dressed in the latest fashions from New York, six-inch heels, expensive perfume, and custom jewelry. The conversation is quick, smart, staccato, the way people talk when they're pumped up and demanding the very best from everyone else. When's the last time you were there?"

"It's been a while," said Dart.

"Would you like to go sometime?"

Dart continued spreading the dough. She wriggled her hands and wrists underneath and transferred the drooping form to a waiting pan. Beside it were two others, the crusts already pushed out and raised on the edges. She lifted the lid from a saucepan on the stovetop, stirred briefly with a wooden spoon, and then began chopping red onions, olives, peppers, and garlic.

"I can't get away," she said. "Too much needs doing."

"I'll tell Amy to give you a long weekend. Everyone needs to have a little fun."

"I like to spend whatever free time I have with Ivan."

"Mothers shouldn't spend too much time with their sons," said Lucky, slipping his wristwatch on and off. "It makes them weak."

"In Ivan's case he needs a lot of weakening."

"I'm serious," said Lucky. "In Native American cultures—and many others, for that matter—sons were taken away from the mothers at an early age. They went to live with the men, and it was better that way. Those older societies knew a lot more than we do. You'd never find a boy as old as Ivan still with his mother. It would bring shame on the whole family. The daughters stayed with the mothers, but never the sons. They belonged among fathers, grandfathers, and uncles. Otherwise, the boys would never become men. They would never understand themselves in the right way, their responsibility in the world. They would never learn to stand on their own, to take what they needed and demand the respect of others. It was considered a disgrace for a son to stay with his mother."

"That's just stupid," said Dart. She tasted the sauce and added ground pepper and marjoram. Then she took a block of soft white cheese out of the refrigerator and began grating it. Long, thin curls mounded up quickly on the other side of the grater.

"No, it isn't. Boys learn values—what things are worth—from men. They can't learn those things from their mothers. It doesn't work that way. Left with their mothers, they would never understand things like honor, courage, and self-reliance. Their characters would never fully develop and they would never become men."

"That's rubbish," said Dart. "Ivan and I already know all the values."

"Come on, that's ridiculous, Danielle. How can you possibly know the value of things? You've never lived anywhere else. Until you've been out in the wider world, making it on your own, having real success, you can't know what anything's worth."

"Well, I do."

"Okay, look here—what do you think this watch is worth? I'll bet you have no idea what it cost."

"Let me see it."

Lucky handed it to her and she quickly gave it back.

"You can get watches like that for less than two hundred dollars from a catalog out of New Hampshire. Free shipping and no sales tax."

"Are you kidding? A watch like this one costs three times that."

"You paid too much, then. My catalogs are filled with watches just like that one. Ivan and I, we know values."

"Wasn't he held back in fifth grade?"

Dart poured red sauce onto the waiting crusts and evened it out with a rubber spatula. Then she sprinkled the cheese and washed her hands in the sink.

"Wasn't he?"

"Yes."

"Why was that, exactly?"

"Because there are no teachers in his school, just testers. In any other school—any good school—they wouldn't get away with that kind of thing. August Helm is the smartest boy around here. He's Pastor Winifred's son and everyone knows how intelligent he is. He uses words like *sachchidananda,* and he and Ivan are best friends."

"What?"

"*Sachchidananda.*"

"That's not a word; it's an insect noise."

"It's a word and August said it. He knows what it means too, and Ivan is his best friend. Ivan keeps up with him, stride for stride. He's just not good at taking tests."

"You're probably right," said Lucky. "Tests don't mean as much as many things, like making it in the world, having success." With a clean napkin, he rubbed flour from his wristwatch before putting it back on. "I'll talk to Amy and get her to let you have some time off so we can go to Chicago together."

"I'm not going to Chicago with you."

"Why?"

"Because I'm not."

"You want to do what's right by Amy and Buck, don't you?"

"What does that have to do with going to Chicago?" she asked. After adding the vegetables, Dart carried the pizza pans to the waiting oven. Lucky watched her slide them in and close the door.

"It doesn't have anything to do with Chicago, but there's a party in Madison two weeks from tomorrow night."

"What party?"

"It's for majority and minority leaders of the state legislature, lobbyists, department heads, notable donors, and other invited guests. There's a lot riding on it. I'm working on a couple promising contracts for Buck, and we're in the last rounds of the elimination process. If the committee accepts our bids it could make all the difference. You probably don't know this, but after Roebuck Construction finishes with that penny-ante nursing home in Red Plain, there are no more major projects lined up. They're just not coming in. People don't want to spend money, because of the bad economy. Buck and Amy are hurting. They've got debts like you can't believe. I probably shouldn't even be mentioning this, but I know too much to keep quiet. At any minute the bank could decide to short-sell this house, for instance, right out from under them. They're just hanging on. So making a good impression at this party could make all the difference. Believe me, my sister understands that. If you go with me it could mean a lot to the family in getting more work."

"What would I have to do?" asked Dart, setting the oven timer and filling the sink with soapy water.

"Just stay close to me, smile, and look good—make everyone remember you."

"I don't have anything to wear."

"I've already talked to a dress shop in Wisconsin Dells. They're waiting for you to come in and try a few things on next week."

"You talked to them about me?"

"Of course. They already heard you were working here."

"No they didn't."

"Of course they did. They'll help you pick out something to wear, something appropriate. And don't worry—it will all go on the expense account."

"Why didn't they call me?"

"I told them to wait until I'd spoken to you first. I wasn't sure you were willing to help out the family this way. I mean, it's a lot of pressure, a fancy party like this one. Many people wouldn't be able to pull it off, not with this much riding on it. I'll have them call you tomorrow and set up the appointment. You can't go into a place like that without an appointment, not if you're serious."

"Does Amy know about this?"

"Not yet. I didn't want to mention it to her, in case you wouldn't do it. I mean, many people won't go that extra mile, and it's not like you have to."

"Is it the dress shop on the corner, across from the bank?"

"That's the one."

After Lucky drove back to his condominium in Madison, Dart took the pizzas out of the oven and carried them to Kevin's room. To the right of the bed, the nurse leaned back in the motorized recliner, her feet up. On the other side, Amy sat on a small pressed-back chair, an antique ideally suited to her grandmother's era, looking both happy to be sitting on it and uncomfortable. Ivan was ensconced in a beanbag chair, busily manipulating a game control while alternately glancing between the game's digital display and the larger television screen, where a feature-length movie had reached its final dramatic scene. Dart passed out paper plates and napkins. Everyone but Kevin began eating.

After having a slice herself, Dart carried the remainder of one pizza upstairs to share with Florence. Soon after, Amy stood up, said she wasn't interested in watching any more movies, and studied Kevin with a worried look. He didn't turn his head and she couldn't tell if he was sleeping, because his eyelids were nearly closed. A clear plastic hose from the medicine bag dropped from the chrome pole, curved across the top of the sheet, underneath a fold, and into the needle in Kevin's right wrist.

For several minutes she watched the drip tube, then nodded to the night nurse and followed Dart upstairs.

After finishing a third piece of pizza, the nurse put her paper plate and napkin on the tray and went down the hall to use the bathroom.

A commercial came on and Kevin muted it with the remote. Then he slowly turned his head toward the game screen in front of Ivan.

"He got me!" yelled Ivan when GAME OVER lit up on the display.

"That's a difficult corridor," Kevin said weakly.

"I know it," said Ivan. He climbed out of the beanbag and took another piece of pizza from the pan. "I never get past this level. That big guy always comes out from behind the door and kills me."

"You have to go hard right as soon as you come to the street with spiders," said Kevin. "Go around the building."

"I tried that. There's no way out of the alley."

"Yes there is. There's an overhead wire and you can climb up to it, walk over, and jump in a window."

"I'll try it," said Ivan. He restarted the game. "How did you get so good at this?"

"It helps to study online cheat codes."

"Yeah," said Ivan, feeding pizza into his mouth with one hand and manipulating the control with the other.

"Watch out for that guy on the second floor."

"I know all about him," said Ivan. "He's not that hard."

"There's another killer above him and if he comes out things really go screwy."

"So what's wrong with you, anyway?"

"What do you mean?"

"Why are you always sick?"

"It's a congenital condition called cystic fibrosis. I was born with it."

"Can't the doctors fix it?"

"Not really," said Kevin and coughed several times. "My immune system is compromised—low cell count, depleted antibodies."

"What's that mean?"

"It's hard to fight infections."

More coughing.

"Where did your grandfather go tonight?" asked Ivan, lurching up out of the beanbag in response to a dire circumstance on the game display.

"I didn't know he left."

"He did, and he hardly ever goes anywhere."

"Is there any pizza left?" asked Kevin, closing his eyes.

"You want some?"

"No, but is it any good?"

"Yup," said Ivan, sitting back down.

"What makes your mom like she is?" asked Kevin.

"What do you mean?"

"I don't know. The way she looks and acts."

"I don't know. She's just my mother."

"What was her family like? Do you have any uncles or aunts?"

"I think my mother had a sister. I heard her talking about her once."

"What's she like?"

"Never met her," said Ivan, leaning quickly to the right to avoid a hand grenade.

"Why not?"

"Don't know. Mother doesn't talk about her family. Except for Grandma it's almost like she didn't have one, and we almost never see her."

"Where did you live before you came here?"

"In town."

"With your mom?"

"Yup."

"Where's your dad?"

"Dead, I guess."

"What do you think happens when you die?"

"Beats me."

"Really, what do you think?"

"I don't know."

"Do you think anyone knows?"

"My friend August might. He's always thinking about stuff like that. You should talk to him."

"He's the preacher's kid?"

"Yup."

"You said something about him before. Does he have any cool games?"

"Nope. His mom won't let him. He's got a bat though."

"A baseball bat?"

"No, a *bat* bat."

"That's weird."

"No it isn't. It's cool."

"Bats are rodents."

"So what, they fly."

"How would he know what happens after you die?"

"I don't know how he knows stuff, but he does. He's my best friend. August's always thinking about things that other people never think about."

More coughing.

"Like what?"

"I can't tell you. Those are secrets between August and me."

"No they're not."

"Yes they are."

"I could get your mom fired. I could tell my mom to make you move out."

"She wouldn't do it."

"Yes she would. I've gotten people fired before."

"I don't care. Go ahead."

"Then you wouldn't be able to play my games anymore."

"They're stupid games anyway."

"People say your mom was a drug dealer."

"Not true."

"Not true that she was, or not true that people say she was?"

"Both."

"Lucky said she was."

"How would he know?"

"He knows some of the same people, I guess."

"Same people as what?"

"Same people who took drugs and bought them from your mother."

"Not true."

"I heard him tell my mom."

"What did she say?"

"I couldn't hear. I asked her later and she said that was just the way people talked. But still, Lucky said it."

"You better never say anything like that again, not to my mother and not to me."

More coughing.

"God, I'm tired of this," said Kevin.

"Tired of what?"

"These fucking tubes running into me, this bed. I'm sick of it all. Do you ever just hate everything?"

"Sometimes. Hey, here it comes."

Kevin opened his eyes. "Go hard right as soon as you see the first spider."

"There."

"Go."

"The wire's too high."

"Push over the dumpster and jump up on it. There, now grab the wire."

"Got it."

"Easy now."

"I got it. No trouble."

"Jump up in the window now."

"I know. I know."

"You made it. Now go down the hall."

"I don't need any more help."

"There's a woman in that room at the end. She's really hot, and you have to get a key from her."

"I can handle it," said Ivan.

"Keep your eye on her. She's got a gun in the drawer."

"I saw that giant turtle of yours," said Ivan.

"When?"

"A couple nights ago. I've been watching for him."

"Where was he?"

"First, he was in the middle of the pond, looking like a big hump. Then he swam over and crawled out. He's a monster."

"I told you. Did you look into his eyes?"

"It was dark and he was a ways off."

"You're lucky. He's the devil. You can see it when he looks into your eyes."

The nurse came back from the bathroom then and told Ivan he had to finish his game and leave. It was time to check Kevin's vital signs and take a blood sample.

When Time Slows Down

Buck and Wally arrived home at the same time. They walked into the house together, and went right into Kevin's room. After several minutes, Wally continued down the hall and climbed the staircase up to his own room. The nurse went to the kitchen to find something to drink, and Buck sat in the recliner next to the bed.

"You smell like cigarettes, Dad," said Kevin.

"I guess I do," said Buck. His spirits were unusually high, having just spent the last hour with his father. Something about being with Wally always made Buck feel good. "I bought a pack and smoked one. Dumb thing to do, really, but I guess we all do dumb things from time to time. Most of the time we get away with it."

"It smells kind of good."

"I know. I like it too. But smoking's a dirty habit. How are you doing?"

"I'm okay. It's after dark. You're late."

"Your grandfather felt like eating steak tonight, so we went to a restaurant near Red Plain."

"I hate steak," said Kevin.

"I know you do, but your grandfather likes it. Did you have some pizza?"

"No."

"Not hungry?"

"Nope."

"You look like you might be feeling a little better though, better than yesterday at least. Is that true?"

"I'm not."

"You will. There have been spells like this before and you've always come through them. You're tough."

"Clearly these infections are tougher. The doctors said this one was that old one, back again, a strain of staphylococcus."

"You'll beat it. You always do. After a while you won't remember anything about times like these. It will be like they never existed."

"What happens when you die?"

"I honestly don't know, but I don't think that's a question—"

"Do you think anyone does?"

"I doubt it."

"Ivan says his friend August does."

"That seems unlikely, but unless you know yourself I guess there's no way of knowing if anyone else does."

"Good. I don't think he knows either."

"That's not quite what I said, Kev."

"I know."

"Ivan and you were talking today?"

"Some. He's out looking for that turtle now."

"Outdoors?"

"He's got a flashlight."

Buck went to the window. In the distance, a small spot of light jiggled along the edge of the water, about halfway around the pond.

"He wants to look in its eyes," said Kevin.

"Why does he want to do that?" asked Buck.

"I don't know."

"Does his mother know he's out there?"

"Probably not," said Kevin, and adjusted the oxygen tubing in his nose.

"Dad, is Ivan's mother bad?"

"Danielle?"

"Is she?"

"Of course not. What do you mean?"

"Would some people call her bad?"

"Some people will call almost anyone bad, but that doesn't mean anything. It's just the way people talk. Doesn't mean anything."

"She looks like she might be bad. How can you be sure she isn't?"

"I'm pretty sure."

"God, I'm tired of this," said Kevin, coughing again.

Buck sat back down and leaned closer to the bed. "You're going to feel better soon, Kev. When you're not feeling well, time slows down. It always seems longer than it is. And then before you know it things are better. I'll give you an example of that, but you have to promise never to tell your grandfather."

"Why?"

"Because that's the rule of the story. It's the only way I can tell it."

"All right."

"Your grandfather was working up on this cherry picker in the summer—that's one of those cages on the end of a telescoping beam. We'd just gotten it, and, fully extended, the cage would run up nearly ninety feet in the air. When it was closer to the ground, you could operate the base from controls in the cage. The base sat low on four wide rubber tires, and when the cage was down it would move three or four miles per hour. When the cage was high up in the air, the wheels wouldn't turn at all. That was a safety precaution, because the whole rig could tip over easily when the lift was extended.

"So there your grandfather was, up about twenty feet in the air, flashing around a chimney. The building next to him was five stories tall, and way up on the roof he sees that someone has planted a pear tree, and there are pears growing in it. So he thought it would be fun to rise all the way up there and pick one. He drove the base about twenty yards to position it beneath the building, and brought the cage up to the level of the pear tree, about seventy-five feet off the ground. But when he rose above the roofline, he saw that there were four girls about your age sunbathing in the nude, lying on blankets. As you can probably imagine, they weren't at all happy about your grandfather invading their privacy. They jumped up, wrapped blankets around themselves, and went for a water hose. By this time Wally was headed down, but at that height the cage came down very slowly, and while it was coming down the base wouldn't move at all. He could only inch away from them. Those girls had a good long time to really soak him before he could get out of range. All of which is to say that sometimes time seems to move very slowly. It probably wasn't very long, in the grand scheme of things, but it certainly seemed like it at the time."

"That's pretty funny," said Kevin.

"I thought so myself, but don't tell him that."

"How were they lying?"

"What do you mean?"

"Were they faceup or facedown?"

"I'm not sure he ever mentioned it, but the way I imagine it was two up and two down."

"That's a good story, Dad."

Wally climbed the stairs to the second floor and stood in the hallway outside his room. Voices murmured from above him on the third floor and he climbed the next staircase. The door to Flo's room was halfway open, and on the other side Flo, Amy, and Dart were talking. Wally sat at the top of the stairs. Though he couldn't make out everything in the conversation, he liked the sound of their voices. The way women talked had a calming effect on him at night. He wasn't sure why. It might have been the rambling talks he and his wife had often indulged in before they went to sleep, speaking of things on their minds in order to settle them down, soothe them into lying flat and keeping quiet, but he wasn't absolutely sure this was the reason. There was also the way that, when he was growing up, his mother and aunt used to talk in the kitchen at night. But in the end it didn't matter. At his age, demanding reasons no longer made sense. Delight was the only guiding light he needed, and he followed it wherever it led.

"Aren't you going to eat any more of that?" asked Dart.

"I have always loved goat cheese, but I think I've had enough for tonight," said Flo, speaking with such deliberation that her listeners clung to her last uttered word in order to make retrospective sense of those that had preceded it.

"You didn't even eat a whole piece."

"Almost."

"Almost only counts in horseshoes," said Dart, glaring at the uneaten portion on Florence's plate.

"Close," said Amy, her voice creating an almost musical tone. "Close only counts in horseshoes."

"That's what I said," replied Dart.

"You said almost."

"They mean the same thing."

"Do you need any more beads, or anything else for making your rosaries, Florence?"

"I work slow and have plenty."

"I'm worried about Kevin," said Amy.

"You don't need to," said Dart. "He's going to be fine."

"Something's different this time."

"That's not what the nurse says. She says he's going to be fine."

"I know, but there are other things too."

"Like what?"

"Last night I had this dream where Kevin was standing out by the road. It was wintertime, and snow lay around him on the ground."

"I don't put much stock in dreams," said Dart. "If it were up to me, I wouldn't have them."

"This school bus came along and Kevin got into it. I was worried, so I followed behind in the car. At every house the bus stopped and picked up another child, until all the windows were filled with faces. As more and more children climbed on, the bus got bigger, until it took up both sides of the road. The bus just kept going on and on, filling up with all the children in the world. It got harder and harder for me to keep up, because my car was old and the school bus was new. It got farther and farther ahead, but I still followed it over the hills, where it would often dip out of sight for a while. Then it stopped and stayed at the very bottom of one little valley. I caught up to it just as Kevin was let out. Then the bus drove away and Kevin was there by himself, standing in fresh snow. I tried to get him in the car with me, but he wouldn't come. 'I don't want to,' he said, just like that.

"'You can't stay here,' I told him, and he said again, 'I don't want to.' That's all he would say, and he wouldn't get into the car. And then I woke up."

"Dreams don't mean anything," said Dart. "They're stupid."

"It must mean something," said Amy. "I'm afraid it means the school bus was driving into the future, and then it stopped and let Kevin off."

"It doesn't mean that," said Dart.

"Then what does it mean?"

"I don't know, but it doesn't mean that."

"It has to, Dart. It has to. There's no other explanation. Why would he keep saying 'I don't want to' over and over again?"

"That's just the way people talk in dreams. Tell her, Flo. It doesn't mean that."

"I never dream," said Florence. "But I agree with Dart. It doesn't mean that."

"You should talk to Pastor Winifred," said Dart. "She knows about dreams and she'll tell you it doesn't mean that. She'll agree with me and Flo."

"I don't know her."

"You don't have to. You can just tell her you know me. Ivan and I were just over there a little while ago, helping her out with her garden. She's got a garden, you know, a fancy one, a long way from the house."

"I couldn't impose."

"Of course you could. Ivan and I do all the time. He's best friends with her son. Besides, people who know more than other people have a duty. What they know belongs to all of us, really. We've got just as much right to it as they do."

"I don't believe in her religion," said Amy.

"I don't either, and neither does Ivan. Religion is stupid—except the rosary religion, I mean. But that doesn't matter anyway. You just go over there, you tell her you know me, and you tell her you had this dream. She'll listen to you and then she'll tell you it doesn't mean what you think it does. You should see her garden anyway. Everybody should. She has a fountain and a deep pool with bright fish swimming around in it."

"What's that?" asked Florence, pointing to the window.

"It's a mysterious light," said Amy.

Wally crept quietly past the half-opened door and looked out the window at the end of the hall. An unsteady spot of light moved along the edge of the pond, reflecting on the water, drawing him toward it like a voice in an empty house.

Wally went downstairs and stepped outside. He stood on the deck and felt the night air, warm and moist, against his wrinkled face. Insects, frogs, and toads sang a riotous chorus. An owl hooted in the distance. Midsummer smells swarmed in to compete for his attention: honeysuckle, pond scum, tree resin, damp earth. The sky above reeled with thousands of indistinct points of light silently shifting toward new configurations. Enthralled, Wally contemplated a familiar expectation: that his deepest hour was about to begin.

Across the pond, the flashlight continued bobbing, the light streaming toward him over the watery surface in a narrow line. Wally marveled at the unfathomable fact of position—how the light line extending from the flashlight would seem to be aimed directly at him from anywhere around the edge of the pond, encouraging the universally held but nonetheless false impression that his occupied space was favored. Closing his eyes to better savor this delusional feeling, Wally stood there for several moments.

Then, after finding the walking stick he'd left leaning against the side of the house, he climbed down from the deck.

"What are you doing?" he asked, catching up.

"Looking for that turtle," replied Ivan. "I want to see its eyes."

"Mind if I come along?"

"That's fine," said Ivan. "But try to keep quiet. If we find him we can both look into his eyes and see if he's the devil."

"Lead on," said Wally.

July Montgomery's House

When Jacob opened his repair shop in the morning, the radio had already been tuned to a folk-country station, and the smell of hot metal, sizzling flux, and ozone assaulted his sleepy mind. Blake was welding in the corner, surrounded by a thicket of silver smoke with a tiny bright white center.

Jacob raised the double doors and the long metal panels clattered noisily as they rolled up above the overhead supports. Dew-heavy morning air and the sudden gloss of ambient light poured in from outside.

"Hey," said Blake, pivoting the black welding hood over his head, flashing teeth, looking more wide awake than anyone should before eight o'clock. "Hope you don't mind. I came in a little early, made coffee—brought some from home."

Jacob poured a cup and set the pot back on the cluttered workbench between the grinder and a rack of deep-well sockets. "What you working on?"

"Turns out my father kept my road bike. I found it in the shed."

"That looks like a new resonator," observed Jacob, pointing to the sculpted metal tube leaning against the arch welder.

"It is," said Blake. "The old one was rusted through so I got a new one, and I'm welding together a better bracket to hold it in place. The old one was cracked."

"Might choke off some of the power," said Jacob. He picked up the resonator and peered inside at the baffles. "I thought half the fun was the noise."

The younger man nurtured a momentary suspicion that Jacob might be teasing him, but quickly let it go. "I just want to get back to riding, not advertise where I am. Besides, they tune these resonators to the engine displacement. Not much power is lost."

Blake felt good. He'd had the best night he could remember, slept nine hours without waking up. The day before, he got the bike running and rode it for a couple of miles. It ran rough. The four carburators needed to be boiled out and reset, and he needed new plugs and brakes on the front, but when he twisted the throttle and sped into the open country, the future expanded inside him like a primal flame. And then later that afternoon—even without the matched pistons thrumming beneath him—he could still feel the vital burning, steady and reassuring.

Last night, lying in bed, Blake remembered how in prison, when he couldn't sleep, he'd pictured riding along the rustic road between Luster and Red Plain—twenty miles of curving, climbing, plunging, and twisting, through mostly uninhabited woodland. Lying on his cell bunk, he'd recalled every detail he could remember of the once-familiar road, like fresh water from a deep well: ditches, bridges, intersections, grades, slopes, straightaways, humps, dips, bumps, fences, gorges, and hillsides, even trees reaching out toward the road and the changing view of the horizon. With sufficient concentration, the remembered trip could take over an hour, and often provided the hypnotic solace required in order to fall asleep. With years of devoted repetition, more details emerged, and the refuge he found in the imagined journey became even more welcoming.

He wanted to take that same ride now, to coax the imagined route out of his memory and thank it for the sanctuary it had once provided, joining the past to the present in a way that would cleanse his world of the reasons he had needed a sanctuary in the first place, enabling him to really start over.

But first he needed to return the bike to its former state. Then, after it was running like it used to, he'd be ready to take the ride, and in this way another debt would be repaid. After promising himself and Spinoza's god that this would be done, he'd slept soundly.

"What do you need to get it running?" asked Jacob.

"It's running already, but I need to find someone who can adjust the carbs after I get the cobwebs out."

"There's a little shop outside Luster, owned by a guy about your age."

"Who is it?"

"Walt Black."

"I remember him. He used to hang out with Skeeter Skelton—worked on his bikes."

"That's him," said Jacob. "I think Skeeter owns part of the shop."

"And here's another thing," said Blake, half-lowering the hood over his face and fumbling with the heavy gloves.

Jacob waited, drinking coffee.

"I can't stay at home anymore," he said. "Need a place of my own."

"Jack Station isn't going to like that."

"I know it."

"What's wrong with staying with your father?"

"Nothing and everything. How long would you want to live with your father?"

"Good point. I'm not sure it will work on your parole agent, though."

"Release agent," corrected Blake, tilting the hood back. His face hardened and he paused for a moment, as if he were looking down an alley before walking into it. Then he rubbed the back of his neck and continued. "Technically, they don't have parole agents anymore, because they don't have parole. They don't like the sound of it. Scumbag politicians put an end to that. Giving someone a second chance—except themselves and their rich friends—doesn't strike them as reasonable. Hell, they don't like much of anything that doesn't put money in their own pockets. And the public goes along with it like a bunch of herded sheep."

Jacob turned his head and stared outdoors, where Words was waking up. A door slammed and two dogs barked.

Blake continued, "Those bastards took this country and made it into a goddamn police state. They're building prisons everywhere, locking up everyone who looks the wrong way. The government-industrial gulag is a multi-zillion-dollar business. Why do you think there's all this talk about illegal immigration? I'll tell you why: they want to get those people into their private prisons. It's postmodern slavery, a war on minorities and the poor. The whole system is corrupt."

Jacob sipped his coffee and fondly remembered those mornings, not long ago when he'd worked alone. But he caught himself quickly, remembering also that he'd agreed to this. He'd even promised himself not to entertain regrets. If he wasn't prepared to give it an honest try, he shouldn't have agreed to take Blake on. It was going to take some time. Blake needed not only to work through the last eleven years, but also to find a way to make up for the experiences he had missed while he was incarcerated. His growth had been stunted, and he hadn't yet learned how to resume his life.

On the other hand, it was also true that he was way ahead of himself in other ways. His mind seemed quicker than most, which was probably because he'd had time to read difficult books. He seemed to actually enjoy writers like Spinoza, whose unyielding sentences presented most readers with an incline too steep to climb. Still, while Blake had undoubtedly learned to negotiate brilliant abstractions, his social and emotional life seemed stalled, mired in his early to mid-twenties.

The coffee tasted unusually good, Jacob noticed—robust yet without bitterness—and he looked around for the package it came in.

"All they care about is their wealthy friends and to hell with everyone else," Blake continued. "They've made a mockery of the principles that once made this country great. You know as well as I do that there was a time, not long ago, when the rest of the world looked up to us. We were rightly proud of our democracy, proud of our freedoms, proud of our system of justice, and proud of our schools. You could feel it in the air, waking up in the morning, walking down the street. Everyone felt it. There was a time when . . ."

And that was the problem, thought Jacob, running the lift up to get underneath a garden tractor. When the best days were in the past, what could be done? When just being alive no longer seemed as fulfilling, what could a person do?

For the most part Blake was like everyone else, Jacob thought. He did his work, went home, and took care of all the things people had to take care of. He didn't desire more than he had, but then something would set him off. It didn't happen often, but sooner or later, Jacob feared, something would light Blake up at the wrong time. This morning, for example, he'd come in early, seeming better adjusted than usual, and then he got knocked off course. A fermented thought entered his head, and he simply couldn't leave it alone. Not that Jacob disagreed with his opinion about how the country had taken a wrong turn. Any fool knew there was something to that; but living a grounded, contented life—in good times and bad—had always been a narrow path, and only those paying close attention could stay on it. Jacob certainly knew that. Until he found Winnie and she found something in him—well, he didn't want to think about that. He was vulnerable, to say the least. Living without a center would do that to anyone. People needed a path—they were born needing it and they would die needing it—and if you couldn't find your way back to your path after you strayed from it, you were finished.

"Where'd you get this coffee?" asked Jacob, pouring another cup.

"My dad. He's big on coffee and he wanted you to try it. He gets it from some guy in Missouri who roasts his own."

"It's good. Say, we've got a lot of work to get out of here today. If it's all right with you—I mean, as soon as you're finished with what you're working on—that four-wheeler needs new gaskets."

Blake stared at him blankly for a moment. "You're the boss," he said, and lowered the black mask over his face.

Several days later, Blake's release agent called the shop to tell him to come in for another drug test. Blake explained over the phone that he didn't want to live with his father any longer. Not long after this exchange, Jack Station's blue Mercury arrived. He climbed out, walked past the half dozen or so people standing around in the lot, and came inside, his eyes narrowed into slits.

"Home not good enough for you?" he asked, laughing without humor.

"It's not that," said Blake. "My father's got his own life. I've got mine."

"What do you know about this?" Station asked Jacob, stalking to the other side of the shop and standing with his hands in his pockets. "Did something happen between Blake and his father, something no one bothered to inform me about? Was there some kind of altercation? What do you know about it?"

"About what?" asked Jacob. The people in the lot moved closer to the open door, smoking, drinking soda, and listening.

"Did you know he wanted to change residences?"

"He mentioned it."

"Did you explain to him that any change of residency is contingent upon my approval? Without my personal authorization Blake can't do anything—not so long as the state bears responsibility for him. Did you explain that to him?"

"Not exactly."

"What's 'not exactly' supposed to mean?"

"It means I didn't."

"That's what I thought. It's not likely he could find a place, you know, not one he can afford."

"I've been out almost two months," Blake said.

"Have you found a place?" demanded Station. "Have you?"

"Not yet. I thought I better talk to you about it first."

"Where exactly do you want to live?"

"Maybe I could find a room."

"Not likely. You'd have to tell the landlord you're an ex-con. You know that, don't you? Your landlord would also have to be informed of the conditions of your release, the felonies you were convicted of—transporting drugs, assaulting an officer of the law—and your record of uncooperative behavior while you were incarcerated. They'd have to know all that."

"Of course."

"And you were intending to come clean on every detail. Right?"

"Of course."

"Just a minute." Station stepped outside, unfolded his cell phone, and dialed a number. The people gathered there moved away. Then he came back inside. "I can't believe this. There's no service here. I can't believe it. What kind of a place is this—something out of the Dark Ages?"

"The hills," said Jacob.

"I need to use your phone."

"It's on the wall."

Station dialed, talked for several minutes, hung up, and scowled.

"Guess what?" he said.

Silence.

"The department is no longer funding tracer bracelets for release programs in rural areas."

Blake and Jacob remained silent.

Station stepped outside and stood for several minutes, looking in. "Don't forget to come give us a urine sample," he said. "Before six o'clock. And if you find another place to stay, give me a call and I'll come look it over."

Then he walked back to his car and left.

After he was gone, Jacob asked Blake if he'd told his father about wanting to move.

"Not yet—in case I couldn't find a place or that bastard Station wouldn't allow it. Besides, it might hurt his feelings, and then if I didn't get to leave anyway, I mean—"

"Good point," replied Jacob. Just then a pickup pulled into the lot. There were two white-bearded men inside it, and a lawn mower in the back. Upon its arrival, the younger people who had been gathered in the lot drifted off. "You and your father still getting along?"

"It's impossible not to get along with my father. He enforces getting along. Sure, Dad and I get along just fine, but he needs more room and so do I."

Three days later, Jacob drove Blake to an abandoned farmhouse one mile out of town.

"What's this?" asked Blake, standing in the weedy yard.

"This is a house you could rent," said Jacob.

"Whose is it?"

"It used to belong to a friend of mine, July Montgomery. Now it belongs to a trust set up by a couple—a Madison lawyer and his wife—who are both dead now. Their children sold off the farmland a couple years ago, before the economy turned sour. They kept the house as a summer place, but the inconveniences of living in the country didn't appeal to them, so they never used it. There's a For Sale sign around here somewhere, or at least there used to be."

"You talked to them about renting it to me?"

"Winifred did," said Jacob, watching as a crow descended from the sky, landed briefly on the chimney of the house, and then flew away.

"And the family was okay with, you know, the ex-con stuff?"

"I guess they were. Winifred is fairly persuasive, so long as she can avoid antagonizing the people she's talking to."

"So this is where July Montgomery lived?"

"This is it. Do you remember him?" asked Jacob.

"Can't say I do," said Blake, staring up at the brick house.

Weeds, vines, and bushes grew riotously around the foundation, as if they were trying to pull the house into the ground. The windows needed caulk and paint. The bricks had been worn down, rounded by many seasons. And the roof's integrity was questionable.

"I heard about him, though," offered Blake. "My dad hauled cows for him several times and they went to auctions together. I guess Dad and July once unloaded silo blocks together until they couldn't move their arms."

"Sounds like something he'd do," said Jacob. "He liked to work."

"My dad's like that too," said Blake. "There was a guy in Waupun who used to talk about July Montgomery a lot. According to him, when July was a little kid he survived for a long time—maybe ten years or longer—in an underground room. That's what he said. Later, his wife was murdered by the government and July hunted down the perpetrators and killed them one by one. Then he came here. It made a good story, but I never knew how much of it was true. Most of the stories you hear in prison are like that."

"All stories are like that," said Jacob.

"You knew him pretty well, then?"

"Not well enough."

"What do you mean?"

"He died out here alone. He was a good friend to me and I should have been a better one to him."

"Why weren't you?"

"I don't know. Mostly blind ignorance, I guess—not paying attention."

"You were concerned with your own stuff," offered Blake, somewhat surprised by Jacob's candid manner, and by his own response to it. He was usually more guarded.

"I suppose."

"Memories like that drive you crazy in prison," said Blake.

"They drive you crazy out here too."

"It's not the same. Out here you can make up for things. Behind bars all you have are the regrets. Prison holds you in place while the regrets work you over. It's one of the many ways the system is set up to turn you into cinder."

A dark silence radiated from Jacob. Blake felt him withdrawing.

"So, what was he like, July Montgomery?"

"Hard to describe. He didn't care about the things most other people care about. And when you were with him you didn't either. He lived an intensely private life, didn't even own a television."

"Can we look inside the house?"

Jacob took the key out of his pocket and handed it to him.

"Aren't you coming in?"

"No."

Blake took several steps, stopped next to a thistle, looked from the house to the key, and asked, "How did he die?"

"July was caught in a power take-off. Right over there." Jacob pointed toward the wire corn crib, which rose up out of the ground beside the barn like a cylindrical rib cage.

"That's bad," said Blake.

"Winifred and I found him."

"No kidding. Right over there?"

"In some ways I never got over it."

Blake felt compelled to say something meaningful, and his anxiety began churning away at gut level. "Did you ever think maybe there were some things you weren't supposed to get over? Things that would take the rest of your life to work through?"

"It's a fair thought."

Blake felt relieved. At least he'd responded appropriately. And then he remembered what Winnie had said during one of her visits to the prison: unresolved traumas were gifts, she'd said. They were psychological chariots sent by grace, to be used for moving to better places. He wondered if he should tell Jacob. But perhaps he'd heard her say it too. Perhaps Jacob already knew that he was taking credit for something he had no right to, vulgarizing what had been a spiritual idea and presenting it drained of all religious content. Oh well, he thought, at least I recognized something good when I heard it. That counts for something. Besides, if people were required to use only original thoughts, it would take all day to simply say hello.

"You're hoping to ride your bike at night, aren't you?" said Jacob.

"I guess so."

"That's a bad idea."

"I know it."

"You may not have noticed, but your release agent is hoping to give you enough rope to hang yourself. I hope you know that."

"I do," said Blake, staring at the house again. "Will you come in with me? I don't want to go in there alone, not the first time."

They walked up to the house.

Making Ready

Dart and Amy Roebuck went to visit Pastor Winifred, and Ivan came along. On the drive over the two women talked about a dream Amy remembered. Dart didn't think it meant much of anything, but Mrs. Roebuck didn't think it meant nothing. Ivan considered saying something about dreams, but his mother had been unpredictable lately and he was afraid she'd change her mind about him sleeping over. Ever since she'd started looking at herself in the mirror in that new dress, she'd been hard to read.

They drove down the rutty drive and parked near the house. Dart told Amy to just ignore the junk in the yard, but from the way Amy stepped on the boards, tires, and pieces of rusted metal, it seemed clear that she wasn't at all bothered by junk.

Dart pounded on the door. When Winnie opened it she pretended she'd known Amy Roebuck all her life, and they all went inside. Ivan just stood there a moment, wondering why adults did that. It seemed false, totally wrong. No one below the eighth grade would ever do that. It would never happen. If you don't know someone very well, just keep your mouth shut, your eyes on the ground, and your hands in your pockets. Wait and see what happens. You might not want to have anything to do with them.

Inside, a pan of cinnamon rolls steamed on the table. Mrs. Helm poured coffee, then started in on how beautiful Dart's hair looked. She even persuaded her to take off her baseball hat. Amy joined in and the two of them roared off on how fabulous she looked, and how she should be doing more to show off how young she was.

It suddenly occurred to Ivan that he wasn't going to get one of those rolls. "Can I go find August?" he asked.

"Of course," said Winnie. "He's been waiting for you in his room."
Ivan waited until his mother agreed.

"Well, go on, Ivan," she said. "You heard Pastor Winifred. Go on."

Halfway down the hall, Milton came swooping out of August's room and made a couple swirling dives in front of Ivan.

"Hey, Milton," he said, "You'd better stay out of the kitchen. Enemies down there."

At the end of the hall the door was open and he walked in.

"Ivan!" August shouted, jerking his head up from a pile of papers and books. He rushed over. "Did you just get here?"

"Just about just."

They looked at each other and Ivan got that feeling he always felt with August: anything could happen now, and when it does it will be fun.

"What are you doing?" asked Ivan.

"Writing my report on the White Nose Syndrome fungus," replied August, and went on to tell Ivan about the new disease.

"Cripes," Ivan said. "I'll bet you know more about that fungus than anyone else in the world."

"Not even close," said August. "I might hate it more than anyone else though. Oh, I forgot to tell you, tonight is the full moon." Then he went on to tell Ivan about the jar of peaches, the Wild Boy, his meeting with the hermit, and the ceremony to burn the statues.

"Cripes, tonight!" exclaimed Ivan, surprised and a little resentful of all the things August had experienced in his absence.

"It's one of the most significant events in human history," explained August. "We need to camp out tonight and go over there after it gets dark."

"Let's set up the tent," suggested Ivan, "and put it by that dam we built."

"Good idea," August said, and they went downstairs.

The women were gone, and so were the coffee and the rolls. August and Ivan decided they must have carried them out to the garden.

Ivan led the way.

Sure enough, they were over by the fountain, at the little table. Winnie had opened the umbrella, and they were sitting under it, talking and talking.

"Whoa," said August, stopping and looking over the tops of the giant-headed flowers. Ivan looked too, but he was distracted by the sound of the bees and other insects. That was the thing about nature, he thought: wherever you looked something was happening.

"Whoa what?" he asked.

"They're so different," August said, pointing at the three women.

He was right. They were as different as they could possibly be. Ivan's brown mother, who'd been complaining about hot weather all week, had on those ridiculous new bright red shorts of hers, a blazing yellow harness top that didn't reach her waist, a white baseball hat, white tennis shoes, and no socks. Directly beside her, Amy Roebuck's wide, sunburned face was the color of a tomato. Her hair was perfectly arranged, light-brown and curly, and she wore a cream-colored blouse, dark green puddle-hoppers chopped off below the knee, anklebone-length green socks, and greenish-brown wooden clogs. And then there was August's chalk-white mom, taking up only half the width of her chair, with straight hair, a black shirt, and a plain gray skirt that would have covered her black loafers and black socks had she been standing.

They looked like three pieces from three different puzzles. But that didn't keep them from getting along, which they were doing quite well. They all jabbered at once, stopping only to take quick breaths. As they talked on, they shifted positions, crossed their legs, folded their arms, made shapes with their hands, pointed with their fingers, leaned on the tabletop, stood up, drank coffee, and tore pieces of rolls out of the pan, sticking them in their mouths whenever the staccato exchange provided a rare opportunity.

Ivan watched August approach these women. With his hands folded behind his back and in his preacher's-son voice, he said, "Hi, Mom. Hello, Ms. Workhouse and Mrs. Roebuck."

The women froze. They stared at August as if he were a burning fuse leading up to a truck bomb. Ivan smiled. August often had that effect on people. There was something about him they were never quite prepared for. "Hi, August," said Dart.

"Is it all right if Ivan and I camp out tonight?" he asked.

"If it's all right with Ivan's mother," said Winnie.

Dart simply nodded. August took a couple of rolls. On the other side of the garden he handed one to Ivan and they went back to the house to pack the things they needed for the night ahead.

They filled a duffel bag with flashlights, a knife, some rope, August's new bat detector, two water bottles, a snakebite kit, a waterproof container with matches, gifts for the hermit and the Wild Boy, and a handful of candy bars. The hermit would also need reading material, August added, and the Wild Boy would need nutrients to supplement his sporadic intake of honey, insects, herbs, and roots.

"This is a story about a pet dragon," Ivan said, staring at the book's cover. "You really think the hermit will want it?"

"It has an uplifting ending," August said. "And Mr. Mortal, I'm afraid, is in danger of losing his faith."

"In what?"

"Mankind."

"What's this?" asked Ivan.

"A jar of strawberry jam."

It took them the rest of the afternoon to set up camp beside the creek. They put August's tent right next to the dam, and built a ring of firestones not far from the entrance.

The pool of water seemed as deep as ever. "Hey," called Ivan, "there's something down there."

August came over and looked. "You're right," he said. Something glimmered on the bottom.

"I'm going to get it," he said. Then he dropped to his knees and stuck his arm in up to the shoulder.

"I'd go easy with that," said Ivan. "Could be a snapper down there."

When his arm came up, August had a big hunk of crystal on the end of it.

"What is it?" asked Ivan.

"Quartz."

"We didn't put that in there," Ivan said. "No way."

"It was the Wild Boy," said August.

"Why would he do that?"

"I don't know. And I also don't know where he possibly found such a large piece."

"Let me hold it."

August was right. It was as big as a loaf of bread and stunningly clear.

"We better put it back," Ivan said, and they did.

When August's dad came home they went in for supper. A prayer was said by August's mom, and they ate vegetables, soup, cheese, and grainy bread. There was a lot of talk about the ex-prisoner working for Jacob. He'd recently moved in to a run-down farmhouse outside Words. Winnie was worried about him.

"He'll be fine," Jacob said.

"I hope so," said Winnie. "That house hasn't been lived in for years. It's in terrible condition."

"Blake needs a place of his own. His motorcycle is running now and he's feeling fairly good about everything. Nate took a load of furniture out for him. They've got a couple rooms set up."

"There's no central heat, for goodness' sake."

"Blake won't miss it any more than July did."

Mrs. Helm paused, closed her eyes for a moment, and continued: "I don't know how you could bring yourself to go out there, Jacob. Every time I decide to go I get no farther than the drive. It's too hard to go back."

"It wasn't so bad this time."

"And you went inside the house?"

"Blake didn't want to go in alone."

"What was it like?"

"Time had settled everything, but I could still almost imagine July walking out of one of the rooms."

"Don't talk like that, Jacob. It betrays your superstitious nature. Ivan, don't listen to him. Apart from several extremely rare examples of theophany—where a divine image of God appears to someone in less-fortunate countries—there are no ghosts."

"I know," replied Ivan.

"I thought you were going to invite him over for supper," she said to her husband.

"I was, but he and his father were going somewhere to eat smelt. Nate found a restaurant he hadn't been to before and he was bringing his cousin along—someone named Bee. She wanted to ride there on the back of Blake's motorcycle."

Winnie looked disappointed.

"I'll bring him another time."

"Could we be excused?" asked August.

"I suppose," said Mrs. Helm, looking from her lap to her uneaten plate of food and then back to Ivan. "Ivan, are you sure you've had enough to eat?"

"I'm sure," replied Ivan, and the two boys went off.

Later that night, the full moon lit up the campsite. The air was hot, and loud with the sounds of insects and other creatures. They made a fire out of the best wood they could find.

"What time is it?" asked August.

"Time to leave," Ivan said, and then they both heard something coming toward them out of the darkness.

Jacob sat down next and stirred the fire with a stick. "Are you and Ivan thinking of going anywhere tonight?" he asked August.

When August didn't answer, he said, "I just wanted to let you know that I spoke with Lester a couple days ago. He mentioned that you might be coming over. I told him that would be all right with me and your mother."

"So it's okay?" asked August.

"Yes. Lester's a good man. Some of the things he does are a little different, but you don't need to be afraid of him as long as you remember to be respectful."

"Of course," said August.

"If you're not back before midnight, I'll come looking for you," he said. Then, after stirring the fire again, he threw the stick in and walked back to the house.

Burning the Past

August and Ivan sat by the fire and discussed which path they should take over the ridge. One of them had bigger trees, less underbrush, and less light. The other path was more in the open, weedier but longer. They decided in favor of the former route and walked away from the campsite. Somewhere far in the distance a band of coyotes began yapping, a sound that cut through the steady drone of insects. After a little while they took out the flashlights and split one of the emergency candy bars. Ivan burned the wrapper so they wouldn't leave behind any signs.

Milton seemed glad to have August and Ivan outdoors at night. He was at home in the darkness, and he swooped around catching insects, making clipping sounds when his leather wings snapped together. Every so often he'd fly off for a while, but he never stayed away too long.

"Can we can trust this hermit guy?" Ivan asked.

"Absolutely," said August.

"How can you be sure?"

"It's hard to explain. When you meet him, you'll know."

"Other people meet him and they don't know. They think he's nuts."

"You'll know," said August.

On the other side of the ridge, on the bottom of the first valley, they found a path littered with bottles and cans that winked with moonlit eyes. An owl hooted and something else made an even creepier sound. Milton came flapping back and lit on August's shoulder.

"What does that mean?" asked Ivan, shining his light into the bat's eyes.

"What?"

"Him on your shoulder."

"It doesn't mean anything."

"Everything means something," said Ivan.

"It doesn't mean anything important."

"There's someone else here. I can feel it. Someone is watching us."

"You're just imagining things," said August, and they continued along the path.

Ivan was trying to watch where he was going, but he stepped on an empty bottle. It didn't break, but the lumpy hardness under his shoe was a really bad feeling. And before he got over it, there they were—on the edge of the melon field. Everywhere were melons with moon shadows beside them.

"I don't want to go out there," Ivan said. "Is there another way?"

"There isn't," said August. "And if we went another way he'd know that too."

"How?"

"I think he has trip wires, detectors, and even tunnels leading away from his hut."

"Let's rest a minute, this bag is getting heavy."

"I'll carry it," said August.

"No you won't," Ivan said, and shifted it to his other shoulder.

"Let's go across," August said, and started through the field.

They were about halfway across when a flame shot up on the edge of the trees on the other side.

"What's that?"

"A torch," whispered August. "Keep your voice down, he can hear you."

"Cripes," whispered Ivan. "I wasn't counting on a torch."

The bushy orange flame burned brightly, illuminating a furry form beneath it.

"Come on ahead," said a gruff voice.

"We're coming as rapidly as possible under the circumstances," replied August. "It's not easy walking through these melons."

"It's not supposed to be," said the voice. "Who you got with you, August?"

"I told you, my friend Ivan. And Milton is here as well."

"I was hoping to see him again," said the voice. "What's your friend carrying?"

"Our stuff," said Ivan, testing his own voice. "Rope and matches, a knife, stuff like that. And candy bars—three of them."

"In truth, we could use a good rope."

August had already described Lester Mortal to Ivan, but in the torchlight the hermit looked like a bear dressed in army clothes.

Then he laughed suddenly, in a crazy way.

"What's so funny?" asked August.

"Your flashlights bobbing along look like boats on a bumpy sea."

"Well, take whatever pleasure you find," said August. "That's what my mom says—so long as it comes free and clear. Ivan and I don't mind being laughed at."

"I wasn't laughing at you. I was afraid you wouldn't come," said Lester.

"I said I would," said August. "I wasn't sure Ivan could make it, but nothing would stop me."

"Good man," said the hermit.

"Mr. Mortal, this is my best friend, Ivan," said August when they reached him.

"Hello, Ivan," he said, extending a furry paw.

"Hey," said Ivan. He set the duffel bag on the ground and shook hands with the creature. Pulling the book out of the bag, he handed it to him. "Here, this is for you."

Lester held the torch closer.

"Oh, I've seen that one around," he said. "There's supposed to be sequels. Do you have those as well?"

"I'll bring them next time," said August.

They followed him beneath the trees to his hut, the torch making the leaves and grass glimmer orange. "Here we are," he said, and reached into an overgrown hillside. Then he set the torch into a holder and walked into what appeared to be an entrance. "Come on," he said.

Ivan had never walked into a hill before, and it reminded him of the root cellar behind the equipment shed at the Roebuck place. It certainly smelled like that. The tabletop and the wooden counter seemed clean, however, and there was a general sense of orderliness.

"Can I get you something to drink? A cup of tea, perhaps?"

"No thank you," said August.

"Why do you have so many guns?" asked Ivan.

"Each one's different, I suppose. I didn't intend to have this many. They just added up."

"There must be a hundred," Ivan said.

"Not quite that many."

"So where are these statues August told me about?" asked Ivan, looking around.

"I set them in the back room. Let me get the wagon."

He went back outside. While he was gone August hurried over to a closed door on the other side of the room and put his ear against it. Ivan joined him, but neither of them could hear anything on the other side. Ivan tried the knob, but it was locked.

They heard rattling and the hermit came back in.

"That isn't a wagon," Ivan said. "It's a shopping cart."

"In truth, yes," he said. "But I put bigger axles and wheels on it."

"How far do we have to go?" asked Ivan.

"Not more than a quarter mile. Are you up for it?"

"Sure, why not?"

"I'll bring them out," he said, and disappeared again, this time into the room in back.

"Someday," whispered August, "we need to see what's in that locked room."

Ivan was dumbfounded when the hermit carried the first statue out of the back room. August had told him how lifelike the carvings were, but it was still a shock to see one. In the lamplight it looked almost as if the hermit was carrying a real person.

He set it down beside the shopping cart and went after the other one. The boys were both shocked when he returned with it.

"That's awful," said Ivan. "How do you make them look so real?"

"You can do almost anything with enough time. Now you boys give me a hand and we'll wrap these figures in some sheets and then tie them into the wagon."

"Why are you wrapping them up?" asked Ivan.

"So they don't get scratched."

"I thought you were going to burn them anyway."

"We are," he said. "But we don't want to bruise them beforehand."

Then the hermit went off to find more sheets and Ivan whispered to August, "Do you know what he's talking about?"

"I believe so," said August. "The ancient Hebrew temple cult demanded that all sacrificed animals be without blemish, especially on the day of atonement. Other primitive religious rituals of appeasement had similar requirements."

"I knew I shouldn't ask."

A short time later they were rolling the full grocery cart through the melon field. The hermit led with his torch, while Ivan pushed and August pulled. Above them, a thunderhead moved in from the west. It became harder to see without moonlight, and the boys began bumping into melons. Then the sky started booming and flashing. Wind rattled the leaves on the melon plants like flapping ground-wings.

"Doesn't this seem a little strange?" Ivan whispered to August. "I mean, who would have thought we'd be out here in the middle of nowhere, pushing two mummies through a field in a shopping cart?"

"You're right," said August.

At the far end of the melon field, they followed the hermit along a path leading uphill through a stand of pine trees. "What are those?" Ivan asked.

August pointed his flashlight at a tree. The beam hit a shiny object.

"It's a can," he said, and examined it more closely. "There's a photograph taped to the outside."

It was a snapshot of the hermit when he was much younger, maybe just out of school, dressed in a uniform and smiling proudly.

A little later, there was another can tied to a low-hanging limb, and another picture.

"The path is marked with these old soup cans," whispered Ivan.

In the picture taped to this one, the hermit was older, wearing a different uniform, standing with other soldiers.

Farther along, more cans and pictures hung from the trees, marking the trail. The hermit was progressively older in the snapshots, until he appeared almost as he was now, with a beard and long hair. In some, the scenery behind him looked like a jungle, in later ones like a desert. The hats and the uniforms changed color too.

Then they started down the hill. The rocky ground grew thick with stunted trees and bushes. Large jagged stones lurched up out of the ground.

They came around a sandstone corner and saw light glowing faintly from somewhere in front of them. After another turn between rocks, the boys found themselves on the edge of a steep drop-off, where the rock fell away into darkness. Around this hole, which looked to be forty or fifty feet across, the hermit had put burning candles inside brown paper bags weighted with sand.

"Down there," said the hermit, holding his torch over the seemingly impenetrable blackness.

Milton flew in and out of the torchlight.

August aimed his flashlight down to a rocky bottom some twenty feet below. The sides of the hold were steep and jagged.

"How are we going to get these mummies down there?" asked Ivan. "It's impossible."

"No it's not," said the hermit. "One of us will go down, the other two will stay up here and lower the cart with the rope."

"I'm not going down there alone in the dark," said Ivan.

"I'd prefer to remain up here with Ivan," added August.

Lester laughed. "I'll go down," he said. "You boys lower one of the figures at a time. Otherwise the cart might be too heavy."

"We can do that," said August.

"Good man," said the hermit. Then he started down the rock sides, holding the torch in one hand and moving slowly from foothold to foothold. Five minutes later, he reached the bottom.

"All clear," he said, his voice echoing up to them. "Lower one down, boys."

Ivan suggested they wrap the rope around a nearby tree so the trunk would act like a pulley, but August had problems with that. He said the rubbing would injure the tree.

"Then we need gloves," said Ivan. "This rope will tear up our hands."

"We can use our shirts," said August, and they did.

"Be careful, boys. It's heavy."

"Not too heavy for us," said Ivan.

After one mummy was lowered into the stone bowl, the hermit took the statue out of the cart and gently set it beside him. Then the boys pulled the cart up and sent the second one down.

"Good work, men, now pull up the wagon and leave it there. Then come down."

There weren't a lot of places to step, so it took August and Ivan a while going down. After they reached the bottom they could see why the hermit had chosen this place.

"This is stupendous," whispered August. "Look." He pointed up.

The thunderhead had blown over, and above them the full moon and stars stood out with unusual clarity. The stone bowl seemed to magnify everything in the sky. The bagged candles were just out of sight above the rim, providing a flickering glow.

There were two flat boulders sitting side by side in the middle of the bowl. After unwrapping the figures, the hermit balanced them on the stones and adjusted their positions so they faced each other. Then he brought out a handful of kindling from a hollowed-out place in the side of the rock and piled them between the legs of each statue.

"It's going to take more than that," said Ivan. "A lot more."

"They'll burn," replied Lester. "While I was working on them I rubbed raw linseed oil in to keep the wood from cracking. They're soaked through."

The three of them stood back and looked at the figures facing each other. The light from the torch made it seem as if the stone bowl were slowly breathing in and out.

"You know what this feels like?" said August.

"What?" they both asked.

"Jonah inside the whale," said August.

"Only you would think of that," said Ivan.

"I thought he would be here," said August to the hermit.

"Oh, the child is here. I thought you knew."

"Where is he?"

"Just over the rim."

"Why doesn't he come down?"

"Probably studying Ivan."

"Me?"

"You're quicker than your friend August, more impulsive."

Then the hermit reached into his pocket and pulled out a homemade straw man, some six or eight inches tall, with two bristled legs, arms, and a head. Stepping up onto one of the boulders, he tied a thread around the neck of both figures and hung the straw man between them.

"What's that for?" asked Ivan.

"That represents me," he said, taking a match from his pocket.

"Wait, Mr. Mortal," said August. "Please wait until the Wild Boy comes down. I think he wants to be here. Ivan and I will stand as far to this side as we can."

They did just that, and then August handed Ivan the jar of jam they had brought and told Ivan to take it—slowly—all the way to the other side of the bowl and set it down there.

Ivan could feel everyone watching him as he walked. Then he set the jar down, looked up, and went back to August.

"It's all right," said August in his normal voice, looking up to the rim. "You can come down now."

"I thought you said he couldn't talk," whispered Ivan.

There was a quick movement along the rim. The slim figure froze, looking from side to side. And all at once the child came down, leaping from place to place. Staying mostly in the shadows cast by the flickering light from the torch, he moved like an animal, quick and wary.

"There he is," whispered Ivan breathlessly. "There he is."

Ivan couldn't see him very well, but it looked as if he was barefoot, and he was unusually skilled in keeping the hermit, or the statues, between him and the boys' line of sight. Ivan was able to glimpse a part of his clothes and some shaggy hair, a thin arm or leg, but he kept mostly hidden as he made his way over to the jar of jam.

They heard the snap of the sealed lid coming off, and then there was nothing but silence.

"Can you see him?" whispered Ivan.

"No," said August.

"Did he taste the jam?"

"I don't know."

Next the hermit wrapped both the sheets around himself until he was all white from top to bottom, except where his face stuck out in an explosion of fur. He began walking slowly around the two figures, reaching out and touching them, and talking to them. As he walked the Wild Boy moved, keeping his body behind the walking mummy.

The hermit explained to the statues how much he appreciated them, how they had stayed with him longer than other figures in his past. He thanked the bigger, noble statue for giving him a desire to mold his character in a certain direction. He thanked the dying man for a glimpse of his own death and an understanding of his own evil. And then he began saying good-bye to them.

"He's talking like they're real," Ivan whispered to August. "He really is crazy."

"It's ceremonial talk," said August. "Like in a theater."

The hermit took out the match again, struck it, waited until the flame burned steady, and finally touched it to the straw man. It caught right away and the small flame crept upward, growing bigger quickly. Soon, all of it was burning. One of the threads holding the straw man between the two figures burned in two; the flaming man swung down, hanging only from the neck of the heroic figure. Then the remaining length of thread burned and the dark clump of flame fell onto the kindling. The flame spread into the sticks, then to a leg.

The fire grew in a fierce manner, yellow and orange flames leaping up, madly seeking more paint and oiled wood. When both legs were in full flame the fire spread onto the painted wooden hands and arms, peeling off the color. Soon the entire figure blazed like a giant wick and the heat began to peel paint from the other figure. Then it too caught fire and the sides of the stone bowl glowed fearfully from the dancing light. August and Ivan were sweating from the heat. Milton began flying in and out of the bowl, diving down and out, feeding on all the bugs that were attracted to the light.

August was falling into one of his moods again. Ivan could feel it. He looked worried.

"What's wrong?" asked Ivan.

"Those flames near the faces. I don't like them."

"They're just flames," Ivan said, and put his arm around August.

Ivan could see what he meant though. The heads burned with different colors, and from time to time a flame sprang up a foot or more away from the main body of fire, into the open air, as if something were coming quickly to life and then disappearing.

"Those flames are called strangers," whispered August. "I've read about them."

As the faces of the figures burned, their expressions changed. The screaming guy suddenly took on a heroic face; the warrior's look became terrified and pleading.

"August, I've never seen anything like this," said Ivan. "August?"

"He's gone," said August, looking around for the Wild Boy.

"That's bad," said Ivan. He'd wanted to watch the boy climb back up the wall, but he hadn't been able to look away from the burning figures.

The boys watched until the fire had burned the statues down to a couple of charcoal stumps.

When Ivan put his hand in his pants pocket, he felt something that hadn't been there before: a smooth stone about the diameter of a quarter.

"How did this get in my pocket?"

"The Wild Boy," said August. "He came over while we were watching the fire."

"Right here?"

"Directly behind us."

"Why didn't you tell me? He put this in my pocket?"

"I didn't know he was there either, but look, he put one in my pocket too."

The hermit walked around the burning chars several times, then sat down. "It's over, boys."

August and Ivan thought they should leave, and after thanking the hermit for inviting them, they climbed up the side of the ceremonial pit and started walking away.

"You have to admit it," Ivan said to August. "That was a great fire."

But August just kept walking.

When they heard something behind them, they walked back to the stone bowl and looked down. The hermit was sitting on the stone floor next the two charcoal stumps, hunched over and shaking, still wrapped in the sheets.

"What's he doing?" asked Ivan.

"Weeping," said August.

Beside him squatted the Wild Boy, watching the sobbing hermit.

The New Dress

Danielle Workhouse had never owned a dress like the one she had now, and the unfamiliarity heightened the experience. Inside it, she never stopped noticing the merriment of silk against her skin, the soft brush of the hem against her leg, the tug on her shoulder, the affectionate fabric hug around the waist. And she was equally unfamiliar with how delightful her feet appeared in the right shoes. An alarming gaiety leaped into her each time she looked down.

Because the mirror in her apartment failed to provide an adequate view of her new outfit, on several occasions she carried the heels down the hardwood hall, slipped them on, and stole a couple treasured glances in the larger mirror in the entryway. She looked good, and she wanted to look good in a way she couldn't remember ever wanting before.

When Danielle was growing up, her father and later her stepfather had ruled their decrepit home with such holy, tyrannical fear that she and her younger sister tried to the very best of their abilities never to attract notice. Dart and Esther crept from room to room with the trained vigilance of mice. They were never encouraged to look good, only to be invisible. During those times when domestic life threatened most ominously—when a hulking embodiment of irrational maliciousness lumbered nearby, drunkenly lecturing inanimate objects, boasting of former and future deeds, proclaiming the inalienable right to alienable freedoms—they hid in closets, cupboards, and clothes hampers. As they grew older, their skills of concealment grew proportionately.

Ridicule, badgering, and beatings were common, though never routine, when Dart was growing up. In fact, nothing could ever be predicted. Signs read from a parent's expression at the breakfast table at seven thirty could be rendered meaningless by nine o'clock. Everything was uncertain. It was best to always remain on guard, even when it seemed reasonable to feel safe for a short time.

Dart learned how to detect the slightest changes in human posture, voice, breathing, skin color, even smell—revealing a new disposition coming to the fore, or deviation from normal thought patterns. She also learned to trust even the slightest impressions informing her of intentions on the part of others. Her sister, Esther, took this cautionary principle a step further, completely banishing from her mind all the empathetic susceptibilities that made benign assessments possible; she didn't just dismiss favorable judgments of other people, she never made them. Esther simply assumed that everyone wanted to harm her, regardless of what they might say or do. The consequences of not being prepared far outweighed whatever vagrant peace she might enjoy by assuming the coast was clear.

Soon after their father was returned to prison for beating their mother (never for beating them, of course), Dart and Esther's mother met the man who would later become their stepfather. With him came a new form of tyranny, in addition to the old demands for rigid compliance with all drunken proclamations. This stepfather became virulently religious following his extended bouts of alcohol- and drug-addled depravity, and at those times God's commandments, righteousness, and humble submission became the orders of the day. Dart and Esther were constantly accused—from the ages of ten and eleven—of putting on airs, flaunting ungodly values, and exciting lust in others. Hiding in closets progressed to hiding in clothes.

Esther never managed to escape from the nightmare prescribed by their childhood, and Dart still thought of her sister often. Each time she remembered, Dart curled up inside, and the warming comfort of her grief often seemed to want more than she could give. And when she couldn't give herself over to it completely, the grief lurked on the edge of her awareness, sulking, waiting. Dart wondered if this was what people meant by never getting over something. In order to be free from the past, she reasoned, surely you would need to forget about it altogether, because how could you still remember those earlier times and not come under their influence?

These days, however, Dart had the strange impression that things might eventually be different. The last two months had been filled with many unexpected successes. Each day gave her more reason for optimism. She'd applied for a position that everyone knew would be difficult to obtain and was hired by a widely respected couple. They were decent folks with productive habits. They lived with purpose and order. They accomplished things, made things nice, got things done, cleaned up, and put away.

She could talk with Amy and Buck—and for that matter, with Florence—and they listened. They almost always did what they said they would, and didn't try to deceive anyone. They were predictable. Dart could disagree with them and they wouldn't get angry. They never hit each other or even threatened to. Yes, they sometimes argued, shouted, and occasionally swore, but they didn't lash out and they didn't lie about money. And Buck never intimidated anyone physically—in spite of how big he was. Even on the nights when he came home and it was easy enough to tell what he wanted from the way he looked at Amy (and sometimes at Dart), Amy didn't act any differently. She just went about what she was planning to do without changing anything. It was clear that Buck had no more authority over her than he would have if he were four feet tall.

For the first two or three weeks she spent in the Roebuck home, Dart waited for Buck's big blowout. She was convinced that when the right time came, he would do what he really wanted. He'd have his way. It simply didn't make sense that someone dealt a trump card that high wouldn't play it. But the blowout never came, and Buck continued getting up in the morning and going to work, coming home at night, watching ball games on television with Kevin, answering phone calls, sitting on the deck with his father, and then finally going to bed. Once he even bought a pack of cigarettes, smoked one, and gave the rest of the pack away.

The same was true of Amy. With all the opportunities she had to demonstrate the natural law decreeing that Dart had to be Dart and Amy had to be Amy, she never did. In fact, from the very first day she seemed to view Dart as someone she could have been herself, if circumstances had been different. She found commonalities rather than differences between them. She even seemed to care about what Dart thought of her, and often thanked her for the work she did.

Dart had little experience with people like this. And then her apartment was clean, and every single thing in it worked. Dart felt safe there. When she closed the door and set the lock at night, she never had the feeling that someone would try to get in. After a few weeks of staying there, Dart took the knife she kept between the mattress and box spring of her bed and returned it to the kitchen drawer.

The work was long and sometimes hard, but she'd been given a raise already, and she overheard Amy telling Buck to go over to the cleaning agency and hire Dart away from them. "And don't let them talk you out of it, Buck. Whatever hold they have over her, get your lawyer to break it. They shouldn't be taking a third of her salary, not after this long."

Now she and Ivan had health insurance through the construction company. They'd both visited the dentist and had their eyes checked. The Bronco was paid for, and she'd been able to put in new wipers, tires, wires, and plugs. She could drive it anywhere, leave it on the street, and not worry that it wouldn't start when she came back.

And then it was also true that Amy was becoming more than an employer. Dart hadn't told her anything personal yet, but the possibility was still there, the sense that they might someday talk about their real lives—what they were like before, what they were like now, and what they wanted to be like tomorrow.

"Just look at that," Amy said to Wally as they noticed Dart rushing back to her apartment in her new dress, carrying her new shoes. "Do you remember how it used to feel to be all dressed to go out somewhere?"

"Sure do," said Wally.

Later, however, Wally drove over to the construction site. He found his son hoisting floor joists from inside the crane cab, peeling the bundles from the flatbed. When the load had been transferred to the men on the top of the scaffolding, Wally went over to him. "It's no good, Buck. No good at all."

"What's no good?"

"That new gal you hired."

"Her name's Danielle, Dad. What did she do?"

"It's not anything she did, at least not yet. It's what's going to happen. And it won't be good."

"You're not being too specific here."

"You'll think I'm an old fool."

"Of course I won't. Say it."

"She got this dress from Lucky, and that in itself is reason to worry. In fact, it's reason to worry plenty. If Lucky gave me a dress I'd take it and stuff it up his—"

"I get the point, Dad."

"Well, see, it's not just that she got this dress from Lucky. Her hair's all curly wild and smells like fruit. And she's been putting that dress on and she looks like a million bucks in it. I'm not kidding."

"She's cute, Dad. Even Kevin thinks so."

"Are you listening to me, Buck? We're not talking cute here. Anyone can be cute. Hell, people even used to think I was cute. This is more than cute. Having her smile at you when she's all decked out is like falling into the North Sea."

"We're kind of busy here, Dad."

"I know. It's just that I've been having these dreams, and nothing good can come from that new gal you hired looking as good as she does in that dress. That's all I'm saying."

"There are good-looking women all over the world."

"Those don't concern me. This one does. Did you know she was going to get to looking like this when you hired her?"

"If I remember, we hired her together. It was Amy who really wanted her, but you were there too."

"I know I was, but she didn't look like this then. She hardly looked up from the floor. Now she looks right at you. Something's going to happen, Buck. Where does she think she's going, looking like that?"

"Lucky's taking her to a party in Madison tomorrow night. I understand it's at the governor's mansion."

"What party? What's it for?"

"Just a bunch of government people and others who hang around the capitol."

"Why?"

"I guess they're getting together to eat and drink and make themselves feel important."

"Lucky was invited?"

"He runs in those circles. He thinks he's going to get us a state contract and this is part of the process—that's what he calls it, 'the process.'"

"For what?"

"Storage units, barracks, holding tanks, and an office building—he's mentioned all of 'em."

"Where?"

"Mostly Fort McCoy. I don't know where the office building is supposed to go."

"Who's submitting the bids?"

"He's working with Raymond."

"So they're having a party, these big shots?"

"Look, Dad, I'm afraid I have to get back to work here."

"Sure, Buck."

"Where you going now?"

"I'm thinking about driving over to that repair shop in Words. The guy who owns it has a garden behind his house with a pool and some exotic fish. Anyway, I was hoping I could see them."

"Who told you about them?"

"Ivan."

"How does he know?"

"He's friends with the boy who lives there."

Dawn

Blake's first night in the brick farmhouse passed almost as slowly as a night in prison. Everything felt foreign to him. The previous occupant had never bothered to remodel, or even to repaint. And because all the original features of the house had been retained, the sparsely furnished rooms evoked a dimly lit earlier era. A musty pungency lurked throughout as well, proudly defying all association with the present.

Blake felt uneasy about living this far away from everyone else. He'd never lived in open country before. There had always been other houses, slamming doors, lit windows, and occasional voices relatively nearby. In prison, of course, there were way too many other people nearby, but this farmhouse felt like the other extreme. Looking outdoors, the lonely vacancy of the farmyard and surrounding landscape seemed to be waiting to capture him inside an old photograph.

The building itself seemed hostile to Blake's presence as well. The staircase resented his inability to understand its narrow, steep design. The fieldstone basement mocked his failure to find anything quaint or charming about it. And after dark, every noise in the house seemed to be amplified to levels of urgency.

And there were a lot of noises. Mice caravanned through the walls and under the floors. Carrying a small flashlight, Blake investigated clomping sounds in the attic, only to discover a full-grown raccoon. Before lumbering down the stairs and out the front door, the masked creature looked up at him as if to ask, "What are *you* doing here, anyway?"

Later that first night, when Blake unsuspectingly turned on the kitchen light, a garden snake slithered across the cracked linoleum and into a hole in a cabinet baseboard.

Twice he got out of bed to let swooping bats out of the house, and as he returned, spiders monitored his movements from inside gossamer fortresses. Half the animal kingdom, it seemed, had been making use of the residence he hoped now to claim.

The morning, however, had an altogether different story to tell. After washing in cold water, dressing, making coffee, and carrying a steaming cup of it outside to drink, his surroundings unfolded before him in a way Blake had never experienced before. The preying vacancy of the night before had been replaced by the silent marvel of dew and plant life shaking off sleep, regrowing the world. A new sun rose in the east, and the beads of moisture hanging from the spokes of his motorcycle burned like blue diamonds. A chorus of wild fledglings sang about the significance of eating weed seeds, having feathers, and flying wherever they wanted. The air felt alive, and he participated in its vitality with every breath.

Blake sat down and stared. This morning was like none other he could remember—something he imagined his father might experience, but never himself. If he weren't living out here on his own, away from the architecture of his childhood, he might have mistaken the morning for one that didn't belong to him, something loaned by others, handed down. But here he was. Only he could testify to its burgeoning wonder, and unlike the few other times in his life when he'd encountered something extraordinary, he did not ask, Is anyone else seeing this? His mind did not leap toward a need for verification, or a desire to share. The morning and he simply communicated. Blake felt authenticated, as if he was catching up.

As far back as Blake could remember, he'd felt behind, born too late, an unneeded afterthought in a long march of human events that had already prescribed the nature of everything around him. Monuments to earlier events were everywhere. His father had a father who'd had a father, and there were stories of all of them doing things Blake could never hope to equal. Likewise, his mother had a mother, and so on. They acted out of habits passed down from generations before. The laws governing what couldn't be done, the kinds of work people engaged in, the ruling order of traffic lights, convenience stores, row farming, drive-through windows—everything had been determined earlier. The streets were named for families who no longer lived along them. His father's house was called the Old Sanders Place, after a family he'd never met. The schools he'd attended had dates chiseled into the cornerstones. Even the prisons he'd been locked inside had come ready-made, part and parcel of a time-honored penal practice that dated back hundreds of years and depended upon developed traditions, enacted laws, and evolved conventions of social and economic power that remained as far removed from questioning as they were from understanding.

But now, as he sat on the sagging front step of his new residence, Blake participated in something the rabbit traps of civilization could never snare. The morning enlisted him in a secret but nonetheless universal rebellion. The past would not prevail. Everything important was not simply being mirrored forward through time. Though the past might always appear to be winning because of the despotic power of knowledge and familiarity, the old was being overthrown and Blake was a part of the insurrection. The inexhaustible emptiness of morning would eventually win. Nothing could stand against it.

As he stared into the misty dawn and thought about the commanding reality of renewal, Blake realized he had absolutely no idea what time it was. He was free, or rather had been free in the previous moment before he realized it. The coffee in his cup was cold. He set it on the step and went down to his motorcycle. Brushing beads of moisture from the seat, he climbed on, fired up the engine, and rode down the drive to the road.

His efforts in rebuilding the motor had been well spent, it seemed, and a shadow of his former confidence moved through him. On County Highway Q he followed the winding valley to the four-way stop on 41, turned east, spooled up into fourth gear, sped around a tractor and a honey-wagon, a pickup and an Amish buggy, then climbed onto the next ridge and followed it until the road plunged into another valley and continued for miles and miles downhill into Red Plain.

The temperature inside the combustion chambers had risen to optimum levels for igniting petroleum vapor and the motor ran smooth and strong. Blake found second gear and glided quietly through town as shopkeepers opened, people in terrycloth robes snatched newspapers from yards and front porches, and folks on their way to work pumped gas into pickups and vans while eating sweet rolls and balancing insulated coffee mugs on the tops of their vehicles. A couple of men who preferred to be drunk for as much of the day as possible headed for the taverns, followed by several others who simply wanted company.

He avoided the street he used to live on, unprepared for the sight of the old rooming house where he and Danielle Workhouse had once lived together.

In the cement plant's lot, he set the stand and walked into the office.

"Hey, Blake," said Bee from behind the counter. She was wearing a bright orange blouse with a huge white collar.

"Hey," he replied, looking around. The room had changed little in the years since he'd come here looking for Danielle.

Blake put a red wallet on the counter. It bulged inelegantly with pictures, credit cards, coupons, expired lottery tickets, keys, movie stubs, car wash tokens, stamps, safety pins, and change. "You left this the other night," he said. "Dad's on the road again today. He asked me to run it over before you missed it."

"What a ninny," said Bee, hanging her head in an exaggerated theatrical way. "Thank you. Have you had any coffee yet? I've got some in back."

"No thanks."

"It's the stuff your father gets from the guy who roasts his own."

"I know—had some already."

An expectant silence opened up between them, and was broken by Bee.

"So, did you go over and talk to Danielle yet?"

"Why, did you see her? Did she say something?"

"No, I just wondered if you'd gone over to talk to her."

"I didn't."

"Why not?"

"No reason, I guess. I don't really think about her much."

Blake could see Bee's eyes laughing behind her reading glasses.

He quickly left the office, climbed on the bike, and rode out of town. To clear his head, he accelerated enough to bring the front tire off the road between gears, and leaned into a tight corner.

On the summit overlooking the descent of the rustic road into the valley, Blake came to a full stop and closed his eyes. This was the time. He summoned memories of the ride that lay ahead of him from the countless nights he'd imagined it in prison. Then he pulled the clutch, notched into first gear, opened his eyes, and started down.

For the most part, traffic was nonexistent. Few people lived along the steep-sided valley, and even fewer took this twenty-mile-long road between Red Plain and Luster, because of the neglected surface, the abrupt curves, and the poorly banked corners.

The ride was mostly as Blake had remembered it. A couple of new vinyl-sided homes had been put up, and several of the old houses had fallen into disrepair or been abandoned. Others had been taken over by the Amish, who built on additions and painted them white, added hitching posts and outhouses, and left their buggies and horses in plain sight. The hilly terrain did not allow for much agriculture, but there were a few foraging goats, small plots of corn and soybeans, calf hutches, wooden beehives, and chickens hunting for insects.

As Blake rode, his whole body remembered what traveling along this road had felt like at the age of eighteen, nineteen, twenty, and twenty-one. Moisture welled up in his eyes as he realized for the first time that prison hadn't stolen all his youth. Though he had been damaged, he still had access to the unwounded delight that lived beneath all the damage. He pulled over on the narrow shoulder and climbed off the bike. A crowd of wobbly, small white and yellow butterflies flew up around him and scattered. His tears fell onto the faded blacktop and he did not attempt to stop them. The memories of lying sleepless on his cell bunk receded. They were out of step with his surroundings.

With his motorcycle beneath him again, he finished the ride to Luster. He briefly explored the little town, then checked the clock in front of the bank. When an old woman with a walker scowled at him, apparently finding his sudden presence beside the crosswalk an unwanted intrusion into her day, Blake returned to the same road and headed back to Red Plain.

Though he wasn't late for work, he wanted to cover the same territory in less time. Leaning into the corners and accelerating briskly along straight stretches released an old and welcome exhilaration. As he became more acquainted with the limits imposed by the surface of the road, and the responsiveness and maneuverability of the bike, he began testing them.

About halfway to Red Plain, a deer jumped into the middle of the road ahead of him and held its position with a straight-on startled stare. At the speed Blake was moving, stopping was not an option. He could only guess which way the buck would go. Blake's intuition told him left and so he focused on the opposite space in the road, a width of less than four feet. He leaned into this committed course with little conviction that he would make it through, but the deer bolted in the direction Blake hoped he might, and the motorcycle passed through the narrow space without obstruction. With an ever-widening distance between them, a shiver of relief passed through both sentient beings. Blake felt endorsed by fate. His good fortune seemed to suggest that perhaps Spinoza's god didn't want to kill him, after all. He twisted the throttle and thundered on faster.

Each morning and night he returned to the twenty-mile stretch between Red Plain and Luster, learning the curves, grades, and straightaways more intimately, going faster and faster. The present moment, it seemed, was slowly embracing him anew.

At the end of the week, Jacob invited Blake home for supper with his family. Blake washed, shaved, and changed clothes in the shop's bathroom. They pulled down the front doors and drove out of Words.

At the log home, Blake parked his bike off to the side and they went in together. Cooking smells filled the house, and Blake tried to identify them as his eyes wandered through the well-lit rooms. "Sit down anywhere," said Jacob. "I'll try to find Winifred and get us something to drink."

Blake had often tried to imagine what Winnie and Jacob's home looked like, and finding himself inside it gave him a satisfying sense of closure. Welcome details emerged from everywhere he looked, grounding his sense of Jacob and Winnie in a domestic opulence that his imagination never could have conjured up. There were pictures, pieces of furniture, colors, lamps, telephones, magazines, growing plants, utensils, marred wooden floors, and curtains unremarkable in every way except that they remarkably belonged to Winnie and Jacob.

The kitchen area opened into a combination dining and living room, dominated by a wood-burning stove in the middle. Off to one side was a small study with walls apparently made of books, a small desk with leaning towers of more books, and a cloth-covered overstuffed chair with more books stacked to the sides and balanced in several places on the oversize arms. Blake could easily imagine Winnie reading there, and he wanted to go in and explore the titles.

Then the door closed behind him and Winnie walked in from outside, her face ashen. Jacob went to her, gently taking hold of her upper arms. "Winifred, what's wrong?"

She brushed him aside, straightened her posture, and composed her face. "We have a serious problem," she said. "Something happened earlier today. When August and Ivan get back here we're going to have to get to the bottom of it."

"What happened?" asked Jacob.

"There's been some trouble," she said.

"What kind of trouble?"

Before she could answer, a blue sedan pulled up behind Jacob's old jeep. August and a boy Blake had never seen before got out of the back door. The driver waved but did not get out, and after the boys closed the door he backed up, narrowly missing Blake's motorcycle, and drove back down the drive.

Winnie waited in the open door for the boys to come in.

They slipped past her, their eyes glued to the floor after first shooting dismissive glances across the room, where Blake stood beside the stove. He was clearly outside the area of their concern.

"Go over there and sit down," said Winnie, pointing to the sofa.

They crossed the room and sat together on the edge of the cushions. August's face was marked in several places, and one eye was swollen. His white shirt was ripped and soiled with dirt, grass stains, and blood. The smaller boy looked mostly intact.

"Now," said Winnie, walking over and standing in front of them, "tell me everything."

They remained silent.

Jacob had not followed Winnie into the living room. He closed the door and remained standing not far from it. The take-charge manner he demonstrated at the shop clearly did not extend to his home.

"August, tell me," said Winnie, her voice soft but demanding.

"There was a slight problem," said August, without looking up.

"What happened?"

"It was complicated," he said.

"Did you give your talk on White Nose Syndrome?"

"Yes," said August.

"And then what happened?"

"After my presentation concluded, I answered several questions as well as I could."

"I want to know what happened," said Winnie.

"Well, I gathered my notes and supporting material together, left the building, and began walking through the parking lot."

He stopped again, but Winnie was insistent. "Yes?"

"Several boys walked over and questioned some of the conclusions I had drawn in my talk."

"What did they say?"

"I'm not sure I remember exactly."

"Try as best as you can."

"They saw no benefit in the survival of bats—any kind of bats—and they had a vulgar way of expressing this."

"Did you say something to antagonize them, August?"

"No."

"What did you say?"

"I suggested that if they studied the existing literature they might naturally wish to reconsider their position."

"What happened next?"

"One of them pushed me."

"And is that when you struck them, August?"

"I never struck them," said August, looking at his mother. "I promise, Mom, I never did."

"What happened?"

"I explained to them that by resorting to physical intimidation they were essentially admitting that their position lacked merit."

"What happened then?"

"One of them hit me."

"Then what?"

"After I adjusted to the impact, I attempted to offer a few more words in defense of bats and the many beneficial services they provide. That's when both of them jumped me, knocked me down, and began hitting and kicking me."

"August, is that when you attacked them?"

"I never did," he said, hanging his head.

"Well, someone did," said Winnie. "Those boys' parents are threatening to bring charges. That's what the sheriff said. They were beaten up pretty badly. I saw them. Tell me how that happened."

August stared down silently.

"August, tell me. Who beat those boys?"

August remained silent.

"I'm afraid that would be me, Mrs. Helm," said the boy sitting next to August.

"Ivan, you?"

"I'm sorry."

"You did all that damage?"

"I didn't mean to."

"Don't you know that violence is wrong, Ivan?"

"Yes, I do, Mrs. Helm. I really do. But when I saw them kicking August, I mean, right then I didn't know."

"But you're smaller than August," said Winnie. "Those boys were both bigger than August."

"They're not that big," said Ivan. "I used to be in their grade, before I was held back. They're bullies. I've had run-ins with them before, when they said things about my mother."

"Violence is wrong, Ivan," said Winnie. "Even retaliatory violence."

"I know," said Ivan. "I know. But I couldn't know it then. When I saw August being kicked, I knew they had to pay."

"What would your mother say about what you did?" asked Winnie. "I'm fairly convinced from what I know of her that Danielle would never approve of such rash behavior."

"Let's just hope she doesn't find out," said Ivan.

At the mention of Danielle, Blake sank into the chair next to the wood-burning stove. He stared forward like someone who had been woken by a loud noise in the middle of the night.

"And apparently that's not all," said Winnie, turning her attention back to her son. "Is it, August?"

He remained silent, staring at the floor.

"You had your bat with you, didn't you, August?"

Silence.

"You promised me you'd never take him into public areas. We talked about that many times and you promised."

Silence.

"He bit those boys."

"He was in my pocket," said August. "After they started kicking me he came out. He was hurt and frightened."

"And he bit them."

Silence.

"August, look at me. Look at me. Do you know what this means? When a bat bites someone they have to test whether it has rabies or some other disease. It has to be done, it's the law. I talked to the sheriff and Mr. Brandson, the city council lawyer. I also talked to Mrs. Williams, the township chair. I spent most of the last hour with them. When a bat or any other creature bites someone, they have to conduct tests."

August stared at the floor.

"You promised me, August. You promised."

"I know I did. I'm sorry, Mom, but Milton doesn't like me to leave him at home."

"If you hadn't taken him, August, if you hadn't taken him . . ." Winnie's voice wandered off. Then she asked August where Milton was now.

"In my pocket," he said.

"Give him to your father," said Winnie.

"No."

"Don't you dare say no to me, August. Give him to your father. We have to make him available for testing immediately."

"No," said August. "He didn't do anything wrong. Biting is his only defense. It's an instinct. It wasn't his fault."

"He bit a human being," said Winnie. "Give him to your father. Now."

"They'll kill him," said August. "I know about those tests. I've read about them. They'll kill him and he didn't do anything wrong."

"August, give that bat to your father. Right now."

With tears running in his eyes, August carefully took the bat out of his pocket, carried him across the room, and placed him in Jacob's hands. Then he went down the hall and slammed the door to his room behind him.

Winnie sat on the sofa next to Ivan and put her head in her hands.

"Can I be excused now, Mrs. Helm?" asked Ivan. "August needs me."

"Yes, Ivan, go on."

Ivan hurried through the living room and down the hall.

Jacob walked over and sat next to Winnie on the sofa.

Blake stayed where he was, staring at the floor.

Then he stood up and walked over to them.

"I'm sorry about this," said Winnie, looking at Blake for the first time. "I'm sorry that . . ." and her voice wandered away again.

"Forget it," said Blake. "I've been honored just to be inside your home, Mrs. Helm. I'll come back another time. I'm going to leave now."

He remained standing, however, and extended an open hand toward Jacob.

"Give the bat to me," he said. "I know all about those laws and the people who enforce them. They'll kill him before they test him. It's what they always do. Give him to me. I'll take care of it. I hate bats."

Jacob handed Milton to Blake and put his arm around Winnie, who had begun to weep into her hands.

Blake walked out the front door and rode away on his motorcycle.

The Party

On the drive into Madison, Lucky explained the rules to Dart.

"Stick close to me for the first half hour," he said. "I'll point out the players. Smile a lot and keep everything simple."

"What do you mean?" asked Dart, watching the sun sink into the horizon.

"Keep everything simple—a lot of motion, eye contact, laughing, smiling, and striking poses. Don't talk about anything that takes longer than two seconds to explain. When you're introduced, say, 'I'm Danielle with Roebuck Construction.' By the end of the evening you should have said those exact words about two hundred times. 'I'm Danielle with Roebuck Construction.' 'I'm Danielle with Roebuck Construction.' You don't need to tell them your last name. If someone asks for it, tell them, but nothing more than that about yourself. If asked what you do, say you're a consultant and mention Roebuck Construction again, the leading contractor in southwestern Wisconsin. If asked where you live, say, 'Not far from Roebuck Construction's main offices.'"

"Shouldn't I have business cards to hand out?"

"No, no, no, don't be an idiot, this isn't that kind of party. Everyone who matters has already heard about Roebuck Construction. I've made sure of that. Jesus, trust me."

"Then why am I supposed to say it all the time?"

"After tomorrow, when a certain five men and two women see the name Roebuck Construction, I want them to think, *Danielle*. And that's another thing to keep in mind—five men and two women. After I point them out you should see only those seven people in the room. None of the others matter. I don't want you to snub anyone, of course, but the entire time you're at the party you'll be trying to find a way to talk to, make eye contact with, smile at, stand close to, or at least bump into one of those seven people. Even if you're not talking to one of them, if you're near enough to hear them say something that's supposed to be funny, laugh and smile. And laugh loud enough that they can hear you. When one of them gets away from you, move on to another. With the men, if you get a chance, touch them in some way as often as you can. Take hold of an arm, a shoulder, a hand. When you've interacted with all of them in some way, you'll know which ones are easier to get close to. You'll feel it. Follow through with that."

"Doesn't sound like a lot of fun," said Dart, trying to catch a glimpse of her reflection in the side window.

"It isn't," said Lucky. "But along with a lot of work that's already been done, and a little hard cash, it generally pays off. What I'm saying is that all the important steps have already been taken. I'm just bringing you in at the end for the final touch."

Dart wished she could see how her hair looked. The window refused to hold a reflection that stayed together long enough to inspect, and she was afraid Lucky might disapprove of pulling down the visor mirror. Then she began to wonder where the new-car smell inside Lucky's car actually came from. How did the makers get it into them? The factories themselves surely didn't smell like that. She made a mental note to look up how much his car was worth when she got back home. And she would check about the smell. It would be nice to have that in the Bronco.

When they reached the Middleton suburb, a row of streetlights lit up as they drove beneath them. As Lucky continued into Madison, Dart saw the main campus of the university sprawled along the lake. Students darted in and out of the streets with daring disregard of moving vehicles. Others rode bicycles and crowded around storefronts with book bags. A lot of them looked Asian, and Dart wondered what it might be like to be twenty and going to school in another country. When her imagination failed she went back to watching the lights.

The governor's mansion was on the other side of the lake. Lucky rolled up the drive and pulled in behind four cars and a limo. As soon as they came to a stop, a man in a short gray jacket came and opened Dart's door. "Good evening," he said.

Dart smiled and prepared to tell him she was Danielle from Roebuck Construction, but he was at the other side before she could. "He's the valet," whispered Lucky. "You don't need to talk to them."

That was a first, she thought, climbing from the car. Nobody had ever told her there were people who did not need to be talked to. She thought about it while adjusting her dress. God, her feet looked great.

As she and Lucky walked up to the mansion, Dart didn't know what to think. Everything seemed fairly unreal. The yard was immaculate. Then Lucky opened the door, someone inside took their coats, and everything changed too fast to keep up with. She saw an intimidatingly gorgeous woman standing to her right, behind the person who'd taken her coat. Then someone else stepped forward and said, "Follow me, please."

Lucky started walking, and as Dart fell in step beside him she noticed that the intimidating woman did as well. Upon closer inspection, she turned out to be Dart's own reflection in a mirror.

"What are you laughing about?" asked Lucky.

"Nothing."

At the end of a hall—wide and tall enough to drive a semi down—stood a set of double doors. They opened into a room filled with fancy chairs, tables with appetizers, an enormous punch bowl, an ice sculpture of golf clubs recently presented to the governor by the Chamber of Commerce, and about sixty or seventy elegantly dressed people. Dart was one of the younger people in the room, and she could feel the attentive gaze. It felt great.

Five people came over. They seemed to know Lucky, and Dart didn't hesitate with a first round: "Hi, I'm Danielle with Roebuck Construction." A few other people joined them, and after more introductions the little group moved to the drinks table. Lucky asked a man in a white coat behind the punch bowl for two, and he handed Dart one of them with a small square napkin.

Cinnamon was a nice addition, she thought, sipping and glancing around the room. She'd have to remember that the next time she made punch.

There was simply too much to take in, and all of it was completely unfamiliar. She followed Lucky and another half dozen people came toward them, precipitating another round of self-introductions.

"He's on the committee," whispered Lucky.

"Who?"

"That last one, Thomas. He's an investor."

"With the green tie?"

"Yes. His wife's an avid horsewoman."

"Is she one of the seven?"

"No."

"Then I thought she didn't count."

"She doesn't, but you might want to know that for later on. Heads up, to your right, there's another one coming."

Dart met Larry Parksletter. He smiled broadly in response to her introduction and asked, "Are we having fun yet, Danielle?"

He appeared to be about fifty. He was balding, but nice-looking in a whole-wheat kind of way. The inanity of his question put her strangely at ease. It was the kind of thing she'd often overheard people say in bars.

"Yes, we are," said Dart. "And we're going to have even more when this punch ripens and one of these yahoos starts trying to golf with one of those ice clubs."

Parksletter roared with wheaty laughter.

"I'll make sure to look you up later," he added.

"I sure hope you do," she said, and took another drink.

The catering crew roamed through the room in white jackets, carrying finger food and drinks, shuttling between ever-changing clusters of drifting conversations and the kitchen. One of the servers asked if she would like something. The voice seemed oddly familiar, and when Dart turned she discovered Vicki Well holding a half-filled platter of crackers and crab meat. She and Vicki had worked together several years ago, in a bar in Luster. It was the first job Dart could find after leaving the cement company.

"Vicki!" she said.

Vicki stared at her wearily.

"It's me. We used to work together, remember?"

"Nope."

"Sure you do—in Luster. You parked your green Oldsmobile next to the dumpster one night, and the truck guy rammed into the side of it. We even shared a crappy apartment for a month, before my son drove you crazy and you moved in with the guy who rammed your car."

"Oh, yeah. Now I remember," said Vicki. "Now I remember. Jesus, what happened to you, Dart? How did you get to looking so fabulous? And what are you doing at this party?"

"No idea," said Dart. "How's the job?"

"Beats the bar in Luster to death. You know, that guy always said he'd fix my car. Never did though. Bastard. Hey, Dart, we had some good times together, you and me. We both got fired on the same night, if I remember right. You still got that kid?"

"Still got him."

"I'd go easy on the punch, Dart. They've got some real rotten stuff in there. Stick with the wine or bottled hard stuff."

"Thanks," said Dart, setting her drink down and meeting Lucky's eyes from halfway across the room. "Look, I've got to go. Old Lucky Two Shoes is glaring at me, and I think that means I should go over there. I'll talk to you later."

"Good to see you, Dart. And congratulations on whatever happy hole you managed to fall into."

Dart joined Lucky and a new group of polite, well-dressed people. She introduced herself dutifully. Four musicians arrived and set up at one end of the room. After an opening number, they settled into light, almost whimsical renditions of classic tunes picked at random from the last forty or fifty years of popular music.

A wave of latecomers washed into the room. "I'm Danielle with Roebuck Construction . . ."

Because of the novelty of her surroundings, Dart's mind attempted to familiarize her situation by calling up all the related memories it could find. Relying on the mad inclusiveness of dream association, no analogy was too loose. While listening to a white-haired woman named Carmen talk about the places not to get a manicure, Dart found herself thinking about the first day of school each year. She and Esther always dreaded it, confronted as they were with other kids whose parents not only drove them to the school and went inside to meet the teachers, but had bought them new clothes, shoes, pencils, notebooks, and filled their pockets with lunch money. She and Esther never had any of those things, and lunch money was always a problem because unless they could dig change out of the sofa or steal it from their mother's purse or stepfather's bureau, they were out of luck. Asking for money was grounds for a later whipping under the pretense of some other infraction. Anything reminding their mother or stepfather of their shortcomings would precipitate some form of abuse. Esther once had a teacher who couldn't in her wildest sheltered imagination picture parents sending their daughters to school without clean clothes, lunch money, or notebooks. Thinking that something must surely be wrong, she made a few phone calls. Social Services sent out a case worker and miraculously picked an afternoon when their mother was sober and could carry through with a reasonable defense. That night their stepfather plugged in the iron, stripped Esther, and threatened to iron her pussy shut if she didn't drink a bottle of hot sauce. Esther vomited four times before she was allowed to stop. They could sometimes be insidiously clever that way, devising ways of hurting them without leaving marks.

"So don't ever go to them," the woman continued. "They make you feel rushed and don't give advice on lotions and creams. Please promise me you'll never go there. What did you say your name was again, dear?"

"Danielle. I'm with Roebuck Construction."

"Oh, yes. I remember now."

"Let me get you another drink," said Dart.

"Oh, thank you."

"Would you like something else to eat?" asked Dart, understanding for the first time that the shame she had felt for being unable to protect her sister had actually added to their stepfather's pleasure in hurting her.

"No, thanks. The drink will do just nicely."

Carmen was one of what Dart now thought of as the Magnificent Seven, and she rushed off to refresh her cocktail. As she did so, Dart thought again how remarkable it was that her lifelong hatred of rich people had come into question of late. Her disgust for all the greedy pricks who fed off the top layer of the food chain had been carefully nurtured into a foundational pillar of her thinking over many years. But her experience working for Amy and Buck had challenged this structure, and by this point she had come to conclude that those earlier assumptions were simply mistaken. After all, in the end Amy was Amy, Buck was Buck, Kevin was Kevin, Flo was Flo, and Wally was Wally.

And as for tonight, she was meeting rich people she couldn't deny liking at every turn. A couple of the better-dressed women were so outgoing and jolly that they almost seemed nicer than anyone else Dart knew. She could hardly believe it.

And to think that Lucky Two Shoes had said this wouldn't be fun. It was great! She couldn't remember ever having had such a good time.

Lucky brought someone over to introduce while she was getting another drink for herself and Carmen.

"Hello, I'm Danielle with Roebuck Construction."

After the man left, Lucky said, "Don't drink so much."

"Okay, I won't."

Some people started dancing at about that time, in front of the band. She got a couple of invitations, but every time she accepted Lucky scowled at her because she wasn't with one of the Magnificent Seven.

After a few minutes, a couple of drinks were dropped, someone fell against the punch bowl table, and a man with a Spanish accent tried to pry a piece of the ice sculpture off and put it in his glass. And then the woman Dart most liked came over and asked her to dance. She was maybe forty, with a long, narrow, and kind face. Her name was Frieda and her legs seemed longer than the rest of her.

"I'm not much of a dancer," said Dart.

"I don't believe that," said Frieda, jewelry latticed across her tanned chest like glittering mail. "If you can walk on those heels, you can dance. Now that man," she pointed, "he can't dance. He's my husband. And most of the other men here as well, you'd think someone shoved a pole up their ass. It comes from sitting in front of those damn computers all day, reading about mergers, equity, and points. And then they go jogging to keep in shape. Jogging. God, I hate jogging. Come on. Wait. First drink this, all of it. Go on."

Then they drank another. Frieda said drinking and dancing should never be separated.

Dart followed her companion into the designated area in front of the band, where Frieda was transformed into, well, Dart didn't know what. She'd never seen anyone dance like her, and she tried to keep up.

"You're really good," said Dart.

"Thank you. What was your name again?"

"I'm Danielle with Roebuck Construction."

"Right, Danielle. My mother had my sister and me going to ballet classes before we could walk, and from there we branched out. My sister became a professional dancer, but I quit sometime after I went to college. I've always loved dancing, though."

"I can tell," said Dart. "You can really move. You've got every guy in this place looking at you."

Frieda laughed. "Thanks, honey, but they're not looking at me. I thought I'd bring you out here to give the old boys a treat. Ten years ago they might have been looking at me, but now they're looking at you."

"That's rat rubbish. You move much younger than I do."

"You think so?"

"Sure I do."

"Thanks."

Just then the musicians began a much livelier song, and Dart's companion shouted, "I just love this one! Wait here. This necklace keeps biting me." Frieda undid the clasp behind her neck and hurried the jewelry over to her husband, who put it in the inside pocket of his coat.

She returned to Dart. "There!" she yelled over the music.

Wow again, thought Dart. Without her diamond harness, Frieda was even more of what Dart could find no word for. Her limbs seemed to have joints everywhere, and they followed paths that could never be predicted, always in perfect rhythm. The musicians adored her. At one point the sax player even came out and walked around the two of them as he played.

At the end of the song, Dart saw Lucky Two Shoes frowning at her again. She excused herself and went looking for Whole Wheat, who was watching her from behind the punch bowl. He handed her a fresh drink and told her about the summer kitchen his grandmother used to have. "It's where they did most of the canning, in a separate building next to the house," he said. "That way they could keep the heat out. They also had more space for hulling and washing produce."

"Very sensible," said Dart, using one of Amy's phrases. "Canning always makes a big mess."

"I'll say," he said. "How come I've never seen you before?"

"Maybe you just don't remember. I have one of those forgettable faces."

"Never," he said with a coughing laugh. "Besides, there's plenty more to you than a pretty face."

"Very clever, Larry. I'm sure you could have forgotten those other parts too."

"No, no, you're new all right."

"Is that good or bad?"

"I'm not sure. Are we having fun yet?"

"Just about there."

Then Frieda came up behind Dart, grabbed her around the waist and arm, and pulled her toward the dancing area. "Come on," she said. "I can have more fun with you than anyone else." She stopped and got them another drink as they made their way across the room.

Dart smiled. Thinking of herself as fun had a strange appeal. Why had no one ever said that to her?

Lucky Two Shoes came over then, took the drink away from Dart, and tried to pull her away. But Frieda was having none of it.

"She's mine," she said. "You go ogle with the rest of the boys."

"There are people Danielle needs to meet," he said.

"I'll report you to the party-pooper police," threatened Frieda, taking the drink back from him and handing it to Dart. "I have friends in high places."

Dart smiled reassuringly into Frieda's eyes. "It's okay. I'll be right back," she said, and went with Lucky to the other side of the room.

"Turns out the Thomas couple own a summer place somewhere near you," whispered Lucky. "They want to talk. So chat them up on local stuff. And give me that drink."

"I can handle it."

"Give it to me now," he said. Something ugly flashed from Lucky's eyes. "I've spent too much time on this to have you mess it up."

She handed him her drink.

Curt and Darlene Thomas told Dart about their property along the Thistlewaite River. They pronounced the names of their horses with the cherished inflections most people reserve for their children, even though their names were Smarty, Fudge, Noodle, and Sweet Treats. They all came from long lines of champions, whose names were provided with the same adoration, as if they were all family members. Their boat had even been named after one of their favorite horses.

All too soon, people were starting to leave.

Dart found another of the Magnificent Seven and proposed a toast to prosperity. Lucky Two Shoes cornered three men and two women near the lounge area and surrounded them with his facts. When one of them finally broke free, his hold over the rest of them shattered, and they fled.

The musicians were packing up. A group of men and women began playing poker at a table near the exit doors, and a second table was designated for the same purpose. Ties and suit coats were coming off like autumn leaves, tossed over the backs of chairs. Someone went to look for poker chips. Two men carried a punch bowl over and put it nearby. The catering staff carried in coffee.

"Is it all right to smoke?" asked someone.

"No," came the obvious reply.

Lucky Two Shoes came over and said it was time to leave. Dart found her purse and they walked across the room, behind the poker players, toward the open doors.

"Good night."

Dart realized she'd had far too much to drink. Her mind was dancing about crazily to its own accompaniment. She looked longingly back into the room. Then she looked down at her feet, and fixed on the ends of several painted nails poking out of the ends of the shoes. They still looked great, but for some reason her connection to them seemed tentative. Then a little voice started up in the back of her head.

That's a terrible idea, she thought. You're not making any sense.

Lucky was shaking hands with the last person in his circuit around the poker table, a gray-bearded man with a jaunty flat-brimmed hat. She waited, feeling increasingly nostalgic about the preceding four hours. Someone had actually called her fun.

Across the room a plate dropped, clattering horribly against a table and then the floor. Everyone turned to look. Dart couldn't believe it had happened—the coordinated sequence, its timing and rhythm, as if it had been planned by fate and anticipated by the cautionary voice in her head. Her participation seemed almost scripted, and she reached into the lining of the nearby coat, found the necklace, and slid it into her purse.

On the ride back to his condominium, Lucky Two Shoes was silent. As they drove through liquid darkness, the lights seemed fuzzy and wavy.

Twice, she put her hand into her purse to feel the sharp edges of the jewels, giddy yet appalled that she had actually taken them.

Inside the condominium, Lucky wasted no time coming after her. This didn't surprise Dart. In fact, she had expected it. She owed him a piece of her for the evening. No one ever gave you something without getting something in return. She knew that. Still, the up-closeness of Lucky was so unpleasant that at one point she pushed him away. The malicious expression returned to his eyes, and Dart simply resigned herself to a deal she hoped never to make again.

A Long Lament

The first few days of hot weather came as no surprise. The residents of the Driftless Region took them in stride. Their summers always seemed to include a few mornings in which striking a match or toasting a piece of bread seemed thermodynamically ill-advised, and a few nights when the possibility of boiling the Arctic Ocean seemed a more than reasonable trade-off for using air conditioners set on high.

As July turned to August the blistering heat intensified and the humidity rose accordingly. Drawers swelled shut. Cutting boards refused to be pulled out of kitchen cabinets. Blackened by mold, refrigerator gaskets dripped water, and a frosty gasp accompanied the opening of freezer doors. Guitars, fiddles, mandolins, violas, and pianos went horribly out of tune. Attic floors buckled, prying four-inch nails out of joists. People carefully considered all alternatives before venturing into direct sunlight, and in shade moved as slowly as possible to avoid making currents in the thick, oven-like air.

To make matters worse, it hadn't rained for three weeks. Despite the tropical humidity, plants withered and the soil cracked open in places. Runoff streams dried up, ponds turned pea-green stagnant, and rivers sank to dangerously low levels, discouraging fish and depressing fishermen. Trees clenched leaf-fists, holding on to the little moisture they still contained. Grasses stopped growing, turned brown, and sequestered their precious plant spirit in underground roots, desperate each morning to suck the manna of dew with the tips of leather-dry tongues.

August Helm sat under the fan in his bedroom, looking out the window. His mother, concerned that he had not come out for breakfast, insisted he eat something for lunch.

He mumbled a civil refusal and returned to staring outdoors.

Several hours later, he got up, dressed, walked to the bathroom, and filled his canteen. When Winnie saw him she said, "August, there are storm warnings this afternoon. Don't go too far from home."

August walked out through the garden, past the brittle leaves and drooping flowers. The morning sun had already been covered by a milky haze. Adjusting his cap, he moved the canteen strap to the other shoulder, then headed into the woods and down the valley. A cloud of biting flies swarmed around him, attacking exposed areas of skin.

At the trail leading to the melon field, August noticed that the litter, cans, and bottles were gone. On the edge of the field, the melons were hardly bigger than the last time he'd seen them. Halfway across, he wondered why Lester Mortal had not come out of his hut.

Perhaps he's not home, August thought, and continued through the field to the edge of the woods. When he reached the hut, the thick front door stood open, and the vines covering the windows had been removed.

"Mr. Mortal," he called into the open doorway. "Are you home?"

"Yes, August. Come in, come in."

Inside the hut, everything had changed. Ample light entered the windows. The weapons and ammunition were gone and the wood chips swept away, down to the hard-packed dirt floor. The crude furniture had been washed, along with the table, chairs, shelves, and counters. Pictures hung on the walls, in appealing shapes with bright colors.

When the hermit walked out of the back room, August hardly recognized him. His beard was gone, his hair was cut short, and he was dressed in tan shorts, tennis shoes, and a bright blue button-up short-sleeve shirt. Only his lumbering manner and eyes betrayed his earlier self.

"Hey, August," he said. "I didn't expect to see you today. Very hot out there."

"What happened here?" asked August.

"What do you mean?"

"You've changed your appearance, Mr. Mortal."

"I have," he agreed. "Would you like something to drink or eat?"

"I would," said August. "I haven't eaten for several days."

The hermit went to a hand-dug hole in the floor, lifted a wooden cover off, and drew up a plastic bucket with a rope. "I have a little aged Swiss, homemade mustard, brown bread, and ginger tea."

He set a place for them at the table.

The food and drink were cool and delicious.

"Where's Milton?" asked the hermit.

August hesitated, tried to speak. Then he muttered, "Milton was betrayed by everyone, Mr. Mortal. In the end he was murdered by a convicted felon who said he hated bats."

"I see you also have a shiner," said the hermit.

"That's nothing," said August, waving his hand dismissively. "My friend Ivan repaid them three times over."

"I'm really sorry about your bat, August."

"Thanks, Mr. Mortal, but I'm afraid I have no desire to live in this world any longer. My soul has been poisoned. What happened to all your weapons?"

"I sold most, gave a few away."

"All of them?"

"Yes, all of them."

"That's too bad. I was hoping I might borrow one."

"Why?"

"I feel a need to learn to shoot. Many things, it seems, could be solved by a rapidly moving lead bullet."

"That doesn't sound like you, August."

"That's the point, Mr. Mortal. The world is no longer the place I imagined, and I'm ashamed for the way I used to think. What a fool I was."

"That sounds a little harsh."

"Perhaps you didn't see it that night, then."

"See what?"

"Strangers—the flames leaping from the faces of your burning figures, sprouting into the open air and disappearing."

"That's what happens when oil-soaked wood burns."

"Perhaps, Mr. Mortal, but your ceremony did not succeed. The evil you hoped to remove from the world is still here. In fact, it's even worse."

"It wasn't my intention to remove evil from the world, August. I only wanted to make peace with myself."

"I know what those strangers were," said August. "I didn't at the time, but I do now. They were demons entering this world from beyond."

"Demons?"

"Yes, Mr. Mortal. Your ceremony opened a channel and demons came pouring in."

"From where?"

"The lowest regions of hell. The seven heavens and seven hells are not nearly as stable as most people think. Along with everything else, they change. Right now, the earth is moving from the neutral zone it has occupied since the first recorded scripture—between the angels of light and the dark principalities of the air. Our planet is turning into a new region of hell, and the demons are coming."

"That's a little extreme, August."

"No, it's not, Mr. Mortal, and you should know better than most. The evidence is everywhere—senseless wars, torture practiced openly, needless starvation, homelessness, higher and higher suicide rates, pollution, species extinction, and the greedy arrogance of the thousand hired thieves in government."

"More cheese, August?"

"No, thank you, I've had enough."

"Then I wonder if I might share something else with you."

"What is it?" asked August, his voice lacking all interest.

"It's a map. Not many would see its importance, but I believe you may."

"What kind of map?"

"It was drawn freehand by my uncle."

The hermit lumbered off into his bedroom. When he returned he was carrying a piece of fiber-rich paper, as thick and limp as a blanket and lined by many folds. When he spread it flat on the table in front of August, the map took up the entire surface and flopped over the sides.

"First you should know that Uncle Ray was one of my favorite people when I was growing up. He worked most of his life in a local logging crew, cutting and hauling trees out of woodlots throughout the Driftless—as far away as Iowa and Minnesota."

August stared into the map.

"Check out this area," said the hermit, directing August's attention to the upper-middle portion of the map. "This is where we are right now, and the map covers the major forested areas for fifty miles around."

"What are these X's?"

"I hoped you'd notice those, August. There are more than one hundred of them on this map."

"They don't seem to form any particular pattern," said August.

"I noticed that myself, and so did everyone else in my family. See, after Uncle Ray passed away the family set to squabbling over everything in his estate, which was worth a considerable amount. I don't mean Uncle Ray was wealthy by any means, but over the years he had acquired more than most, certainly more than the other loggers working with him. And no one understood exactly how he'd managed to do that. He had never married, he didn't leave a will, and he had no children. Still, open warfare broke out between the different factions of my family over who would get his house, investments, savings account, twenty acres of walnut trees, and a number of valuable pieces of antique furniture and silver inherited from his grandparents."

"And that's when they found this map?" asked August.

"Exactly," said the hermit. "They found it in his safe, and they chose to ignore the fact that it was inside a manila envelope with *For Lester* written on it. Everyone recognized right away that it was a map of this area, and by consulting with Uncle Ray's diary they identified the plots where he'd been assigned to cut trees, and some of them corresponded to places marked with X's on the map. So off they all went, hunting for the money they thought Uncle Ray must have buried in those locations, digging up everything in sight."

"Seems highly unlikely," said August.

"I agree," said the hermit. "And sure enough, they found nothing. Just weeds, they said, just dumb weeds. They gave up after three or four days. After they decided the map had no financial value, they presented it to me in a brief show of pomp and sentiment, and returned to squabbling over the rest of Uncle Ray's estate. See, they all knew Uncle Ray and I saw eye to eye on most things, and naturally they hated me for it."

"Why did they hate you for it, Mr. Mortal?"

"Because the friendship between Uncle Ray and me was truly valuable, and they knew they could never have it. I'm afraid that's the way most of my family is. At some level they are capable of recognizing truth, but they never involve themselves with it."

"And you probably asked yourself," said August, "why would a man keep a record of the places he'd visited if he didn't intend to return someday?"

"Exactly," replied the hermit. "I had the map for over a year, and then it came to me."

"I know," said August, apologizing for interrupting by nodding. "Those X's indicate the places where your uncle noticed ginseng growing in the woods. That was his gift to you."

"August, you're a gifted human being. No wonder you have a friend like Ivan. You figured it out. One of the reasons I've been able to live out here like this is by cultivating plants that grow in the places my uncle first discovered. This has been my secret and my joy."

August looked away, drawn back into his despair. "I'm afraid my life no longer contains any joy, Mr. Mortal, and I don't think it ever will again. Thank you for sharing your map and attempting to turn my attention from the horrors of living without the companionship of my beloved Milton, but I'm afraid it hasn't helped."

"Give yourself some time to get over this, August. You can't think your way out of this kind of pain. It takes time."

"You don't understand, Mr. Mortal. I stand at the root of the most terrible facts. I am the one who betrayed Milton. I took him out of my pocket and turned him over myself. Why did I do that?"

"Okay," said the hermit. "Why did you do that?"

"At first I told my mom no. But then she said in an angry voice that I had to hand him over, so I did. But why did I?"

"Because your mother told you to, August."

"I know, but it wasn't her fault. I should have protected Milton. I never should have agreed, no matter what anyone said. He was my bat and he depended on me. It's all my fault. If I hadn't brought Milton to the fair, he'd still be here. It was me, Mr. Mortal, it was me. I was given a sacred trust, and I failed miserably."

"You couldn't go against your mother, August."

"I'm not so sure about that, Mr. Mortal. What's wrong with me? July Montgomery never would have betrayed a sacred trust."

"July Montgomery?"

"He was a friend of my father's who used to live around here. He had principles and he never betrayed them, even unto death."

"Do you mean that shy guy who used to milk a few cows on a little farm outside Words? The one who sometimes hid when the mailman delivered his mail?"

"Did you know him?"

"A little."

"Then you know that he never would have done what I did. His cords were tied with much stronger fiber."

"To the best of my knowledge, July never had a pet bat."

"Well, if he did, he never would have betrayed him. He wasn't a sniveling coward like me."

"But he didn't have one, so nobody knows what he would have done."

"Milton would be alive today if I had only resisted, but the better part of me didn't speak up. It went into hiding, and the other part of me, the demon part of me—the believe-what-you're-told-and-do-what-they-say part of me—took over. I could have taken a stand. I could have . . ." August's voice trailed off.

"Come on, let's get out of here," said the hermit. "I'll show you some of my ginseng plants, teach you how to identify them, how to tell when the roots are ready to come up."

"Is this another attempt to change the subject from the horrors of being August Helm?"

"No, it's a way for me to have some company while I check on my plants."

"Fine," said August. "But let's look for the Wild Boy too. I've decided to join up with him. I've lived in civilization too long."

They walked across the melon field and into the woods, moving slowly through the oppressive heat, stopping frequently to drink from August's canteen. Here and there, the hermit pointed out ginseng plants, growing in shady, moist areas and along hillside runoffs.

"They like wet conditions," he said. "You can't pick them until there are at least five rings on the neck and three sets of leaves. It's not legal to sell anything younger than that."

"Who buys ginseng?" asked August.

"Most of Wisconsin's ginseng goes to Asia. And oddly enough, if you buy ginseng in Wisconsin it probably came from Asia."

"Why?"

"Wisconsin is one of the few places in the world where ginseng grows wild, and wild ginseng is worth ten times what the cultivated varieties bring. Asians value it more than we do."

"How can anyone tell the difference?"

"By the root color. Wild-grown is darker, the rings on the neck closer together."

"Why are you snipping the leaves off that one?" asked August, wiping sweat from his forehead.

"Other ginseng hunters started coming through here after the DNR began charging license fees, and I don't want them to find this one. The root still grows, even without the leaves. In fact, when a field has been grazed for many years and then the livestock are taken away, very old ginseng sometimes comes up again the following spring."

"Why does buying a license mean there will be more hunters?"

"Not necessarily more, just more determined. When people pay for a license they expect some return. It used to be that ginseng hunters were more casual. Most of the people who found it were loggers or fence builders. But the new license requirements changed all that. Now people think, By god, if I bought a license I'm going to find some."

"What are you doing now?" asked August, watching him crush red seed berries.

"These seeds have matured early, so we'll pick them, crush them, and plant them in a circle around the mother plant, starting a future crop. It takes about ten years to grow a big root."

"What's that plant?" asked August, pointing down.

"Jewelweed," said the hermit.

"It looks like little pieces of jewelry strung on heavy green thread."
He reached for the plant.

"Easy there, August. Jewelweed is a touch-me-not, a succulent. They shrink up if you pick them. Best to enjoy them where they are. Their juice is also a natural treatment for poison ivy."

They moved along slowly, observing more plant life, and after several hours the air became even more humid. The milky haze covering the sun darkened to greenish purple, and the lazy breeze died. The birds, squirrels, and insects grew silent. It was as if the entire valley were holding its breath, waiting.

"You'd better be getting home," said the hermit. "A big storm's coming."

"I don't care if I never go home again," said August. "I want to join the Wild Boy."

"Well, I'm heading back myself. Come with me if you want. This is going to be a gully-washer."

They climbed up onto the nearest ridge and followed it in the direction of the hermit's hut, then descended into an open meadow where even the butterflies remained still, clutching the tops of coneflowers, their wings folded tight.

The hermit stopped. "Listen," he said.

"What?" asked August, looking into the darkening sky.

"The plants are talking to each other about the approaching rain. They can already taste it."

The heads of prairie grasses jiggled and danced, and the leaves on distant trees turned on their stems and began to rattle and hum. The ground quivered. A few warm drops fell out of the sky, plummeting to the ground like arrows of clear glass, disappearing without a trace.

They picked up the pace, moving quickly through the thigh-high prairie grass. The drops increased, along with a louder rattling of leaves and faint, distant thunder. Layers of the greenish purple western sky ignited briefly along the horizon.

Reaching the end of the prairie, the hermit and August followed a deer trail uphill, climbing through bracken, young white pine, and scrub oak. Up ahead of them on the trail, a shape darted in and out of view. A little ways farther, August saw it again, moving between trees.

"It's—"

"I know," said the hermit. "The child's been with us for an hour or so."

"How can you know that?" asked August. "It's not like I haven't been paying attention."

"You have to know what to pay attention to."

The rain picked up in intensity, and thunder shook the limbs of trees, then tore into the sky. The first bolt of lightning leaped into jagged view, bright and searing.

As the hermit started into the next valley, the Wild Boy stepped into plain sight in the distance. He stood on a piece of rock at the top of the hill.

"It would be best for you to go home now," said the hermit, looking from the child on the rock to August. "We're going to get a lot of water here."

"I told you," said August. "I want to join up with him."

And then August took off, running uphill.

The hermit continued into the next valley while August ran up the hill. But when he reached the top the Wild Boy was gone.

That makes sense, thought August, feeling abandoned and winded. What would he want with me, anyway? I'm nothing but a traitor and a coward. I don't even want myself.

The full fury of the storm was now directly overhead, and the locomotive sound of the wind against the trees was broken only by the thunder and lightning. The rain fell in buckets, blown into slanting sheets and waves.

August felt his way under a protective overhang in the rock. He tried to bring his breathing under control. He swung his legs over the ledge, leaned back on his arms, and watched the wall of rain.

An hour or so later the rain began to let up. The sky turned from black to gray.

The earth had absorbed all it could, and now water poured out of the rocky sides of the hills across the valley, turning the little creek at the bottom into a raging torrent. August watched on as the water moved beyond its banks, forming a river beneath him. Soon the valley floor was covered by brown rushing water, carrying limbs, branches, rocks, leaves, and uprooted plants.

After another twenty minutes, the clouds cleared enough to allow the sun to break through, and a double rainbow arched across the sky. Still, the valley floor remained under roaring water, and the smell of soaked earth rose up.

August left the protection of the overhang and slowly began to make his way down the hill. By the time he reached the bottom, the river had returned nearly to the banks of the stream, surrounded by a muddy prairie. The prairie grass had been flattened, and clumps of moss, twigs, and leaves deposited in woody shrubs about two feet in the air, marking the earlier water level.

The melon field was too muddy to walk through, but August found what looked to be the safest path and continued on. He'd left his canteen somewhere behind him, but he didn't care enough to return and look for it.

When he finally arrived at home, August took off his muddy shoes and headed for his room. The sight of the sofa struck him like a blow to the chest. The scene of his shameful betrayal three days before unfolded in his memory in dreadful detail.

In his room, August took off his wet clothes and put on dry ones. Then he lay down on the bed and fell asleep.

Minutes later, the door opened silently and Winnie looked in. Her hair was matted against the sides of her face and her clothes were soaked, muddy, and alive with leaves and clinging pieces of humus. Her arms were scratched and bleeding in places. She held in her hand the strap attached to August's canteen.

Fortunes Never Spent

The morning after the flood, Wally and Ivan took the four-wheelers out for a ride. Some of the flooded areas were bigger than baseball fields. They parked and waded into the backwater with landing nets, looking for fish that had washed over the riverbanks.

If the fish were still gulping air, they carried them to the river and put them back. Wally figured they saved some seventy-five of them, and he kept track of the different kinds in his notebook. If the fish were already dead, they threw them into coolers with ice.

When the two coolers they had brought were full, they took them back and put the fish in the freezer in the back of the pole shed. Most were carp and other bottom-feeders, and they didn't bother with any that were less than a couple of feet long. At the end of the morning they had the freezer filled with what Wally called "our turtle food."

Then they found a big tractor-tire inner tube, inflated it, tied a rope to it, and attached the other end to a coffee can filled with concrete. That was the anchor. When the tube was fully rigged they rowed out to the middle of the pond and left it floating there with a couple of dead fish hanging from lines. All day long the tube floated out on the pond like a giant bobber, with the dead fish dangling several feet down into the water.

They were after the giant turtle. They wanted to catch him, or at least to see him close up. But first they had to form a relationship, make a connection. That's what Wally called it, a connection. In time, he said, they'd find the right place to anchor the tube and get the big turtle's attention. Once he started eating the fish, they'd feed him more and more, until he got used to coming to the same place every day. Then they would have him.

After no luck the first day, they moved the tube to a different spot. The next day they rowed out and pulled up the fish tied to the tube. They had clearly decayed, but none of them had been touched.

"Maybe we should replace these with fresher ones," Ivan suggested.

Wally declined. "Turtles smell underwater," he said. "Before long he won't be able to resist. The more rotten those fish are, the more they'll smell like a morning bakery shop to that turtle."

Then he took out his notebook and wrote, "No. 289: The smell of baking bread."

Ivan rowed farther away from the dock, towing the tube. "What's the point of writing down all those things you're going to miss after you die? It isn't going to change anything."

"I don't want to be surprised."

"What difference does it make?"

"A great deal, I think," Wally replied, relaxing in the back of the boat and gazing over the pond. "You see, Ivan, after my wife died there were many things about her I missed, and I was unprepared for most of them. I knew I'd miss her, but I didn't know I'd miss her when I got up in the middle of the night to go to the bathroom. And there were all kinds of things like that, like how she hummed when she drank coffee in the morning. That little habit seemed like nothing at the time, and I paid no attention to it. But after she was gone, for crying out loud, remembering those things nearly killed me. I should have just sat there in the kitchen every morning and done nothing but listen to her hum while she sipped coffee and looked out the window. It was like having a fortune in my own house that I never bothered to spend. I should have paid closer attention."

"Well, why didn't you?"

"Because I was a damn fool, Ivan. I didn't have enough sense to know what I was going to miss. Like this one time twenty years ago or more. I was driving down the road and saw something that looked like a white camel standing in a pasture. I just kept on going, and I wonder to this day what it was. But I don't intend to miss anything from now on. I finally woke up."

"How about here?" asked Ivan. They were just beyond the edge of some floating weeds, twenty or thirty feet from shore. The flat shiny leaves rolled in the waves made by the boat, and minnows darted just below the surface.

"This looks pretty good," said Wally.

Ivan helped him pick up the cement-filled coffee can and throw it overboard. It made a sploshing sound and then sank down quickly through the water, yanking yellow rope after it.

"Do you think he might be close by?" Ivan asked, staring into the water.

"You bet," replied Wally. "One thing for sure, he knows about every movement on this pond, every ripple. This is his kingdom. He sees all, hears all, and knows all. He's the boss of this pond world. Every time an oar slides into the water—no matter how quietly—his eyes pop open."

"Then he knows we're here now? He knows about these dead fish?"

"He sure does."

"Why hasn't he eaten any yet?"

"He's still watching, thinking, waiting for us to move them into just the right place. He might even wait and see what happens when something else eats one or two of those fish before he does. See, that's why those government men couldn't net him when they dragged the pond. They moved too quickly, without showing respect for his age and intelligence. I bet that turtle just dug a hole in the bottom of the pond and climbed into it. And he lay there smiling as the net passed over him."

"But we're going to catch him, aren't we?" said Ivan, looking into the water and wishing he could see the turtle.

"You bet we are."

As Ivan rowed back to the dock, Wally wrote something else down in his notebook.

When they went inside, the house was empty. Dart had gone shopping, Amy had driven Kevin into town for a checkup at the hospital, and Buck was in Red Plain at the work site. Wally went upstairs to his room to lie down. The afternoon light was just right for dreaming, he said.

Ivan went into Kevin's room, fired up one of his video games, and was just getting into it when the doorbell rang.

It was the ex-prisoner, standing on the other side of the door in a tight-fitting black T-shirt, jeans, and boots. Ivan hadn't heard anyone drive up, but now he saw the motorcycle out in the front lot.

"I'm Blake," he said. "I don't know if you remember me, Ivan, but I met you the other day at your friend August's house."

Ivan said he remembered. Then he noticed a couple of insects flattened against the man's face, and a whole lot more splattered on his T-shirt and arms.

"Is your mother here?"

"She went to the grocery store."

"How long do you think she'll be gone?"

"Maybe an hour."

"Do you think it would be all right for me to wait here until she comes back?"

"Maybe," said Ivan.

"Is there someone else here I should ask?"

"Wally's taking a nap and Flo is beading, so it's probably better not to disturb them."

"I'll just wait out here then," he said. "Is that all right with you?"

"Sure."

Ivan closed the door and went back inside.

About ten minutes later he came out again. Blake was sitting on the front steps, smoking. When he saw Ivan he flipped the cigarette into the yard.

"What do you want with my mother?" asked Ivan.

"I need to talk to her," he said.

"What for?"

"We used to know each other."

"When?"

"A long time ago."

"Were you a friend of hers?"

"I'd like to think so."

"Does that mean yes or no?"

"Mostly yes."

"You took August's bat from his dad," Ivan said. "You said the government testers would kill him, and you said you hated bats."

"That's right."

"August would rather have died himself than have his bat die."

"I feel really badly about what he's going through," said Blake. "Really, I do. It's hard to get over something like that."

"He'll never get over it," Ivan said. "Other people might, but not August. He wasn't made that way. He's different. Once something gets inside him it never comes out."

"He'll get another bat," Blake said.

"See, that's just what I mean. People always say things like that, but to August that doesn't mean anything. Milton wasn't a bat for him. He was Milton."

"Ivan, I promise your friend will get another bat," said Blake.

"I know him a lot better than you do, and I promise he'll never get over Milton. I know him better than anyone. Nothing will ever come between us."

"How did you two get to be such good friends?"

"It just happened, I guess."

"Are you in the same grade at school?"

"This year we will be. They're making me do fifth grade over again."

"That sucks."

"No kidding. But at least August and I will be together."

"When I was your age I would have given anything for a friend like that," said Blake. "And as far as that goes, I'd give anything now."

Ivan sat down next to him on the step. Blake smelled like cigarette smoke.

"So, how do you like living here?" Blake asked.

"I like it fine and so does Mother."

"It's an awfully big house."

"It doesn't seem that big anymore."

"A person could get lost inside a place this big."

"Naw," said Ivan. "If you want, I could show you around. I mean, while you're waiting."

"Do you think it would be okay?"

"It's my house too," said Ivan, and with that they went inside. After Blake took off his boots, Ivan showed him the first floor.

"Someone's been doing a lot of work here," he said in the dining room.

"That's Mrs. Roebuck. She's getting everything just the way she wants it. We all help her, but mostly she does it herself. This house used to belong to Flo, and Mrs. Roebuck wants it just the way it was back then."

"I see," he said.

"This is our apartment up here on the right, and this here on the left is the kitchen and pantry."

"I suppose your mother spends a lot of her time in there."

"She spends a lot of time everywhere."

They went out on the back deck and looked over the pond.

"Impressive," Blake said. "How deep is it?"

"Real deep," replied Ivan. "See that black tube out there?"

"What about it?"

"Wally and I put it there. We're going to catch the devil. Kevin says he's hiding inside a giant turtle. Wally and I are after him."

"Good luck with that."

On the second floor they walked around whispering because they didn't want to wake Wally. Ivan took his guest through the old billiard room and past the door to Buck and Amy's bedroom, then up the back stairs to the third floor. They crept past Flo's room and Ivan showed him the door to the library.

"You've got a library up here?"

"Mrs. Roebuck's grandfather used to teach college. He kept his books here—thousands of 'em."

"No kidding."

"They keep it locked, but the key's right here in this crack in the base-board. I'll show you."

Ivan opened the door and they went inside. All four walls were covered with books. There was a table and two chairs, and nothing else but the smell of old paper.

"Why do they keep this locked?" whispered Blake.

"Something about protecting books. Mrs. Roebuck says she's going to wait to the very end to fix this room up. It's what she calls her jewel—something to do with her grandfather. I guess he wrote some books himself."

Blake walked from shelf to shelf, studying the books. "What did he write about?"

"Something to do with studying God a long time ago."

He stopped at one place, selected a book and thumbed through it, then took out another.

"You know," said Ivan, "they wouldn't mind if you want to borrow a book."

Then Ivan and Blake heard a car coming up the drive, and hurried out of the library. Ivan locked the door and replaced the key. They went downstairs.

Outside, Ivan's mother was standing in the lot holding a big sack of groceries, staring at the motorcycle with a hard look on her face. Blake just stood there motionless on the porch, looking at her. Then he and Ivan walked over.

Dart looked up from the motorcycle, and when she and Blake looked at each other their eyes got watery big. Blake's hands were shaking.

"What are you doing here?" Dart demanded.

"I came to talk to you," he said.

"We've got nothing to talk about, Blake. Nothing."

"Yes we do," he said.

"No we don't," she said.

The look on her face was like nothing Ivan had ever seen before. It was as if she were crying and madder than blazes at the same time. Her whole body was shaking, and when Ivan looked over at Blake again, he was shaking too. And their faces looked like they were both freezing.

"It's good to see you again, Danielle," he said, his voice breaking up.

"Get out of here!" she shouted. Tears streamed down her cheeks.

"Ivan and I have been talking," Blake said.

That's the first time she noticed Ivan. "Go inside," she snapped. "Now."

Ivan went toward the house, but only as far as the front porch.

"I wanted to come as soon as I got out," said Blake. "I thought about you every day, and then I asked Bee about—"

Dart threw the sack of groceries at him. "Get out of here!" she yelled. "Get out of here. Leave me alone."

The door behind Ivan opened. Wally came out and sat down beside him. "Is that Blake Bookchester?" he asked.

"Yes," replied Ivan.

"I thought so. Do you think I should go over there?"

"I wouldn't if I were you. You might get hit by a can of soup. Now be quiet, I'm trying to hear what they're saying."

But even with Wally not making a sound, it was hard to tell what they were saying. Blake was talking in a normal voice, which was hard to hear from that far away, and Dart's words came out too fast to separate them.

"Getoutofhere!"

"You never wrote after I . . . later then when . . . I didn't understand."

"Youleftmealoneyoubastard!"

"I tried to . . . then after that . . ."

At that point Dart went over to the motorcycle, shoved it over onto its side, and started kicking and jumping up and down on the tank.

"Danielle, stop that."

"Getoutofhereleavemealoneyou'regoingtoruineverythingyouonlycame heretohurtmegetoutofhere!"

Weed War

After the heavy rains, Winnie weeded her garden. The soil's friability allowed for a strategic victory over enemy plants. Even the most stubbornly rooted species complied, and Winnie found delicious satisfaction in pulling on damp weedy stalks and feeling them yield all the way down. She smiled as she remembered previous times, when even the tiniest invasive plant necessitated the intervention of trowels, diggers, and shovels. And then when they finally did come out, their roots either busted off, seeding the next weed war, or came up clinging to sizable chunks of earth. Now, the weeds slid out cleanly, ready for stacking.

Rather than feeling badly about extinguishing the life of a happily growing organism, Winnie reasoned that when growing conditions were optimal—the soil moist, fecund, and alive with the mineral magic of life—the earth simply let go of its weeds. Even better, on this particular morning some had already been pushed up an inch or so, as if the ground itself had ejected the weeds to make room for plants with giant colored heads, elegant stems, and extravagantly veined leaves, plants painstakingly selected from seed catalogs in the depths of winter. Rich soil reveled in exotic plants that needed assistance in reaching their full potential, while the more hale and hearty varieties grew everywhere. Winnie understood that a well-kept garden was an expression of the invisible splendor of the dirt beneath it.

And yet as she crawled from place to place, leaving behind mounds of extracted weeds as big as muskrat houses, she struggled with a far more menacing internal adversary. By noon, she had won the ground war but been battered to defeat by this more personal struggle, and gave up the pleasure of gardening altogether. The sight of her soiled hands, wrists, arms, elbows, knees, and clothes mirrored the condition of her soul, and she walked over and lay down on the painted bench next to the fountain. Curled up on her side, she wondered what she was going to do with herself.

The last several months had been an ongoing psychic disaster, culminating in the recent debacle with her son. How could she have been so negligent? She knew August did not understand the potential consequences of carrying his beloved bat around in public. She also knew he had been taking Milton out with him more and more often. She knew the time and place of his talk on White Nose Syndrome, and she knew the subject meant a great deal to him. She knew young hooligans often attended the county fair where August was scheduled to speak, and that she should be present. She knew her meeting with the church's board of trustees could be postponed, and she knew that when August was with Ivan the chances of him getting into trouble increased exponentially. And finally, she knew that if something very bad happened it could drive a wedge between her and August, choking off all the joy in both their lives.

And yet she had let it happen. In fact, she was guilty of an even more serious infraction. Curled up on the bench with her eyes closed, she tried appealing to a higher court, but the judge in that potentially more forgiving venue had apparently gone on vacation.

Winnie knew that her loyalties were no longer in their proper order. It was not just that she had been negligent about August taking his bat to the fair, but also what she did after everything went bad. Called away from the board of trustees to meet with the sheriff, the two youths who had assaulted her son, and their parents, Winnie was thrown into a state of supreme agitation. Accusations flew, making her feel like a harried bull in an arena.

She admitted that her son had a pet bat. No, he did not have a permit to keep a wild bat, nor did she or her husband. Yes, she agreed that people should obey the law, and yes, that included state laws regulating wildlife. The bat had been seen regularly by a veterinarian, and checked for communicable diseases, but no, that did not mean owning a bat was a particularly good idea. She agreed there was no excuse for a bat biting someone, and she was very sorry the boys had been bitten. And no, being sorry did not make everything right, and of course no one would want to be bitten by a bat even if someone else felt sorry about it. Yes, she understood very well that her son had given a talk about bats at the fair and advocated for costly measures to protect bats, and yes, she was aware that these were difficult economic times. There were many people out of work and many more without health insurance, and yes, the price of gasoline was rising. No, she did not think bats should come before people. Yes, she understood that many people had strong feelings about bats, but she did not agree that because many people had strong feelings about bats, their feelings should be respected above those whose feelings were less strong, though she agreed in general about respecting other people's feelings when they were in a state of high dudgeon, even when they weren't especially respecting yours. No, she wasn't trying to talk fancy. Yes, she agreed that if a rabid bat bit someone and that person went untreated they could possibly die. Yes, she agreed that her son had done something wrong, but no, she did not think carrying a bat in his pocket was the same as packing a concealed weapon. She did not agree that her son had attempted to cause any trouble, nor that he had goaded the bigger boys into knocking him down and kicking him repeatedly. Yes, it certainly did appear as if the two boys who attacked her son had gotten the worst of it in the end. No, she did not condone violence, not for any reason. Yes, there obviously had been some violence here, but no, she did not agree that the initial assault was perpetrated by a couple of good-natured boys just being boys, only to be followed by the real violence. Yes, she knew that her son's friend had occasionally been in trouble at school, and that he would be repeating fifth grade. Yes, Ivan's mother was unmarried, and Danielle's father and stepfather had both been in prison, but Winnie didn't see how this was relevant. No, as far as she knew, Ivan and his mother were not Muslims, and never had been. No, she didn't have proof of that. Yes, she was a Christian pastor. And no, she was not the kind of pastor who didn't believe in the Bible. She was not aware that the two boys who assaulted her son were both model students who had never been in any kind of trouble before, nor that they had both won prizes in the junior rodeo competition in Marengo. No, she did not know that their fathers were members of the Lions, and that one of them had served on the chamber of commerce. Yes, her husband, Jacob, owned the Words Repair Shop, and he did employ a convicted felon. And yes, she had even encouraged him in this. She did know Jack Station, and that he

were no longer yielding meaningful benefits. Established ways of thinking had led her astray, and the spiritual life she had always wanted to live was slipping away.

Obviously, the time had come to leave the church.

At first appearance, this idea seemed so foreign, heretical, and insane that Winnie's whole body lurched. Sitting up on the bench, she prayed for forgiveness. I didn't mean it; the thought wasn't mine.

From an early age she'd found refuge inside Christianity. Its psychological truths had sustained her, given her hope, courage, and helped her form a valid identity. Then she had fastened onto the mystical branch of her faith like a vine twining toward sunlight. Leaving the church would be like leaving her true home, abandoning everything she believed in, giving up her part of the shared responsibility for mankind.

I'll just get a cart and haul these weeds away, she thought. And I'll completely forget I ever entertained such an absurd idea.

But even as she carted the extracted weeds out of her garden and placed them into the composting cage Jacob had made from the shell of an old baler, she already knew the idea of leaving the church was not going away. Despite her objections, it now resided in a secure region of her mind, watching her.

Oh no you don't. Stay there as long as you like, but I won't ever think about you again.

Finding a new reservoir of resolve, she finished hauling all the weeds away from her garden. As the sun set over the western ridge, she sighed with satisfaction over how happily her flowers were growing and how nice they looked. Inside, she showered, dressed in light, comfortable clothes, chopped up vegetables for a stew for dinner, and cooked it in a cast-iron pot.

When Jacob came home he devoured three-quarters of it, while August picked around the edges of his plate and went back to his room without saying more than three words. The splinter in her heart worked in deeper.

"It takes time," said Jacob.

"Oh, I believe that," said Winnie, carrying tea for them both over to the sofa. "Or at least I'm trying to. That's one of the problems with time. It's hard to trust."

"August is resilient," said Jacob. "You're his mother, after all."

"Nonsense," said Winnie, and began to explain how all this was her fault. Jacob stopped her. He didn't like it when she talked that way. It upset him. So instead she offered, "He's strong in a weak way, Jacob. His pain has always been difficult to eradicate."

"I know," said Jacob, sipping from his tea. He wanted sex. It had been almost four days, which was a long time for him. Winnie was thankful for the diversion.

Later that night, after Jacob had fallen asleep and the only noises in the house other than his breathing came from insects and boards adjusting to changing moisture content, Winnie quietly climbed out of bed and crept down the hallway. The door to August's room was not quite closed, and she nudged it open a crack, just enough to look inside. There were no lights on, but light coming in through the window allowed her to see the outline of objects.

The bed was still made, flat across the top. August was sitting in a chair next to the open window, wearing his faded blue pants and a T-shirt with the words *There's Something Out There* stenciled on the front and back. His homemade bat detector rested on the sill, its white wire running up into his ear.

Winnie silently collapsed in the doorway.

August moved the detector, changing its angle, then moved it again. He leaned back in the chair and after a while looked as if he might fall asleep, a position Winnie had found him in several mornings ago. For some reason it comforted him to slip away while listening to the crackling sounds of bats flying through the night sky.

Bats, thought Winnie, I hate them. She leaned against the doorpost, pulled her robe more tightly around her, and thought about going to sleep herself.

Suddenly August rose to his feet and pressed the detector flat against the screen.

Winnie stood up, pushing the door open. August didn't notice. She could sense him trying to contain his excitement. He took the screen out of the window so he could point his detector directly up at the sky. She could feel his heart pounding inside her.

Then she heard the faint clicking of a bat in the room. Its dark shape appeared first in one place and then another, darting about frenetically, swooping toward August again and again, fluttering around him like a butterfly around a butterfly weed.

August turned on the desk lamp and a reddish-purple bat landed on his shoulder. He took the creature in his hands, inspected it, and carefully removed something attached to one of its legs. Then he found the magnifying glass in his desk drawer and looked through it at a tiny piece of paper. Winnie felt the pure emotion burst open inside him as he turned in the direction of his parents' bedroom and cried, "Mom, Mom!"

Winnie rushed into the room and August placed the tiny piece of rolled-up paper in her hand. In minuscule print, it read: Milton + Dye = Our Secret.

"He's back," said August. Then, choking on his words, he continued. "Mom, I'm currently experiencing a joy that is strangely too heavy to bear. Is it possible to be too fully alive?"

"No," said Winnie. "It isn't."

"I'm afraid I've been very wrong about some things."

"Me too," said Winnie, and they both began laughing and crying at the same time. When Jacob came into the room they handed the piece of paper to him. After reading it, he cried and laughed harder than both of them together. "Well, okay, then," he said. "In that purple color I wouldn't have recognized him myself."

Heresy

The day after the return of August's bat, Winnie had several committee meetings to attend at the church, and in the evening she led Bible study. After everyone had gone home, she remained in the church for several minutes longer, sitting in a pew and praying. Then she turned out the lights and locked the door behind her when she left.

It took less than five minutes to drive over to July Montgomery's old farmhouse. Following the headlights of her little car up the long driveway, she parked next to the shed and climbed out.

The farmyard seemed unusually still, dark, and welcoming. She remembered the several times she'd been here since July's death. The feeling then had been decidedly different, empty and unwelcoming. Now she could smell honeysuckle growing somewhere nearby.

Apparently Blake had never installed a yard light. July never had one, either. He had always liked to see the night sky.

Winnie walked over to the empty corncrib and stood in front of it. This was where July had died, caught in his tractor's power takeoff while loading ear corn into a wagon. The experience of finding him had reoriented her life, forced her into deeper levels of engagement and higher planes of commitment. She took a deep breath and smelled the honeysuckle again. She remembered eating breakfast with July once. If she could relive that time now it would be different. She would treasure every morsel of biscuit, every movement of eye. She would prolong her departure, ask if there were any chores around the farm that she could help with, set aside her own agenda, and live completely in the moment.

Winnie followed the dirt path to the house, climbed up the steps, and knocked on the front door. As she waited, she looked around. The porch and everything else seriously needed carpentry and paint. In fact, everything around looked rundown and shabby.

After knocking again, she tried the door. It was unlocked.

"Hello," she called. "Blake?"

Nothing.

She opened the door. It was even darker inside.

"Blake? Blake? It's me, Winnie."

She found a light switch, turned it on, and stepped into the kitchen.

The old-fashioned green linoleum was worn down in places to the black underlayment. The house smelled of mold, mildew, and dust from an earlier era. A good scrubbing was clearly needed here, but Winnie repressed her cleaning instincts and indulged a few moments longer in the complex set of smells, letting it open up memories. It had been almost fifteen years since July lived here. August hadn't even been born. In fact, she and Jacob were not together yet then. Her long hair, when combed out, had fallen below her waist.

"Blake?" she called again, feeling increasingly self-conscious about the naked sound of her voice in his home. The darkened doorway into the next room beckoned. She wondered what lay on the other side.

She resisted the urge, turned out the light, and went back outside, closing the door behind her.

The farmyard seemed unusually quiet and welcoming. She sat down on the top step, and once again her store of memories opened for business. She browsed its narrow aisles, letting old feelings wash over her.

She felt at peace for the first time in many months, perhaps years, and while she dissolved pleasantly into this sensation she noticed a spot of light moving along the horizon. It advanced rapidly, flying low over the dark landscape. The single beam changed direction slightly, and then sped ahead again.

When the light reached the drive, it turned in and rushed down the lane. Once in the farmyard, she could hear the engine and the tires on the gravel and dirt.

The motorcycle moved across the grass and stopped at the foot of the steps. Blake climbed off.

"Mrs. Helm," he said, walking up to her. "Is something wrong?"

She could smell his leather jacket and the fifty miles of night air clinging to him. His dark hair bristled like a weedy hillside in the skylight. The motor-cycle's engine sighed and snapped as it cooled.

"I wanted to thank you in person," she said.

"What for?"

"You know what. Don't fool with me about something like this."

"Oh, Milton. August came into the shop today. He thanked me already."

"I know he did, but I wanted to thank you myself. Where have you been?"

"Riding," he said.

"You shouldn't be doing that," said Winnie. "It's breaking the terms of your release."

"I know, but sometimes the difference between doing something and not doing it is like the difference between living and not living. Let me take you for a ride."

"No," she said. But even as she declined, she heard in her voice something different. "I've never been on one of those things," she added. Then she thought for a moment and spoke again. "We couldn't go very far."

"Done," said Blake. He hopped off the steps and started the engine. "Climb on."

Winnie walked down and stood behind him. "Don't look," she said, hiking her skirt up enough to allow her to climb onto the seat behind him. She hooked the heels of her loafers behind the foot pegs.

"Ready?" asked Blake, feeling her behind him, fitting around him.

"You know, this seat isn't very comfortable."

"Sorry," said Blake. "Passenger seats are a bit of an afterthought on bikes like these."

They moved down the driveway, onto the road.

"Why is there a hole in the back of your jacket?" she asked.

"In memory of Spinoza, I poked a knife through it."

"But Spinoza was attacked by someone else."

"I know. But in my case I have no one else to blame for the time I spent in prison. It was a Blake-on-Blake crime. Is there anything else you want to say?"

"Not really. Why?"

"Because it's time to go fast."

Blake turned the throttle and they shot ahead. Winnie's hair blew away from her head, and she felt as if she were being pulled into a vacuum in the sky. What in the world was I thinking? she wondered, as the dark landscape peeled by. It was the most frightening thing she could ever remember experiencing. And yet on the very edge of her fear she began to detect a different version of herself. This new Winnie had no second thoughts about flying along winding roads at night with her hair in chaos, her skirt pulled up to her hips, and her red car coat flapping behind her like a libertarian flag. She laughed out loud at this realization.

Five miles later, back in the farmyard, Winnie climbed off and straightened her clothes and hair. Blake shut off the engine, set the stand, and stepped away from the bike. "Come in," he said. "I'll make you a cup of coffee."

"I can't drink coffee," said Winnie. "My normal state is already too nervous."

"I've got tea," he said.

She followed him inside.

"In case you're wondering, Mrs. Helm, there were a lot of bats here when I moved in. It wasn't very hard to catch one. No one will ever know the difference, of course. The esteemed officers of the law got their pound of flesh, and we got Milton."

He seated her at the kitchen table, went over to the refrigerator, and set a bowl of giant red grapes in front of her.

Winnie chewed one and swallowed. "These are excellent," she said.

"I know it," he said, putting on a pot of water. "My dad found them at a farmers' market somewhere in Ohio. Take a bag home with you. I don't really like grapes, but there's no way to refuse my dad when it comes to food. I'm sorry it took me so long to decide on the right dye to disguise Milton. In the end I just used Kool-Aid. It will wear off in a couple weeks, but by then it shouldn't matter. I also checked into licensing a wild bat, which isn't very hard. Your veterinarian can help you."

"I'm leaving my church," said Winnie, eating another grape.

"No, you're not," said Blake.

"I am. I can't preach any longer." She could still feel the imprint of the wind against her face, the tug at the roots of her hair.

Blake took off his jacket, threw it over the back of a chair, and sat down across from her. "This is serious, Mrs. Helm. You'll probably feel different tomorrow."

"I won't. I know I won't."

"You can't leave the faith, Mrs. Helm."

"Call me Winnie."

"Okay, but Winnie can't leave the faith, either."

"Yes I can."

"You can't be saying this. Religion isn't something you just walk away from. Where in the world would you go?"

"Others live without it."

"That's fine for them, but not for you. It's part of who you are."

"I'm afraid that's the point. As a preacher I've become someone I don't particularly like."

"What difference does that make? Of course you don't like yourself. That's the first definition of being religious."

"I think we're talking about two different things."

"No we're not, and I should know. I've taken every course on the subject of self-loathing."

Blake got up, poured them both a cup of tea, and set Winnie's in front of her, along with a paper napkin and a spoon. A wind rattled the window in the door as he sat back down across from her. While they drank the steaming liquid, they looked at each other.

"I need to leave the church," said Winnie, breaking the silence.

"Even Spinoza couldn't give up religion," said Blake. "He was excommunicated from his own Jewish community, cast out like a diseased dog. Then he was renounced by the official Christian church. But not even Spinoza could stop worrying about the maddening mystery of spirit and matter. He couldn't stop trying to find a way to see the world as a good place, to find the sacred in the ordinary and live a decent life. The only way to really quit religion is never to have begun thinking about it. The only people who can walk away are those whose imaginations never embraced the idea that behind everything real is something more real, more alive, and more profoundly beautiful. Only people who never thought that way in the first place can be free from religion. People like you and me are doomed."

"I forgot how much I enjoyed talking to you," said Winnie, smiling as she reached for another grape. "You're right, of course. It isn't possible for me to leave my faith, though I admit that when I first thought about leaving the church, it seemed like the same thing. You're right. I just can't preach any longer."

"Keep talking," said Blake, drumming his fingers on the wooden tabletop.

"I'm tired of constantly defending what religion and faith are supposed to be. The ministry forces you to do that. Your success depends on mounting a strong defense, and then what you end up defending are often institutional practices, hierarchical ways of thinking, ceremonies and rituals that you don't even believe in yourself. I mean, maybe you believed in them at one time, but even after you grow out of them, you keep on defending them. Or at least it feels that way to me. The same institutions that first point us toward higher ground later prevent us from reaching it. Maybe other preachers don't have the same problems, but I keep finding myself doing things that embarrass me whenever I think about them."

"Be specific."

"I want the people who pay my salary to approve of me. I'll say things, do things, and even find myself thinking things that will please them. I also discover myself shading what I know to be true in order to conform to what they like to hear. It's not really lying, but it's not completely honest either. Isn't that pathetic?"

"No."

"And worst of all, I find myself all too often doing conniving things—arranging a committee meeting in a particular way, for instance, including details that present me in a favorable light, or pretending I'm better than I am—in order to increase my hold over my congregation. I act in ways intended primarily to make me more secure, to bring me more power."

"How much power can you possibly have in such a little church?" scoffed Blake.

"Power is power."

"Do you still have your own private faith?"

"Of course, and I've been telling myself that for years. I still have my own private faith, but how much does that matter when so little of my time is spent with it? I mean, the life I always wanted to live is escaping me. I want to live in a more authentic way, to believe in nothing yet have faith in everything."

"I see what you mean," said Blake, standing and pacing back and forth between the refrigerator and table. "It's like prison. Everything about it conditions you in exactly one way—to make you bitter, angry, and mean. It's part of the design. The police who bring you in, the warden, the guards, even the other prisoners and people on the outside—everyone expects you to be bitter, angry, and mean. And if you relax for even a minute, that's the shape you'll take. If you don't pay attention, don't fight back, that's exactly what will happen. The forces are constant, like gravity almost. The only way to be true to yourself in prison is to persist in remaining a decent and compassionate person. I failed many times, to be sure—but at least I was always aware of that."

"I don't see how that's at all the same," said Winnie.

"Well, it is," said Blake, sitting down again and looking across at her with blazing eyes. "I don't know how to explain it, but it's the same."

"Too much of my life is spent fighting that particular fight," said Winnie.

"What else would you do?"

"I don't know. And my family does need the income."

"I'll bet if you talk to Jacob about this, he'd tell you to quit. He'd want you to do whatever you think is right. He'd insist on it, actually. He loves you."

"I know."

"You could begin by living on grapes," said Blake, opening the refrigerator and taking out a sack. "Here."

"Thank you," said Winnie, standing up from the table.

"I didn't mean to suggest that you leave."

"I know, but I should be going."

"Wait," said Blake, "I'll walk you to your car."

Blake grabbed his coat and waited for her by the door. Winnie had never taken off her coat, and she walked over toward him. They stood close together in the doorway. Their eyes found each other, and with an astonishment that didn't really astonish her, Winnie noticed a monstrous surge of energy. An organic gate snapped open and a path of passion appeared, filled with slippery events that would not have been possible before. A swelling physical sensation threatened to crowd out all her past. She could feel her face flushing, her heart beating faster.

Blake's face flushed as well and he reached out with both hands. Winnie put her hands into his and Blake drew her toward him.

"Mrs. Helm," he said, "you've honored me with your visit. As long as I live, I'll never forget it."

Then he walked her out to her car and Winnie drove back home. As she followed her headlights around darkened corners, she smiled upon recognizing that there clearly was a submerged part of her, beyond the control of her personality, that never slept. In fact, it was always planning new ways of engaging her. She drove faster, hoping to preserve the excitement aroused by the unexpected encounter in the doorway for later use with her husband.

Jacob was waiting up for her, reading a magazine.

"After Bible study, I went over to visit Blake," she explained. "I wanted to thank him in person."

"I thought that's probably where you were."

"He was out riding his motorcycle, breaking his curfew."

"I know. He's going to get in trouble. What's in the bag?"

"Grapes."

Coming Alive

After work, Blake rode to Red Plain and waited in the cement plant's parking lot for Bee to come out. When she did, he asked if she had time to talk.

"I'd like that," she said.

They walked several blocks and sat down on a bench along the sidewalk. Blake bought two cans of soda from a machine along the way, and they drank them overlooking the back of the feed mill and the front of a secondhand store. Light traffic moved slowly along Main Street, one block away. Occasionally a car or van would turn off and drive past them along the alleyway. Most of the drivers waved, and Bee waved back.

"Let me say right out, I'm not comfortable talking about this," said Blake. "I'm not. But I have to, and I didn't know who else—"

"It's about time," interrupted Bee, smiling uncomfortably and sipping from her can of cola. "How did it go?"

"How did what go?"

"You must have seen Danielle."

"How did you know?"

"Just a lucky guess. How did it go?"

"Not very well," said Blake.

"Maybe she just needs a little time to get used to the idea of seeing you again."

"It seemed a lot worse than that. She knocked my bike over and stomped on the tank. I pulled out the dents and polished them down, but one left a crease. You can still see it, even with new paint. It looks terrible. I'll show you."

Blake ran back to his motorcycle, rode it over next to her, and parked it.

"See?" he said, sitting back down on the bench.

"Sorry, I don't."

"It's right there when the light's right. It's awful."

"Maybe you should have called before you went over."

"Then I wouldn't have seen her at all."

"Did you meet Ivan?"

"Yes."

"What did you think of him?"

"Nice kid. He looks a lot like her."

"Who else does he look like?"

Blake frowned and rubbed his hand through his hair.

"Look," he said. "I need to tell you something, but I don't know how to say it. Prison does that to you. Those few good memories you carry in there, you think about them so much they become hard to talk about. They're like private rituals. But this is important, probably the most important thing in my life."

"Okay," said Bee, waiting.

Blake turned and looked directly at her. "I love Danielle," he said, as if he were confessing that he had tuberculosis.

"I thought that might be true," said Bee.

"You couldn't have," he said. "I've never told anyone, not even her. I've never said those words out loud before, and I might never do it again. You couldn't have known."

"I love your father," said Bee. "So I'm at least a little familiar with the feeling."

Blake's face went blank. What she just said had nothing whatsoever to do with what he was talking about. Absolutely nothing. The consuming passion he felt for Danielle could not possibly be associated with any love she might have for his father. The two were simply incompatible. The latter type of love was buoyant, friendly, cheerful, and familial; a comforting convenience, good for everyone involved. The former was a smoldering febrile disease, heavy, sorrowful, alienating, and cursed, the greatest suffering Blake could imagine. No one else had ever experienced it before, certainly not in the same way, and if they had they probably hadn't survived very long. The word used to talk about the two feelings was the same, admittedly, but it referred to planets with completely different temperate zones.

"I don't care who she might have slept with," he declared. "That means nothing to me. It means less than nothing. You have to understand. I love her, everything about her."

"I always thought Ivan looked a little like you," said Bee.

"What? Like me?" The blank stare returned. "No."

"Yes he does."

"No."

An uncomfortable silence settled between them, as if thoughts were burning like old tires inside it.

Then the bones in Blake's face dissolved.

"God, I never thought of that," he mumbled.

"This surprises me," said Bee.

"What a fool I am," he replied. The rest of the bones in his body softened and he sagged on the bench like an empty jacket and pair of pants.

He looked away from Bee. At ground level, life throbbed on a more manageable scale. A red ant hurriedly carried a yellow speck of something through a dense forest of grass blades, followed by another ant of the same color and size that wasn't carrying anything. They moved in a jiggling manner, lurching to the right and then the left, but generally heading toward the sidewalk. An identical third ant joined them, and they jiggled around briefly in a six-legged circle dance before moving off in a different direction, and disappearing into a patch of clover.

"Can I talk?" asked Bee.

"Please do."

"When Dart came to work at Cement, I think it was her first real job after her sister committed suicide—"

"Stop right there," said Blake. "Stop right there. I knew she had a sister, but I never heard anything about her sister offing herself."

"You should have. You probably should have known a whole lot more about her than you did."

"She never talked about herself."

"You should have asked her, Blake."

"Why did her sister kill herself?"

"I don't know for sure, and I'm not sure anyone else does either. She dropped out of school, and people always said her stepfather had put her in a family way."

"Surely not."

"That's what people said."

"Why didn't Danielle tell me?"

"She probably didn't trust you enough yet."

"She should have."

"Should, should, should."

"What else?"

"After Danielle was hired they put her in the warehouse, where we keep the mix, stone, and sand. It's rough, dirty work. They also used her to clean tracks and inside the mixers—another job no one else wanted. She kept to herself, ate her lunch alone, hardly ever said a word for the first six or eight months.

"About a year later," Bee continued, "the plant manager brought Danielle out of the warehouse and assigned her to work in the office with me. That's when I got to know her."

"Why are you telling me this?"

"Because the learning curve is steep in the real world, and there are things you need to know. You're pretty far behind, Blake. You've got to catch up."

"Being in love with my father doesn't make you my mother, you know."

"I'm aware of that, genius."

"Go on."

"After you and Danielle started seeing each other, she changed."

"What do you mean?"

"She began opening up, talking a little. She wasn't so closed off. She'd look out the windows, hoping you'd come by, answered the telephone right away. She'd tell me about races you'd won, the places where the two of you went to eat, what you ate. She took more interest in everything, dressed better, stood with better posture, walked faster, occasionally laughed, and—"

"Why didn't anyone tell me this?"

"Because you're an idiot, Blake, that's why. You and your father both. Most of the time there's no sense telling either of you anything. You simply don't hear. You don't understand what's important until it's too late. No one should have to tell you these things. You should know them. You've got to stop feeling sorry for yourself, and catch up with everyone else. We all carry things around inside us that hurt too much to examine, but you've got to be able to move on at the same time. You have to try to understand how others feel, and make that a part of you."

"My father and I are completely different, but I'm listening, really."

"Then stop staring at your motorcycle."

"I can't help it. That crease really bothers me. I'm going to have to completely redo the whole tank."

"You and Danielle started living together after a couple months, isn't that right?"

"Right."

"Danielle seemed content with that. She thought she finally had something good."

"I never knew what she thought," he said. "She never talked about herself, never told me anything. I spent most of my time trying not to make her angry. She never told me about anything."

"After you got arrested and thrown in prison, Danielle went back to the way she was before you met her, guarded and defensive. Only now she was pregnant and even more scared. She wasn't even eighteen years old. You abandoned her, Blake."

"She seemed as old as I was."

"She never finished high school. She actually lied about her age to get hired. She's three years younger than you, Blake. Was then, is now."

"I never abandoned her!" Blake shouted. "I loved her. Okay, so I agreed to run a package from here to Milwaukee. I did it three or four times. This guy I knew at the foundry would give me three hundred dollars for each trip. That was a lot of money to me. But that's it, no more. Then that guy got busted and the authorities made a deal with him. He turned me and three others in, and they let him go. He told them the exact time I'd be showing up in Milwaukee, and they were waiting for me there."

"You abandoned her."

"I didn't!" yelled Blake, jumping to his feet.

"I'm telling you what it felt like to her."

"I loved her. One of the arresting officers was from around here. He knew I lived with Danielle, and he said he'd been hoping she would be with me. He said he was looking forward to arresting her, to turning her over the trunk of his car and then taking her into the backseat for a long ride to the station. With my hands handcuffed behind me, I head-butted him, knocked him down, and kicked one of his ribs into his lung. They nearly beat me to death with their clubs after that, but I didn't care. Nobody was going to talk that way about her."

"You idiot!" shouted Bee. "That doesn't show you loved her. That just shows how stupid you are. You show how much you love someone by being there for them when they need you, by knowing what they need and anticipating those needs. And do you have any idea what it must have been like for your father to get that call after everything that had happened? Do you have any idea what it's like to raise a child alone? Do you have any idea how—"

"Stop it!" yelled Blake, leaping to his feet again. "She never wrote to me!" he yelled. "Not once."

"Dart had seen her whole family ruined by drinking, drugs, and dealing. She couldn't trust you."

Blake climbed onto his motorcycle and sped off down the street.

Two miles out of Red Plain, he came to a full stop, threw out the stand, and walked around his motorcycle, cursing and spitting on the pavement. The shadows were growing long, the light golden. It was time to get home.

Everyone had turned against him.

Okay, maybe he should have considered the possibility that Ivan was his son. But why hadn't anyone given him a hint? He couldn't be blamed for not knowing. Why hadn't Danielle told him? It wasn't his responsibility to know. He was in prison. Why hadn't Winnie told him on one of her visits, or his father? They must have known, and if they didn't they should have. It was their responsibility. Danielle should have written him a letter.

A slow-moving vehicle climbed the hill. The young driver slowed down even more, stopped, rolled down the window, and asked, "Anything wrong?"

"No," said Blake. "Everything's fine."

"I just wondered," said the youth, poking a cigarette into his mouth and lighting it. "Say, aren't you Blake Bookchester?"

"Unfortunately."

"I heard about you when I was doing time in Portage. You hit a guard at Waupun. We all heard about it."

"How long have you been out?" asked Blake.

"Couple weeks."

"How's it going?"

"Not bad, I guess. Say, what are you doing out here?"

"How old are you?"

"I'm as old as you were when they first sent you up. You want a cold one?"

"No thanks."

"What's the Lockbridge supermax like?"

"What do you want to know?"

"I've heard about it so much I can see it in my mind clear as anything. I can picture just what the center hold looks like, with that narrow aisle leading into it, the exercise cages to the side and back, and the long wire rack between the two main buildings. Is that pretty close?"

"Pretty close."

Blake climbed back onto his motorcycle. "I should be going."

"Maybe I'll see you around. You come out here often?"

"Not really."

As the young man drove off, Blake started his engine and felt it idle beneath him. He could see the crease in the tank.

A month ago, his first ride on the twenty miles of road between where he was now and Luster had taken about forty-five minutes. After nearly daily practice, his best times were now between fifteen and seventeen minutes. He wanted to get below fourteen, but conditions had to be perfect. Other traffic was the biggest obstacle. A farmer with a manure spreader, a utility truck, people on bicycles, and animals in the road—all were hazards that posed temporal setbacks. The road surface was a factor as well. Mud, sand, and leaves on the corners, water and gravel thrown up from the shoulders—they all imposed limits. Even humidity affected the grip of the tires.

He checked his watch, waiting for the second hand to swing up to twelve, and arrived in Luster fifteen minutes later. En route, he flew through two Spinoza spaces—one between the ditch and a melon-sized chunk of sandstone that had fallen into the road from a nearby out-cropping, the other along the center line between two approaching cars. When he entered those spaces, he didn't know if he would make it. When he did, it confirmed that he belonged on the other side.

He backed off the throttle coming into Luster, then glided slowly through the little town, wondering what he was going to do when he got home. At a stop sign, he thought about going back, seeing if he could make it in fourteen minutes. Nah, he decided. I need to get home.

Two blocks later, he parked in front of a small restaurant that served bacon cheeseburgers with a fried egg on top—a jolt of fatty protein perfectly suited to his current appetite.

There were only three others in the one-room eatery, and Blake sat in a booth, next to a window on the street. Drinking from a glass of grape soda, he thought about what Bee had told him. He felt his blood pressure go up. Then he remembered his conversation with the young man on the hill, and he felt even worse. What could possibly be sadder than someone fondly picturing the interior of a prison? Unless, of course, it was swapping stories about hitting a guard. It was one of the most ignorant things he'd ever done. It added at least three years to his sentence and made him feel smaller and meaner for doing it. He'd lost his temper and taken it out on someone who was just trying to get from one day to the next, like everyone else.

He wondered how it was possible to rise up, like Bee had insisted he must, and to carry his share of the world's grief and still keep moving. The shame he felt made it difficult to do any lifting.

When his burger arrived Blake added extra salt and ketchup, then bit into it, relishing the unmistakable taste of an open grill. The grainy beef was satisfying, and Blake paused before taking another bite. He wondered if this might be one of those moments that—were he ever in prison again—he would look back on with cherished longing. What a joy it was to desire a particular food, act upon that desire, and completely fulfill his expectations.

Just then Bud Jenks walked by outside.

Blake put down his burger and stepped quickly out onto the sidewalk.

He followed him for two blocks and then watched him go into a tavern. Blake sat down across the street, waiting on the concrete steps of a closed bakery.

After a while, Blake almost convinced himself that he'd been mistaken. Bud Jenks belonged to the world of prison, not this one; his presence here violated the law of separate categories. Blake's memories of prison had slowly been receding, increasingly replaced by the reality he was trying desperately to catch up with, and it seemed almost impossible that Bud Jenks could suddenly appear in his full-bodied 285-pound form. It was like a returned veteran meeting one of the enemy in the grocery store.

But when Jenks came out of the tavern a half hour later, Blake knew he had not been mistaken. Jenks looked slightly out of character in a faded short-sleeve shirt and sweatpants, carrying a white paper sack filled with carry-out food. But his size and lumbering shuffle were the same. Blake followed him back past the restaurant, then another three blocks. Jenks walked up to a green one-story house and went inside.

It was an open block, with no place to linger without attracting attention, and Blake returned to his motorcycle. He sat next to it on the curb in front of the restaurant. He tried to think, but every idea melted into a confused and angry fear.

"Excuse me."

He turned around and met the waitress from inside. "Are you finished with your burger?"

"Yes," said Blake.

"Do you want to take it with you?"

"No."

"Were you thinking about paying for it?"

"Oh yeah," he said, and handed her several bills. "Sorry."

Back at home, Blake wandered through the empty barn before going into the house. From the front door, he watched Jack Station approach in his blue Mercury. This time he didn't even slow down at the drive.

Blake closed the front door and went from room to room, looking for a place he could feel comfortable and safe. He ended up in the attic, sitting on the bare wooden floor and staring through the small filmy window. He remained there a long time and then noticed something wedged into the corner of the windowpane, crumpled up and shiny. He picked it out and unfolded the foil from a piece of gum. Someone else had once sat where he was now. That person had taken out a piece of gum and put it in his mouth. Then he'd stuck the foil into the crack between the pane and the wooden frame, perhaps thinking he'd make the window fit tighter. He imagined it might have been July Montgomery, and for some reason this made him feel better.

Blake absently put the foil in his pocket and went downstairs to call his father. He would tell him he'd talked to Bee, and assure him everything was all right.

Hunting the Devil

When August came to visit Ivan at the Roebucks', Danielle introduced him to everyone. Even Flo came down from the third floor. Ivan had talked about him so much she wanted to see for herself. She shook his hand, asked a few questions, and gave him a rosary that glowed in the dark.

August smiled, blinked a lot, and answered politely. Danielle had always thought August was shy, but Ivan knew he was just cautious, and until he figured out the rules of wherever he was he talked nervously and used big words. Otherwise he might go out of bounds, and Ivan knew his friend never wanted to do anything that might embarrass his parents.

After the introductions were over, Ivan showed August his room. An extra bed had been moved into it, and two drawers emptied. August was staying over for three nights. He opened his suitcase, folded everything away real neat, and showed Ivan his new flashlight. It could be set to flash on and off, a warning signal.

Danielle came in then, and said they had to help Mrs. Roebuck in the garden at three o'clock. That gave them just two hours.

The boys went out back and walked around the pond, skipping stones. August told Ivan about Milton coming back, and showed him the little piece of rolled-up paper that had been wrapped around Milton's leg.

"Do you have Milton with you?" asked Ivan.

"No, I had to leave him home. It's too bad; he would love this pond."

Ivan pointed out the floating tube and told August more about the giant turtle that he and Wally were trying to catch. August wanted to know everything. How big was its body? How big were its head and neck?

What color was it? Was its shell smooth, wavy, or spiked with ridges like dorsal fins? Why did Kevin say it was the devil?

As they continued walking around the pond, Ivan told him everything he knew, and after that August started going over and sticking his hand into the water every so often. Once again, Ivan had the feeling he always got when August and he were together—he just knew something was about to happen, and he knew it would be fun.

"You've described an alligator snapping turtle, *Macrochelys temminckii*," said August. "It's related to the common snapper, but bigger—the longest-surviving reptile known to science. It retains many features common to the Triassic period. And they're indigenous to North America."

"Why is he so hard to catch?"

"I don't know," replied August, checking the water temperature again with his hand.

"Why do you keep doing that?"

"He should be in the warmest water in the pond. Gator turtles prefer milder climates. In fact, they don't usually come this far north. They're more commonly found in southern states, as far north as Kansas, Missouri, Illinois, and Iowa."

"So he likes warm water," Ivan said.

"It's a good guess."

"Let's get the boat," suggested Ivan.

"And a reliable thermometer," August added.

They ran inside and moved silently through the house, finding their way to the kitchen. Ivan went for the meat thermometer.

"Oh no you don't!" yelled Danielle. "Put that back!"

"We just want to test the water in the pond," pleaded Ivan.

"That's for food," she replied. "Those disgusting pond germs could kill us all."

"But we—"

"Put it back, Ivan."

When they went back outdoors, Wally was on the deck with a cup of coffee. He set down his mug, tucked his shirt into his pants, and said, "Come on, boys." They followed him into the pole shed.

"Up there," he pointed. Ivan scrambled up on the workbench and took down a wall thermometer with a picture of hybrid seed corn.

The three of them went out and got into the boat. Ivan rowed. Wally sipped coffee and lowered the temperature gauge into the water, calling out the numbers. August wrote them down in the back of a little notebook, inside a little drawing of the pond.

It took a long time.

Wally didn't know anything about the Wild Boy, so they told him.

"We've seen him up close, as close as we are now," said Ivan.

"Where does he sleep?"

"Wherever he wants. And look, he slipped this into my pocket." Ivan showed him the flat, round rock.

"Can I hold it?" Wally asked. Ivan handed it over. He rubbed it for a long time with his old fingers. "That's real nice," he said. "Real nice. Give me back that notebook for a minute." August did, and he wrote something down before handing it back.

"What does he eat?"

"Mostly roots, insects, grass, and honey, we think, but folks give him other stuff too," explained Ivan. "August and I are the only people he trusts, though, except for Mr. Hermit."

"His real name is Lester Mortal," said August. "He's a decorated war hero who fought in three foreign countries and hunts wild ginseng for extra money."

"And he lives inside a hill," added Ivan.

"I used to know Lester," said Wally. "He was about ten years younger than me, and probably still is. He worked at the co-op, and then he joined the military after his father died. He was a nice fellow. I'd like to see him again."

Just then Kevin came out on the deck with his mother. Amy waved and Ivan rowed over.

Amy smiled with a pained look on her face.

"That's my boat," said Kevin angrily. He was as white as cooked fish, and still in his pajamas.

"We know it is," said Wally. "And we've got room for you right beside August here. Come on, Kev. We need your help."

When Mrs. Roebuck frowned, Wally added, "He'll be fine, Amy. He will. Come on, lift that tank down here. August, keep an eye on the tubing. With the four of us, that turtle doesn't stand a chance in hell."

"Wally, don't talk that way around the boys," said Amy as she helped

Kevin into the boat. Kevin wobbled over and sat next to August, setting the boat to sloshing.

"Wait," said Amy, and handed down a big hat to put on Kevin's head.

Ivan rowed out to the middle of the pond.

Kevin asked what they were doing and August explained, "We're trying to find the location of the highest relative water temperature, so we can better position the necrotic lure."

"You talk funny," said Kevin.

"I know it," said August. "My mom says my unfortunate verbal habits make many people uncomfortable. I sincerely hope you won't feel that way."

"I don't care," said Kevin, and coughed underneath his hat.

"Excellent," said August. "You have a fine boat."

"Ivan says you have a pet bat."

"That's true, but I don't want too many people to know about him, at least not until my application for a wildlife rehabilitation license has been approved."

"Stop rowing," said Wally. Then he lowered the thermometer into the water and read out the number to August.

"This is the place," August said. "Each time we've sampled this area the temperatures have been higher."

"Let's move the tube over," suggested Ivan.

"If we find him, will we kill him?" asked Kevin.

"That will be up to you, Kev," said Wally.

"Good," said Kevin, coughing again.

They towed the black tube over to the warm area of the pond and tossed in the anchor. August pulled up the four strings and checked the fish, which were still hanging there white-eye dead.

"You know what?" said August.

"What?" they asked.

"If we duct-taped my flashlight to the tube and taped one of the strings over it in just the right way, a tug on the end of the line would turn on the flashing light, giving us a signal."

"Let's do it," said Kevin. "There's a roll of tape in my room."

Ivan rowed back to the dock. Kevin told Ivan where to look for the tape, and then on the way back Ivan picked up August's flashlight and another cup of coffee for Wally.

Later, while they were taping the string to a little piece of wood that would go over the flashlight switch, Danielle came out on the deck and yelled, her voice jumping across the water.

"It's three o'clock, Ivan. You're supposed to be helping Mrs. Roebuck in the garden. You don't want me to have to come out there and get you."

"All right," said Ivan, and started rowing back. But then Amy came out on the deck, stood next to Danielle, and they talked for a few minutes. Then they pushed each other, laughed, and Danielle yelled, "One half hour, Ivan—no more."

They had just enough time to get everything done. The flashlight was set and aimed at the house.

When they had finished their work, Kevin went back to his room and Wally went upstairs to take a nap. August and Ivan pulled weeds and dug in the dirt out front.

Sometime later, Lucky's shiny car pulled up next to the pole shed. The motor revved up before it shut off. He got out, locked the doors, and walked over to Amy. She took off her gardening gloves as she talked to him. The boys couldn't hear what they said initially, but they could see Amy frowning and looking at the ground. They were clearly arguing.

"Where is she?" Lucky asked, raising his voice to an audible level.

"Inside," replied Amy.

Lucky went into the house.

Amy put her gloves back on, dug a few holes with her trowel, then stood up again.

"I'll be back," she said to the boys, and went in after Lucky. The boys could hear them arguing again just inside the door, but they couldn't make out the words. Then they couldn't hear anything more.

August and Ivan looked at each other. "Go on," August told him. "If anyone asks, I'll say you went to take a pee."

Ivan went into the house, took off his shoes, walked a little way down the hall, and listened.

Amy was sitting by herself in the dining room, staring into space. Danielle and Lucky were talking in the kitchen, so Ivan went down and stood near the doorway.

Lucky said something about government contracts being announced in three weeks. Everything had gone just as he'd hoped, just as he'd planned, just as he'd said.

"Fine," said Danielle.

"We should get together tonight. Go into Madison, back to my place."

"Ivan has a friend over. I can't go anywhere."

"Tomorrow night, then," he said.

"August is staying until Monday, and those two can get into trouble quicker than politicians tell lies."

Then Lucky's voice changed.

"You and I aren't finished," he said.

"I gave you back the dress. I had a nice time that night, met a lot of nice people, but—"

"But what?" he snarled.

"I'm not going anywhere with you again. Never."

Lucky stepped closer to her and his voice turned mean. "There's been a reward offered," he said. "A big reward." He waited for her to respond, but she didn't.

"A diamond necklace was stolen," he said.

"That has nothing to do with me."

"What do you think Amy would say if I told her I knew what happened to that necklace? What do you think Buck would say if I told him?"

Ivan's mother didn't say a thing.

"Ten years in prison, do you hear that?"

A brief silence followed. "I'll pick you up next week," he said.

When Lucky walked by he didn't notice Ivan standing against the wall on the other side of the doorway. He lit a cigarette as he went down the hall. Ivan's mother stayed in the kitchen.

Back in the garden, Ivan told August everything.

"What do you think he meant about the necklace?" asked August.

"I don't know," said Ivan.

"Things often seem worse than they are," said August. "Don't worry."

"You shouldn't talk about not worrying," replied Ivan. "And just for the record, I really hate that guy Lucky."

After supper, Kevin said August and Ivan could play one of his video games, so long as they did it in his room. He'd changed out of his pajamas and into a pair of too-big blue jeans and a red long-sleeve shirt. He looked as if he was feeling better, but he still had the hose running up his nose.

August was no good at video games, and after an hour or so Ivan could see that Kevin felt sorry for him. He set his laptop down and showed August some things he could do to get better scores.

It didn't help.

"You're hopeless," said Kevin.

"My fingers won't move the way I tell them to," explained August.

Amy stuck her head into the room just then, but she didn't say anything. A little while later Buck came in. August hadn't met him yet, so he just stared at him.

"Hello, boys," he said. "How's it going?"

August and Ivan thought Kevin would answer, since Buck was his dad, but when he didn't say anything August spoke up. "Excellent, Mr. Roebuck."

"You must be August Helm," said Buck, sitting down in the chair next to Kevin's bed.

"I am."

"I've heard a lot about you, all of it good."

"I'm afraid I have absolutely no skill in these games, though."

"Neither do I," said Buck.

"That's okay for you," said August. "But at my age a proficiency in fine-motor skills is practically a prerequisite for existing."

Buck laughed.

"He talks funny, doesn't he, Dad?" said Kevin.

"He talks just fine. It's hearing the word *proficiency* again," said Buck. "It's like an old song that hasn't been played in a long time. Say, is there any supper left?"

"Mother always leaves some for you," said Ivan. "You know that."

"You're right, I do, and I'm going to see what it is, if you'll excuse me."

He stood up and headed for the door. Before going out, though, he looked out the window. "There's a light blinking on and off out over the pond."

By the time the boys got outside, Wally was already on the dock next to the boat.

"Ivan, you and August help Kev down here, and hurry," he said.

It was dark, and the air felt heavy and still, as if it were listening. Across the pond, the flashlight was still signaling, its light-lines flashing across the water.

"Easy there," said Wally in a low voice. "Easy does it."

The boat rocked back and forth as the boys climbed in. Somewhere far away two dogs started barking. August untied the rope and tossed it into the front of the boat. Then he climbed in and pushed them away from the dock.

The oars slid into the dark water quietly, and Ivan rowed toward the blinking light.

Wally lit a kerosene lantern and set it in the front of the boat.

"What if he attacks us?" whispered Kevin.

"If he does, he'll be sorry," replied Ivan.

"He could kill us all if he wanted to," said Kevin. "If he thought it was time for us to die, nothing could stop him."

"Kevin makes a point," said August. "There are several unsettling reports of alligator snappers. One gator actually ate a small chicken—after it was dead."

"What?" Ivan asked.

August said he'd read about a farmer in Louisiana who caught an alligator snapper in the swampy land around his farm. After lugging it home, he decided to make it into a gumbo stew for his hungry family. He cut off the turtle's head and it rolled onto the ground. Then a young chicken came over to investigate and the severed head bit it.

"Wait a minute," said Ivan. "How could a head bite something?"

"Deep reflexes," said August.

They pondered that silently for a while. The boat drifted a little, and Wally had to remind Ivan to keep rowing.

When they reached the inner tube, August snapped off the flashing light. For some reason that seemed to make everything grow even quieter. They could hear the dark water lapping against the boat.

"Who wants to do the honors?" asked Wally.

"I'll do it," said Kevin. Wally helped steady him as he stood up. August held up the lantern.

"Is it heavy?" asked Ivan, staring down the string and into the water.

"No," he said, and pulled up a gray-white fish head.

He pulled up the other strings too. The fish had been eaten. Even the eyes were gone.

"What a ghastly sight," said August.

"Do you think he's underneath us?" asked Ivan. "Right under the boat?"

"He's nearby," said Kevin. "I can feel him."

"Me too," offered Ivan.

"Me too," said August and Wally in unison.

They thought about this while the dark water rocked the boat, and then Wally said, "Well, boys, we've got his attention. What's the next step?"

"I've got an idea," said Kevin.

"What?" asked Ivan.

"We'll bait the strings again, but this time with the tube closer to shore. And the time after that we'll put it even closer to shore. Then we can start setting dead fish out on the bank, and he'll have to come out of the water to eat them."

"Excellent," said August.

"That's very good, Kev," said Wally. "We can even get one of the security cameras from the construction company, set it up with motion detectors, and record him when he comes out."

"Should we bait the strings tonight?" Ivan asked.

The others nodded, and Ivan rowed back to the dock. Kevin and Wally waited in the boat while August and Ivan ran off to the pole shed for more dead fish.

"Now this is impressive," said August, looking down into the freezer.

"No kidding," said Ivan, and they chipped four of the dead fish off the top and carried them back to the dock.

After they'd moved the tube closer to shore and tied four more dead fish onto the strings, Wally said he was ready to go to bed. Ivan rowed back and he went inside.

Kevin, August, and Ivan got out of the boat, sat on the dock, and talked. Kevin told them about a time when the turtle pulled a goose under the water and ate it. August asked Kevin why he thought the turtle was the devil, and Kevin said that when August saw it for himself he would feel the same way.

"The devil wants to kill me," said Kevin. "It's the reason he's here."

"The devil doesn't usually do that," said August. "I mean, in Christianity the devil is supposed to make us repent. That's his only job."

"Right," Ivan agreed.

"Why do you need extra oxygen?" asked August, changing the subject.

"I have a congenital defect that makes it hard to get enough. Nature made a mistake with me," offered Kevin.

"I don't believe that," said August. "Nature doesn't make mistakes."

"It did with me."

"No it didn't," said August. "The way you are is the only way you could be made. There was no better way for you to be just like you are."

"That sounds stupid."

"It's not, though."

"August is right," chimed in Ivan. "Nature doesn't make mistakes. It can't."

At that point Amy came out. She said Kevin's tank was getting low. It was time for him to take more medication. The two of them went back to Kevin's room.

August turned to Ivan after they were gone. "What's the matter?"

"Nothing," said Ivan.

"Something is wrong," replied August. "I can tell something is bothering you."

"Let's go back outside," he continued.

"You go ahead. I'll be out in a minute," said Ivan.

August went out and Ivan went to find his mother. There was a light on in the living room, but he didn't see her anywhere. She wasn't in her bedroom, or the bathroom either. He finally found her sitting in the little kitchen, in the dark.

When Ivan went over to her she didn't look up.

"What are you doing?" he asked.

"Nothing."

"The light's off," said Ivan.

"I'm resting my eyes. Where's your friend?"

"He's outside."

"You'd better go out, then."

"That turtle ate the dead fish."

"That's nice. Go on, Ivan. Your friend is waiting."

"Should I turn the light on before I leave?"

"Leave it off. I'm resting my eyes."

When Ivan turned it on anyway, she just sat there and didn't look up. Then Ivan turned it off and left.

He found August down at the dock again, looking over the water.

"What's the matter?" he asked.

"Something's really wrong," said Ivan.

"I wish we knew what it was," replied August.

"You want to see where I like to sit at night? It's up here."

They crawled under the deck. August agreed that this spot offered a good view of the dock, the pond, and anyone coming and going out the back door. It felt safe and totally fortified.

"Do you come out here a lot?" he asked.

"Sometimes."

"Does anyone else know about this?"

"Nope."

Just then they heard a loud splash.

"Did you hear that?" asked August.

"Yes," said Ivan.

"What was it?"

"I don't know. Could be anything. A jumping fish, frogs, raccoons washing food, deer pawing."

"Maybe we'll hear it again."

They waited and listened.

"Maybe a limb fell into the water," whispered August.

"There aren't any limbs that close," replied Ivan.

At that moment a dark shape walked up from the edge of the water. August pointed at it. Ivan swallowed and nodded.

The shape looked human, and it stood for several minutes without moving, just at the bottom of the landing below them. It stood there as if it were listening, then walked over to the side of the house. It stopped, continued to where the two parts of the house came together, and moved into a shadow.

August and Ivan stayed quiet, knowing it had to come out sooner or later.

Then the shape climbed out of the shadow and up to the house, slowly, quietly, higher and higher.

"Cripes, do you see that?" whispered Ivan.

"Of course I do," said August. "This is probably the most curious event I have ever seen in my whole life."

The shape reached the roof window on the third floor, stood on the roof, crouched down, and climbed through the window.

"Cripes," said Ivan again.

Kevin opened the back door and came out on the deck. His feet were right above them.

"Psssst," Ivan whispered. "Down here."

"Where are you?"

"Down here."

When Kevin found them they told him about the shape. Ivan expected him to be scared out of his wits, but he wasn't.

"I knew something like this would happen," he said.

"How?" they asked.

"I've been hearing things for a couple weeks now."

"What kind of things?"

"Sounds that don't belong in the house at night," he said. "When I try to find where're they're coming from, I always end up on the third floor, and then nothing."

"Shh," said August.

The shape came out on the roof again, climbed down the side of the house like the phantom of the opera, walked over to the pond, and continued along the far edge until it disappeared.

"It's the devil," said Kevin. "I knew he was in the house. I could feel him."

"Where's your oxygen tank?" asked August.

"Sometimes after someone beats on my back and I breathe that medication, I can do without it for a while."

"So you think the devil's coming into the house—the turtle shape-shifting?"

"I'm sure of it," said Kevin.

Undoing Destiny

"Did you finish turning out the wagon shaft?" asked Jacob. He was looking for a half-inch bolt three-quarters of an inch long, fine threaded all the way down. The old oil pan with the shop's premium supply of used bolts, washers, and screws appeared to have every other imaginable size.

"Over there," said Blake from the workbench.

"Did you write up the tag?"

"It's over there too."

"We have the four-puller, two riders, and a haybine to get out of here before the truck comes in on Tuesday." Jacob found a suitably sized bolt, poked it through a lock washer, and turned it into the brush hog's threaded hole, pulling tight a loose castor.

"I know it," said Blake. "Is it always this busy?"

"Every summer gets worse. We need a bigger shop."

Winnie's car pulled up outside. She and August came in.

"I have to run over to the church for a couple hours," she told Jacob. "And August wanted to spend some time here."

"Fine," said Jacob, wiping grease from his hands and checking his watch.

"I'm late," said Winnie. "I'll be back."

She climbed into her car and drove off, the small engine discharging a large volume of sound through the lower gears.

"We better get a muffler on that," observed Blake.

"I know it," said Jacob. "August, can you work with Blake while I pick up some parts in Viroqua? They've been waiting down there almost a week."

"Sure," said August.

Jacob left.

Minutes later, four motorcycle riders rode up to the shop, parked, walked around the lot looking for something to be interested in, and then came inside.

"Hey," said Blake, not recognizing any of them. Two were in their early to mid-twenties, in T-shirts, torn jeans, and tennis shoes. The shoes looked like the kind worn for jogging, but neither of the men could be imagined running or moving quickly in any other way, at least not in their current glassy-eyed state. The others were older, heavier, in bulky clothes; one had a shaved head, the taller one had long stringy hair that kept getting in his face.

"Hey," said the man, brushing hair out of his eye with one hand and unbuttoning his jacket with the other. "You work on motorcycles here?"

"We work on everything here. What do you need?"

"Are you Blake Bookchester?"

Blake nodded.

"That your Gixxer out front?"

"That's it," said Blake.

"You've been riding that stretch of road between Red Plain and Luster."

Blake waited.

The man continued. "Skeeter Skelton noticed. You know who Skeeter Skelton is?"

"I did at one time," said Blake.

"He says to tell you welcome back."

Blake waited.

"Skeeter will be waiting outside Red Plain Thursday night, at ten o'clock."

"That's three nights from now," said the man with a shaved head.

"I know when it is," said Blake.

"He'll be at the top of the hill, waiting."

"I'm not sure I can make it," said Blake.

"Then don't," the man replied, brushing his hair out of his face again. All four walked back outside.

Blake followed them. "Nice bikes," he said.

"Thanks," said one of the younger men. They climbed onto their

Harleys—a Super Glide, an old Shovelhead, a Fat Boy, and a Softail—and roared out of town.

"Who are those guys?" asked August.

"People who used to have good jobs and now don't know what to do without them," said Blake, watching the motorcycles turn the last visible corner. The sound continued.

"What's going to happen to this country, Blake?"

"Hard to say. The folks who stole all the money are trying to figure out if they can get along without the rest of us. Don't worry, August. Everything comes around in the end."

"Why do some people seem so dead?" asked August.

"You mean those guys who were just here?"

"Yes, the ones who weren't talking. Their eyes were dull. Why?"

"Does that bother you, August? That dull, drugged, stupid look?"

"It bothers me a lot."

"That's the face of ignorance."

"Those men frightened me," said August.

"Good. There's nothing more dangerous than ignorance—nothing."

"Why is Skeeter Skelton going to wait for you outside Red Plain?"

"He's just an old friend, August. Hand me that wrench and see if you can find the can of penetrating oil."

August began searching. "If you meet Skeeter Skelton you'll be breaking your release conditions," he said.

"With only a couple weeks before the DOC relaxes some of my restrictions, that would be really stupid, wouldn't it?"

"Yes," said August.

"Tell me about your friend Ivan."

"There's nobody like Ivan. When we first became friends I felt like I finally belonged. Most people think I'm really weird."

"What most people think isn't worth thinking about."

"Even if you don't think about it you can still feel it," said August. He followed the row of shelves to the workbench, looking for the penetrating oil.

August was fond of his father's shop. In addition to friendly oil-smells, each area had its own collection of machinery and dark wood. And a durable history of utility resided in every location. The workbench, for example, was originally constructed out of new oak planking, blond, straight, and level, with visible wood grain and sharp edges and corners. What now remained of it resembled a miniature battlefield, with blackened and burned areas, gouges, valleys, foxholes, and no straight or sharp edges anywhere. The bench was a page from long ago, written on over and over again, one account on top of another, so thick with history that separate events could no longer be read, embedded as they were in a blackened mass of oil, grease, dirt, and wood scars. Soaked in layers of service—every hammer blow, hot torch laid down, leaking battery, file stroke, drop of blood, chiseled wedge, and slipped wrench—the bench absorbed all the light around it. Several inches of darkness hovered over everything placed on its surface, pulling them into its record of time.

The tools themselves were no different, made venerable by decades of constantly working hands. Each retained a record of hard, prolonged use. There were screwdrivers with bent shafts, rounded almost smooth by thousands of turns inside screw-slots that did not quite fit, prying open frozen crankcases, paint cans, gearboxes, and being driven between stuck-together iron plates. There were sockets beaten into dome shapes, burnished to a dull silver, cans with illegible labels, dents, and missing nozzles.

"Found it," said August, handing Blake the penetrating oil.

"Good fellow."

The telephone rang on the wall. Blake answered it. His father invited him to come over after work. Nate had found some local pork chops—butchered on the farm, two inches thick—and new red potatoes, hard as bricks. He also had second-ear white sweet corn with no dented kernels. Bee was bringing homemade butter, freshly ground basil, and an old family photo album. They were going to use the charcoal grill, and hickory chips soaked in apple vinegar.

"I'd like to, but better not," replied Blake. "Thanks though."

"Why?"

"I've got things to do."

"We can bring supper over to your place," said Nate. "We'll load up the grill. Did I mention the orange chutney to go with the chops?"

"No, you didn't mention that, Dad, but could we do it another night?"

"Tomorrow night? That's my last night before I'm back on the road."

"Okay, I'll be there."

"What are you doing tonight?"

"Things that need doing."

"Are you out of coffee yet?"

"I've got plenty."

"Grapes?"

"Still got some."

"See you then."

Blake and August finished with the rider and were almost done with the four-wheeler when Jacob returned. An hour later, Winnie came back, picked up August, and drove him to the library. A chain saw came in needing a new bar, sprocket, and tune-up. Then Harvey Mortimer drove his golf cart, which he used for everything except golfing, through the front doors. The clutch was slipping, the idle rough.

After work, Blake went straight home. He noticed that his lawn looked better for having been mowed a second time. There were plenty of thistles, chicory, and dandelions that a more conscientious person would dig out, but it still looked much better.

Inside, he ate a handful of grapes, drank a glass of water, and lifted weights for a half hour.

Skeeter Skelton must be getting old by now, Blake thought, his heart galloping in his chest. When he was finished with the weights, he went to the practice bag he'd hung in the living room. He put on padded gloves and began punching, searching for a satisfactory rhythm. The truth was, Skeeter had seemed old years ago—vigorous, but old. He wore his age well, though; the countless times he'd gone down—on roads, circle tracks, motocross courses, and hill climbs—shone like victory flags from his face, arms, and legs. Skeeter had nerve, always ready to turn his throttle a little farther than the next guy, lean deeper into the corners, take the risk, seize the prize. He also had uncanny instincts, and had somehow managed to make a little money from them. And ever since Blake could remember, Skeeter had a group of road-runners following him around, hoping his charm would wear off on them.

Blake took off the gloves, drank another glass of water, showered, and changed into clean underwear and a T-shirt. He pulled the same sweatshirt and jeans over them, found his newly borrowed book on Spinoza, and resumed reading at the place he'd left off the night before, in the upholstered chair next to the window.

The reading was difficult. The meaning of individual words seemed to shift, as if they were living organisms with unstable personalities. He looked out the window. Far above the tree line stretched a horizontal cirrus cloud. The long ribbon of mist changed shapes frequently. When part of it rose slightly higher in the fragile atmosphere, the condensed water vapor dissolved into clear blue invisibility; in other places the moisture collected out of the air, giving the impression of something passing into and out of existence.

After looking out the window for several minutes, Blake took a deep breath and returned to reading the book. Four hours later, he woke up, still in the chair. He had an odd, lingering sensation of having just seen something that should not be seen, heard, or thought—something forbidden. He found the light switch and checked the time: a little after midnight. Even though the house always seemed unusually still, tonight it felt subterranean.

At the kitchen table he sat in the dark and ate grapes to help his body wake up. Mice scratched beneath the floor, announcing a loneliness that spread outward, and soon the rest of the house filled with melancholy.

Suddenly Blake knew what he was going to do, and he stopped resisting it. The rest of his life spilled out before him, exposing his future in a rare moment of clarity. He was going back to prison. It was inevitable. He'd known it the first time he saw Bud Jenks in Luster—understood it the way a bee understands how to find its way back to the hive. He simply could not forget everything that had happened. The corridors of prison, the sound of steel doors closing, were still more real to him than anything else. He'd never get over it. Maybe if he hadn't seen Jenks—but it didn't matter now. He was going to find him and make someone pay for the civilized cruelty in the world. One of the thousand burning coals in the furnace of organized injustice was about to go out. A small part of what was wrong with the world would be set right. Blake would get even.

The melancholy grew calmer, more beautiful. His only conern was for his father, and he went to the phone and dialed his number. Nate deserved to know, to understand that everything had to be the way it was. He appreciated what his father had done for him, everything he wanted for him, and Nate's steady, benevolent spirit would always burn in Blake's heart. But living on the outside wasn't going to work, not with Bud Jenks walking around in Luster. The world was the way it was and Blake was the way he was. Things would happen. They had to. He could feel the pieces of his own destiny falling into place.

The phone rang six times, tripping the answering machine.

Blake smiled. Nate was driving his cousin home. They still didn't have the courage to spend the night together. Such deferential caution was something that Blake both envied and didn't understand. He hung up without leaving a message.

He thought about calling Danielle Workhouse and telling her how much he loved her. But he didn't have the number, and it didn't matter anyway. His feelings for her had been hidden so long that exposing them might change their vital content. The wild longing he felt for her would have to remain within him for the rest of his life. He put on his boots and jacket.

On the ride to Luster, the stars burned brighter than usual, the air smelled sweeter, more welcoming.

The little town waited for him, its streetlights spreading dramatic shadows. A few windows were lit in otherwise-dark houses on empty streets. He turned onto Main and an owl silently launched from the top of the grain elevator, opened its white wings, and glided into the darkness. Somewhere a motor turned over several times and started. A cat ran down an alley.

Blake had come here three times before, looking for Jenks. He'd seen him each time, either inside the tavern or walking from the tavern to the house where he apparently lived, sometimes carrying food. Twice, he'd been walking with other people, an old woman once and a younger man. He'd argued with the old woman, though not in a serious way—like neighbors who had to see each other again no matter what.

The tavern lights were on, the beer sign glowing red and green. Three pickups and an old Honda wagon stood out front, a beat-up utility van farther down. The Honda had a broken window on the passenger's side. The other side—he noticed while parking his bike next to it—had been sideswiped. The mirror was gone.

Blake walked to the curb. Next to the street drain lay a length of pipe, rusted but solid, threads on one end, about a foot long. Blake picked it up and shoved it into the back pocket of his jeans. The sidewalk had been swept clean. Two Styrofoam cups had blown out of the alley and come to rest against the side of the building.

Blake hadn't been inside a tavern for a long time, and when he pushed the door open the yellowish light and smell of booze, beer, and bar food welcomed him inside. There were three people sitting on stools—two older men sipping from short glasses, and an old woman by herself, slumped over and maybe asleep, her head cradled in her arms, her left cheek flat against the bar top. Two couples sat talking in booths, mixed drinks and hot sandwiches before them. A pair of younger men sat at a table; between them, two tall glasses rose up, half-filled, between eight or nine empty beer cans. The man behind the bar had stooped shoulders, silver hair, and a trimmed beard. A country song played on the radio near him.

"One from the tap," said Blake.

"Regular or light?"

"Regular."

The bartender tilted a glass under the spigot and unhurriedly filled it, as if enjoying a ritual.

"Bud Jenks in tonight?" asked Blake.

"He will be before long," said the man, looking through bushy silver eyebrows and collecting Blake's two dollars. Down the hallway, a black Labrador slept on the floor just inside the back door, between the restrooms, the tips of her muzzle hairs white with age.

The woman roused, looked at Blake out of one eye, and said something like "Whadda wan' wuth Buddy? Whadda—" Half of her teeth were missing and there were deep lines in her face. Her pale blue eye refused to focus.

"Take it easy, Rosa," said the bartender. "Nothing to concern yourself with."

"Ba-bastards," she mumbled, as if naming something she'd been trying to remember for a long time, and again cradled her head in her arms.

Blake carried his beer over to the empty booth nearest the door while the bartender walked to the back wall and made a telephone call.

The cool liquid went down easy and he savored the taste. The two young men at the table began laughing and talking loudly about something that had been on television the day before. "Liberals, conservatives, it's all a bunch of bullshit," said one.

"It's the rich and the rest of us," said his friend, and then repeated it, "the rich and the rest." A different song began playing on the radio, steel guitars but no fiddles.

The door behind Blake opened and he turned around. Bud Jenks seemed even more massive than Blake remembered. His blue pants looked as if they might be guard-issue, but not the green nylon jacket or untied boots. He shuffled heavily over to the bar and sat on a stool next to the old woman.

The bartender nodded. "Evening, Bud," and held up an expectant glass.

The back of Bud's head shook. "No thanks," he said.

The woman turned toward him. "Ba-bastards," she said again. Then she put her head back down, her gray hair stringy and matted.

Blake stood out of the booth and pulled the length of pipe out of his back pocket.

Bud stood up from the stool and turned to the old woman. "Come on," he said. "Come on now."

Blake moved to the side, blocking the door.

Bud picked up the old woman and turned around.

The old woman swore.

"Time to go home, Mom," said Bud, ignoring her complaints. He held her carefully, protectively, and began to move forward.

Their eyes met. Bud saw the pipe and recognized Blake. Blake understood that Jenks had come to take his mother home.

Blake called up the past, summoned the divine fear he'd felt in prison, along with its vicious twin, hatred, but the channel wouldn't open. All he could see was Bud Jenks holding his mother, taking her home.

Blake opened the door with his left hand. He held it open and stood back as Bud carried his mother out into the street. As Bud passed through the doorway they exchanged another look and Blake felt something inside him die. What he had come for would never happen. What there had been between him and Bud Jenks was over, blown out like a flame too weak to live.

The door banged closed and Blake continued to stand just inside, feeling a relief he'd never experienced before—something so deeply private and fundamentally right that he could not imagine ever telling anyone else about it. Something so profoundly good had happened that he almost felt embarrassed.

He shoved the piece of pipe back into his pocket, drank the last of the beer in his glass, and carried it to the bar.

"Another," he said.

"You bet," said the man with bushy eyebrows. He refilled the glass and pushed it over the counter.

"And a whiskey, straight up," added Blake. He went back to the booth.

As the alcohol began its dull, happy work, he celebrated his good fortune by trying to figure out what it meant. He'd been so sure of what was going to happen. On the way over, the sky, air, and everything else had seemed to confirm his passionate mission. The town seemed to be waiting, even eager for him, as had the piece of pipe beside the drain slot. Even the way the bartender said "He will be before long" seemed to imply that he knew what Blake had come for.

That was all wrong, of course. More importantly, everything that had seemed to point to a single imagined outcome had just led to another, completely unanticipated outcome. He'd come over here to confront the Bud Jenks he'd known in prison, and instead he'd met a man he didn't know at all.

"Another, please," he said, back at the bar. "Both of them."

"You bet."

At his booth, he continued drinking and thinking about the two Bud Jenkses. It had been a long time since he'd felt the effects of alcohol in his brain, and he was astonished by how pleasantly it enhanced the thinking process. It was almost as if—

"Hey," said one of the two young men who had been drinking at the table ten feet away. They had both come over to his booth. "Hey," one of them said again.

"Hey what?" said Blake.

"You're sitting in Big Jim's booth."

"Who's Big Jim?"

"He's a guy who doesn't want anyone sitting in his booth," said the other one, grinning in a twitchy way.

"When he gets here he can have it," said Blake.

"Big Jim doesn't like people to sit in his booth—even when he isn't here," said the man who had spoken first, pushing his upper lip out over his lower lip in a way that might mean he often made the same facial movement for no particular reason. Blake wondered if they were brothers, or if they simply bought their clothes at the same crappy store.

Blake shrugged and climbed out of the booth. "I'll sit somewhere else, then," he said. He carried his glass up to the bar and had it refilled. He put a five on the counter. The two men followed him over and stood on either side of him.

"No trouble here tonight, guys," said the bartender. The way he said this made Blake think he'd said it before on earlier occasions.

The two men went back to their table. The bartender found a couple dollars of change in the cash box and placed them on the counter.

Blake left them and carried his beer back to the same booth. He tried to resume his thoughts from earlier. He tried to reconcile these two dramatically different identities of Bud Jenks. On the one hand, the brutal prison guard, on the other, a caring son. Maybe something had changed inside him. Maybe the prison had imposed new rules, given the guards a raise, and held them to a higher standard. Or maybe the Bud Jenks Blake had come looking for no longer existed except inside Blake's mind.

"Hey." The two men had come back. "You're still sitting in Big Jim's booth."

The two couples who had been drinking and eating sandwiches got up, carried their coats down the hallway past the bathrooms, around the sleeping Labrador, and out the back door. The two older men sitting at the bar moved farther down.

"No trouble in here, guys," said the bartender, walking around the bar and coming toward them, but stopping ten feet away. "We'll be closing up before long. It's getting late."

"Big Jim wouldn't like you sitting in his booth."

"I've had enough of this," said Blake, climbing out of the booth, his right hand closing around the piece of pipe in his back pocket.

He could feel the same holy anger he'd carried into the tavern earlier returning. Apparently it wasn't necessary to address grievances from the past, he thought, because the present moment would always provide ample opportunities for violence. The threat of man-on-man violence had always characterized the society he lived in, and it almost felt good to have all that atmospheric hostility suddenly come together and take shape, confirming once again that at this moment in history, man's deepest social instinct was his antisocial instinct.

At that moment Blake's father came through the front door in his light tan jacket and shorts. He carried a six-pack under one arm and nodded at the bartender.

"Evening, Larry," he said.

"Evening, Nate."

"Thanks for the call. I appreciate it. You two," Nate said in a friendly voice, "what are you drinking?"

They looked at each other and said, "Beer."

"I know that," said Nate. "But what kind of beer? That's what I'm asking."

"The regular kind."

"I'd like you to try this new beer I found last week. I don't know, maybe you've already tasted it. It's called sour beer, and it's made by leaving the top off the fermenting cask, so the wild yeast in the air can do its work. It's sour, fruity, and strong, almost like wine but not really. Have you ever heard of it?"

They shook their heads.

"Neither had I. That's what I'm trying to tell you. This is something new, brewed and bottled right here in Wisconsin. Try it. You'll see what I mean. It's different."

The two men looked at each other and then one of them turned to Nate. "Are you some kind of salesman?"

"No, I'm some kind of truck driver. My name's Nate. Here, go ahead, take a drink. See what you think." He handed a bottle of sour beer to each of them.

They twisted off the caps and took a drink. "It's okay," one said.

"Not bad," said the other.

"Come on, it's better than that," said Nate. "Much better than that. You wouldn't want to drink it every day, but when you're in just the right mood, nothing else will do. Here, you can have these bottles too. Larry, you should get a supply of this. People would really like it."

"They might at that."

"I'll bring you a case tomorrow. Come on, Blake, we've got to get you home." He took his son's arm, pulled the piece of pipe out of his back pocket, and led him out the door.

Bee met them in the lot. "Hurry," she whispered. "The police do a sweep around closing time." Nate's pickup was parked in the street, with a seven-foot aluminum ramp leaning into the bed. Bee rocked Blake's motorcycle off the stand and pushed it toward the ramp.

The three pushed the blue and white Suzuki into the back of the truck, tied it in with rope, and tossed the ramp in with it.

"Get in," said Bee.

Blake sat between her and Nate.

Nate drove out of town.

"You're a certified idiot," said Bee to Blake. "Do you know that?"

Blake ignored her. "Where'd you find the beer, Dad?"

"Son, I'd appreciate it very much if you didn't say anything for the rest of the way home."

Stepping Out of the River of Time

The Words Friends of Jesus Church did not have an ideal room for its monthly business meetings. Sunday school rooms were simply too small, and after months of prayer and discussion the Spiritual Oversight Committee had decided to reserve the sanctuary—which provided adequate seating for over one hundred adults—for events of a more holy nature. And so the fifteen or twenty members of the faith community who assumed responsibility for the upkeep of the church building and the coordination of its many functions had been conducting their meetings in the basement, seated on metal folding chairs, at tables with collapsing tubular legs and mustard-brown Formica tops.

Though no one complained, they encountered notable difficulties in the basement. The concrete walls and floor—coated with three separate applications of a glossy gray epoxy enamel believed by the trustees to adhere to damp surfaces and resist mold and mildew better than ordinary paint—conspired with the fiberboard ceiling that concealed the wiring, water, and sewer pipes to create an acoustic environment resembling the inside of a small gymnasium. Even when a microphone was plugged into a portable amplifier, some people couldn't hear much of anything, and others couldn't hear well enough. Consequently, speakers often had to repeat themselves, which took extra time and diminished the vitality of the initial communication by removing it from the immediate context and order of business from which it had been delivered.

The metal folding chairs provided further encumbrances. They became increasingly uncomfortable over extended periods of time, frustrating even the most creative efforts to find a satisfactory sitting position. And much time was required for these meetings because of the thorough manner in which all revenue was duly noted by the treasurer and assistant treasurer, and then all expenditures were duly noted by the treasurer and assistant treasurer and discussed by the meeting at large, before expenditures were anticipated for the coming month, presented one item at a time by the treasurer and assistant treasurer, and discussed at length, item by item, by the meeting at large. Following the pastor's monthly record of her activities, then, reports on actions taken and activities organized during the month were presented by chairpersons of the Building and Grounds Committee, the Spiritual Oversight Committee, the Education Committee, the Missions Committee, the Hospitality Committee, the Social Concerns Committee, the Youth Committee, and the Community Outreach Committee.

Interruptions to these deliberations were common, as more than a few members whose attendance was critical to the final resolution of the more complicated matters involving finance and spiritual oversight—church officers, chairpersons, clerks, and other venerated individuals—required help in climbing up and down the steep concrete stairway leading to the only bathroom on the first floor. Some of the oldest members, including Violet Brasso, actually traveled the length of stairs sideways, in order to avoid pitching forward or backward on the steep incline. Violet often joked that her crablike walking style took a little longer, but provided a better view of the concrete walls, a bit of good humor suggestive not only of her generally cheerful nature, but also of the part she had played, as the head of the Spiritual Oversight Committee, in placing the sanctuary off-limits to business meetings. Some congregants thought that Violet had perhaps weighted her position with regard to restricting the sanctuary too heavily in the direction of a narrow interpretation of *holy* due to the sacrifices that were imposed upon her because of it. But no one except her sister, Olivia, ever said this out loud, and on each of the three different occasions when she had raised the point, she was told by Violet in no uncertain terms that it simply wasn't true.

The tables in the basement were also far from satisfactory. While providing a useful horizontal surface for those needing to confer with documents and write things down in hardbound administrative notebooks, the tables posed an insoluble dilemma for those who arrived with knitting, shopping lists needing a few additional items, sewing projects, birthday and get-well cards to be addressed and filled out, brochures, and other light reading materials that were hard to attend to beneath the table, and too brazenly obvious when placed on top.

An additional problem with the tables—and with the basement in general—arose from the members' well-established interests in food, juice, desserts, and coffee with cream and sugar. After sitting for an hour in a location where they normally ate meals, it was hardly surprising that people got hungry, they wanted a cup of juice, coffee, or bite of cake with whipped frosting and found it difficult to concentrate on the business at hand or offer any reasonable suggestions for the peaceful resolution of difficult business matters.

Because of these and numerous other considerations, the Spiritual Oversight Committee finally agreed to reconsider the sanctity of the sanctuary. The committee prayerfully deliberated on this subject for several years, and then decided that business meetings could be held in the upstairs sanctuary, provided they were conducted in a reverent and worshipful manner. The committee's final reasoning rested on a solid foundation, they believed. Since the administration of the church was necessary to the proclamation of the kingdom of heaven and the ruling order of Jesus Christ, and with it the spread of the blessed gospel story and the hope of salvation into all lands, monthly meetings for business could be considered a vital part of the sacred mission of the Words Friends of Jesus Church. Food and beverages still were not allowed inside the sanctuary, of course, just as they had not been allowed in the inner court of the Jerusalem temple during the time of Jesus. And, the committee further resolved, all items of business must be carefully considered before they were presented in the presence of the living God, whose holy spirit was usually thought to be more present in the holy sanctuary than it was anywhere else.

And so it was that on this Wednesday evening, eighteen people gathered toward the front of the sanctuary, sitting in the first three pews to the left of the center aisle. Facing them—just before the elevated platform at the front, out of which the lectern rose like a wooden obelisk—were Oskar Hamilton, head of trustees; Violet Brasso, chair of the Spiritual Oversight Committee; and Violet's sister, Olivia, who had recently accepted, much to the surprise of nearly everyone, the position of church business clerk.

Olivia's responsibilities included taking brief yet accurate minutes of all business discussed and all decisions made, with particular attention to matters involving finance. The three wooden chairs these authorities were sitting on had been carried in from the nearest Sunday school room. Their papers and notebooks rested in front of them on a large oak desk with a single drawer and tapered wooden legs. Simple yet dignified, not quite in the Shaker tradition but drawing on the same stark simplicity, this piece of furniture had been donated by Oskar Hamilton's grandmother in 1934. And just before the meeting commenced, it had been carried in from the main entryway, where it normally sat dutifully, providing a base for the church guest book and the weekly stack of bulletins.

Pastor Winnie sat in the first pew next to the aisle, wearing a long green skirt and a white blouse. She was not expected to be up front and in charge of business meetings. Even the prayers at the beginning and end of the meeting were delivered by Oskar Hamilton, though on occasion he called on Violet to give them because she excelled in delivering prayers and never failed to remember every name and cause that needed mentioning. Her sister, Olivia, was actually better with the religious phraseology, but she lacked Violet's tone and sensitivity to the unspoken yearnings in the room, and often went on much longer than the occasion called for.

Business meetings were delicate matters. Drawing on traditions that dated back to high priests and kings of old, those possessing spiritual authority could sometimes be out of harmony with the authority of those who controlled the purse and made the laws under which spiritual power could be exercised. The tension between these two kinds of authority often surfaced in business meetings, in part because those with financial power often lacked subtlety in wielding it. They were awkward, blunt, and highly sensitive to criticism—particularly compared with Winnie, who had been practicing her form of social authority for more than fifteen years.

Winnie knew her place, and on this occasion she sat sideways in the pew, in order to be able to make eye contact with everyone in the room. Jacob and August sat together in the middle of the second pew. As usual, August was the only person under thirty in the room. And Jacob looked so stiff and uncomfortable in his white shirt and green tie that his usually ruddy face appeared ghostly white. They were here in support of Winnie, of course, but they did not sit next to her, in case something came up that demanded her full attention. On another level, this spatial separation also acknowledged that in church Winnie belonged as much to the rest of the congregation as she did to them.

The meeting had been stuck for several minutes on a single point of business. A steel floor jack had been used to temporarily support a section of the church while repairs were being made to the foundation. The jack had been borrowed by the Building and Grounds Committee from a relative of Abraham Johnson, a trustee, and it had disappeared sometime between last Thursday night and Saturday morning.

"What color was it?" Elizabeth Fitch asked from the second pew.

"It was red," said Abe Johnson. "Tall and red, with a black ratchet arm, in perfect condition."

"Oh," said Elizabeth. "No, I don't remember seeing a red one."

Violet Brasso laughed briefly, trying to free some of the nervousness in the room. Abe Johnson was very upset about his relative's missing jack, and everyone knew he believed that Oskar Hamilton—or someone in his family, in any case—had taken it. The two men owned large farms on opposite sides of Words, and their mutual distrust sometimes spilled over into open hostility. Both contributed heavily to the church, and together they provided more than two-thirds of the annual thirty-thousand-dollar budget. Their wives also attended nearly every official church function, and were well known in the wider community.

"Did you see a floor jack of some other color?" Violet asked Elizabeth.

"No, I didn't," replied Elizabeth. "I just thought the color might jog something loose."

"Well, someone took it," said Abe Johnson. "Jacks don't just walk away by themselves."

"How much is a jack worth, anyway?" asked Rita Fry. She was knitting a red and green scarf for one of her grandchildren.

"It's not just a matter of money," said Abe Johnson. "It's a matter of trust."

"No one said anything about the jack being stolen," said Oskar Hamilton.

"I did," said Abe Johnson. "I said it and I'll say it again—someone stole that jack."

"Maybe a better word would be *misplaced,*" suggested Florence Fitch, not looking up from her folded hands.

"Not if it was stolen," said Abe Johnson. "If it was stolen then the right word is *stolen.*"

Olivia Brasso stared at her lined tablet and wondered how much of this she should be writing down. Keeping minutes involved a great deal of diplomacy. Records were kept to be read in the future, when the people participating in the meetings often did not want to remember what they had actually said at the time. And so it was important to preserve the facts in a way that erased the uncomfortable details and favorably represented the church body as a whole to any outsider who might find reason to read them.

"Has the Building and Grounds Committee . . . conducted a formal search . . . for the jack?" asked Oskar Hamilton with halting solemnity.

"No, we have not," said Ardith Stanley, that committee's chairperson.

"I've conducted a search," said Abe Johnson, his voice rising, "and it's not there."

Winnie felt awful when members of her congregation argued with each other. Discord of any kind reflected badly on her leadership. Personal animosities did not belong in church, and to keep them out pastors were brought in from outside the community. Unencumbered by family ties and longstanding feuds between members, incoming pastors were like houseguests. Simply dressing up wasn't enough, though tonight Winnie wondered if some kind of dress code for business meetings might help. She had noticed over the years that when people dressed up, it had a pronounced influence on the way they acted; partly for that reason, Sunday mornings were always the best times for getting along.

The pastor was the glue that kept this little community together, and a great deal of Winnie's time was spent gluing. This part of her job was so important, in fact, that she could never allow herself to become friends with anyone—not in a close, personal sense—because it could lead to perceptions of favoritism. In practical terms, this meant she hardly ever spent time with anyone she actually liked. She had support, but no friends in the group.

"There's a floor jack in the shop," said Jacob. "I'd be glad to bring it over."

An uncomfortable hush settled over the meeting. As a general rule,

Jacob's suggestions were seldom acted upon. This had concerned Winnie for many years, until she finally understood that it had nothing to do with Jacob and everything to do with her. The spouses of male pastors didn't have this difficulty; in fact, the "pastor's wife" had become nearly a cliché of social utility within rural communities, her script written and rewritten over hundreds of years by earlier wives of ministers. But no similar tradition existed for the "pastor's husband," and so no one knew what to expect from him.

It wasn't that the congregation did not approve of Jacob, it was that they didn't know how to go about doing it. They'd deliberated long and hard before calling a woman "pastor," weighed the drawbacks and benefits. Over the years since taking that step, they had ironed out most of the wrinkles, and successfully adjusted to the still-somewhat-unusual situation. But then Jacob came along, and for some reason this hurdle couldn't be cleared, or at least it hadn't been yet. The congregation could understand why a woman might want to aspire to a position that had formerly been reserved for men; what they couldn't understand was why a man would want to marry such a woman, and how to fit that circumstance within the traditions of the church.

"That's reasonable," said Violet hopefully.

"What color is it?" asked Elizabeth.

"Gray," said Jacob.

"With a green handle," added August.

After thinking about it for as long as he could, Abe Johnson dismissed the notion that his anger could be appeased by agreeing to let Jacob bring in another jack from his shop. He initially wanted to say that the substitute jack would not be of comparable value to the one borrowed from his cousin. But because he didn't know this for sure, he refrained. He deliberated about it for several seconds longer, and finally took a less compromising path.

"This isn't about a jack," he said, staring at Oskar Hamilton. "This is about a thief."

Oskar Hamilton slowly folded his notes on the table, pushed them away from him, and began to get up.

At that point Winnie rose to her feet and walked between the table and the front pew. She climbed onto the elevated area in front, took a

Bible from the pulpit, and opened it before coming down again and resuming her position between the table and front pew. She turned to Abe Johnson and looked at him for a long time. Eventually he was reminded of when his teenage daughter had not returned home from school one evening. Winnie had gone over and wept and prayed with him and his wife until three o' clock in the morning, waiting for the police to call or drive into the farmyard with the dreaded news. When his daughter had finally come home, vomiting from her first drinking binge, Winnie convinced Abe that beating her half to death might not be the most reasonable way of expressing his gratitude for her return. In fact, she conveyed, it might endanger his future relationship with her and her mother, who was still crying hysterically in the other room. Then Winnie walked with him around the farmyard for an hour as he calmed down.

With similar eye contact, Oskar Hamilton was reminded of the many times Winnie had come to the hospital during his open-heart surgery last winter, and also later, when the incision had become infected and visitors were required to don gowns, masks, and gloves before entering the isolation room. She had read to him from the Bible, smuggled in corn bread and other fatty foods in Tupperware containers in her purse, brought him updated reports on the farm, took back instructions for how to build the new feed bunk and where to plant the oats, and repeatedly assured him that his young wife was spending her few idle hours either at home in the farmhouse or with her sister in Luster.

These and other actions had increased Winnie's moral capital to such an extent that she could sometimes spend some of it in a business meeting, where moral capital had to be used with great discretion because it didn't go very far. Without the support of Oskar Hamilton and Abraham Johnson, Words Friends of Jesus Church would not exist. And just so everyone understood that too-easily-forgotten reality, from time to time the two men faced off against each other like rams on a hillside.

Winnie looked down into the opened Bible, closed it, pressed it against her like an infant, and sat down again.

"I propose that the Building and Grounds Committee hold a search for the missing jack," said Abe Johnson with a giant sigh, "and report back to us next month."

"Is that agreeable to you, Chairperson Stanley?" asked Oskar Hamilton.

"Call me Ardith," she said.

"I'm following *Robert's Rules of Order*," said Oskar.

"This is a church, not a card game," said Ardith. She had never played a game of cards in her life, but she had heard that such games were strictly governed by a rule book that sounded something like *Robert's*. "I trust I can speak for the rest of the committee when I say that conducting a search is agreeable to the Building and Grounds Committee."

The rest of the committee—Larry Fry and Florence Fitch—nodded.

"Thank you," said Oskar. "Now, Clerk Brasso, would you please read the last minute to be sure we have reached closure on this issue."

"Now?" asked Olivia.

"Yes, now."

"'The floor jack was discussed and the Building and Grounds Committee will report back next month on where it is.'"

"Shouldn't it be mentioned that the jack belongs to my cousin?" asked Abe Johnson. "Just for the record, I mean."

"The owner's name was recorded in last month's minutes, when it was noted that the Buildings and Grounds Committee would be borrowing it," replied Olivia.

"Would you please read that minute, Clerk Brasso?" instructed Oskar Johnson.

"Certainly," she said, turning back a page in her notebook, "'Chairperson Ardith Stanley reported that the Building and Grounds Committee had located a floor jack suitable for the repair work on the basement foundation, and the committee moved to borrow it from Cecil Johnson, with Ardith Stanley motioning and Florence Fitch seconding.'"

"Thank you, Clerk Brasso," said Oskar.

"I think it should be mentioned somewhere in there that the jack was red," said Elizabeth Fitch.

"Last month's minutes have already been approved by this committee," said Oskar Hamilton. "You can't change minutes after they've been approved."

"Then I move that a new minute be added, making it clear that the jack was red," said Elizabeth.

"*Is* red," added Olivia.

"That's what I said."

"No, you said *was* red."

"But we only know for sure that the jack *was* red. We don't know what color it is now. Someone could have painted it."

"But we didn't know what color it was before we borrowed it either," said Olivia.

"Elizabeth makes a good point," said Larry Fry. "I second the motion with *was*."

"I'm sorry," said Florence Fitch, looking away from her devotional literature, "I didn't hear the first motion. Could you repeat it?"

After all the committees had finished giving their reports, Winnie presented the monthly pastor's record. During the last month she had preached at four Sunday-morning worship services and four Sunday-evening worship services. She had preached at the Grange Nursing Home on a Tuesday morning, taught five Wednesday-night Bible studies, spoke briefly at Family Night, attended ten committee meetings and a prayer vigil for Horace Grover's sick grandson, visited fifteen separate homes, two hospitals, and three nursing homes, met with the local Ministers Association, gone bowling with the two teenagers in the church, and delivered used clothing to Goodwill and canned goods to the food pantry in Red Plain. From the Pastor's Mileage Fund she had withdrawn $35.46, which the treasurer and assistant treasurer both acknowledged, explaining that the Pastor's Mileage Fund had to be replenished from the special fund donated by the family of Oskar Hamilton after the departure of Mildred Hamilton, who died in her home after a lengthy illness at the beginning of June.

Then Winnie found the courage to stand up a second time. She announced that she had decided to submit her resignation, which would become effective as soon as Words Friends had succeeded in finding another pastor to replace her. She and her family would continue to attend the church as regular members, but she firmly believed it was the Lord's will for her to step down at this time and allow a new shepherd to minister to the flock.

A blanket of stunned silence fell over the room. Violet's eyes filled with tears.

"What will you do?"

"The Lord hasn't made that known to me yet," said Winnie, "but I have faith a door will be opened in the future. In the meantime, I shall apply myself to prayer and gardening."

"Gardening? Did you say gardening?" asked Florence Fitch.

"Yes, gardening."

Winnie could tell that this made no sense to anyone. With few exceptions, to be sure, everyone in the room either had a garden or frequently worked in one. But gardening wasn't something one did, it was simply something one had. Compared to preaching it amounted to, well . . . nothing.

"Did someone say something unkind to you, or do something to discourage your ministry among us?" asked Abe Johnson, staring in a threatening manner at Oskar Hamilton. "Lord knows you haven't had the kind of support you deserve from some."

"No, no, no, no," said Winnie. "My years as your pastor have been the most precious gifts anyone can imagine. It's just that the Lord has other plans for me, I guess."

"I object," said Olivia.

"To what?" asked Winnie.

"To your resignation. We won't accept it, or at least I won't. After the anointed are called out of the world to live as ministers to the Holy Word, they can't ever quit. They've been set apart. My own father preached in this very church for over thirty years, despite untold hardships and with no regard for his health and personal welfare. And all that time he had a garden too."

"Twenty-five years," corrected Violet. "It was twenty-five years, and he never stepped foot in that garden."

"Just the same, he didn't leave the ministry until death was nearly upon him," replied Olivia.

"Is it the money, Pastor Winifred?" asked Oskar. "Lord knows your salary is hardly enough to keep a rabbit alive, and yet I know someone in this room who was opposed to giving you a raise last year, in spite of the fact that the rest of us were in favor of it."

"That's a lie," said Abe.

"I think we have a minute to that effect," said Oskar, knotting his hands into fists. "Clerk Brasso, would you please find the minute from last year, the one referring—"

"Please don't, Olivia," interrupted Winnie. "This has nothing to do with my salary. You all have been more than generous. I'm asking you to release me now."

"This is terrible," said Violet.

"Why are you doing this?" asked Florence.

"I told you. It's the Lord's will."

"Yes, I know, but why are you really doing it?"

"I have to stop. The forms are going empty inside me."

"I move not to accept Pastor Winifred's resignation," said Olivia. Silence.

"And I second it," she added.

"You can't do that, Clerk Brasso," said Oskar. "It's against *Robert's Rules*."

"Then I move that we postpone this item of business until next month, when Pastor Winifred will have changed her mind."

"Second," said Violet.

"All in favor," said Oskar.

The meeting ended in prayer, and a short time later, Winnie and Jacob's cars were the only ones in the parking lot.

"August and I were thinking about driving into Grange for some ice cream before we go home," said Jacob. "Why don't you come with us?"

"You two go. I have some things to do here."

"We can bring you back something," said August. "The choices are practically unlimited."

"I'm afraid it would melt before you get home."

"No it won't, Mom. Dad will drive fast."

"Then bring me something with bananas in it."

"Will do," said Jacob. "Let's go, August."

Through the sanctuary windows along the west-facing wall, Winnie watched them walk across the parking lot. The sun lay low in the sky, and the colored light made the air look soft and embracing. August's face glowed as he climbed into the old jeep next to his father. Her son was trying to explain something with the help of many hand gestures, and Jacob was nodding and smiling.

Winnie turned away from the windows and sat down in a back pew. The sanctuary seemed provocatively quiet, and Winnie remembered the first time she had come here, many years ago. She'd lived in the parsonage behind the church. She was young then, and the rough country around her had seemed even younger, as if it had just been formed and inhabited.

Winnie began to think about a river of history flowing through this place, connecting her to the past. Many years ago, the area had been taken over by immigrants—homesteaders arrived from Europe with their families, farming methods, and cherished religions. Reminders of those sturdy folks were everywhere, in many cases walking around inside their descendants, who had grown taller and generally lived a lot longer, but still looked alarmingly like them.

She shivered with gratitude for having been allowed to participate in such a unique drama—one that would never again be performed in exactly the same way. After their homes were built, those homesteaders had constructed churches with wood hewn from local trees, and flocked into them Sunday after Sunday to sit reverently and listen to someone hired to stand in front of them and read from translated historical writings that themselves originated in a place they had never seen and from a tradition they did not understand, someone hired to instruct them on how to enter a place of eternal salvation called heaven, to condemn them for having sinful thoughts and desires, and to lead them to a heightened state of remorseful bliss.

Throughout the Midwest, these churches grew and grew, filled with pictures, stories, and children's drawings of camels, donkeys, Egyptian water jugs, miniature stables, and thin people with long hair and white head scarves living in deserts. While growing crops and raising children, the immigrants reserved a sacred place in their minds for imagined events from over two thousand years before. They thought about them deeply, in many cases identifying so profoundly with these stories that they believed themselves in moments of unusual clarity to be in direct relationship with the characters themselves, referring to them by first names such as Moses, Jeremiah, Jesus, Paul, Simon, Mary, Martha, and John. They even gave these names to their children, hoping in some way to empower them with a remnant of that ancient mythical power.

Even when scholars rose up among them, studied their holy scriptures in distant theological schools in Chicago and New Haven, and returned with the news that Moses did not write the five books of Moses, and that Jesus, if he lived at all, was not born on December 25 and would not have recognized the concept of the Holy Trinity, they listened patiently and quietly discounted everything they heard.

It seemed like simple foolishness to their parents. How could children not know that there were different kinds of facts? There were facts that depended on objective, verifiable evidence, and then there were those evinced through a thrilling verdict in the heart. So long as those old stories still resonated, they were true. The holy traditions had been set in place by holy ancestors, and they still held individuals and families together.

Sunday after Sunday, generations of Midwesterners had poured into the pews and prayed with flowing tears and gnashing teeth, then rose from their pews and sang at the top of their lungs—songs with joyful images of faith, courage, reunion, strength, celebration, and triumph, songs written by inspired men and women who had been filled with the same resurgent spirit that filled the singing and offered transport from their often bleak and difficult lives.

Winnie had been part of this. How many Sundays, she wondered, had she stood behind the pulpit and spoken of the great miracle, when the divine came alive in the most humble human circumstance? Through this same progression, wonder, love, and compassion would eventually overcome political and military power. She had stood in front of the church and explained how there was hope for a better tomorrow. "The despair you feel is a lie. It will pass away. Jesus will heal every wound, ease every sorrow. No matter what happens on earth, or in the wicked mind of government, the future has a home for you."

Such fundamental belief made it possible to endure the great disappointment when advances in science and technology seemed initially to promise that modern societies need no longer fear destruction by more-primitive societies, only to witness the resurrection of barbarism among themselves. Such belief even made it possible to look into the open abyss of the nineteenth and twentieth centuries, when the world's most advanced, well-informed, and cultured civilizations proved to be brutal, murderous, and evil.

Even now, sitting in the back pew and having just resigned her position because she could no longer continue in her role, Winnie trusted in the possibility of redemption. Life would not end in an apoplectic implosion of frustrated desires, foiled schemes, and defeated dreams, but rather in revealed glory.

I can't help it, she thought. I'm a daughter of the Midwest, and I never was sophisticated enough to be cynical. Blake was right. Once the imagination takes hold of the world in a certain way, nothing could possibly change it. When properly heeded, even the land itself insisted upon a magical sense of reciprocity. She would never be free of religious thinking, and she couldn't imagine ever wanting to be. She just needed a new schedule for her faith, one whose appointments with the divine were arranged not only through sermons, songs, and scripture, but rather on a walk-in basis with rocks, water, air, blood, space, and time.

Winnie walked to the front of the church, knelt at the carpeted altar, folded her hands, and wept for joy. Then she went outside into the parking lot, got into her car, and drove away without looking back.

Catching Up

Blake pulled to the edge of the deserted road, set the stand, and climbed off his motorcycle. The warm night enveloped him. Miles away, he could see houselights on the next ridge, remote and unmoving. He took off his jacket and laid it across the seat. A streak of yellow briefly marked the northern sky—a meteor or some other piece of space mineral burning up.

It was hard for Blake to conceive of astronomical speeds. What would it be like, he wondered, to move at the velocity of a meteor or comet?

His memory drew on the few grand-scale concepts he knew to apply to topics like these, and he reminded himself that motion was relative. Without the embrace of a gravitational field, you would have no sense of how fast you were moving until you came upon something moving at a different rate.

Everything on a galactic scale was hard to imagine. What would north, south, east, and west mean in deep space? There would be no orientation until you put yourself in relationship with something else, and arbitrarily decided that you and that something would serve as a basis for north, or south, or east, or west.

He'd recently read somewhere that space itself was expanding. Volumes of newly created intergalactic space were moving galaxies farther apart. In some cases whole orbital systems were moving away from each other faster than the speed of light. Some of the stars now visible in the sky would soon be disappearing, going out like switched-off nightlights along a dark hallway. Whole regions would soon go black, no longer visible from other regions, forever separate.

If Spinoza had known about expanding space, he might have been forced to conclude that God was not just changing from minute to minute, but growing. Would Spinoza's god feel this as personal growth? Would God's experiences all be subjective and interior, the way people feel emotions, thoughts, memories, and pain? Had Spinoza thought about this?

Probably not, thought Blake.

He emerged from his thoughts and once again discovered that he was alone on top of a hill, looking at a billion stars and listening to the ubiquitous sound of insects. He breathed deeply and felt humbled. For now, things were complicated enough without wondering about the larger picture.

He was glad Skeeter Skelton had not showed up. Blake had almost not come himself. Meeting people from the past was difficult—hard to know what to say, and even harder to know what they might be thinking. This was especially true of someone like Skeeter, who occupied a significant place in his memory.

Blake had the same problem with Danielle.

He heard a noise in the distance. Of course Skeeter would be late, thought Blake. The sound of an engine moved closer and closer, out of the valley below.

After clearing the last corner, a single headlight lit up the two hundred yards of steep road between them. The sound accelerated rapidly and the beam of light rushed forward. Probably third gear, thought Blake. Then the engine noise ended abruptly and the light went out.

Rising silently out of the darkness, Skeeter Skelton coasted up the hill in neutral. His momentum died a couple feet away from where Blake stood.

"Hey, Blake," said Skeeter. "Welcome back."

Blake smiled. He couldn't help it. Skeeter hadn't forgotten how to make an entrance.

"Nice to see you again, Skeeter."

In the milky skylight Blake noticed Skeeter had acquired some gray in his brown hair. Except for that, he looked much the same—short, wiry, still probably weighing less than 130 pounds. His face and the back of his hands were scarred and road-burned. His right leg—below the knee—had been replaced with a prosthetic. The refashioned body part had been made to look like several lengths of stainless steel pipe and black metal; when he climbed off his bike it gave the impression that part of the machinery had been dismantled.

Skeeter's handshake was quick, breaking away after the first hard bony squeeze.

"Still running tracks?" asked Blake.

"Don't race much anymore," said Skeeter, unzipping his tight-fitting leather jacket. "My sponsors started telling me which races to enter."

"What do you do now?"

"Pick my own. Things changed while you were away."

"How's that?"

"New people, different. I'm semiretired now."

Skeeter walked around Blake's motorcycle. "Looks like the same Gixxer you used to have," he said, fondling a fender. "Old one with carbs."

"I see you're still riding Ducks."

"So, what's it like in prison?"

"Some days are better than others."

"Someone said they sent you up for drugs."

"That's right."

"Didn't know you were into that."

"Only takes once."

Skeeter leaned against his own motorcycle, took a small cigar out of his coat, and lit it. "You still with that same woman?" he asked.

"Afraid not."

"Damn, she was nice."

"I didn't think anyone else knew that," said Blake.

"Never works that way. I looked for her after you were gone. Found her too, but she wouldn't have nobody. She could ride nearly as good as you."

"I know it," said Blake. "I taught her."

"She's got a kid now."

"That's what I heard."

"Does he belong to you?"

"He might."

"He looks like you."

"I heard that too."

"Have you seen her?"

"Once. I'd like to see her again, but—"

"But what?"

"But nothing."

Skeeter laughed, took a last pull from his cigar, and flipped the remainder into the ditch.

Skeeter was different, thought Blake. The risk-loving that had once characterized his racing seemed to have influenced the way he talked. He seemed to assume a greater familiarity than actually existed between them. It felt a little like a psychic invasion.

Skeeter spoke again. "You were the only guy around here who could keep up with me. You ran dirt and hills, short track and quarter mile, and then you spent the last three years in supermax. A couple nights ago you were ready to jump Jim Clay and Bobbie Jackson in the bar in Luster— both of 'em cage fighters. You live alone in the middle of nowhere, in a farmhouse most people think is haunted, and yet you're afraid to go see that little gal who works as a live-in outside of Grange."

The night had turned cooler. Blake put on his jacket. "How'd you know all that?"

"Way too many people talk to me," said Skeeter, walking around Blake's bike again, crouching and looking at the engine.

"I'm not afraid of seeing her."

"Yes you are."

"Why would I be?"

"She's got something you can't live without."

"I'm living without it now."

"You hope you might get her back someday, and you don't want to live without that dream."

"What business of yours is this?" asked Blake, bristling.

"The few exceptional women in the world belong to everyone. She has something that can't be named. If people knew what it was they'd sell it by the pound and you could snort her up a paper straw and stay higher than a kite."

Fighting against the older man's presumption of closeness was becoming more difficult for Blake. He felt himself giving in to his more charismatic companion. "I'd like to know what it is," he said. "I mean, I agree with you that she has it, but I'd like to know what it is."

"Wouldn't be what it is if you knew what it was," said Skeeter.

"I'd still like to know," replied Blake.

"Big mistake," said Skeeter. "That's why most people don't know shit."

Skeeter sidled back over to his bike. "Let's start," he said, zipping up his jacket and climbing on. "First one to go past that tavern in Luster wins."

"That's right in the middle of town."

"Something about that bother you, Blake?"

"No, just checking. How many people know about this?"

"Not too many. And to make it more interesting, let's do this without lights."

Blake started his engine and lined up beside Skeeter's reworked Ducati. Blue smoke rolled off their back tires.

Blake found himself ahead of Skeeter after the first corner, but he quickly became aware of the drawbacks of being the leader. All Skeeter had to do was keep up for twenty miles, letting Blake take all the risks, then try to take the lead at the end.

Blake felt like a fool. How did he get himself into this?

After three or four miles of riding as fast as he dared without a head-lamp, Blake backed off a little, to see whether Skeeter intended to ride his tail all the way into Luster.

Sure enough, he stayed behind him, even along a straight run of sky-lit highway that could have been traveled twenty or thirty miles an hour faster than they were going.

After another couple miles, Blake tried to see how familiar Skeeter was with the road. By going wide on several corners that should have been taken on the inside and watching in his rearview as Skeeter followed him, he gathered that Skeeter did not know the road very well. This assumption seemed to be confirmed when a set of headlights came toward them in the distance; Skeeter narrowed the length between them, hanging close behind, afraid something unforeseen might happen with the vehicle, leaving him with too much distance to make up before Luster.

Blake smiled. In the old days, Skeeter never would have played it safe.

A doe standing in the road caused a moment of hesitation before both bikes raced by it on the left.

Three miles outside Luster, Blake felt his body tighten. While Skeeter might not be very familiar with the road they had traveled to this point, surely he was well acquainted with that part of it just outside of Luster, which is why he'd set the race up this way. Still, the caution he sensed in Skeeter's riding gave him an unanticipated confidence in himself.

On the outskirts of town, Skeeter nearly came alongside Blake, bidding for the inside on the last corner. They leaned into it together and came out side by side, headed into town.

Both bikes accelerated through the four-way stop and on past the tavern. Blake nipped Skeeter by a tire length.

They continued through Luster and pulled into a little park on the north side of town. Neither rider got off.

Skeeter, who almost never lost races, looked like someone had just poked him in the eye with a stick. But he smiled and sat there on his bike, shaking his head. "You've got a damn long third gear, Blake."

"Listen," said Blake. "No one is going to hear about this from me. I don't want your reputation, Skeeter. You can have it. But I need you to do something for me."

"Name it," said Skeeter.

"I need to know if Danielle Workhouse is seeing someone. If she is, I want to know as much as you can find out about him."

"I can do that," said Skeeter.

A siren came toward them through Luster.

"I'll take this," said Skeeter. "You stay here."

Skeeter turned on his headlamp, rode out of the park, and waited for Luster's deputy sheriff to see him. He led him out of town before opening the Duck up, putting an eighth of a mile between them, and then taking the bicycle trail over the ridge and into Thistlewaite County.

Blake remained in the park long enough to reflect on his recent victory. For several minutes it seemed significant, and then all the importance drained out. Skeeter had gotten older. In his prime—back when Blake had really cared about beating him—he was still untouchable.

Looking up at the sky, Blake smiled and rode back home.

Two Lives Collide

Amy Roebuck was working in the garden on the north side of the house. Dressed in faded denim overalls, a leather apron, canvas shoes, and an enormous straw hat that fastened under her chin with long pink ribbons, Amy transplanted a row of perennials along the edge of the lawn, carefully moving the plants from black plastic pots into evenly spaced holes in the ground.

Dart watched her from the window in the laundry room. She was stacking clean towels and facecloths into rising towers on top of the washer and dryer, staring outside periodically and wiping perspiration from her forehead.

On her knees, Amy spread out the delicate roots of a purple New England aster and pressed them gently into loose soil sprinkled with organic fertilizer. She pulled more dirt into the hole with her cupped hands and patted it down, making sure the plant stem poked straight up. Then she carefully added water from a galvanized can with a narrow curved spout. The liquid spread into a black puddle around the plant, then shrank from the outside in, leaving a dark, concave indentation. She added a little more water, leaned back on her ankles, put her hands in her lap, and tried to imagine what it might feel like to be plucked from the nursery's niggardly container of vermiculite and implanted in the wet earth, to feel your life grounded and reaching down into the world.

Dart's fluffy tower of facecloths grew unstable. The vertical reiteration of monogrammed *R*'s running up one side was in danger of bending. She began another stack, and searched through the basket for more facecloths to pile on it. Then she turned toward the window again.

Amy finished her row and refilled the watering can from the green hose snaking away from the house's stone foundation. One by one, she added more water to the asters, soaking the soil around them. At the end of the row she set the can down, folded her arms, and looked at the new line of plants in relation to the rest of the garden. For a delightful moment, she could see the garden of her childhood, the way it had looked when she would visit her grandparents. She had loved it here—away from town, away from the incessant demands of school, away from mocking classmates, neighbors, and the familiar anguish of her daily routine. As soon as her father's old Plymouth came to a stop at the end of the drive, she'd throw open the back door and run madly toward the house, as if she were rushing into the refuge of the afterlife. Amy had always felt a strong connection with her grandparents. They shared the same emotional rhythms. Being with them always felt right.

Dart finished folding the laundry and set the towels and facecloths in an empty basket, to distribute later through the house. She looked out the window again at Amy. She'd never known anyone so private, gentle, and contained. A terrible sadness bloomed inside Dart—remorse without bottom, beyond tears, as if someone had split open the skin of rage to reveal its bitter contents. She took the sheets out of the washing machine, put them in another basket, and carried them out to hang on the clothesline.

As she walked across the yard, Amy intercepted her. Dart set the basket of laundry on the grass.

"Do you think your friend Winifred would be willing to come over and help with the garden?" asked Amy. "I keep seeing her annuals, especially the patch of marigolds next to the fountain."

"I don't know," said Dart, looking away from the taller woman. "She's not really my friend, anyway."

"Dart, what's wrong?"

"Nothing," she snapped. She tried to find the courage to look directly at Amy, but her hat framed her face in such an alarmingly beautiful way, accentuating her eyes and cheeks. Dart had to look away.

"Tell me."

"Ivan and me," said Dart. "We're leaving at the end of the week."

"What?"

"We're out of here Friday afternoon."

"What do you mean?" Amy took her hat off and held it by the long ribbons hanging from the sides of the brim, looking both surprised and hurt.

"I quit. Ivan and me, we're moving on to better opportunities."

"Oh really. Which ones?"

"None of your business."

"I thought you liked it here."

"Well that's just stupid."

"Why are you doing this, Dart?"

"It's time to move on. We've been here too long. I've got to do what's best for my son. You should be able to understand that."

"Look at me," said Amy, dropping her hat and taking Dart by the shoulders.

"Take your hands off me," said Dart.

A brief gust of wind carried Amy's hat several yards away.

"Look at me."

"No."

"Look at me."

Dart pushed Amy's hands away and stepped back.

Amy stepped forward and took hold of her again.

"Look at me."

Dart looked at her.

"Tell me."

Dart's eyes moistened. "I stole the necklace."

"What necklace?"

"This one," said Dart, taking it out of the pocket of her jeans and placing it in Amy's open hand.

Amy spread the necklace and the lattice of diamonds fell open like a minor galaxy. Her eyes hardened and a look of resigned disappointment swept over her face. "Dart, this isn't mine," she said breathlessly. "I could never afford something like this. Where did you get it?"

"I would never take something that belonged to you," explained Dart.

At that moment Buck's truck drove up the driveway and parked next to the shed.

Dart looked frightened.

Amy put the necklace in the pocket of her leather apron.

"Go inside," she said sternly. "Now."

Dart went into her apartment, locked the door, and began packing.

Slippery Slopes

In a truck stop just off I-10 in New Orleans, Nate was eating a bowl of gumbo. He remembered a time when he didn't like okra. Since then his tastes had expanded, and a good meal was now more complicated, open to the influences of mood, opportunity, and whim. The favorite dishes of his childhood were still important, of course, but he had also discovered many other good foods and ways to prepare them. He finished off with a piece of peach pie, and while he was forking in the first bite he remembered canning peaches with Bee in her kitchen.

The pie was exceptional—the crust chewy yet flaky, with a bumpy sprinkle of cane sugar on top, the peaches not too sweetened by a custard that had a lemon afterthought. His second bite only reinforced the first impression.

His thoughts turned to Bee again, and he noticed the absence of the distress he often experienced when thinking of his relationship with her. Testing this new circumstance, Nate took another bite. And again, the nagging shame that had always accompanied his feelings for his cousin—the familial dark taboo—was no longer there.

Nate celebrated his good fortune as he finished the pie and explored how it might have come to light. The new freedom of his imagination was surely not an inevitable result of having lived longer and experienced more. Individuals had little control, Nate believed, over the moral alarms instilled in early years by their families and cultures. With age, the alarms often became more sensitive, easier to trigger, reinforced by earlier eruptions. Cousins were off-limits. There were good reasons for that, and the happy fact that Bee was no longer of child-bearing age had utterly failed to dampen the feelings of distress surrounding his longing for her—until this current moment in a humid truck stop in Louisiana. But whatever the reason, his desire for Bee now acknowledged no obstacle to securing its prize.

When Nate returned home three days later, he went to see his cousin and learned that she had—a week or so earlier—experienced a similar freedom to imagine herself entwined with Nate. Her first encounter with this phenomenon began, she said, on the drive back from the tavern, after she and Nate picked up his son. Something about the way Nate shifted gears that night had opened the gate. She hadn't said anything, though, because she didn't want to rock the boat and because she was older and thought Nate might need a couple more years before his own imagination found this new authority to go places formerly forbidden to it.

"We should be careful," said Nate. "We could be talking ourselves into this. The old demon may still be waiting to catch us in the act."

"Maybe," said Bee. "But I know how to find out. Let's spend some time in Slippery Slopes. If there are any taboos lurking, they'll turn up there."

As children, the two cousins had frequently visited their grandparents' home in Slippery Slopes, Wisconsin—a little town seventy miles north of Grange. The long sleepy drive on country roads had always made it seem as if they were traveling to a foreign country. On more than a few occasions their respective families had visited simultaneously, bringing Nate and Bee together. The house occupied a prominent place in their shared memories; it was a reservoir of initial encounters, explorations, and early adventures in places other than home. It was also the embodiment of family traditions.

The old Slopes mining community was named after its hilly terrain. Comprising a three-block-long collection of stores and other businesses surrounded by an expanding kaleidoscope of homes of different sizes and shapes, it sheltered about eight hundred residents. Built before the advantages of modern construction equipment, most streets connected through precarious inclines, and to children raised on flat, isolated farms, it seemed marvelous to walk a short distance downhill from your home and find yourself inside a grocery store or barber shop.

Bee had tasted her first buttermilk pancakes inside the summer kitchen toward the back of the house. The maple syrup was always warmed, which she didn't like at the time because it seemed thin and watery. But now she always heated the syrup when she made pancakes, to evoke those earlier days.

There was a dark alley behind the towering three-story buildings along Main Street, and a rickety wooden staircase on the back of one of them led up to a tiny apartment on the third floor. An old woman lived up there and hung her laundry out on the roof—a wondrous fact for a rural child, and the knowledge had lived on to this day in a special place inside her. The alley ended after several buildings, sheds, and rubbish bins in a used-car lot with grass growing up through cracks in the concrete, where a soda machine stood—a locked red refrigerator—guarding the cars for sale.

Nate, on the other hand, remembered many features from inside the house particularly well: pictures, furniture, flooring, windows, wainscoting, and deep bottle-fly-blue and violet glass vases and pitchers, which his grandmother collected and set in the bay window. The rooms were small and the hallways narrow, as if the place had been built by dwarves for the occupancy of children. The walls were papered over with vegetative designs, and the beds were high and lumpy with noisy springs. The thickly varnished wood floors creaked loudly, and the banister going upstairs consisted of a water pipe with fittings on the ends, painted glossy white. He remembered seeing his first harmonica in a cabinet drawer in the living room. He picked it up, blew through it, and made a broad, fuzzy sound. Then Bee—whom he had just met for the first time he could remember—took it away from him and put it in the pocket of her yellow dress. "You're too little," she said. "This is a very expensive mouth organ and I'll keep it for you. That way it will stay safe."

Bee claimed to have seen Nate a number of times before this encounter with the harmonica, when Nate was too young to remember. She remembered carrying him around, feeding him, changing his diapers, getting him to stop crying, and taking him for walks in a stroller. Nate always enjoyed hearing these memories of which he had no recollection, though he often wondered how much Bee herself contributed to their content. Somehow the details surrounding the time when he was a helpless infant and she a competent girl with precocious child-rearing skills always seemed to exceed the narrative material available from other periods in their lives.

It didn't take long for Nate and Bee to make a decision. And so Nate called their uncle Dan and asked after their grandparents' house.

Daniel Bookchester, now in his eighties and talking on the white phone in the beige room of his retirement home, explained to Nate that the old couple who rented the house for fifteen years following the death of their grandparents had recently moved out to live with their children. The real estate agency that managed the property had made repairs, replaced the furnace, refrigerator, and stove, repainted, and listed it again. It was currently unoccupied.

"Would it be possible for Bee and me to stay there a couple days?" asked Nate.

"What?" said Uncle Dan, adjusting the little knob on his hearing aid.

"Could we rent it for a short time?" asked Nate again.

"I don't know," said Uncle Dan, his voice rising with uncertainty. "I don't have anything to do with it anymore. Call the realtor."

"Which realtor is it?" asked Nate.

"I don't remember. Look it up. How many can there be in Slippery Slopes?"

"We'll find it," replied Nate.

"Who did you say this was?"

"Your nephew Nathaniel."

"Oh, right. Is that boy of yours still in prison, Nate?"

"He's been out awhile now and he's doing real good."

"No kidding. What do you hear from your cousin Beulah? I don't think she ever got married, did she? Cute girl she was, but strange as a one-eared donkey. Gave my sister fits. Anyway, I've got to go now. It's lunchtime."

At work the following day, Bee talked to a woman at the real estate agency in Slippery Slopes. She agreed to rent the house short-term, though Bee said she had to talk to Nate before setting a firm date.

When she spoke to Nate, Bee explained that if they were going to do this—the two of them, really do it—she hoped they would try to get it right. There was no sense going to their grandparents' house to confront the hoary past and see if they could finally become lovers in the most unambiguous and consummated sense if they didn't intend to stay long enough to have a meaningful experience, ten days at the very least. Otherwise, they might as well not go at all.

"That means," said Bee, "I'll have to find someone to stay with Mother, and you'll have to get that shipping company to give you a vacation."

"Are you sure you want to do this?" asked Nate. "Ten days is a long time."

"Not if you don't want to."

"Oh, I want to."

"So do I," said Bee. "I can get Rufus to stay with Mother, or Gladys or even Margaret. Do you think they'll give you some time off?"

"No problem," said Nate, though he knew it was a stretch. Ten days was a long time in the transit business. In this bloody-knuckled economy, shipping companies were constantly looking for excuses to hire new drivers who spoke no English and were willing to work longer hours for less money and no benefits. Unlisted contractors trained them, licensed them, marketed them, and whisked them out of the country if problems arose.

The agreement Nate finally made with the dispatcher and freight manager was for one week, but he also agreed to check his phone messages daily and be available for an unlikely emergency. He did not tell Bee about this improbable contingency though, and merely explained that he had the week off.

Bee didn't know if one week would be long enough, but she decided to go ahead anyway. If they were still bound by the old rules after that much time, then there was nothing to be done. The past would have its victory and she would go on living as she had for this long.

Nate and Bee drove up in Nate's pickup, and when they arrived in Slippery Slopes they discovered that the town had grown considerably since they'd last seen it. Excepting the downtown area, the streets had been widened and there were now four sets of stoplights instead of one. Pastel vinyl siding covered most of the homes, and only a few people kept gardens in their yards. There were also signs of encroaching tourism: antiques and gift shops, two motels, several B and Bs, and three restaurants on the six-lane strip leading to and from the interstate.

They parked behind their grandparents' house and stood in the backyard, reluctant to go inside. The backside of the steeply peaked house looked especially imposing, if smaller than they remembered.

"Maybe we should walk around town for a little while," suggested Nate.

"No, we should go in," said Bee. "We need to get these groceries in the refrigerator. Oh my, look at that." She pointed to a bent iron hook on the door leading down into the cellar. "It's the same one."

"I remember," said Nate, opening the tailgate on the pickup. "It has an odd shape. And look up there."

Halfway up the linden tree, a platform of rotten boards rested between three branches. "You helped build that," said Nate.

"I didn't help build it," said Bee. "I built it all by myself to give Rufus something to do, so he'd stop following me around."

"He practically lived up there for a couple days, lowering strings to haul up things he needed," said Nate.

"You were with him much of that time," said Bee.

"I know. The strings were my idea."

"And a dumb one at that." Bee snorted. "Everything you pulled up there fell down at some point."

Nate felt the more recent stages of his life unraveling, peeling off in irrelevant episodic scrolls. He and Bee were reverting to their younger selves, and they hadn't even gone inside the house yet.

"This isn't going to be easy," he said.

"Come on," said Bee in a commanding voice. "No time to waste. Let's get this stuff inside."

The key they'd received from the real estate agent fit perfectly and turned smoothly in the lock. The back door opened silently. They walked into the kitchen, plugged the cord attached to the refrigerator into the wall, and stuffed it with food.

"You go get the luggage and boxes," said Bee. "I'll open some of these windows."

For the rest of the day Nate and Bee explored the sparsely furnished house. Many of the wood floors had not been carpeted over. The light switches, doorknobs, and electrical outlets were all the same, as were the basement, the attic, the windows, and the sink in the summer kitchen.

Two of the upstairs bedrooms shared a single large closet that could be entered by doors in either room. Like much of the rest of the house, the closet was empty, which made it seem remarkably different from earlier times, when moving through the secret passageway included a hanging jungle of aromatic old-people clothes, many of them with silky textures. Yet standing inside it now still brought a glimmer of the old enchantment. Nate and Bee put their clothes in this closet.

The bed in their grandmother's old room was the biggest one in the house, and so they put the sheets on it, along with a green and red blanket. An empty silence surrounded them as they worked, the air monitoring their movements.

"I'm a little scared," said Bee, sitting on the bed.

"Me too," said Nate.

"After all those years of you lusting after me, what if I don't measure up?"

"You didn't know how I felt about you back then."

"It was pretty obvious. Even when my mother insisted you couldn't have such feelings for me, I knew you did. The hands in your eyes were always on me."

"You never gave me any sign," said Nate.

"Of course not. What did you expect?"

"You might have encouraged me a little."

"I was older, and every time I thought about letting you close to me I'd explode with shame. That would be taking advantage of you, acting out the part of the sodden farm girl drunk with incestuous impulses."

"I know," said Nate. "It was one of the reasons I got married so young— to force my feelings for you away."

"You never should have felt guilty about me, Natie. You were younger. It was natural for you."

"I didn't have the right to think about you in that way."

"There are no rights, just feelings and the things that hold them in place."

"You were older. I didn't have enough experience to look directly at you and explain how I felt. All I had were these emotions I didn't understand and couldn't tell anyone about. I wanted to please you, hurt you, be you, all at the same time. And the impossibility of that somehow made the desire even stronger. It was a lonely time, and it went on for years and years."

"That's the way it works," said Bee, resuming her vaguely superior voice. "Besides, everyone would have excused you and blamed me."

Nate put sheets on the bed in the room on the other side of the shared closet while Bee made buttermilk pancakes. After eating them, they listened to several radio dramas and slept separately, restlessly.

The next day they walked around town, ate in restaurants, visited

Slippery Slopes Cemetery, put flowers on several graves, and talked about the obstacles preventing them from doing what they wanted to do. Who would disapprove, really? The names of several particularly righteous relatives were suggested, then cautiously dismissed. They had either been dead a long time and little was known about them beyond the frozen rectitude staring out from old photos, or developments in their own lives had sufficiently disqualified any potential criticism of what Nate and Bee were contemplating.

By the third day they agreed that it was their own habit of denying themselves to each other that rose up like chaperoning dragons between them. It seemed as if those fearful forces came from outside—the wider family and the community. But in truth these forces were less important. The cousins felt like separate individuals who had wanted to drink from the same forbidden fountain their entire lives, but when finally given the opportunity, they couldn't decide if they should or not.

They told each other that the most rigidly held family embargoes and societal norms meant absolutely nothing to them, and yet such brazen disregard for the rules seemed the wrong approach, like burning the ancestral home in order to enjoy the flames. Indeed, one of the most compelling features of Nate and Bee's love for each other issued straight from their shared associations and familial sensibilities, which both drew them together and kept them apart.

"I think it's against the law for first cousins to marry in Wisconsin," said Bee.

"I know," said Nate. "I looked it up when I was eight years old."

"I have an idea," said Bee. "You leave this to me."

Nate watched Bee leave the house and drive away in the pickup. To pass the time before she came back, he took a long walk, lingered inside a few stores, bought a flannel shirt at a secondhand shop, dug out a nickel embedded in an asphalt parking lot with his pocketknife. He talked to one older man sitting on a park bench about the local fishing; then another man standing in front of the bakery told him how the human body completely replaced itself every seven years with new cells, except the teeth.

"That's hard to believe," said Nate.

"I know it," said the man, before stepping into the bakery.

When Nate returned to the house, Bee was in the kitchen.

"I hope you're hungry," she said.

"Starving," said Nate.

"Wait out there until I call you," she said. "I have a surprise."

Nate sat down in the living room. When Bee came out, she told him to close his eyes, then led him to the table and helped him sit down.

"Don't look yet," she said, and put a steaming plate in front of him.

"I can smell it," said Nate. "Can't quite place it though."

"You can open your eyes now."

Nate looked down on hot chipped beef in a white sauce on toast, with a side of canned peas.

"I want you to eat every bite before you leave the table," said Bee.

She had even managed to find some nutrient-free white bread that closely resembled the brands they grew up with. Nate cut a piece of soggy toast and lifted it to his mouth. As he chewed, the salty yet bland taste invited memories of countless meals served to him as a child. This had been his most disliked food, and he remembered well the dismal combination of frustration and resignation required to get through it. Revisiting an often-thought but never-spoken question from childhood, Nate wondered how anyone could actually like this food.

Unlike years ago, however, Nate now knew the answer to this question: he and his sister were always hungry, and their parents were always busy. Chipped beef on toast was easy to make, and it provided calories, starch, and protein. And there were also more-limited choices back then.

The simple truth was that fifty years ago his family felt differently about eating. Their attitude was entirely appropriate at the time, but things changed and now Nate cared in a different way about food. The evolution from one attitude to another required a convolution of economic, scientific, and technological developments, all of which would be impossible to comprehend completely. Times changed.

Nate stopped eating halfway through these ruminations, and stood up from his grandmother's table.

"You sit right back down there, Natie, and finish your supper," snapped his older cousin, her eyes flashing.

"I will not," said Nate, coming toward her.

"Good," said Bee.

The Trial

When the knock came, Dart had three suitcases and a cardboard box packed with clothes.

"Just a minute," she said.

"Come out here right now," said Amy.

Dart opened the door.

Amy's face was white, her lips tight. "Come with me." She turned rigidly and walked away. Dart followed her out to the SUV. Amy got behind the wheel and started the engine. "Get in," she said, and Dart sat beside her in front.

"Where are we going?" asked Dart after ten minutes.

"Don't talk to me. I'm angry, I'm scared, and I'm trying not to cry."

An hour and a half later, south of Madison, Amy pulled off the interstate, drove along a county road, and turned up a long drive between overhanging trees. They stopped in front of an enormous stone house with a side yard as spacious and evenly maintained as a nine-hole golf course. A bronze sculpture of a nude dancer rested on a brick patio between a tennis court and a five-car garage. Amy shut off the engine.

"This is where Frieda and Harold Rampton live," she said. "She's the woman you stole the necklace from."

"How do you know?"

"Buck called some people. The police are involved and a reward has been offered."

Amy took the necklace out of her purse and handed it to Dart.

"Why are you giving this to me?"

"Because you're giving it back."

"I can't do that," said Dart, her eyes wide, moist, frightened.

"Yes you can."

"Are the police here? What will she do when I give it to her?"

"I guess you'll find out."

Dart opened the car door, then turned back to Amy.

"I can't do this."

"You have to."

"Will you come with me?"

"All right," said Amy, getting out.

They walked to the front door and Amy pushed the plastic button.

A woman in a light blue work dress opened the door.

"Can I talk to Frieda Rampton?" asked Dart.

"Come in," said the young woman. They stepped into a beige-tiled entryway.

"Wait here." She gestured toward a couple of chairs next to the bay window.

Neither Dart nor Amy sat down.

After several minutes a thin, casually dressed woman approached from a long hallway to the left. She was wearing a crisp white sleeveless blouse, white shorts, and flip-flops. Her legs, as Dart remembered, seemed longer than the rest of her, slender and reedlike.

"Hello," she said in a formal manner. "I'm sorry, do I know you?"

"My name is Danielle Workhouse," said Dart, stepping forward with the jewelry hanging from her right hand. "We met at a party and I took your necklace."

Frieda looked at her for a moment, and then a flash of recognition bolted across her face. She took the necklace and held it for a moment as her expression filled with dark anger. Without warning, she struck at Dart with her open hand.

Instinctively, Dart stepped back, escaping the blow. Then she stepped forward again and closed her eyes.

"I'm sorry," she said. "Go ahead, hit me."

Frieda drew her hand back, but before her arm lashed out again the darkness in her face had receded. She took a deep breath. "I can't do it now," she complained. "You shouldn't have ducked the first time."

"I'm sorry," said Dart, opening her eyes.

"Are you her bodyguard?" Frieda asked Amy.

"I'm Amy Roebuck, and I'm her friend."

Frieda turned back to Dart. "Why did you take my great-aunt's necklace?"

"I didn't want to leave and I was just standing there and—"

"Tell me the truth," snapped Frieda.

"I wanted to keep something beautiful from that night," said Dart. "I didn't know it was worth that much. I'm sorry."

"I liked you," said Frieda. "We had a good time together."

"I liked you too," said Dart. "You will never know how much fun I had that night. But there are no excuses. I took your necklace."

"I'm calling the police right now," said Frieda, walking over to where a cordless phone rested on a table. "They know how to deal with people like you."

"Go ahead," said Dart.

Before she finished dialing, Frieda hung up and walked back to Dart and Amy.

"I remember now who you are," she said to Amy. "You and your husband own a construction company outside Grange."

"That's right," said Amy.

"You're a big gal," said Frieda. "Almost statuesque."

"I've heard that before," said Amy, smiling.

"How did you become friends with her?"

"It just happened."

"And you don't care if your friend is a thief?"

"I care very much, Frieda. That's why I'm here."

Frieda turned back to Dart. "She made you come, didn't she?"

Dart nodded.

"Have you been in trouble before?"

Dart nodded again.

"How long ago?"

"A year or two."

"What did you do?"

"Took a battery out of a new Escalade."

"Why'd you do it?"

"The owner, he owed me."

"Is that the only other time?"

"Twice before."

"What happened?"

"I broke a guy's leg to keep him from hurting my son."

"It's not easy to break a man's leg."

"It wasn't that hard. I had a piece of angle iron."

"And before that?"

"I stole a cart of groceries."

"A big cart?"

"Big enough for a month."

"Do you just do everything you want?"

"No."

Frieda looked down at the necklace again, spread it open, inspected it carefully, and put it in the pocket of her white shorts.

"I have to admit, I'm glad to have it back." She went to the door, opened it, and stood waiting for them to leave.

"Aren't you going to call the police?" asked Dart.

"No."

"Why not?"

"I'm just not going to. You're not the only one who can do what she wants."

"But the police are already involved."

"Get out of here before I change my mind. Thanks for bringing her, Amy," she said, and held out her hand.

"You're welcome," said Amy, pressing Frieda's hand inside both of hers.

Outside, Dart turned around. "You really do dance better than anyone I ever knew," she said.

Frieda smiled, then stepped toward her and slapped Dart smartly across the face.

Dart and Amy got back in the SUV and drove off.

"That really hurt," said Dart, rubbing her cheek.

"It sounded like it," said Amy.

"Do you think it will leave a mark?"

"Probably not."

"Nobody ever did anything like that for me."

"Slapped you?"

"No, stood up for me the way you did. Never."

"You're welcome."

Forty miles later, Amy asked Dart if her face still hurt.

"Is it red?"

"I'm afraid so. Look for yourself; there's a mirror above the visor."

"No thanks," said Dart, and a mile later added, "My sister always wanted to look at her marks after she got beat. She'd check on them several times a day. I never wanted to see mine."

"Dart," said Amy, "that's very distressing."

"I know it. But that's just how we lived. We didn't think much about it. We had to hide the bruises and burns from the teachers and social workers, of course."

"No child should have to live like that."

"I never told anyone about it. I remember it all the time, but I've never told anyone."

"I can understand that."

"Really?"

"Of course I can."

Ten miles later, Dart's face stopped hurting. As the sting receded, a buoyant sensation followed. Her whole body felt light.

"Why did you go in with me?" she asked. "Why did you do it, Amy?"

"I'm your friend."

"I never really had one of those," said Dart. "I had my sister, but never a friend."

"I didn't either," said Amy.

"That's hard to believe. Your family had money."

"I was always two sizes too big, and all my time was taken up being a sister, daughter, and granddaughter. The happiest day of my childhood came when I finally graduated and got out of that wretched school."

After several more miles, they got off the interstate and drove along the edge of Wisconsin Dells.

"Are you still going to fire me?"

"What do you mean?"

"Are you still going to make Ivan and me leave?"

"I never said anything about you leaving."

"You didn't say it, but you meant it. You were really mad. Your face got white and you looked like you hated me."

"I was worried for all of us. But I never said anything about you leaving. I do, however, remember asking if you liked working for us. And you said, 'That's just stupid.'"

"I didn't mean it. That was only because I thought you wouldn't want us anymore. Do you still want us to leave?"

"No."

"Are you sure?"

"I'm sure."

"Then say it, please. Say you want me to stay."

"Dart, stop it."

"I can't help it. If this big old fancy car of yours didn't have a top I think I'd float right out. I can't remember ever feeling this way before, not for a long time, at least, like the world actually likes me. I mean, Frieda could've called the police. I thought she would. I knew she would. I was sure of it."

"I'm glad your face stopped hurting," said Amy.

"Then you don't want us to leave?"

"If you ask me that again you're fired."

They looked at each other. "I knew it," said Dart.

Then they both started laughing, and Amy had to pull into a parking lot to keep from ramming into someone. When they stopped laughing, they got embarrassed and started in all over again. Then Dart noticed that the tavern they were parked next to was one she'd been in several years ago. It had a marble bar, leather seats, and booths that made you feel like nobody could see you.

"Let's get something to eat," said Dart. "I'm starving."

They went inside, sat in a booth, and ordered tuna fish sandwiches. Dart added two Bloody Marys to the order, with extra vodka and lemon.

"I haven't had anything to drink since I got pregnant with Kevin," said Amy.

"Nothing?"

"Wally is a recovering alcoholic, so we never have liquor around the house. Buck never liked to drink to begin with. I always thought it made me act too silly."

"Come on."

After an hour, the sandwiches were gone and they were still talking and laughing, exploring the new freedom between them. Dart asked Amy if she had gone out with many men.

"Not many," she said. "I was always a foot taller than my dates, sometimes more."

"That shouldn't be a problem, but I imagine you thought it was."

"The second happiest day of my life was when Buck and I got engaged and I could finally stop dating. How about you?"

"I was only with one guy, really. Then he got sent to prison."

"You mean Blake Bookchester?"

"That's him."

"Dart, you said you'd never met him."

"I know, but one thing you have to understand is that there are two of me."

Amy took a drink and set her glass back down on the napkin.

"The normal me is afraid all the time. She's suspicious and thinks the worst of everyone. She lies to keep bad things from happening, and to keep Ivan from knowing things she's afraid might harm him. The past bleeds right into her and makes her think thoughts that frighten her even more. Whenever she imagines that things will get better, a voice snicker-smackers inside her, mocking her for thinking such a thing. And then there's the me that's sitting here now, ready for whatever comes next, seeing everything that's happened and knowing it doesn't have to mean anything about me now. They're both the same person, but in some ways they aren't, and you have to understand that."

"So you knew Blake Bookchester?"

"Yes. But I never knew he was into drugs, never saw any signs. And believe me, I knew how to look for them, because of my father and step-father. They could hide a needle, vial, cooking spoon, or foil packet inside almost anything, and I can spot a glassy eye, itchy nose, and face twitch from clear across the room."

"You liked him then?"

"Sure I did—the part of him I knew. But that's the trouble with men, Amy, they won't show you everything. They get what they want and then spring the rest of it on you when you aren't ready. They aren't like us."

"Would you ladies like another drink?" The waitress had streaks in her hair, and she looked too young to drink herself.

"Amy's the only lady here, and of course we would," said Dart. "Bring us two more."

The waitress walked away and Dart looked at Amy.

"So, do you think you know everything about Buck?"

"Not everything, I suppose," said Amy, a little fearful of the new territory that was developing between them. "The other day, for instance, I learned that Buck didn't know we had two different sizes of forks—long ones and short ones. After almost seventeen years together, he still couldn't tell a salad fork from a dinner fork."

"See what I mean?"

Amy laughed nervously.

"Men don't know jack about the finer things, but in most other ways Buck seems like a good catch to me."

"I'm happy with him," said Amy, in spite of the fact that most of her inward self rebelled against openly talking about herself and her husband. Putting such feelings into words seemed to create impossibly simplistic images out of complicated and private dramas that couldn't possibly be explained to anyone. At the same time, the novel pleasure of drinking with another adult in a bar in the middle of the afternoon was undeniable, and talking this way seemed to be a natural enhancement of those other natural activities.

"I'll tell you about Blake if you tell me about Buck," said Dart.

"This is childish, stop," said Amy, squeezing lemon into her drink.

"I don't care. I want to tell you. There was this one time when Blake came home from the foundry after his night shift. It was around dawn, and I hadn't gotten out of bed yet. He came inside, hung up his coat, and wanted me in the worst way. He'd won a race the day before—against about sixty other riders—and we hadn't had time to be by ourselves and celebrate like we usually did when he'd won a race, so I should have known what was coming. I should have known it because whenever he felt real good about himself he tried to turn that into something between us. Anyway, when he came in the room that morning it was just killing him to be outside of me, like a fish out of water, you might say, like he couldn't hardly breathe, couldn't live without what I could do for him. He knew it and I knew it, because at that time our feelings talked to each other without any misunderstandings, on account of us living so close together. We only had two tiny rooms, and that bed took up all of one; there was just a sliver of space along one edge, so that you had to walk sideways. There wasn't enough room for two people to think separate thoughts, and our feelings kept nudging into each other until sometimes I didn't know if I was having a good time or if he was. Anyway, that morning he started yanking off his clothes like they were on fire and telling me how he'd thought about me all night at the foundry. And then he started reaching for me and I told him I wasn't interested because I'd just woken up and my head was stuffed full of that sweet cotton that wants sleep more than anything else in the world."

"Do all men want it in the morning?" asked Amy, sipping her drink.

"You'd have to ask someone with a lot more experience than me, but I think it's true 'cause about half the time they're ready as soon as they wake up. They can't help it."

Amy took another drink and Dart continued. "Anyway, I managed to keep my night-top on and I got away from him, ran across the top of the bed and into the other room, where the kitchen and living room and everything else were, and he came right after me. 'Oh no you don't,' I said, throwing on this old coat that hung on the wall, and I hurried out the door, down the steps, down the hall, and outside. He came after me without a stitch on but his wifebeater and red boxers. We lived in this rooming house in Red Plain. There were cars parked along the street and a sidewalk running along the front, and I headed down it as fast as I could run, with him right after me. Like I said, it was just getting light outside, and the cool air had this glowing grayness with shafts of blue. There were several neighbors outside picking up their newspapers, and as we ran by they looked at us like we were crazy."

"Go on," said Amy cautiously.

"He chased me all the way to where the street ended, across the field where the high school team sometimes practiced, under the fence, across the creek, and into this big old drafty shed of stored hay. By this time I was all woken up and ready for him to catch me, of course. Anyway, inside the shed we started going at it hard and fast. And then the guy who owned the building came out of his house and backed his trailer up to the front door of the shed. He'd come to get some hay. I didn't want him to see us, but that dumb Blake wouldn't stop. I tried to tell him someone was about to come busting in, but it was like he couldn't hear nothing 'cause the end was coming for him, and his face pinched together the way it always did, like he was thinking about something really important. That's how he always was; he'd get desperate, like someone dying of thirst and trying to get water up out of a deep well with a hand pump. But finally he understood the situation just enough to get off and we scrambled between two big round bales and hid there for almost half an hour, until that guy finished loading hay into his trailer, closed the door, and drove away. I looked down at Blake then, and he was still ready. He'd stayed alert that whole time. I started laughing and he came at me again, but by this time I had my coat back on and I took off through the side door. When I reached the middle of the field he hadn't come out of the shed yet, so I stopped and waited for him. When he finally came out I yelled, 'Come on, old man.' He set out after me again. I was only seventeen at the time. He was maybe three years older. Running felt really good then, and the morning still had that bursting grayness, cool against the skin, the grass wet against my feet. He chased me all the way back up to the rooming house, and then down the hall and up the stairs and into our room. He didn't even shut the door, and you know what, Amy, that was one of the best times ever. That's when I got pregnant with Ivan. I mean, he wanted me so much that's all he could see in the world. But I never knew anything about him being into drugs. I promise I never knew, Amy. And after he went to prison and Ivan was born, I knew I could never, ever see him again. I knew absolutely nothing about love, not the caring kind, and I knew that I loved him so much I might eventually forget he was into drugs, just the way my mother always forgot everything she didn't want to know about the men she was with. That wasn't ever going to happen to me, and it wasn't ever going to happen to Ivan. It just wasn't."

"That's quite a story," said Amy.

"Why are you smiling?" asked Dart, spilling an ice cube and some of her Bloody Mary on the table. "You're thinking of something now, and you have to tell me."

"No, no, no, no, I can't."

"Yes, yes, yes, yes, you can. I told you. Fair is fair."

"I can't. It's just that your story reminded me of, it reminded me . . . never mind."

"Don't you dare do that, Amy. Friends don't do that."

"This friend does."

"Hey," yelled Dart to the waitress. "We've got a mess over here on the table."

The waitress arrived with a damp towel and wiped up the spill.

"Okay, I'll tell you," said Amy. "It was quite a while ago. Buck and I, we liked to go camping. Still do, but we never do it anymore. Something about tents, I guess. Being inside them was . . . well, it was exciting for both of us in a way that's difficult to explain. This was after we'd been together for over a year, just after we got engaged and told our families and everything. Before that it didn't seem right to me. I kept putting him off."

"Of course," said Dart. "They should have to wait."

Amy continued. "We'd gone up north to the Boundary Waters, and we canoed back to a small island of pine trees that you could smell every time you took a breath. It was spring and the sun was going down over the lake. The water was bumpy all the way out, but quiet. We started a fire and cooked our dinner, and both of us knew that this would be the night."

"What did you have for dinner?"

"Some fish we'd caught that afternoon—rolled in flour."

"What else?"

"We boiled rice and threw in some fiddlehead ferns, wild asparagus, and ramps we'd found after we tied up the canoe."

"What did you cook the fish in?"

"Butter, we brought some butter. That was one of the problems, but I'll get to that later."

"That's all you had?"

"That's it. After we finished eating and cleaning up, we sat looking out at the water and listening to loons until it was dark. Then we went into the tent. That's when we heard it."

"Heard what?"

"This chattering and growling outside. Buck was half-undressed, but he stuck his head out of the tent, and on the other side of the fire pit was a bunch of raccoons, trying to get into our cooler. They could smell the butter. Buck jumped out of the tent and yelled at them, but they just stood up on their hind legs and stared at him, their faces lit from the coals. I don't know if you've ever seen a raccoon standing on its hind legs, but it's as strange a thing as you will ever see, and almost all of them were standing that way and staring at Buck. They were looking at him like he was even stranger than they were, and I was looking at them from between his bare legs inside the tent. He yelled at them again and they just looked back, so he ran forward and they took off. He chased them along the edge of the lake, running flat out while they were humping along. I came out of the tent and watched until he stopped chasing them. Then he turned around and ran back to me with a big smile on his face, breathing harder than ever, and . . ."

"And what?"

"It was just funny, that's all. I laugh every time I remember it."

"And what, Amy?"

"I'm not saying any more."

"You have to."

"No I don't."

Two hours later, Buck and Kevin were sitting on the front porch, Buck on the railing and Kevin in the glider. They watched the SUV move up beside the shed and come to a jerking stop.

"Mom's back," said Kevin.

"Looks like it," said Buck. He watched both women climb out and come toward the house, laughing and talking in whispers. When they saw Buck and Kevin, they veered off toward the garden. Amy stumbled and took off her heels, which were sinking into the lawn.

"Your hat is still out here," said Dart, running off. "I'll get it."

She put it on Amy's head, tying the ribbons under her chin. "There," she said.

"Go inside," said Amy, taking the hat off. "I want to put some more water on these plants."

Dart walked along the edge of the garden, heading for the side deck. Amy picked up the hose, twisted the nozzle, and sprayed Dart from the back.

Dart turned around into the spray, picked up the half-filled water can, and ran toward Amy, yelling.

"Why are they doing that?" asked Kevin, watching his mother and housekeeper running around in the yard, laughing and shrieking.

"Your mother's finally getting a chance to have a childhood," said Buck, watching Amy with a look of immense fondness.

"Mom had a childhood," said Kevin. "Everyone does."

"Your mother was young, but she was never a child."

"Why not?"

"Everyone expected too much from her. You should know about that."

"I do, but you're not supposed to have fun with people who work for you. It isn't right."

"There can't be rules about those things," said Buck.

Kevin studied his father.

"I don't like Dart," said Kevin.

"Yes you do, Kev. I can tell you do. You just don't like what she sometimes brings out in your mother, and maybe in you. That's different."

"I wouldn't want her for a mother," said Kevin, launching into a sudden fit of coughing.

"You don't have to," said Buck.

"I pity Ivan."

"He probably feels the same way about you. Where is he, by the way?"

Kevin coughed several times more, swallowed, and seemed to be over it. "He and Grandpa are out back. We got a video of that turtle coming out of the pond after a dead fish. They're repositioning the camera so when he comes out again we can get a better look at him."

"Is that Helm boy coming back again?"

"In two days—that's what Ivan said. He's going to bring his pet bat—if he really has one."

"Do you get along with him?"

"Well enough. But I don't get why he's friends with someone who has to repeat fifth grade."

"Did you ever ask him about what it's like after you die? I remember you said Ivan thought he might know."

"I don't think he knows. But Ivan was right about him, he thinks about things more than most other people."

Amy and Dart finally wore themselves out in the yard, turned off the hose, and climbed up onto the deck leading around the house to the back door.

"Do you think they'll make us something to eat?" asked Kevin.

"I wouldn't count on that," said Buck. "Are you feeling well enough to ride into town? We can go get something."

"Yes, I've been better lately, a lot better—those drugs help."

"Good. Should we tell your grandfather and Ivan that we're going?"

"No, we can bring them back something."

"Sounds good," said Buck, picking up Kevin's oxygen tank and helping him stand out of the glider.

Boy's Nature

August came to visit Ivan again the following Saturday morning and brought his bat with him. Everyone stood around in the entryway while his mother explained that Milton was a highly educated bat who had been checked out for diseases and would not hurt anyone. And to prove this point she took Milton out of August's shirt pocket and put him on her shoulder. Then she handed him around so everyone could hold him. "He's cute," she said.

"No he's not," said Kevin, staring at Milton as if he were a poisonous snake with wings. "That thing is definitely not cute."

Amy's face wrinkled up because Kevin had said something that might offend Winnie, but Winnie quickly took care of everything. "I probably should have said that in a different way." She laughed. "I mean, once you get used to him you begin to think of him as cute."

"I never heard of a red bat," said Kevin.

"Hopefully they're the most harmless kind," suggested Dart. She had declined to hold him when he was passed around.

"I'm afraid Milton got into some purple dye," explained Amy. "I think it looks rather distinguished, though."

"Can he fly?" asked Kevin.

"Of course he can," offered Ivan.

August looked at his mom and she nodded. He tossed Milton up into the air. The bat opened his wings, swooped down, rose up, and flew up and down the hallway three times. Then he circled August and dove into his shirt pocket.

"Jesus," said Kevin.

"You may have noticed," said August, "that Milton needs some elevation in order to begin his flight. It's difficult for mammals to take off, because they're heavier than birds relative to the amount of air moved by their wings. It's why they sleep upside down in the air, so they can just drop into flight."

"What does that mean?" asked Kevin.

"If Milton is on the ground he needs to climb up on something to jump off," said Wally, scribbling something into his notebook.

"That's correct," said August. "Bats always begin flight with a gravity-induced swoop."

"I forgot how funny you talk," said Kevin.

Amy winced again, but August and Winnie just laughed. "Both August and I are overly verbose, I'm afraid," she said. "But we both mean well most of the time."

"How about the rest of the time?" asked Flo, her eyes dancing between August and his mother.

"At those other times you should just ignore us."

"Does he catch mosquitoes?" asked Amy.

"He consumes on average a thousand insects each hour," explained August, "and many of those are mosquitoes. That's when he's hunting. But bats help control insect populations even when they're not hunting, because insects avoid gardens and other areas that bats often visit."

"Why do they do that?" asked Flo.

"Many insects can hear the echolocation signals that bats emit. They probably sound something like sirens to them, but no one knows for sure. And just as people will avoid areas where there are frequent sirens, so will insects."

"How do you spell *echolocation,* and how often do bats emit signals?" asked Wally.

"E-c-h-o-l-o-c-a-t-i-o-n. When bats are hunting for insects, they emit navigational signals about ten times a second. But once they locate a possible target, the emission rate increases to about two hundred a second, and continues at the increased rate until they intercept it."

"Unless the bug gets away," said Kevin.

"That's right, unless it gets away, which happens about twenty-seven percent of the time, though this varies according to atmospheric conditions and the density of vegetation within the hunting environment." ·

"Well, your bat is welcome here," said Amy.

"Not in the kitchen," added Dart.

And then Amy, Dart, and Winnie went out to get a bunch of potted plants from the trunk of Winnie's car. Flo went upstairs to her room, and Wally went out to the pole shed.

"Come on," said Kevin. August and Ivan followed him into his room, where he showed August a video recording of the turtle coming out of the pond, biting a dead fish, and carrying it into the water.

"Excellent!" cried August, staring into the monitor. "Play it again."

"Just look at that monster," said Kevin, pointing at the screen. "His neck and head are bigger around than a softball."

"What a magnificent specimen," said August. "He's straight out of *The Age of Reptiles.*"

"Wally's making a trap to catch him," said Ivan. "Let's go see if he's done." But before they got out of the house Kevin's nurse came down the hall and said it was time for him to breathe his medicine fumes and do some coughing, so August and Ivan went outdoors without him.

In the shop, Wally had almost finished welding sections of cattle-fencing together, with a hinged panel for the floor. The steel cage was big enough to contain August and Ivan. It was also heavy.

After he finished making it, Wally put the trap on a little trailer and used the garden tractor to pull it slowly toward the pond. August and Ivan rode with the cage, keeping it steady. There were two frozen carp inside.

"You know what happened the other day?" asked August.

"Of course I don't know," replied Ivan. "I wasn't there."

"Skeeter Skelton came to see Blake Bookchester at the shop. Do you know who Skeeter Skelton is?"

"Everyone knows who Skeeter Skelton is. Some people say he's made out of old motorcycle parts."

"I know. I heard that too. Well, he rode all the way into the shop, climbed off his motorcycle, asked if he could have a cup of coffee, and talked with Blake for ten minutes over by the lathe."

"Could you hear them?"

"Not much. Skeeter asked Blake if he wanted to do a little lazy riding together, become road buddies and sometimes go places together on week-ends. Blake said he'd like that, and explained where the coffee he filled up

Skeeter's cup with came from. But after that I heard them talking about your mom."

"What did they say?"

"I couldn't hear very well because my dad started banging with a wrench on a mower blade. But I heard them say 'Dart' six or seven times."

"What else?"

"Skeeter said something about Lucky."

"What was it?"

"I couldn't hear."

"I hate that guy."

"I know. And after he said his name Blake picked up a ball-peen hammer and slammed it into the workbench."

"I've got something to tell you, August," Ivan said.

"What is it?" he asked.

"It's something real big."

"What is it?"

"I think Blake Bookchester might be my dad."

"Really?"

"Really."

"How do you reason that?"

"It's not so much the reasons, it's the way I feel about them. He came over here and talked to me for a long time, and then he talked to my mother. He said he was an old friend of hers, but the way they looked at each other, I mean, it seemed really different. Anyway, he told me you were going to get another bat."

"He saved Milton's life," said August.

"I know, you told me."

"The other day, when he and I were alone at the shop, he asked about you," said August.

"What did you tell him?"

"I told him you were one of a kind."

"Couldn't you think of anything better to say about me than that?"

"Not right then."

"So what do you think about him being my dad?" asked Ivan. "I mean, do you see anything wrong with that?"

"No. He's a man of the highest moral principles," replied August.

"Except that he's an ex-con."

"True."

"And another thing," began Ivan, but just then Wally turned off the tractor.

"Here we are, boys. Let's get this cage unloaded and bait the trap."

The boys jumped out and went to work. Wally had a good plan. It was a lot like an old-fashioned box-trap, he said, simple in design and guaranteed to work.

"We've been setting box-traps since mankind first came down out of the trees and learned to walk on two legs," he said, putting the trap next to the water and tilting it open. "This is our lucky day, boys, I can feel it in my bones."

"What do your bones feel like?" Ivan asked.

"They feel like yours do."

"My bones don't feel like anything," replied Ivan.

"I know," he said. "But when you get older you feel them hurting and rubbing together, except when they know something is about to work out just right. And then you don't feel them at all."

"I think you've got it, Wally," said August, and the old man carefully crept out from beneath the tilted cage. Inside, the two frozen carp rested on the metal trigger. When nudged, this trigger would trip the heavy steel cage, trapping whatever nudged it.

"This is going to work, boys."

"I think you're right," added Ivan. He was trying to feel his bones.

The three of them sat down next to the cage then. They looked out over the shiny surface of the pond and imagined the giant turtle coming out. Milton flew from one end of the water to the other, catching insects and occasionally skimming the surface, picking up floating bugs. After a half-hour or so, August whistled him back. He said Milton shouldn't wear himself out too much during the day. He was, after all, nocturnal.

"Where's Kevin?" asked Wally.

"With his nurse," said August. "It was time for his medicine."

"He'll want to see this."

Ivan nodded. "I'll go see if he's done. You two wait here."

When Ivan got to his room, the nurse was still pounding on Kevin's back. After supper that night, August, Kevin, and Ivan went outdoors to check on the trap. They sat on the bank near the cocked cage and talked. Their young voices moved over the water, rising and falling. As the sun dropped below the distant ridge, a shadow slowly grew over them. Three ducks dropped out of the sky and landed on the pond, spreading circles around them.

"So this Wild Boy, he's real?" asked Kevin.

"As real as you are," said Ivan. "I've seen him with my own two eyes, stood next to him—as close as you are now."

"It's hard to believe," said Kevin.

"I know it."

"And he just moves around and does whatever he wants?"

"That's right, whatever he feels like. August and I think he lives in caves, but he's probably got hundreds of places to spend the night. He just goes wherever he wants. He's a free spirit."

"Where are his parents?"

"I've wondered about that," said August, "but no one knows."

"Were they wild too?"

"No one knows," replied Ivan. "The hermit knows more than anyone else, but even he doesn't know very much about him. And because the Wild Boy can't speak our language, there's no way to ever know."

"What does he do when he gets sick?"

"He doesn't," said Ivan. "He's wild."

"Everyone gets sick," said Kevin. "Wild has nothing to do with it."

"He never gets sick. Diseases roll off him like water. He never catches a cold or anything. His body is tough and he can sleep in subzero winters and baking-hot summers. It makes no more difference to him than it would to a bird or a rabbit."

"But he could have an infection," Kevin offered.

"If he did," replied Ivan, "he'd eat a handful of herbs and cure himself, or make a vegetable bandage out of mashed leaves, berries, and roots. Nothing could slow him down for long."

"How would he know which herbs to eat?"

"Same way he knows how to move around the way he does. It must be instinct. You should see him climbing those rock cliffs. You wouldn't believe a human can move like that—as quick as a cat and as sure as a spider. It's like August said once: most of us are born into nature, but the Wild Boy was born out of it."

"And this hermit looks out for him?"

"He even stays with Mr. Mortal sometimes," said August. "In fact, I think the Wild Boy might stay there a whole lot more than Mr. Mortal lets on."

"Mr. Mortal?"

"That's the hermit," said Ivan. "He has a dirt house beside a melon field. August and I have been there hundreds of times. If he's in just the right mood, he makes us tea with honey."

"What kind of hermit makes tea?" asked Kevin.

"The war-hero, tea-making kind," replied Ivan.

"What do you think the Wild Boy worries about at night?" asked Kevin.

"He doesn't worry about anything," said Ivan. "The Wild Boy has no fears. If he feels like sleeping, he sleeps. If he feels like running, he runs. If he feels like swimming, he swims. If he feels like making a fire, he makes one. Sometimes he sits in a tree next to August's house, just because he wants to. He has even been known to slip into someone's house and take a freshly baked pie if he's hungry."

"He'd get caught if he did that," said Kevin.

"No, he wouldn't. He gave August a jar of canned peaches once. Where do you think he got them if he didn't sneak into someone's house? It's not like he's going to can them himself. He doesn't have any jars. He lets others do the work while he just moves through the country like a young buck—quick, quiet, and smart."

"But what would happen if he got sick or hurt?" asked Kevin.

"Good question," said August, staring out over the pond. "Disease and injury could be a real danger for the Wild Boy. I hadn't really thought about that before."

"Now don't start worrying about that," said Ivan. "You've seen him more than anyone, and you've never seen him sick."

"Maybe we could convince my mom to arrange for a doctor to find him and check him over," offered August.

"Are you crazy? A doctor would kill the Wild Boy in an instant," replied Ivan.

"You're right about that," said Kevin. "Hospitals are full of infections and diseases, and most doctors are in hospitals all the time."

"*Shh,*" whispered Ivan. "*Shhh.*" He pointed out into the pond.

"What is it?" asked August.

"Shhhhh."

Then August started pointing as well, and when Kevin sighted along his arm he saw a dark head sticking out of the water, like a rounded-off wooden post.

"Jesus," Kevin said.

"Shhhhhh."

The head moved slowly and silently toward them across the surface of the water.

"Jesus."

"Shhhhhhhhh."

The dark head took a long time to reach the shore. Then the massive turtle crawled out of the water and onto the bank. It moved slowly, heavily, dragging its body forward with wide clawed feet. It stood for a moment in front of the opened steel cage. Then it turned its thick neck and head and stared at the boys, the moonlight reflecting green in its tiny eyes.

The boys just sat there, motionless.

The turtle crawled toward the dead carp and the cage fell around it, clanking against the metal floor piece. The turtle seemed not to notice it had been trapped, and began eating the fish in quick gulping bites.

"We got him," said Kevin, almost inaudibly. "I don't believe it."

"Shhhhh," said Ivan.

"There's no need to be quiet now, you dope. Jesus. Where's my grandpa? He'll know what to do next."

"He went into town to get something to eat. He doesn't like pizza. But he should be back by now," said Ivan.

"Oh, right. I forgot. He'll never believe this."

"Sure he will. He knew it was going to happen," replied Ivan.

"He just said that to keep our interest up."

"That turtle is even bigger and more reptilian than it looked in the video," said August, staring into the cage. "Its back looks like a burned mountain range. Fascinating."

"Told you," said Kevin, and coughed.

"Why would he do that?" Ivan asked. "He came right out of the pond like we weren't even here. Very, very sketchy, if you ask me. Just look at him ripping into that fish."

"We need a flashlight," continued Ivan. "It's getting too dark to see him."

"We can't all go in," said August. "Someone needs to stay here with the turtle."

"Why?"

"So he doesn't get away."

"He can't get away," said Kevin. "He's trapped. And besides, if there was a way for him to get out of the cage, none of us could stop him."

"Sure we could," replied Ivan. "We could turn him over on his back."

"That's just stupid," said Kevin. "He weighs over two hundred pounds, and he could bite your hand off as soon as you touch him."

"Good point," said Ivan.

Kevin began coughing then, and it continued for a long time in a convulsive, gagging manner. The nurse, who had been standing on the deck, hurried down to the edge of the pond and told Kevin he needed to come inside.

"No," he coughed out.

"We caught the turtle," Ivan told her, but the nurse didn't seem very interested.

"Kevin, you have to come inside now. This damp air is aggravating your lungs."

"Fuck off." He coughed.

Then the back door of the house slammed and Wally came out. He found the walking stick he'd left leaning against the railing, and made his way down to the boys.

"We got him!" hollered Kevin.

"Now that's something," said Wally, staring into the steel cage. "That's really something. Boys, we did it. That's what I call teamwork."

"Kevin needs to come inside now," repeated the nurse.

"And it's up to me what we do with him now, right?" said Kevin.

"Yes, that was the agreement," said Wally, staring into the cage.

"It was your boat," confirmed Ivan.

"You need to come in now, Kevin," said the nurse.

"Let's put the cage in the pond, near the shore where we can still see into it. We'll leave it there, completely underwater," said Kevin.

"Why?" asked August.

"He'd eventually drown, and we could watch that. He would try to get his head out to breathe. It might take a whole week."

Silence.

"I'm not doing that," said Ivan.

"That is completely beyond the pale," said August.

"No," said Wally. "That's not an option."

"You said it was up to me," said Kevin.

"It is," replied Wally, "but your choices don't include that one. I'm not heading into the afterlife with something like that weighing me down."

"But he's the devil," said Kevin, staring into the cage. "I'd like to watch him die."

"If you want to end his life, we'll get someone out here with a rifle. Is that what you want?" asked Wally.

"I don't know," said Kevin. "Do I have to make up my mind now?"

"No, of course not."

"Good. Can we just keep him in the cage until I decide?"

"Sure. But it will get too warm out here during the day. He needs to be in the water. Let's see if the four of us can push the cage a little ways into the pond. Then we can still see him and feed him fish, check on him, get to know him a little better. And then you can decide."

"All right," said Kevin, "but pushing that cage isn't going to be easy. We'll have to watch our fingers."

"We could get some long poles and pry it into the water, one lift at a time," suggested Ivan.

"Good idea," said August.

"Let's go for it," added Wally.

Then Dart walked out. "What's going on?" she asked.

"We caught the turtle," replied Kevin.

"Good work," she said. "Boy, he's a big one."

"He's immense," said August.

"It's time for you two to come in now," she said. "It's after ten. Mrs. Helm wouldn't want August out this late."

"First we have to move this cage down to the water," said Wally.

"Then do it," she said.

"Kevin is refusing to come in," said the nurse. "This air is hurting him."

"He's not refusing," replied Dart.

"Yes he is," said the nurse.

"He just wasn't ready until now, right, Kev?"

Dart picked up the oxygen tank in one arm and put her other arm around Kevin. "Come on, big guy. After we're inside I'll tell you why the most beautiful women in the world always undress from the top down. You don't already know that, do you?"

"No."

"Well, come on, then, let's go."

She and Kevin went inside, followed by the nurse.

And then August, Wally, and Ivan pushed the cage down to the pond, until only a foot of it stuck up out of the water.

Night Ride

When Blake learned his curfew had been relaxed and he could move about with the same relative freedom as everyone else between 8:00 p.m. and 8:00 a.m., he thought he should celebrate in some way. His other restrictions were still in force—no leaving the state without written permission, no fraternizing with other felons, no firearms, no drinking, etc.—but he'd nevertheless reached a higher plateau of liberty, and he felt compelled to mark the passage somehow.

He thought to call his father, but Nate and Bee were off together for ten days in Slippery Slopes, and Blake didn't want to disturb them. They were trying to make a mark of their own.

He wondered what it might be like to call his mother, assuming she was still alive and he could find her. "Hi, Mom, it's me, Blake. I know it's late but I'm here at the farmhouse and just wanted to tell you that my curfew has been suspended."

Of course he'd first have to explain that he'd been in prison for over ten years and was now out and had a job and—

Dumb idea, he decided, and looked out of the window again and imagined other calls he might make.

"Hi, Danielle. It's me, Blake, and I wanted to tell you that . . ."

Dumb idea.

Blake walked around the house, found the book he'd borrowed on Spinoza, and read it until he fell asleep. When he woke up, his familiar heart-hunger was deeper than usual—stronger than any idea he could find to subdue it. Like a child's dimly understood urge to grow bigger, it was impossible to deny.

Blake felt empty. He yearned for a minute-by-minute, week-by-week entanglement with someone who meant something to him. His new-found freedom was burning a hole in his pocket, and he longed to spend every last bit of it. As for the obvious constraints of such an on-going entanglement—the cables potentially binding him to the hopes, dreams, nightmares, foibles, and frailties of another person as broken as himself—as far as his heart was concerned, without someone to love, freedom was nothing more than a worn-out Vacancy sign on a motel no one wanted to set foot in.

He had to go over there again. Otherwise, the tension he felt would tear him apart. Blake picked up the borrowed book, put on his leather jacket, and went outside. The night was clear and bright, the sky immense. As he rode, the night accompanied him from one valley to the next.

Outside Grange, Blake took a couple of back roads before stopping at the edge of the Roebuck property. Just beyond the fence and the wind-break, the pond spread out flat and shiny all the way to the house. The windows he could see from here were dark, and he pushed his motorcycle off the road and into the tall weeds in the ditch.

He moved swiftly along the edge of the pond. A fish broke the surface of the water, and frog-song erupted spontaneously. He waited for several minutes in the shadow of the house, listening. And then, using the sup-ports for the heavy ceramic downspout as toe-holds, he climbed up to the third floor, stood on the roof, jiggled the window open with the blade of his knife, and went inside.

The smell of old paper dust and varnished floors greeted him. Unlacing his boots, he left them beneath the window and indulged for several min-utes in the luxury of knowing that somewhere beneath him—embraced by the same walls, protected by the same roof, breathing the same air—slept Danielle and Ivan. Then he silently crossed the room. With a narrow shaft of light from his penlight, he found the spot he had borrowed the first book from, and slid it back into place between the two other volumes. Then he looked for the second book, which was not in the place he remembered. The little round light danced along the titles.

When he heard a sound like a muffled cough, Blake turned off the penlight. The sound didn't return, so he breathed again, turned the light back on, and resumed searching.

Then he heard another sound, and before he had time to turn off his penlight, a hooded reading lamp on a table across the room flipped on. A wrinkled old woman was seated on an upholstered chair beside it, dressed in a gray housecoat from an earlier time and puffy gray slippers. Her snowy hair glowed, and she seemed almost to be receding into herself. The effect of this aging concentrated her life within her bright blue eyes, which shone out of her face like lit shrines.

"So you came back," she said. Her slow voice sounded dusted with flour, and as she spoke the many fine wrinkles in her face moved along with her small mouth.

Blake could not think of anything to say, and his mute alarm seemed to amuse the old woman. "So," she asked, "did you get through my husband's first book on Spinoza?"

"Three times," said Blake.

"What did you think?"

"Who are you?" he asked.

"I'm Florence," she said, her hands busy with something in her lap.

"What are you doing?"

"I'm making a rosary. Would you like one?"

After a moment of hesitation, Blake replied. "Yes, I would."

"So, what did you think of the book?"

"I'm not sure," said Blake. "I couldn't understand it all. That's why I came back for the second one."

"I'm afraid the next one is no clearer than his first," said Flo. "My husband worshiped Baruch Spinoza, but I don't think he ever really understood him. My husband was too traditional, if you know what I mean."

"I do," said Blake, turning off his penlight. "I'm having the same problem."

"Come over here, young man, sit down," said Flo, reaching for another bead and poking the dark string through it.

Blake sat on the wooden chair next to her.

"You're Blake Bookchester, aren't you?"

"How did you know?"

"Oh, don't worry, I know very little about you—just things I hear, and most of those are probably not true. People are never what other people think they are. So, what didn't you understand in the book?"

"Well, for one thing, your husband writes that Spinoza's god has no reasons for doing anything."

"Oh, that's true," said Flo, pushing the new bead down on top of others. "How can that be?"

"If God acted out of a compelling reason, or toward a particular end, that would mean there was something beyond God to achieve. And Spinoza never could have accepted that. For Spinoza, God was everything, perfect and complete in every way."

"Then God never acts, never does anything?"

"What could be acted on?"

"The world."

"But God and the world are not separate."

"Then God doesn't act?"

"Not the way we do. We're incomplete, in pieces, constantly needing to hold ourselves together, attach to something else, running this way and that. But God is already everything, and everything is in God. The divine doesn't do anything; it is simply here."

"That's really hard to understand."

"I know. Like I said, I'm not sure my husband ever completely understood it either. That's why his books are so opaque."

"But you understand it."

"Sometimes I do, but only for brief moments."

"You just explained it to me."

"I learned the words, but I rarely understand them."

"Tell me more."

"At my age it's best to just keep quiet about most things."

"Please tell me."

"You probably won't understand until you get older, but people need something to keep their mind busy—something repetitive, routine. For me, it's making rosaries. I set my mind to work making rosaries so it will leave the rest of me alone. Then I'm free to roam around, and occasionally I experience blissfully connected things, like how becoming can be in every moment, emergent yet unchanged. What seems like change could also be a futher manifestation."

"Yes, emergent yet unchanged," replied Blake. "That's what I want to understand. That's the key. Changing characters disguise the unchanging story. The shifting details always trip me up."

Flo reached for another bead, then continued. "Sometime around the age of eighty-three it occurred to me that I'd already had all the thoughts

I was going to have, and for the rest of my time I was just going to rethink them. I understood I'd have to find a way to climb out of my mind so I could live my own life. That's why I make rosaries. For my granddaughter Amy, restoring this place to an earlier condition provides hundreds of repetitive chores. Having a mind is like having a child—you won't have any peace until you can keep it busy."

"They've relaxed my curfew," said Blake. "I can go where I want now."

"Congratulations. You've done well."

"Thank you."

"You'd better leave now," said Flo. "Wallace usually checks on me around this time of night. The dear boy wakes up because he has to pee. If I'm not in my room, well, you know."

"You're right," said Blake.

"Here, don't forget my husband's second book." And with that she handed a slim volume to Blake, along with a glow-in-the-dark rosary taken from the pocket of her robe.

"I don't know how to thank you," said Blake.

"It's not necessary. It's been nice talking to you. Now run along and be careful going down the side of the house. It would be a long way to fall."

Blake put the book inside his jacket and the rosary in the pocket of his shirt. He put his boots back on, climbed out of the window onto the roof, and descended to the ground in the moonlight. When he got there, however, he was surrounded by August, Ivan, and Kevin.

"It's you," said Ivan.

"What were you doing up there?" asked Kevin. When Blake didn't respond, he added, "If you don't answer I'll call my dad and he'll pull you apart like a roasted chicken."

"I borrowed a book from your great-grandmother."

"Let's see it."

Blake held out the book, and August shined his flashlight on the cover.

"She knows you borrowed this?" asked Kevin.

"Of course," said Blake. "I wouldn't just come into someone's house on my own. What kind of guy do you take me for?"

"You're a felon," said Ivan.

"Who ingeniously saved Milton from destruction," added August.

"Give me a ride on your motorcycle and I won't tell anyone," said Kevin.

"I know you have one, and you probably rode it over here. Everyone says what a hot shit you are on that bike. Give me a ride."

"That's out of the question," said Blake.

"Go ahead, give him a ride," said Ivan.

Blake looked at Ivan. He felt something small and mute opening inside him. "Why should I give him a ride?"

"Because it's the right thing to do."

"Come over here," said Blake.

He and Ivan walked a couple of yards away, where they could talk without being heard by the others. Blake looked into Ivan's eyes, and with that look a wild ox began walking around inside him, making room for a new and terrible joy. Then the ox began to bellow, and Blake felt the spirit of the boy inside him. His hands shook and he realized that his new life had begun before he even knew it, and that he was already a good way downstream in it. There was no time to wonder if he was prepared, or if he could ever be as much to this boy as his father was to him. There was no time to think or know anything, only to keep up with what was already happening.

"Kevin doesn't get to do much," said Ivan, "and he might never get another chance."

"That kid doesn't look healthy," whispered Blake. "What if something happens to him?"

"Like what?"

"Like passing out or having a spell or something."

"Actually, he's been better lately. He usually lugs around an oxygen tank."

"Okay, Ivan. If you want me to, I will."

"We better hurry. If my mom wakes up she'll go off like a word bomb."

At the bottom of the long drive, the boys were waiting for Blake.

"Jesus," said Kevin, climbing onto the motorcycle behind Blake, "this seat is really uncomfortable."

"Sorry," said Blake. "Now put your arms around me and lock your hands together."

"Go," said Kevin.

Blake eased down the road, trying to keep his pipes quiet. Several corners later, he nudged the throttle. The tachometer needle rose and he felt Kevin's thin arms tighten around him. The headlamp burrowed into a straight stretch of road, and Blake shouted, "Hold on!"

The dark foliage on either side of them shot past. He found third gear and smiled as Kevin gripped him even tighter. He could feel the boy's exhilarated fear.

Blake backed off and the bike slowed down.

"Are you all right?" he shouted.

"Oh yeah," said Kevin.

Blake could feel the boy's heart beating.

They rode through the curving valley, the wind lifting their hair. Climbing onto the ridge road, another long straightaway stretched open before them. Because of the additional weight, the front end of the Gixxer rose up more easily than usual and remained above the road most of the way through second gear.

They took a corner and another stretch opened up. The tachometer needle leaped up, and at the end of second gear, Kevin shouted, "Faster!"

Blake jumped into third gear, but as the engine spooled up, he began to feel anxious. The weight of the boy made it harder to handle the bike. He was going about as fast as he felt comfortable with.

"Faster," shouted Kevin.

They rode along the ridge, cruising the deserted blacktop, the remaining universe directly above them, dark valleys yawning open to either side, the distant light of houses and small towns dotting the blackness. Blake could feel Kevin moving his head, looking right, then left, and up at the stars.

"Go down there," said Kevin, pointing into a welcoming valley.

Blake turned, opened the throttle a crack, and headed down. They took several corners and Blake accelerated again. And then with no warning they entered an aisle of dense fog. It was impossible to see anything. The road disappeared. He could feel Kevin pressing his face against his back, bracing himself for a collision that was certain to come.

And then suddenly they were released. The blacktop opened again in from of them, the sky star-filled with wonder.

Blake decelerated, pulled to the edge of the road, and stopped.

"Did you feel that?" he asked Kevin.

"Yes," said Kevin.

"What did it feel like?"

"Giving up."

"Exactly. You know what that means, don't you?"

"No."

"The future wants you in it, Kevin."

"You're right," said Kevin. "It does feel like that."

Riding slowly, they continued down into the valley. "Can you outrun Skeeter Skelton?" asked Kevin.

"No," said Blake.

"Really?"

"Really. Say, have you ever heard of Baruch Spinoza?"

"Sure. He's the guy my great-grandfather wrote about. You have one of his books in your coat. What about him?"

"Did you know he gave away his family inheritance?"

"No. Why did he do that?"

"He thought he could never see the world clearly so long as he had the privileges of money. He wanted to work for a living. But that's only one of the reasons he could see things others couldn't see. He was also sick most of his life, and he died young."

"Why was he sick?"

"Breathing glass dust, but that's not the point. The important thing is that people who are sick sometimes see the world the way it really is. Not always, but sometimes it happens. People who have things too easy can't do this. They're too easily influenced by the self-serving thoughts that march out of good fortune. Do you know what I mean?"

"Of course I do. I'm not stupid."

"Good, because you have that same chance. You can see things the way they are. You could be like Spinoza, and he was one of the greatest men who ever lived."

"Could you give me another ride someday?"

"Sure, if it's okay with your folks."

"It won't be, but it would really mean a lot to me. This has been one of the best times ever, and I want to do it again—during the day. I'm missing too much in the dark."

"I can't promise," said Blake. "But if the opportunity comes up again, we'll take it."

When they returned to the house, August and Ivan were waiting for them at the bottom of the drive, immersed in some animated discussion.

"We'd better get back," said August, and the three boys started up the drive.

"Ivan," said Blake. "Come here."

Ivan walked back to Blake, a puzzled look on his face.

"If you ever need anything, call me, okay?"

"Why?"

"Because no matter what, I'll come."

"Do you mean it?"

"I do."

And with that, Blake rode off. The boys continued walking up the drive, then turned through the side yard so they could enter the house from the back.

Standing on the deck, August pointed over toward the pond. "Look," he whispered.

In the distance, a moonlit figure stood at the edge of the water near the turtle cage.

"It's him," said August. "It's the Wild Boy."

Then Kevin and Ivan saw him.

"What's he doing?"

"I don't know," said August.

"Let's go over there," said Ivan.

"He'll just take off," said August.

"Let's go anyway," said Kevin, coughing. "That's our turtle."

Dart Ventures Out

After Dart fed everyone breakfast and started a lentil soup simmering for lunch, she poured a cup of coffee and sat down with it at the kitchen counter. Morning light filled the room, much of it colored by the blue curtains.

There was nowhere more relaxing than a clean kitchen, she thought. Pans and utensils hung securely from hooks; herb, flour, and sugar jars rested silently in place; smooth closed cupboards and the cat-faced clock on the wall all seemed to join her in taking a couple moments for herself. Inanimate objects made excellent company.

She blew into her cup and sampled the black coffee. It was still too hot.

For some unknown reason an old song flared up in her memory, and for another unknown reason she started humming it, though this was something she rarely did. At first her humming burbled along in a shaky, unsure manner, but after a short time it grew thicker, steadier, and more satisfying. Then it assumed a life of its own, a loop in the corner of her mind, and she could entertain thoughts and memories while the hummed song continued all by itself.

She remembered how her sister used to hum to herself, especially when she walked for any distance. They would be walking along a sidewalk or through a field and Esther would be murmuring like a tuned engine. Dart never could recognize the songs, and she never asked, respecting the privacy that seemed to accompany the habit. Esther's humming had always comforted Dart, perhaps because she imagined it comforted Esther.

Suddenly Dart realized she was crying. Tears moved down her cheeks and onto the backs of her hands and the countertop in warm, wet splotches. She stopped humming, wiped her eyes with her sleeve, and burned her tongue with a long swallow of hot coffee. The forces she'd put in charge of her personality simply did not allow weeping, and she was more than a little frightened that such unlawfulness could be going on inside her. Her security system had broken down. What was wrong with her?

She found Amy in the basement, refinishing an old sideboard with a leaded glass front.

"Can I have the rest of the day off?" she asked.

"Why?" asked Amy, scrubbing the wood with a wad of steel wool.

"I want to visit my sister's grave and do some other things I've been neglecting."

"Would you like some company?"

"No, thank you. I need to do this myself."

"Don't forget that Buck and I—"

"I know," interrupted Dart. "You're going backpacking for a couple days. That's no problem. We can handle everything. No need to worry. Ivan's going to visit August, and Kevin's been feeling as well as I can remember. And Flo, well, you know, she's never any problem."

"Are you sure? It seems a little reckless. Buck's in the middle of things at the construction site, and I can't imagine how long it's been since we—"

"I told you, Amy, it's not a problem. You need to go. Everything will be fine here. You can both leave in the morning and there is no need to worry about anything."

"I hope it will be all right," said Amy. "I'd never forgive myself if something went wrong. In any case, take the rest of the day off. I'll feed everyone lunch."

"There's soup on the stove and sandwiches in the refrigerator," said Dart, "and there's lettuce and sliced tomatoes to add to the sandwiches. The crackers Kevin always wants with his soup are in the pantry, to the back, and the—"

"Thanks, Dart. I'll manage."

Several miles outside Red Plain, Dart pulled off the road in front of a small cemetery that was set off from a cornfield by a short wire fence with a gate in front. Dart walked over and sat down by her sister's grave. A hot wind blew down the valley and the wide corn leaves rasped against each other, making it seem even hotter. It had been several weeks since the cemetery was mowed, and many of the grass tops had seeded out.

After lingering for over an hour, Dart took off her homemade leather-and-bead necklace and placed it on top of the flat stone, circling the name.

"If someone takes it," she explained, "they'll remember your name. I had a nicer one for you, but it didn't work out."

Dart closed the rusty gate on the front of the cemetery and drove to Words, where she parked and stared out of her windshield at the repair shop. Then she drove to Winnie and Jacob's log house, and found Winnie's little yellow car parked in front. She walked around it and continued to the edge of the garden. At first she didn't see Winnie sitting on one of the painted benches, staring into a patch of red bergamot. Then she did, and hurried over toward her.

"Dart," said Winnie, standing up and smoothing her skirt over her hips, as if she'd just stepped off a train after a long journey. Around her grew hundreds of plants, arranged to express something that could not be expressed any other way.

"I need to talk to you," said Dart.

"Good. I was wanting to talk with someone."

"Am I interrupting something?"

"Definitely not."

"What were you doing?"

"I was just trying to find a better way to pray."

"A better way?"

"Much of the time all I really want to do is pray, and it seems important to find the best way."

Dart laughed a short, loud, two-note laugh, then stepped forward and hugged Winnie. "I simply love how odd you are, Pastor Winifred," she said. "I've always wanted to tell you that."

"Call me Winnie," she said, looking at Dart with some apprehension.

"Now, I need you to tell me about Blake," said Dart.

"What about him?"

"I need to know about his drug problem."

"Neither Jacob nor I have seen any sign of it."

"Maybe you're not looking."

"That might be true, but we haven't seen any sign of it. And I'm pretty sure Jacob has been paying attention. He's a lot more suspicious that way."

"Drugs are why Blake was in prison."

"I know," said Winnie.

"He was tried and convicted."

"Actually, he pled guilty right away—never said anything but that one word at his hearing. I know because Jacob wanted to see his case file before he'd let him work at the shop. He wanted to be sure there weren't any more serious charges against him. Blake was sentenced for carrying over two pounds of brown heroin—that's what the file said—and with resisting arrest and assaulting an officer of the law."

"Assault," repeated Dart.

"That's what the file said."

"Where did they catch him?"

"Somewhere in Milwaukee. Blake said there was a guy in the foundry who would pay three hundred dollars for every delivery made to Milwaukee. Apparently he did it three times and never knew what was in the packages. Then the guy who was paying him turned him in, set him up. Why do you want to know this?"

"Because I don't think I can stay away from him much longer."

"I don't understand."

"Not that long ago I spent the night with someone, slept with him. He didn't mean anything to me, and it wasn't a good experience at all. It was awful, in fact, and it made me think that maybe I'm all used up. Maybe that part of my life is ruined for good."

"I'm not sure what you're saying," said Winnie.

They sat down on the bench, and Dart continued. "There was a very short time when I felt good about myself, and the guy who made me feel like that was Blake Bookchester. The ways he was weak, I was strong. Blake knew it and I knew it and though we always had a lot of problems on account of him being so quick to act and not thinking about the consequences of anything he did, whenever I was with him I didn't feel alone. And with all the other men I've known in my life, I always felt alone. But it wasn't that way with Blake. Sure, I was mad at him most of time, but I never felt alone with him, never, and now I can feel myself slipping, going back to him in my mind, and before long I'll go see him. I'm going to do it, I know I will—drugs or no drugs. And I need you to tell me something to keep me from doing it, because I keep forgetting that a person like that can never be trusted. When he came over a while back I thought it would be different. He was in prison so long, and I thought it would be different. But it wasn't.

That thing inside me lit up again, and when it does it makes me need something I don't have so much I can hardly stand it."

"Dart, I'm still not sure exactly what you're saying, but you would never act solely on a raw physical urge, would you?"

"Of course I would."

"We're not biological brutes, Dart. We can make informed choices about how to conduct ourselves. Our destiny is in our own hands."

"Excuse me for saying this, Pastor, but that's just stupid. Things build up. I see what other people have and I want those things too. I want to be full of someone else, and have them full of me. I want him back."

"Go talk to Jacob. He knows more about the trouble Blake got himself into."

"You can't send me over there. Blake works in the shop."

"He's not there now. I took a lunch over about an hour ago, and Blake and August weren't there. Jacob said they'd gone to Blake's father's house to water plants, mow the yard, and see if they could stop the toilet from leaking before Nate and his cousin return from Slippery Slopes. He took August along to help him."

"I'll be going then, thanks," said Dart.

"Are you bringing Ivan over in the morning?"

"If it's still all right. Amy and Buck are going away for a few days, and it would make everything easier."

"We're always glad to have Ivan over."

"Thank you, Pastor Winifred." And with that Dart turned and left.

At the Words Repair Shop, she hesitated for a moment before getting out of the Bronco, walking through the five men clustered in the shade of the yard, and going inside.

"Hello, Dart," said Jacob, looking up from the bench.

"Hi," she said. "Your wife sent me over here."

"Good for her. What can I do for you?"

"I need to know some things that are no one else's business."

Jacob wiped the grease off his hands and went outside with her. Together they walked down the road.

"I need to know if Blake's got a habit."

"Not that I can tell," said Jacob. "He's completely unpredictable, no habits at all. In fact, if you don't keep him focused, he'll wander off."

"That's not what I mean. I mean drugs—dealing drugs, taking drugs, sticking needles, popping pills, snorting, shooting it under his toenails, rubbing it in his gums."

"He passes all the drug tests they give him, and they spring them on him all the time."

"Then maybe he's just dealing."

"Not that I can tell."

"Do people come in, look out of the corners of their eyes, stay for a short while, and leave?"

"There are a lot of people who do that. This is a small town. But I know what you mean, and no, I haven't seen anything like what you're talking about."

"Where is he now?"

"He went over to his father's house to take care of things while Nate is away. We're kind of slow this afternoon, so I told him to take August with him. Also, there's a man from the government coming over in a little while, and I thought it would be better if Blake and August weren't here."

"What's he coming for?"

"I've applied for a small-business loan. We need more room."

"Well, thanks for talking to me. And could you please not tell him I was here?"

"Sure," replied Jacob.

Driving a Picture from the Past
into the Future

Buck and Amy left early the following morning for the North Woods, leaving some confusion about who was in charge. Dart and the nurse argued about whether Kevin should ride along when she drove Ivan to August's. The nurse said he couldn't go, but Dart brought him anyway, after his blood pressure, pulse, and temperature were recorded in the notebook.

When they pulled up by the log house, August came outside. He told Dart how good it was to see her again and thanked her for bringing Ivan. She walked past him dismissively and went inside.

August hurried over to Kevin and Ivan and started waving his hands excitedly as he talked. He said that the day before, he and Blake had gone over to Blake's father's place to mow the yard and do some other chores. While taking a break for a glass of water inside the house, Blake played back the messages left on his father's answering machine. Most of them were from tired women with nervous voices trying to sell stuff. Blake erased them one by one. But the last message was from the trucking company. The male voice said Blake's father was to take a load to a town called Wormwood, in Iowa. All the other drivers were busy; it needed to be done right away, and he was supposed to call back as soon as possible.

After hearing the message, August said Blake had paced around the kitchen and living room. Then he'd called the trucking company and told them his father, Nate, would take the job. The trucking company told Blake that someone would bring the loaded trailer over the following evening and drop it off. All the papers were signed and ready. The brown wrapping paper and plastic cling were to be delivered to the packing plant in Wormwood by eleven o'clock at night.

Then August asked Blake how his father was supposed to get the message from his answering machine if he wasn't there to listen to it. Blake showed him. "Just dial the number," he told August, handing him his father's phone. August dialed Nate's number and when the answering machine picked up Blake told him to punch in the number two, followed by seven. "You have one message," the machine said. Then Blake told him to punch the number five. When he did that the machine played back the message from the trucking company, and August could hear it through the phone. "See," Blake told him. "When Dad calls home, he'll get the machine to play back the message. That way he'll know."

"Everybody knows how answering machines work," said Kevin. "What's the big deal?"

"I'm trying to tell you something important," said August. "I don't think Blake's father is ever going to hear that message. I think Blake is going to take that load to Iowa himself, and if he gets caught he'll be in serious trouble, because that's a violation of the conditions of his release."

"Why can't he leave the state?" asked Kevin.

August and Ivan tried to think of a reason.

"Well, each state is different," said Ivan.

"Ivan's right," added August. "And some things that are against the law in one state are legal in other states, like buying fireworks."

"Other states probably have the death penalty for carrying drugs," added Ivan.

"The death penalty?" scoffed Kevin.

"He's already served his time for that," said August.

"Sure," Ivan said, "but that might not mean anything in other states. They might just be waiting for him to come into their territory so they can electrocute him."

"Surely not," said Kevin, but Ivan could tell that neither he nor August was sure.

"I'm going with him," said Ivan.

"How are you going to do that?" scoffed Kevin.

"I don't know how, but like I've told both of you, I think Blake Bookchester is my dad, and I'll find a way to go with him. He might need me."

"That's crazy," said August.

"You don't even know for sure that he is your dad," said Kevin.

"I'm pretty sure."

"Did you ask your mom again?" asked August.

"Mother and I aren't getting along too good right now, and anyway she has always said that my father is dead."

"And you don't believe her?"

"I just think she needs to tell me that for some reason."

"So you can't ask her again?"

"Not right now, but if we could get inside Blake's house and look around, I'm sure there's something that would tell."

"You might be right," replied August. He was quiet for a while, and then he added, "We can do that tonight if you want. After Blake leaves to drive his father's truck down to Iowa, it would be easy to get into his house. It's only a mile, or less, out of Words. We can ride over on our bicycles. I have one for you to ride."

"Are you two completely nuts?" asked Kevin. "You can't break into someone's house."

"Yes we can," said Ivan. "I'll bet he doesn't even lock it."

"That doesn't make any difference. There could be other ex-cons staying there, hiding from the law. There could be two or three of them, with knives, guns, and sexually transmitted diseases."

"You're just imagining things," said Ivan.

"Maybe, but a lot of the things I imagine end up being real."

"My dad would know if there were other people living with Blake," said August.

"Sure, but he might not tell *you*," said Kevin. "Listen, I've got a really bad feeling about this."

"Maybe he's right," said August to Ivan.

Then Dart came out of the house and walked toward them, frowning.

"I'm not kidding," said Kevin. "Stay away from there, promise me."

"I can't do that," said Ivan. "Some things are important enough to take risks."

"No," said Kevin, but by then Dart was there and she drove away with him in the front seat, leaving Ivan and his suitcase standing next to August.

The two boys watched the Bronco leave, then went inside the house and told Winnie they wanted to camp out overnight by the hermit's hut. She had a thick book with fine print in her hand, and she looked up over the tops of her reading glasses and said that was way too far away. It was fine to camp out, she said, but it had to be close by. August said they wanted to see the hermit again, and look for the Wild Boy, but she just repeated that it was way too far away, making it clear this time that it was useless to argue.

The boys put up the tent in the woods beyond her garden. After supper, they made a fire and let it burn down and unrolled their sleeping bags inside the tent. Then August said they were running out of time. They started playing back the tape on which they had recorded their conversation for the last couple of hours, so when August's parents walked out to check they'd hear their voices inside the tent.

August's bikes were in the garage next to the house, and they got them without being seen. It was hot and the ride took longer than August had planned for, but they got to the road in front of Blake's farmhouse just before dark. Ivan looked through the binoculars August had brought. He could see the motorcycle parked in front of the house.

"Maybe you were wrong," said Ivan. "Maybe he isn't taking the load to Iowa."

"Maybe," replied August.

They waited a few minutes on the other side of the road, crouched down in the ditch. After a little while Blake came out of the house, got on his bike, and came down the driveway toward them. They got down lower and he turned the corner and raced off without having seen them.

They looked for a place to hide the bikes in the farmyard, then leaned them against the far side of the house.

"Maybe he locked it," said Ivan, looking in one of the windows.

"We'll find out," said August. "Let's try the back door first."

"I'm a little surprised you're doing this," Ivan said to August as they walked back around.

"Me too," he said. "But this was July Montgomery's old house, and I asked myself what he would have done if his best friend—who was my dad at that time—wanted to find out who his dad was. And when I asked myself that I just knew that we should do this."

They tried the back door and it opened right away.

"I'll go in first," said Ivan, stepping inside.

Almost immediately, he wished he hadn't come. It was dark in there, and something horrible was hanging in the air in the middle of the room.

"That's Blake's bag," explained August, snapping on his flashlight. "He uses it to exercise. It's a punching bag."

They went on to explore the rest of the room, and then the kitchen it opened into. Six bulging garbage bags were stacked up against the wall, and bits of old wallpaper and chunks of plaster on the floor led the boys to assume that Blake had been cleaning up the place. They checked the drawers and cupboards as well, then looked through the other room downstairs. The book written by Flo's husband was on a chair next to the window.

Upstairs were two relatively empty rooms. The room Blake slept in had a single bed and two bureaus. There were more books scattered around, along with some motorcycle magazines, empty soda cans, wrenches, and screwdrivers.

"You'd better look at this," said August, looking down into the top drawer of one of the bureaus.

Inside were several pictures of Ivan's mother when she was younger. In one of the pictures she and Blake were laughing, their faces close together and their eyes watching each other.

Ivan had seen only a few pictures of his mother before he was born, and none of them looked like these. He couldn't stop looking at them, even when August said he saw something outside. "Nate's semi is coming down the drive," he said, "turn your flashlight off. We've got to get out of here."

Ivan just stood there, looking at the picture of Blake and his mother. It was cracked and dirty around the edges, as if it had been picked up and held too many times. Still, it was the key to the empty places inside him. He studied how his mother and Blake looked at each other, the way their eyes cocked sideways, and then the way they were laughing. It seemed like a real laugh, but Ivan couldn't imagine what kind of laugh it was. What could ever happen that would be laughed about like that? And the more he studied the picture, the more puzzled he was by this image of his mother. She looked so young and so wild, as if she had just stepped into the world and wasn't sure what she was doing there. Ivan simply didn't recognize this earlier version of her, and the effect was unsettling.

"Ivan, come on!" yelled August again. "Turn your light off. He'll see it."

Ivan turned off the flashlight and they felt their way out of the room, along the hall, and down the stairs. Then they heard beeping, and when they looked out the kitchen window, they saw the back end of the trailer approaching. They hurried into the back room, heading for the door.

Outside, they crept around the side of the house to where their bikes were. Then they looked around the corner.

Blake unbolted the trailer and swung the doors open. Then he went into the house. He came out a minute later carrying several garbage bags. He threw them into the back, then returned for more.

Ivan took the picture out of his pocket and shone the flashlight on it again.

"Turn it off," said August.

Blake came out with two more bags, tossed them into the trailer, and went back inside.

"I'm going with him," Ivan said to August.

"What?"

"If he gets into trouble in another state, he might need me."

Ivan could hear Blake rustling around the kitchen. He ran to the open trailer, climbed onto the bumper, crawled between the garbage bags, and scrambled down the narrow aisle between the crates, all the way to the front of the trailer.

Blake came out again with more garbage bags, tossed them in, and closed one of the double doors. Then he went back inside, and when he did August climbed up just as Ivan had, crawled back through the trailer, and crouched down beside Ivan.

"I'm coming too," he said.

Then Blake came out, closed the second door against the first, and bolted them tightly in place.

It was pitch black inside the trailer.

The boys heard the cab door open and close, and then a couple of minutes later the engine started up, the sound vibrating through the trailer. They felt the trailer lurch ahead. August shined his flashlight on his watch.

For the first few minutes there was a lot of stopping and starting, running through a couple quick gears, bumping around, and corners.

They couldn't tell where, but Blake stopped outside Grange. He opened the back doors and began carrying the garbage bags across the road and throwing them into an open dumpster.

Then they were off again. After another half hour they could feel the truck running through the higher gears, and the hum of the tires got louder and steadier. Every so often a car would pass and tiny holes in the trailer filled with pencils of light, then went dark again.

"Must be on a divided highway," offered Ivan. They walked to the back, looking along the way for a place where they could see out. But the little holes in the sides were too small, and there was too much jiggling.

They climbed up on a couple of the boxes. "We should have brought something to eat," said Ivan.

"We didn't know we were coming."

After a while Ivan asked August how they were going to get out of the trailer without being seen.

"They'll start unloading it as soon as we get there," said August. "We'll slip out when the forklift driver turns around with a load. It will be late and there won't be many workers in the warehouse. Then we'll get into the cab, where the bunk is."

"You make it sound easy," Ivan said.

"What are we going to do if he gets stopped by the police in a different state?" asked August.

Ivan shrugged.

A little later, August looked at his watch again. "It would be a good idea to get some sleep," he said. "It might be a long night."

Ivan had his flashlight on, staring at the picture of his mother and Blake. "There's something about this—"

"Let me see it again," said August. Ivan handed it to him.

Someone honked outside, behind them on the highway.

"I know what you mean. The pictures of my parents before I was born do the same thing to me."

"What is it?" asked Ivan.

"I don't know. But they always make me wonder about much more than you can see in the picture. We really should get some sleep though, Ivan."

"Okay," he said, taking the picture back.

They fell asleep, and when they woke up the truck was stopping and starting again, lurching and turning.

"We must have turned off the highway," said Ivan.

Sometime later the truck came to a stop. Blake climbed out of the cab, and they heard voices.

"We're closed," someone said gruffly.

"Don't you guys have watches?" replied Blake. "It's before eleven. Here's the shipping order."

"Open the gate," said another voice. The cab door closed, and the boys could hear it scraping open.

"Dock fourteen," someone yelled, and they were moving again.

The sounds of animals—cows and hogs—got louder and louder, until they were on both sides, bellowing and coughing.

Someone yelled, "Bring 'er back easy. Easy."

They backed up, then stopped and went forward. Then backward, forward, and backward again.

"I can't see around the corner!" yelled Blake.

"Drive much?" someone yelled back and laughed.

About ten minutes later, after a lot of stopping and starting and starting over, the trailer bumped into something.

"Easy!" yelled a voice over the sound of the animals.

Then Blake climbed out and they could hear the post jacks cranking down, lifting the front end of the trailer.

August and Ivan crawled off the boxes and hid in the narrow center aisle near the back.

"Say," said Blake, "I'm having trouble with my alternator. Is there a place around here to have it looked at?"

"There's a truck stop just off the highway north of town, but I doubt you'll find any mechanics at this hour."

"Can I park here until morning?"

"No. Everybody out by eleven. It's the company rule."

"Okay. Do you need anything else?"

"No. That's it. Sign here. Take it easy."

"Aren't you going to unload it?" asked Blake. "I thought this was a rush job."

"Jackson does that. He'll come in the morning."

Then Blake drove away, and there was only the sound of cows and hogs hollering, along with a real bad smell.

"I didn't count on this," said Ivan. "We could beat on the sides of the trailer and yell until hell freezes over, but no one would ever hear us over the sound of those animals."

"We'll be out in the morning," said August. "But it might get a little cold tonight."

"No problem," replied Ivan. "I've got a couple matches. We can make a fire with some of this cardboard."

Kevin and Wally

Kevin Roebuck rested comfortably on his bed. Though it was nearly midnight, he was staying awake in order to savor the sensation of adequate quantities of air moving in and out of his lungs, banishing the anxiety that usually threaded through his respiratory system—the strained, impotent fury that resulted from never getting quite enough oxygen. He quietly experienced a new strength: his arms and legs joined to his mind through an alert network of muscle tissue and smooth nerves. Impressions from the world around him—the overnight nurse's steady raveling snore, the blinking of electronic devices, the sound of his mother's antique clock ticking in the hallway, even the wind outside the window—were accompanied by frolicsome thoughts. And while he understood on some level that the new corticosteroid responsible for these heightened sensory treasures would sooner or later lose its efficacy just as other new drugs had in the past, this understanding did not enter the contented circumstances he found himself immersed in. It felt almost as if he had never been sick a day in his life, and never would be again.

Kevin climbed from his bed and dressed in the dark, pulling on his clothes with a conscious fondness for both the texture of cloth and the movements that fit them into their proper places. He stepped from the room and put on his shoes, feeling the protective leather cushioning the soles of his feet. And then he quietly slipped out the back door.

The pond and moon welcomed him into their private greenish-blue performance. The clear sky was a speckled kettle placed upside down over the horizon. He breathed deeply and the night air became a willing part of him. Bumping against the dock, the tethered boat spoke in hollow, wooden syllables, a story of abandonment.

Kevin found his grandfather's walking stick leaning against the deck and grasped it with his right hand. Pleased that the shape of his palm and fingers so perfectly conformed to the indentations carved into the wood, Kevin walked along the edge of the pond. A current of cool air brushed against his cheek and he instinctively reached to readjust the sterilized plastic tubing from the oxygen tank. His hand discovered the tubing's absence like a distant memory of a once-tragic event that had become comical.

He lingered at the place where the heavy wire cage rested half-submerged in water. Inside, the head of the ancient reptile rose above the shining water, the moon reflected in its eyes.

"Hungry again?" asked Kevin. The head turned toward him.

The air was rich with clicking sounds, followed by shadows darting in and out of the moonlight above the cage. They looked like bats.

Walking as fast as he could into the house, he climbed to the second floor, went down the hall, and walked into his grandfather's room.

"Wake up. Wake up."

"What's the matter?" asked Wally, emerging slowly from a warm swamp of sleep.

"Plenty," said Kevin. "Get up, Grandpa."

"I'm having a dream."

"Ivan and August are in trouble."

"What are you talking about?" asked Wally, slowly removing the covers from his body, swinging his legs over the side of the bed, and warily locating the floor with the bottoms of both feet. Balancing with one hand on the mattress, he reached over and pulled the cord on the bedside lamp. A phalanx of yellow light invaded the room. Wally's eyesight slowly came to his assistance, and he noticed that his grandson was fully dressed.

"What kind of trouble?"

"Big trouble," said Kevin. "I can feel it."

"I'm not following this, Kevin."

"Get dressed. We need to drive over to Blake Bookchester's rented farmhouse."

"Why do we need to do that?"

"Because August and Ivan said they were going over there tonight, to break into his house while Blake was taking his father's truck on a run into Iowa that will break the conditions of his release if he gets caught."

"I don't think I'm awake enough to understand this," said Wally. "Help me find my glasses."

"Here they are, Grandpa."

"Where were they?"

"On your nightstand."

Wally put them on, found his notebook, and wrote something in it.

"Get dressed, Grandpa," repeated Kevin.

"Shouldn't I understand what this is all about first?"

"I'll talk and you dress," said Kevin. "And try to be quiet, because we don't want to wake anyone up. Don't put on your shoes until we leave the house."

"Where's your oxygen tank?"

"I don't need it tonight."

"I'm not going anywhere without one, just in case," said Wally.

"All right. We'll have to take the heavy one, though. The small ones are empty."

"Where are we going again?"

"Over to Blake Bookchester's rented house in the country."

"What are we going to find there?"

"Hopefully nothing."

When they arrived in the farmyard and climbed out of Wally's pickup, there were no electric lights burning anywhere, inside or outside. The moist, still air was filled with the smells of late summer.

"Come on," said Kevin, shining the beam of a flashlight ahead of them and following it up toward the house.

They knocked on the front door, and tried the knob.

The door opened and they went inside. While searching through the empty rooms, they found the back door open several inches.

"I don't see anyone out here," said Wally, stepping into the backyard. "Maybe Blake just didn't close the door the last time he used it."

Kevin came out too, but after looking around and finding nothing, they went back inside and finished searching through the empty house.

"Well, I guess they didn't come over here, after all," suggested Wally, wishing he were back home in bed. He closed the front door behind them.

"Maybe not," said Kevin, waving the flashlight through the front yard in broad, slow, sweeping arcs. "I still have this queer feeling, though."

"Someone recently backed a heavy truck up to the house," said Wally, stepping down into the yard. "See, Kev, the way the grass is smashed down. By the driveway they dug up some sod. Keep shining that light around."

"I told you," said Kevin. "Blake had his dad's truck tonight."

"Wait a minute," said Wally, pointing off to his left. "Hand me that light."

Kevin gave it to him, and he directed the beam toward the corner of the house, where they both saw something shiny.

"What's that?" he asked, and they went over toward the aluminum rim and spokes. Two bicycles leaned against the side of the house.

"August and Ivan actually came over here, and now they're in the back of the truck," concluded Kevin.

"That's a lot to imagine," said Wally.

"They're in trouble. We've got to go down there."

"Down where?"

"To Wormwood."

"Where's that?"

"Somewhere in Iowa. I've got a smartphone in the truck."

"Shouldn't we call August's parents if they're in trouble?"

"No," replied Kevin. "They'll say I gave them up. Ivan would never let me live it down."

"But telling me doesn't count?"

"You're one of us."

"I'm honored, I guess."

"Besides, I might be wrong, and I don't want to look like a fool," added Kevin. "But I know I'm not wrong. They're in trouble. I can feel it. Come on, let's go."

"We should at least take that woman your dad hired with us."

"No. It would take too long to go back and pick her up, and besides, she already thinks she's too important."

"We should at least tell her we're leaving."

"It's none of her business."

"I'm still going to call and tell her we'll be gone a couple hours. I don't want that gal for an enemy. She'd chase a fella all the way into the afterlife. By the way, wasn't your nurse working tonight?"

"She sleeps like a horse. You can tell Dart we're driving something up to Dad and Mom, and she can tell Gladys if she wakes up."

Kevin began coughing, then quickly recovered.

"Are you sure you're up for this, Kev?"

"I have to be."

"Any idea how we find them?"

"I'll get directions to the plant. There can't be more than one in such a small town."

"Good man," said Wally, pausing before he climbed into the pickup. "I'm going to step over here and take a pee while you're looking that up. Be right back."

They drove south, Wally pushing the upper edge of the speed limit. Kevin looked out the window at the sleeping houses and fields, took a deep breath, and remembered his ride on Blake's motorcycle, the feeling of surrender when they'd ridden into the fog.

They crossed the Mississippi River at Dubuque, its dark muddy water reflecting the lights of slow-moving boats.

When they arrived in Wormwood an hour later, Kevin had fallen asleep, his head leaning against the window. Wally reached over and shook his leg, told him to read the map.

"We're in Wormwood already?" asked Kevin.

"Not much happening," said Wally with a nod. He stopped the pickup at a deserted intersection in the middle of town. Absolutely nothing was moving. "Which way?"

"Take a left, six blocks, and another left."

Kevin pointed and Wally turned and drove among crouching buildings, many of them boarded up. Broken sidewalks lined the street.

"Turn left here."

Around the corner, Kevin pointed again. "There it is," he said.

"I can smell it," said Wally, driving toward a complex of buildings with elevators, sheds, dumpsters, and a row of Porta-Potties. Beyond the parking area—filled with mostly older cars and trucks—were several large animal lots, with loading ramps leading into the main slaughterhouse. They could hear animals bawling. Smoke rolled out of chimneys and a small cloud of steam hovered around a row of condensers. A security fence surrounded it all.

Wally stopped in front of the main gate. A line of spotlights tripped on.

"They've got to be in there," said Kevin.

"How do you know?"

"I just do."

"I'll see if I can wake someone up," said Wally, climbing out of the truck.

As he approached the gate, two security guards stepped out of a booth on the other side of the fence. One adjusted his hat, yawned, and crossed his arms in front of his chest.

"Evening," said Wally, steadying himself against the side of the pickup.

"We're closed," said the other guard.

"I'm afraid we have a problem," said Wally. "Two boys are missing and they might be inside, perhaps in the back of a trailer that arrived several hours ago, around eleven o'clock."

"They aren't here," said the guard.

"Mind if we look around?"

"You're not coming in here, old man."

"It won't take long," said Wally. "We won't cause any trouble."

"You're not coming in here. This is private property."

"Those boys may be in trouble."

"They're not here."

"But how would you possibly know if you haven't looked?"

"This is a private business. We're closed."

"Pretty unfriendly way of doing business," observed Wally.

"We have an unfriendly business," said the guard. "Now beat it."

Wally took out his notebook and wrote something in it. Then he climbed back into the truck, drove several blocks away, and parked along the side of the road.

"What are we going to do?" asked Kevin.

"We're going in," said Wally.

"How?"

"If I'm not mistaken, Buck has a bolt-cutter in the toolbox in back."

They climbed out of the truck, found the cutter, and began walking back in the direction of the plant. For the first time that night, Kevin felt a biting pain when he breathed.

They went between two abandoned cars and a burned-out barrel, then along the row of trailers and shacks just outside the security fence. There was a light on in one of the trailers. An old dog chained to a doghouse got up, moved several feet, and lay down again.

They continued along the line of impromptu dwellings until they reached the stretch of security fencing that ran along the back of the plant. Standing in high weeds, Wally took the bolt-cutter from inside his coat and began cutting through the thick links of wire.

"Excuse me," said a voice behind them. They turned to find a teenager, maybe sixteen or seventeen, his black eyes burning. "You can get into a lot of trouble going in there. The guards are big and mean. The last guy they caught sneaking in was beaten unconscious and thrown into the offal pit. They're afraid of people stealing meat, and they try to set an example every chance they get."

"I'm going in," said Kevin.

"This may not be such a good idea, Kev," said Wally.

"It's like August always says," replied Kevin. "The right ideas don't always seem good."

Wally took out his notebook and wrote something down.

"If you're going in, I can show you a good place," said the boy. He led them twenty yards down the fence, then kicked a stand of horseweed aside, revealing the entrance to a hole.

"Stay close to the stockyards, and if you need a place to hide, go in one of the Porta-potties. The guards don't use them. What are you looking for, anyway?"

"We think there are two boys trapped in a trailer."

"What was it carrying?"

"Wrapping paper and plastic cling."

"They keep that kind of thing over by the animal pens, next to the slaughterhouse."

"Thanks."

"I've got to get back now," said the boy, and disappeared in the tall weeds.

Wally and Kevin crawled under the fence and moved toward the first building through an obstacle course of discarded packing crates, scrap metal, old tires, and abandoned pieces of machinery.

They moved along the side of the building, keeping in the shadows. At the corner, Wally peeked around it. He watched workers come out of the next building to throw pails of something into a dumpster.

Animals bellowed. When they let up momentarily, Wally raised his hand. When the animal sounds resumed, a man walked around the corner of the second building and into the first door.

Wally and Kevin hurried across the lot, ducking behind a metal sewage tube. Keeping the tube between them and the building, they approached the first animal pen, where several hundred cattle crowded together in a space defined by a six-foot-high fence. The wire was heavy, the posts made of concrete. The beasts milled around one another in a state of quivering motion. When they bumped against the enclosure, the fencing banged against the concrete. Kevin's nostrils burned from the acidic odor of urine and manure.

Each lot had a ramp leading up to the side of a building. The ramps turned and ended at a narrow door that led onto the killing floor.

Kevin watched the animals, then reached out and took hold of the sleeve of Wally's coat. "They know," he whispered.

Wally nodded. "You're right. The animals know why they're here. They can smell the blood."

"It's not right that they have to stand in their own shit while they wait," said Kevin.

A thin strip of light shone along one edge of the door at the top of the cattle ramp. Kevin pointed at it.

"That door must be open," he whispered.

"The cleaning crews are probably working inside," said Wally. "If they had the slaughter plant running, cattle would be standing on the ramps."

"You stay here, Grandpa. I'm going up there."

"Be careful, Kev. They have electric wires in the chutes, to shock the cattle if they rear up on their hind legs. You'll have to crouch down. And the door may be hard to open."

"Give me a lift up," said Kevin.

Wally clamped his hands together and Kevin stepped into his palms. Rising up, he clambered over the fence to the other side, then dropped down among the milling cattle. The liquid mixture of manure and urine came halfway up his shins, and the smell was so strong it made his eyes water.

The cattle paid no attention to him as he walked among them.

Kevin paused at the opening to the covered ramp leading up to the door. The line of light still shone through from inside. He saw the shock-wires Wally had described, sagging down five feet above the slotted floor. It was getting cold and he pulled his jacket around him.

Kevin crouched down and started up, holding on to the sides of the chute with his outstretched hands, stepping on the wooden slats. He stopped twice to catch his breath. At the top, he pressed his ear against the door and listened, then placed both hands against the cold metal and pushed. The door opened a crack and he squeezed through.

Inside, he stood on the killing floor, where cattle were shot in the head with a metal bolt, then hoisted up with hooks through the tendons in their back legs, gutted, skinned, and sent down on the conveyer toward waiting knives, saws, and cleavers. The implements needed for this work and the smell of blood and entrails surrounded him.

Below him, Kevin saw men and women in uniforms cleaning the gutters, tubs, and conveyers. He moved to his right, along a small aisle that separated the killing floor from the processing plant below. After twenty or thirty feet, he came to another steel door and pushed it open.

Inside was cool, cavernous darkness. He stepped into it, closing the door behind him.

Moving by feel along rows of storage shelves, Kevin passed through a wide opening leading into the warehouse. At the other end, faint light seeped in from the yard lights outside.

Most of the loading docks were closed, but the back ends of three trucks were visible in the middle. One was open and empty, the other two closed.

Kevin opened the first of these two trailers, prying up the long locking bar.

The trailer smelled of wood and dust, but it was empty.

He opened the doors on the second trailer and was greeted by a cloud of smoke and the sound of coughing.

A narrow light came on and two figures emerged from the smoke and rows of loaded pallets.

"Kevin, is that you?" said a voice.

August and Ivan walked out coughing.

"What's with the smoke?" whispered Kevin.

"That was my idea," said Ivan. "I started a fire."

"Bad idea," said August, coughing. "It took our air. You got here just in time."

"Keep your voices down," said Kevin. "We've got to get out of here."

"How did you find us?" asked Ivan.

"Shut up," said Kevin. "If they catch us they'll throw us in the offal pit."

"What's that?" asked Ivan.

"I don't know, but it can't be good," said Kevin.

"Offal is digestible organs and intestines," explained August. "Most of it is used in pet food."

"Did you bring anything to eat?" asked Ivan.

"No, keep quiet. We've got to get out of here."

Just then a door closed at the other end of the warehouse and the overhead lights came on. The three boys ran to the end of the loading docks and opened the door.

Outside, they jumped down and hid under a trailer, huddled against the back wheels.

"Do you see that line of Porta-potties?" whispered Kevin, pointing across the open lot. "We've got to get to one of them. We can hide inside and then move on to where Grandpa is waiting in back."

"Let's go, then," said Ivan.

"No, wait."

Four guards walked around the corner of the warehouse. One of them stopped and shouted, "There they are, under the trailer!" The boys ran out the other way, along the side of the building, keeping in the shadows.

"Where'd they go?" shouted another man, breathing heavily.

"We'll get the little bastards."

The boys hurried along the Porta-Potties and continued toward the animal pens.

"Over here," called Wally, waving to them from the draining pipe.

The boys ran toward him, through the piles of junk, under the fence, and into the horseweed.

"Come on," said Wally, picking up the bolt-cutter and moving along the edge of the fence.

Back in the truck, the four breathed a collective sigh of excited relief. Ivan said he'd like to stop somewhere as soon as possible to get something to eat. Wally said everything was closed. August said he was sure Kevin's bravery had made July Montgomery smile in his grave, but

Kevin reminded him that July had been cremated, so smiling was out of the question.

"Whose idea was it to get into the back of that trailer?" asked Wally, starting the truck.

"Mine," said Ivan.

"And mine," added August.

"Well, I'm sure you had your reasons," said Wally, driving quickly through town.

"Blake Bookchester is my father," said Ivan. "We found out for sure."

"That's the best news I've heard all year," said Wally. "You okay, Kev?"

"I'm fine, but I'll be better when I get this smell washed off."

They talked all the way back. August and Ivan explained what it was like to be in the bumpy dark for so long. Kevin, breathing through the oxygen tubing, talked about how he knew they were in trouble, and how when he saw the line of light at the top of the packing plant ramp, he knew he could get inside. And when Wally drove over the Mississippi River he told the boys about a time he and Buck had gone down the river as far as they could on a pontoon with an outboard motor.

"How far did you get, Grandpa?"

"Not very far. Neither of us knew anything about what we were doing."

After two hours of driving in Wisconsin, Wally parked halfway down the drive so August's parents wouldn't hear him pull in. Ivan asked Wally and Kevin to wait in the truck a couple minutes, while he accompanied August to the campsite, just to make sure everything was all right.

"Thanks for coming with me," said Ivan, as they reached the clearing in the woods.

"No problem," said August.

"Are you going to stay out here or go into the house?"

"I think I'll stay out here for a while," August said. "I want to think about what happened tonight."

"I thought you would," replied Ivan. "I'd better be getting back, though."

Ivan, Kevin, and Wally arrived back at home just as the sun was coming up. Ivan thanked Kevin again for coming after him. Kevin went down the hall, threw his dirty clothes into the laundry room, took a shower, and went to bed. His nurse didn't wake up.

Wally said he could feel important dreams forming in his mind, and went upstairs.

Ivan heard his mother banging around in the big kitchen. When he walked in she was making biscuits, flour on her hands and arms. She looked up and said, "I thought you were over at August's. What's going on?"

"I need to talk to you about something, Mother," said Ivan, taking the picture out of his pocket.

Grass Fire

After Dart talked to Ivan she carried Flo's breakfast up to the third floor. The two women ate oatmeal with brown sugar and cream, along with fruit jam and biscuits.

"What's the matter with you today?" asked Flo, setting her spoon down.

"Why?"

"You're different."

"There's a grass fire burning in my life and I don't know how to put it out."

"Do you want to?"

"Something is chasing me faster than I want to run."

"Does that frighten you, Dart?"

"Yes."

Florence took a drink of chamomile tea. "When my husband and I first moved out here—this was over seventy years ago, during the Depression—we had two big dogs. We thought we needed them for protection. One was a great dane, the other a German shepherd. They were magnificent creatures, but thunderstorms frightened them both. The dane would cower under the table in the dining room, shivering and whining. The shepherd would attack the rain, snarling and barking."

"Which one did you like better?" asked Dart.

"I liked them both."

"If it were me, I'd have no use for the shepherd."

"Why?"

"I just wouldn't."

Dart felt the blood pounding through her veins. She gathered their bowls, plates, silverware, and cups, and placed them on the carrying tray. "Do you have everything you need for the rest of the morning?"

"Yes."

Dart checked on Kevin and his nurse, and found them both still asleep. Then she drove to Red Plain and walked into the cement plant. A man and a woman were standing at the counter, talking to Bee about having a patio poured behind their house. The man thought they were too expensive and the woman wanted more choices in pattern-stamping. After they left, Dart stepped forward.

"Do you remember me?" she asked, her voice unsteady.

"Of course I do, Dart," replied Bee, looking over the top of her reading glasses.

"I was hoping you'd be here today."

"I just got back from a vacation in Slippery Slopes." Bee yawned. "I'm afraid I'm still a little behind on my sleep."

"I need your honest opinion about something."

"Okay."

Dart looked around the office, reinforcing her memories. "I was so young back then," she observed, more to herself than to Bee. "I was dumb as a post and afraid of everything. I lied about my age when I started working here."

"I know," said Bee. "And you're still young in my book."

"I'm almost thirty."

"That's just getting started."

"Is it true you're going out with Blake's father?"

"Yes."

"Do you think Blake and I could ever . . . I mean, do you think his father could ever . . . I mean, if something terrible was built in the past, do you think the same people who built it could tear it apart? And do you think that after they'd torn it apart they'd still be able to look each other in the eye—"

"Yes," said Bee.

"And do you think people can ever be forgiven for what they don't know about themselves, for paying too much attention to what frightens them and too little to what makes them happy? Do you think there is any future for people who have been so ignorant for so long about everything? Do you think people can really start over? Do you think they can wake up one morning and—"

"Yes, I do."

"Well, then fine, I mean, that's what I wanted to know."

Dart left the cement plant and drove to Blake's farmhouse. She turned down the long drive, parked her Bronco in the farmyard, and walked up to the house. After knocking several times, she pushed in the door.

"Hello," she called, stepping into the kitchen. "Is anyone here?"

The house smelled musty, in need of cleaning. The windows were dirty. "Hello?"

The sound of her unanswered voice annoyed her. She walked through the kitchen and into what had once been a dining room, where Blake's heavy punching bag hung from the ceiling.

This doesn't belong in here, she thought, shoving the bag and letting it swing back and bump her in a not-altogether-unpleasant way. She thought about talking to the leather bag, practicing what she was going to say to Blake, but that seemed really stupid. She shoved the bag again and walked away before it pushed back.

At the repair shop in Words, three men were smoking cigarettes next to a red combine in the parking lot. She asked them where Blake was.

"He didn't come in today," one of them said.

"Is Jacob here?"

"His wife came over and they left together."

"They went over to Nate's," said another one, and added, "Nate is Blake's father."

"I know who Nate is," replied Dart. "But why did they go over there?"

"They didn't say why, but they were in a hurry."

Dart drove the fifteen miles over to Nate's house. From the road she could see a pickup next to the shed. Winnie's yellow car was parked next to it. Farther away from the house, a man climbed stiffly out of a blue Mercury. Nate, Winnie, and Jacob walked out of the house and met him in the yard. The four of them stood close together, talking.

Dart pulled into the drive, parked, got out, and stood beside the Bronco, watching. After several minutes Blake's father walked away from the others and leaned against the pickup. As Dart studied him, the genealogy of their mutual disapproval loomed up between them—the residue left over from forgotten words, jabbing looks, mocking tones, and nuanced silences. She could feel her hackles rising and she tried to retract them, but they were too well trained, determined to protect her even if against her wishes.

Winnie walked over to Nate and touched his shoulder. He turned away and put his head in his hands. Then Winnie saw Dart, said something to Jacob, and motioned for Dart to come ahead while she crossed over toward the man Dart didn't know.

Dart walked over. The man moved away and stood next to the blue Mercury.

"Is Blake here?" asked Dart.

"No," said Winnie, her face stiff.

"What's going on?" asked Dart, exchanging furtive glances with Nate.

"That's Jack Station," said Winnie, talking loud enough to be heard by everyone. "He's Blake's release officer. Blake apparently took his father's semi into Iowa without permission, or at least that's what Station thinks. Patrol cars are waiting to arrest him when he crosses the state line from Dubuque. If he left the state he has violated the conditions of his release."

"Call him on the CB," whispered Dart, looking over at the man leaning against the Mercury. "Tell him to ditch the rig and find another way home. They can't prove anything."

"Nate tried that. Apparently the CB is turned off."

Winnie said Blake had called the shop from a truck stop outside Wormwood, where he'd just had a new alternator put in.

"Is he still in Wormwood?" asked Dart.

"No," said Winnie. "He left a while ago. We think he's probably about an hour from Dubuque, on Highway 151."

Dart walked over to Nate, and they stood facing each other without looking up.

"I can't believe this is happening," she said. "I can't believe it."

"There's nothing anyone can do," said Nate. "He should have called me. I gave him the number. He should have called. He didn't have to drive down there. I could have come back. It was my responsibility. Two hours of road between here and Dubuque and he has the CB turned off."

"Don't beat yourself up," said Dart. "Blake does everything without thinking. He always has. He's as dumb as a box of rocks."

"I know," said Nate. "And he's stubborn too."

Dart looked up and into Nate's eyes, and for the first time she could remember, she didn't look away. "This isn't going to happen, Nate, not now, not this way. The government cheated us out of him once, and it isn't going to happen again."

"There's nothing anyone can do," said Nate.

Dart walked past Jack Station, across the yard, and kicked her Bronco, denting in the door. Then she paced around the yard, running her hands through her black hair in frustration.

"We'll hire a lawyer," said Winnie.

"Won't help," said Station, lighting a cigarette. "After he's caught it's a simple matter of sending him back."

Dart walked behind the house, out beyond the beehives. She looked across the pasture to the rock outcroppings and the trees growing out of the sandstone. A child stood at the edge of the forest, looking back at her.

So that's the Wild Boy, she thought, remembering the many conversations she'd overheard between August and Ivan, Ivan and Kevin, the three of them together. They worshipped that child, and she smiled as she recognized now that there was nothing wild about him. The child looking back at her clearly was afraid of other people, yet also yearning to belong. Someone was obviously taking care of him, keeping him clean, feeding him, making it possible for him to stand on that outcropping with his hands in his pockets, wanting to be seen. Wild my eye, she thought.

Dart raised her hand and waved.

The boy returned the wave, then stepped back into the trees and disappeared.

Dart walked toward the house, thinking about how she'd always thought of love as something that would come to her, seek her out. But now she knew this was wrong. Just as the empty places inside Blake had aroused in her the very things that attracted him, so her own empty places had reached out and excited in Blake the qualities that drew her to him. They were complicit in planting the things they wanted to find in each other. She remembered how she and Blake would ride all night through the Driftless Region, stopping for gas in sleepy little towns, sitting on curbs along deserted streets, owning the world.

Winnie, Nate, Jack Station, and Jacob turned toward the sound of

Blake's bike behind the house. Spitting a stream of sod from the wide back tire, Dart sped across the side yard, climbed the ditch onto the road, opened the throttle, and disappeared in a vanishing blur of blue-and-white noise.

"That young woman is going to kill herself," said Winnie.

"Or someone else," said Nate.

"She can't possibly get there in time," said Jacob.

"She might," said Station, staring into his watch. "When I was younger, I could have."

Rooting Trees

Along Highway 151, approaching Dubuque, Iowa folds into the Mississippi River Valley in a long, gradual descent. Entering town, the decline sharpens and houses begin to appear, tucked into crevices in the sloping terrain like keepsakes in open-shelved cabinets. The buildings grow thicker as one descends, and at the bottom the muddy brown river runs deep, swift, and wide, with railroad tracks along each side, flood walls, barge lanes, and two bridges—the first of them leading into Illinois, the second into Wisconsin.

Blake was driving downhill, occasionally engine-braking, and thinking about Ivan. He knew little about him, far less than his consuming concern for the boy's future would seem to imply. But what Ivan was becoming was of more immediate consequence than what he already was, in any case. And why did he have to repeat fifth grade, anyway? Blake decided that before school started in the fall, he would go talk to Ivan's teachers. Maybe there was some other way. And even if there wasn't, he would be sure they knew who he was.

This train of thought surprised him. Normally too uncomfortable with himself even to go into the public library in Grange and check out a book, Blake was now contemplating going into school to talk with public officials, perhaps even some of the teachers who had once taught him. It seemed out of character, and yet he could feel almost all of himself wanting to do it. Even his interior choir of dissidents, who consistently demonstrated a principled disrespect for anything outside his established traditions, seemed in favor of going. Once again, he was beginning to sense the possibility of a new life already begun.

The road began to descend more rapidly, and every so often he touched the truck's brakes, keeping under the speed limit. He was hungry, and he thought about stopping to get something to eat at the brick restaurant under the viaduct. Eleven years ago, he and Dart had gone there after competing in Dickeyville hill climbs. They ordered full-dress cheeseburgers, sat inside a red booth, and Dart complained that the ground beef had come from round instead of chuck, the cheddar was too gooey sweet, the lettuce wilted, and the tomato slice was without any taste at all. He fondly remembered the sound of her voice, and the way her eyes looked when she was annoyed by something she considered truly blameworthy. But before he could adequately savor this affection he was assaulted by the deathless grief that surrounded all his memories of her. He pushed the recollection aside.

He saw a sign for a farmers' market in the city square and decided to go there instead. That way he could also look for something to take back to his father.

Without the trailer it was easy to find a place to park the Kenworth, and when he arrived at the square in front of city hall, he was glad he had come. There were fifteen or twenty booths, each displaying colorful vegetables and fruit, local meat in coolers, honey, homemade breads, cookies, and a wide variety of chutneys and relishes in polished glass jars with pieces of ruffled cloth screwed tight between the sealed lid and screw top. Shoppers with bags of produce went from booth to booth, and standing among them, Blake closed his eyes and imagined his father's face, felt his love for such scenes. Then he opened his eyes and began searching for the right foods to bring home, talking to vendors as if they were old friends, delighting in the colors, sounds, and smells.

One booth offered boxes of assorted caramels made by a Trappist order of sisters called Our Lady of the Mississippi Abbey. Blake bit into a sample and exclaimed, "This is fantastic. How do you get that chewy, smooth richness? And the buttery flavor? I've never tasted anything like it. How do you do it?"

The sister behind the table confessed she didn't know. She was not part of the team that made the candy, and it was only yesterday that she had volunteered to work the booth. Blake bought a box for Ivan, and then asked on a whim if she'd ever heard of Spinoza.

"Of course," she said. "Spinoza was the first modern philosopher."

Blake was overjoyed. It seemed so improbable to meet someone familiar with Spinoza. The size of the universe shrank to walking distances in all directions.

"Look at this," he said, turning around and showing the knife hole in the back of his leather jacket. "I did that in honor of Spinoza."

"Very clever," said the sister.

"Spinoza wanted to remind himself how dangerous new ideas were," said Blake.

"And did you know he gave away his family fortune?" asked the sister.

"Yes," said Blake, his excitement rising. "I knew that." It felt as if the world had opened a small space in which he could be comfortable, where he could feel at home the way he was.

"He lived a life of voluntary poverty, just as I do," said the sister.

"Excellent!" shouted Blake, taking the plastic rosary out of his pocket to give to her. But just then he glimpsed out of the corner of his eye a woman with no helmet and wild hair pull her motorcycle in front of the parked Kenworth, climb off, and dash across the street into the square, coming in his direction.

Something in her urgent manner ignited his attention. He excused himself from the conversation he was having with the sister and turned away from the booth.

Just as he turned, Dart stopped and they stared at each other across the square. Her face glowed from the wind and Blake held the box of caramels under his right arm. The plastic rosary dangled from his left hand. Then they ran toward each other, meeting in front of a pile of ripe muskmelons.

"They're after you," said Dart, breathing through her mouth and talking at the same time. "They're looking for your truck. We'll have to leave it here and find another way across the river. We need to call your father. He's worried, and Winnie and Jacob are too. We'll tell them where the truck is. They can come get it. How could you leave the state without telling your release agent? How could you risk it? Why would you do that to me? You brought August and Ivan down here with you, did you know that? They were in the back of the trailer, and they almost got killed at the packing plant. They were locked in, and it's your fault. Are you crazy, Blake? You need to think and you never do. Your life belongs to other people now. How could you have left me and Ivan alone all those years? Didn't you know I was pregnant? Didn't you know how lonely I would be? Do you have any idea how hard it is to raise a child alone? Didn't you ever think about that? None of this had to happen. All those years we could have been together. We could have had something nice. Ivan would have had a father. What were you thinking?"

Blake was still falling into her unexpected presence. Her mouth, her darting eyes, how the wind held her black hair away from her tight brown face—it was more than he could comprehend. She'd lived as a static treasure in his mind for so many years, and now that she was real he had a hard time making the adjustment.

"What?" he said.

"Aren't you listening to me, Blake Bookchester? Aren't you? Stop looking at me like that. Stop it. We don't have time to look at each other like that. We've got to get out of here. The police are everywhere, like bugs on rotten fruit. They aren't far behind. Is there anything you need in the truck?"

"I loved you the first time I saw you," said Blake triumphantly, as if he were completing a sentence at the end of a marathon.

"That's just dumb, Blake. The first time you saw me you didn't know anything. We have to get out of here."

"Can you smell those ripe muskmelons? Let's get a couple to take home."

"Are you crazy? We've got to get you back into Wisconsin. Your release officer is about to put you back in jail. I told you, stop looking at me like that."

They ran to the motorcycle. Blake got on and started the engine. Dart climbed on behind, hugging him firmly between her thighs like a grasshopper on a blade of grass.

"This seat is terrible," she said.

"I know," he replied. "Would you rather drive?"

"No. My hands are still vibrating; I can hardly feel them. But you really need to do something about this seat."

They sped away from the truck, looking for someone with a boat to take them across the river.

"Blake, how are we ever going to put all this behind us?" shouted Dart into his ear. "How are we ever going to get over all this?"

"We will!" shouted Blake.

"What?"

"We will!"

"I can't trust you again, not with Ivan and not with me!" she shouted into a third-gear wind.

"What?"

"I can't trust you again."

"Yes you can."

"What?"

"Yes you can!"

"I'm no good at trusting people. I can't help it."

"That's okay. Think whatever you want!" shouted Blake. "It won't change anything. I'll always be here."

"People never really get over the bad things that happen to them."

"We will!" shouted Blake. "We'll rise together out of the past like two rooted trees."

"Like what?" shouted Dart.

"Like two rooted trees!"

"That's just stupid, Blake. Why would you say something like that? Are you trying to make me mad on purpose?"

"What?"

"God, this is an uncomfortable seat. If you don't do a better job of missing those bumps in the road there won't be anything left of my ass. And neither of us would be happy about that."

"What?"

"Never mind!"

The Bargain

On Sunday, Dart made a late brunch of Belgian waffles, scrambled eggs, fried potatoes, sausage, toast, and fruit jam. The entire Roebuck household enjoyed it. When they had finished, Wally carried his second cup of coffee down to the pond and sat on the bank looking into the water. Several minutes later, Kevin and his father joined him, followed by Ivan, Dart, Amy, Flo, and Kevin's nurse.

Buck took off his shoes and socks, rolled up his pant legs, and waded in. He lifted the metal cage out of the pond and carried it onto the grassy bank.

Everyone stared at the enormous turtle inside. The turtle stared back, its eyes round, small, and bright. Ivan called August on Dart's new cell phone and told him everything.

"Are you sure about this, Kev?" asked Buck.

"Yes," said Kevin.

"Maybe you'd like to think on it a little longer," said Wally.

"I don't need to," said Kevin. "I've made up my mind."

"The DNR would be more than happy to take him south," said Amy.

"No," said Kevin. "He came here. This is his pond. It's where he wants to be. If he decides to leave he can go on his own."

"Good point," said Wally.

"And you won't worry about him coming after you again?" asked Dart. "I mean, what if he does?"

"He knows where he can find me," said Kevin. "Turn him loose, Dad."

Buck unsnapped the wire fasteners and pivoted the top and sides of the cage away from the heavy wire on the bottom.

The turtle stuck out its neck, turned its head, and looked at them, then slowly crawled into the water. His broad encrusted back remained for a short time above the surface, then moved forward again and disappeared into the pond.

"He's going deeper and fading away," said Ivan into the phone. "He's gone now."

"It's done," said Kevin.

"Good man, Kev," said Wally, writing something in his notebook.

While the others went back to the house, Flo asked Buck if he would help her walk all the way around the pond.

"Sure," said Buck. He sat down on the bank to put his shoes and socks back on.

"From my room I look out over the water every day," said Flo. "Just once I want to see it from the other end."

"I can understand that," said Buck. Flo took hold of his arm and they inched along the grassy slope.

About halfway around, Flo spoke again. "I'm afraid I have another favor to ask."

"What is it?"

"I want you to drive to Luster and talk to that release agent. I think his name is Jack Station."

"Why?"

"Blake Bookchester can't be sent back to prison, Buck."

"Did something happen?"

"Not yet, but it will. Blake's impulsive, and all he has to do is go into a tavern or show up late for a drug test. Seventy-one percent of all recidivism results not from new crimes, but simply from breaking the rules."

"What do you want me to do, Florence?"

"I don't know exactly," replied Flo, "but you need to go over and talk to that release agent. It would break Dart's heart if she lost him again. I know she's tough, but people have their limits."

"I suppose that's true."

They took a few more steps and then Flo went on, "You know my husband was a teacher."

"I remember, a professor."

"He said every so often a student would come along who wanted more than just the credit and degree. Every once in a great while, he said, a student came along who wasn't looking for a way to succeed in society, but was desperately seeking a way out of it. Those students, he always said, were like canaries in a coal mine. If they couldn't survive, the rest of us were doomed. The success of democracy depended on them."

"Is Blake really our responsibility?"

"Yes he is."

"I'll go over and talk to Station then," said Buck.

Flo stopped. "Here," she said. "This is where I wanted to stand."

As they stood, their feet slowly sank into the soaked grass.

"What is it about this place?" he asked.

"I don't really know," said Flo. "But when I'm sitting in my chair making my rosaries I always wonder what it would be like to stand here with the windbreak behind me. Now I can look at the window and wonder what it would be like to sit behind it."

"Don't they feel about the same?"

"Not at all."

They went back to the house and Buck helped Flo up to her room. Then he went down to the basement, where Amy was putting a new finish on a piece of period furniture. He told her he'd be gone for several hours.

On his way out to the truck, Wally called from the porch, "Where you going?"

"Over to Luster, want to come?"

"Yes," said Wally.

During the drive, Wally asked about Lucky. "I saw he was here earlier this morning. What did he say? Did the contracts come through?"

"They did," said Buck.

"Well?"

"Apparently Lucky went after a job he didn't tell us about. He got it, and he was pretty proud of himself."

"What is it?"

"Building a new prison outside Words. They're going to call it the Words Correctional Program Facility. There's a group of investors putting millions into it, and apparently they have some down-the-road understanding with the right people in the Department of Corrections and the Department of Development."

"How many cells?"

"Four hundred, with a separate building for laundry and a backup power plant."

"Big job," said Wally. "What did you tell him?"

"I told him we wouldn't do it."

"Someone else will build it anyway," said Wally.

"I know it. Lucky was pretty angry. He said he'd put a lot of time into the deal."

"Tough decision on your part," said Wally.

"I'll talk to the crew on Monday," said Buck. "The company building the prison—the second one down on the list—will be needing more help. That's what Lucky said."

"How many do you think will leave?"

"Half, maybe more. We don't have enough work to keep them all on anyway, not after the nursing home is finished. They know that. Our only new jobs are a couple large single-family homes in the hills."

"Hard times for construction," said Wally.

"Does that mean you would have taken the prison job, Dad?"

"Hell no, Buck. Carrying something like that into the afterlife would be like wearing lead clothes into the dreamworld. You and I started out over twenty-five years ago with a wheelbarrow and a manual cement mixer. We did real well, better than I imagined we would and possibly better than we deserved. And by the way, the idea of Lucky being angry just warms me all over."

In Luster, they found Jack Station washing his car in front of his modest house, working with a soapy sponge. They pulled in and got out.

"Who are you and what do you want?" asked Station.

"Most people call me Buck and this is my father, Wallace Roebuck."

"You own the construction company in Grange," said Station.

"That's right," said Wally. "We're here about Blake Bookchester."

"What did he do?" asked Station without looking up.

"He didn't do anything," said Buck.

"He took his father's truck into Iowa. I know he did that, but he didn't get caught."

"That's what we're here about," said Buck. "We want to make sure he doesn't go back to prison."

"Why?"

"Blake's son and his son's mother live in an apartment in my house," said Buck. "She works for my wife and her son is a friend to my son. Blake's father used to drive for our company and his cousin manages our cement company. Blake currently works for a man who occasionally fixes our equipment. His wife has been a pastor in Words for over fifteen years. And on top of all that, my wife's grandmother sees unique potential in Blake."

"Unique potential?"

"I can't say I see it myself, but she does. The point is, if Blake Bookchester goes back to prison it will affect a lot of people I care about."

Station tossed the sponge into the bucket of soapy water, walked several yards away, and sat on the grass.

"I'd appreciate any help I can get," he said. "There's only so much I can do beyond hammering away at these guys not to break the rules. Like taking his father's truck out of state: so long as I'm the only one who knows about it, that's one thing. But when other people find out, that's when it gets out of my hands."

"So you're not trying to find a way to send him back?" asked Wally, taking up the sponge and washing where Station had left off.

"Of course not. People who work with these guys like I do don't want to see them returned to prison. It's the people above us—career guys who've never met an inmate in their lives, and have no understanding of the situations they come from—who push us to send them back, to keep the prisons full.

"Don't get me wrong," Station went on, "there are plenty of guys who need to be locked up—better for them and for the rest of us. But most of them get hauled in because it's easier to keep locking up people who don't need to be locked up than it is to change the system."

"What can we do?" asked Buck.

"Give me your telephone number so I can call you if something happens. You could also sign up as sponsors."

Buck took the sponge from Wally and began washing the top of the car. "We'll do it," he said.

Wally walked around the soapy car, snapped his suspenders against his chest, and asked Station where he was going to put the car when he was finished washing it.

"What do you mean?"

"I mean, where are you going to park it?"

"Right where it is now."

"You need a garage."

"No kidding."

"Buck and I will build you one, at cost."

"What do you mean?"

"We'll build you a garage."

Station stared at Wally.

"What kind of garage?" he asked.

"One big enough for your car, with a couple windows and a side door."

Station stood up, walked over, and took the sponge away from Buck. He continued washing his car.

"I should probably mention that I've got a fishing boat and trailer behind the house, and a ride-on lawnmower on the back porch."

"We could build a two-stall garage," added Buck. "All you would have to pay for is the cost of the materials."

"Two single doors or one double?"

"You choose."

"What if I want to heat it in the winter?"

"We'll insulate it, build you a heated garage. How does that sound?"

"Concrete floor?"

"Poured concrete on clay and sand," replied Buck.

"You could have parties inside, with coffee and cake," added Wally.

"I don't know. I've watched your crews. You've got some pretty young guys on your payroll. Their workmanship can't be the best."

"Buck and I will build it ourselves," said Wally. "The two of us. I've been wanting to swing a hammer again and building an insulated garage seems like just the thing. We'll even mix the cement ourselves."

"Well, I suppose it would be good for the community," said Station. "I mean, a new building in the neighborhood would benefit everyone—looks neater, good for property values."

"Of course," replied Wally.

Winnie in Her Garden

Hidden among the Helms' afternoon mail lay a hand-written invitation to celebrate the marriage of Blake Bookchester and Danielle Workhouse. The reception was to be held outdoors, at the old July Montgomery farm outside of Words. All food and beverages would be provided.

Winnie recognized Dart's handwriting in the body of the invitation, but the blocky signature was definitely Nate's. They had worked on it together. A note at the bottom—also in Dart's scrolling hand, with extravagantly looping *g*'s and little swirls on top of the lowercase *i*'s—requested that August extend the invitation to Lester Mortal on behalf of Ivan.

Winnie smiled and read it again. When she showed it to August he went to his room to retrieve a seventeen-page essay he'd recently printed out on the history of ginseng and its place in human culture. After rolling the pages into a tight tube and stuffing it into his back pocket, he went outside, adjusted the strap holding his canteen around his shoulder, and ran off in the direction of the veteran's hut.

Setting down her cup of tea, Winnie watched through the kitchen window as her son disappeared into the tangled vegetation beyond the yard. An unusual calmness visited her and she no longer wished to be indoors.

On the painted bench in her garden, Winnie studied her flowers. A premonition of autumn had invaded the once-plump summer leaves, thinning them down and in some cases wrinkling the edges brown, but most of the rudbeckia, tall phlox, hydrangea, turtlehead, and echinacea blooms were still in optimal display of orange, purple, white, and gold. Late-summer butterflies with nearly transparent regalia hovered in the air, drifting lazily from flower to flower, landing, sipping up nectar, adjusting their colored robes, and moving weightlessly on. The slightest breeze moved the dainty creatures off course, but this never seemed to distress them, and Winnie admired their aimless good cheer.

She took off her shoes and socks and felt the grass with her feet. She remembered the first time she had thought about making a garden. The idea sprang from her belief that divine inspiration could be received by anyone, anywhere. It seldom was, but she remained convinced that nothing prevented even those in the most squalid or splendid surroundings from participating in numinous luminosity. Nothing could obstruct the advancement of spiritual events, provided the time was right and the recipient open to holy communication.

And yet Winnie also believed—with similar conviction—something almost contradictory: for effective prayer, some places worked a whole lot better than others. When God went looking for individuals, any location they happened to be in would suffice; but when Winnie went looking for God, some places were clearly better to search in than others. And maximizing her efforts in this regard was particularly important to her. From an early age she had known that without searching prayer, her life resembled the meandering of troubled sleep. Reverent prayer helped focus her mind and order her thoughts.

She had chosen the location for her private garden carefully, with an eye to cultivating heightened receptivity.

First, she'd observed the wild creatures in the area surrounding her home. In different seasons and at different times of day, she noted where they dozed, stretched, groomed, ate, nested, stored winter food, and conversed with each other. Next, she spoke to people familiar with the history of the area. A local landowner belonging to the Ho-chunk Nation even informed her of earlier uses of the land, and the location of former sacred sites.

She studied groundcover, trees, and shrubs, and measured the rate of growth from spring to fall. She watched how trunks, branches, and leaves spread their shadows on the ground, paying particular attention to the sound of the wind moving through them, and to the changing textures, colors, and fragrances.

Scientists at the university in Madison analyzed her samples of soil.

She dug holes, filled them with water, and timed how long it took for them to drain. At night, she charted the constellations seen from different places. In the library, she downloaded pictures taken from global positioning satellites and studied them.

For more personal deliberations, Winnie had Jacob tie several turns of scarf around her head and lead her from one place to another. While blindfolded, she related her changing feelings, thoughts, and moods, which Jacob dutifully recorded in a spiral notebook. They repeated the experiment at different times of day and night. Finally, they made love in dozens of locations and rated their respective experiences, then repeated the experiment again in the top-rated spots.

When the findings of all these tests had been evaluated, Winnie selected the grassy plot of ground a hundred yards or so uphill from her home. To the west of her chosen site, sandstone outcroppings rose out of the earth like fossilized layer cake, allowing for a sense of protective enclosure. Congested bunches of aspen, white pine, and birch grew to the north and south. To the east, a sloping view of a narrow valley expanded down an open meadow to a distant ridge, giving the impression that her garden rested in the plugged neck of a land funnel.

The project took two years to finish, and with a modest sense of satisfaction Winnie now sat up, raised her head, closed her eyes, and felt the afternoon sunlight gently push against her eyelids, igniting a lavender glow in front of her irises. As wave after wave of contented relief rinsed through her body, she focused her attention, following them into ever-widening experiences.

At least for the moment, no outstanding tensions or pressing psychic imperatives demanded her life's energy. The house was clean and her chores completed. The people she most cared about were doing fine, and their imagined representatives in her mind did not require her anxious vigilance. August was looking forward to the beginning of school and the prospect of seeing Ivan every day. Their friendship was more secure than ever.

Just a couple of days before, Ivan had called and told August he had something for him to see, something secret and important. August went with him that evening to a remote place not far from where Lester Mortal had conducted his ceremony with the burning statues. As the sun went down, they sat under a rock embankment. "Why are we here?" August asked.

"Wait," said Ivan. "My dad showed me this place. Listen. They're coming."

"What?" asked August.

Before Ivan could answer, there was an unearthly rattle above them. August looked up as the swarming sound grew louder.

And then a river of bats poured out of a deep crevice in the rock above him, gushing into the open and flying in all directions, clogging the air in a mad frenzy of beating black wings. The thick eruption of hungry creatures went on and on, until it seemed as if there would never be an end to the outpouring. The frantic flapping of thousands of individual bats breaking off from the dense cluster and speeding off in their own directions continued until they were all gone, dissolved into the evening light.

"See," said Ivan, and August felt an exhausted contentment that he carried inside him for the rest of the night and into the following day.

Jacob's application for a loan to build an addition onto his shop had been approved, and he was busily consulting with Roebuck Construction, planning the final details and selecting pieces of machinery to install.

The church had finally accepted Winnie's resignation, hired a new pastor, and was collectively swooning over every nuance of his emerging religious character.

Blake and Dart had found a way to resume actively loving each other, and Ivan and his father spent time together nearly every night, including long bouts of video-gaming, walks through the woods, studying math, and punching the heavy exercise bag that Dart had moved out of the dining room and into the barn.

All the forces demanding Winnie's attention seemed to be releasing their grip. Still seated on the bench with her eyes closed, she contemplated this brief freedom, and felt herself falling deeper and deeper into an indescribable peace. Both the falling and the peace had many layers, and she slowly dissolved into them until there was nothing left of her but a single wordless prayer, which she experienced over and over again.

After some time, Winnie began to experience a silent nudging to return to the practical world of everyday events. She felt the outer layers of her consciousness growing firmer, more alert. There was a new coolness in the air. The sound of birds resurfaced in her mind, accompanied by a number of recognizable fragrances.

Slowly opening her eyes, she noticed early evening shadows lying at the base of things. She took a deep breath and looked at her wristwatch. Over three hours had passed since she'd entered the garden. Jacob and August would be home soon and she had things to do.

Then her attention was drawn to a gangly shadow beneath her. Something about it was disturbing. She wondered briefly how a shadow could be there, and soon understood that it was her own, and then—in a rush of recognition—that she was five feet above the ground, levitating in midair.

A west wind came up the valley and Winnie was blown several feet to the east, directly above the painted bench she had been sitting on. She tried to propel herself downward, but without success. Her movements succeeded only in swiveling her around, turning her over, or having no effect at all.

Winnie laughed. She stretched her right foot out beneath her and managed to hook her toes inside the space between the horizontal board on the bench-back and two of the wooden slats connecting it to the seat. Anchored in this tentative way, she exerted pressure against the bench with her toes, and lowered her body several inches in the air. But as soon as she relaxed, she rose back up. Then she lost her tentative grip and floated freely again.

Fortunately, the next breeze that came along blew her farther into the garden, where she brushed against the ornamental crabapple that Jacob had planted for her several years ago. Grabbing the nearest limb, she pulled herself into the center of the tree and attempted to grapple her way toward the ground. By pushing against the fattest part of the limbs she managed to force her feet into the grass, but as soon as she let go she rose back up into the tree.

"Put me down!" She laughed and was suddenly alarmed to find she was not alone.

Dressed in a long-sleeve muslin shirt, red suspenders, gray work pants, and duck boots, Wally Roebuck stood about twenty feet away, watching her. When he saw her startled expression he said, "I'm sorry, Winnie, I should have announced myself. There wasn't anyone in the house, so I came out to look at the fish in your fountain. Ivan told me about them, and I've been wanting to come over and see them for a long time."

"This is very embarrassing," said Winnie, still holding on to the limb above her head and attempting to keep her voice calm. "I've been experiencing something I can't explain."

"I don't understand it either," said Wally. "I've found the key is to eat something, and almost anything will do. Here, eat some of this." He walked over, took a couple of nuts and dried berries from his shirt pocket, and handed them to her. She ate them, and within a few minutes she felt firmly earthbound.

Then she noticed that her feet were cold, and put her socks and shoes back on.

Wally went to the fountain and looked at the fish in the deepest part of the water. Their gills fluttered, but otherwise they were motionless. "I've stopped trying to make sense of everything," he said. "I had to after I began thinking about the afterlife. Acceptance is the only useful logic for me now."

"Do you believe in individual salvation?" asked Winnie.

"I don't," said Wally. "How about you?"

"I used to," said Winnie. "But the thought eventually just wore itself out inside me. Either we will all become fully conscious or none of us will."

"What about those gifted ones who seem so far ahead of the rest of us?" asked Wally.

"Even the scouts are part of the wagon train," said Winnie. "Why do you want to look at my fish?"

"Fish fascinate me. I don't know why, but I dream about them all the time. And yours are beautiful and strangely colored. I imagine your son knows the scientific names for them."

"You could safely bet your afterlife on that," said Winnie with a smile. "I hear you and Buck are going to build a heated garage for Jack Station."

"Yes, and I'm going to get a new hammer. Working with Buck has been one of my greatest joys. I assume you're coming to Blake and Dart's party?"

"I'll be there," said Winnie.

"So will I," said Wally, looking up from the pool. He jotted something into his notebook and turned back to her. "Can you tell me anything about this Wild Boy that August and Ivan keep talking about?"

"I suppose it would be all right to tell you," replied Winnie. "The Wild Boy is no wilder than you or me. Lester Mortal brought him back from a mountain village in Vietnam. The boy lives with Lester and is well cared for in every way. Believe me, I've checked."

"How do you account for the way Ivan and August think of him?"

"Mostly that's just boys being boys, but some of it is probably Lester's doing. He has his reasons, and I suppose we should respect them."

"What are they?"

"The boy is a grandchild of a friend of Lester's. They served together in one of those special units of the army. They were running reconnaissance missions and his friend fell in love with a woman who lived outside their temporary base. They had a son together. After his discharge, Lester's friend returned to Vietnam to be with her. They stayed together for many years, and their son eventually married a local girl in the village. After Lester's friend got sick from Agent Orange poisoning, he returned to the States and Lester visited him in a veterans' hospital several months before he died. He asked Lester to go back to the village and make sure his wife and son were provided for. He made Lester promise, and when Lester finally fulfilled that promise several years later, the village had been devastated by typhoid. His friend's wife and son were no longer alive, and his daughter-in-law had died three years after giving birth to another son."

"What happened to the child?" asked Wally, crossing over to the bench and sitting down.

"The child was badly neglected, partly because his features increasingly resembled his American grandfather's. Isolated and ignored, he had learned very little language. He was six or seven years old when Lester found him, an elective mute living on the edges of the village, scavenging for food, and roaming through the mountains. His face and hands had been scarred by a land mine that was set off when another child stepped on it."

"Lester brought him back here?" said Wally.

"After returning to the States, the child's fear of other people made life difficult. Lester tried to enroll him in a public school, and later he took him to several private clinics. The child resisted all the help that was offered, and after a while Lester began to resist it too. Every time the child was given a new label, his spirit dimmed further. He persisted in not speaking, and his health declined. I should also say that Lester had come to a place in his own life where all he thought about was protecting the child. You might almost say that civilization and Lester had fallen out. He'd come to the end of one phase of his life, and except for that child, he had nothing good to begin the next one with. And so he decided to keep the child beyond the grasp of anything resembling modern society. The child had already been damaged, and Lester vowed that he wouldn't be hurt again. He was also afraid that the boy's right to be in this country would be questioned, and perhaps there would be some attempt to deport him."

"So Lester came here," said Wally.

"Nature was the only thing that consistently appealed to the child, and Lester was determined to hide him in the Driftless—away from the great urban centers, hidden away from institutions and other people. He wanted him to be able to roam about as freely as he had in the mountains of Vietnam. And so Jacob helped him purchase a piece of land. Jacob also helped him register the child for homeschooling with the Department of Public Instruction, and makes sure that Lester has all the books he needs for the child's curriculum. He also helps him market his ginseng. And he still checks on them both every couple weeks."

"So Jacob knew about this child before anyone else?"

"Yes, and Lester made Jacob promise never to tell anyone. He even made him promise not to tell me, and Jacob kept that promise until very recently, when August became fascinated with the child. Jacob asked Lester if he could tell me, and when he had I went out to Lester's hut. I saw the child's room, which was clean and in good order, and I saw the medical reports from the doctors, and watched from a distance as Lester and the child conversed in sign language. It was perfectly clear to me that they are both reasonably happy."

"So Lester became a hermit and frightened people away in order to protect the child," said Wally. "All these years he's been protecting him."

"Lester worked at cultivating the image he wanted, and for the most part it worked. People stayed away. And according to Lester, living in nature—among plants, animals, and changing seasons—restored the child's intelligence and spirit. Along with his health."

"But Lester couldn't expect to hide him completely."

"He knew the child would be seen from time to time. It couldn't be avoided in the beginning. He made mistakes and once in a while someone saw him. But whenever anyone went looking for him, Lester chased them off. And as the boy became more knowledgable about the area, he was seen less and less often."

"Ivan says he and August have visited Lester's home many times."

"Lester says he's fine with the boys coming. Usually the child hides in his room, but Lester imagines that over time he will become more comfortable with them, and may even start interacting with them. But Lester wants to take it slow. Like I said, he's protective."

"Fascinating," said Wally, and wrote something in his notebook. "What does Lester call him?"

"JW."

Strawberry Wine

On the day of the wedding an ominous cloud rose out of the west. It grew darker and threatened to rain on Nate as he turned the pork over the fire pit at the end of the driveway. Several drops seared into steam as they struck the hot coals. Dart came out of the farmhouse to check on the meat sauce and yelled at the sky. By ten thirty the clouds had cleared.

Bee took over the job of roasting pork while Nate and Blake brought folding tables from the basement of Winnie's church. In the farmyard, they arranged them in lines of five around two tables that would soon hold the large platters of food: pork, barbecue chicken, corn on the cob, homemade beef bratwursts, potato salad with pickles and sweet onions, zucchini bread, green beans with almonds, baked beans flavored with maple syrup, wild Wisconsin rice, sliced tomatoes, fruit and nut pies with homemade frozen custard, and an assortment of locally made beers and wine from rhubarb, peach, apricot, and strawberry.

Dart covered each table with tightly stretched wrapping paper, and Nate and Blake went back for the folding chairs. Ivan set blue jars of wildflowers and grasses with seeded-out heads on the tables.

Guests began arriving mid-afternoon, and despite having been told that food and beverages would be provided, most of them brought something to add to the abundant feast. In a short time there was hardly any room to put plates down on the tables.

When the Roebucks arrived, Wally went directly to the roasting pig. He wanted to talk to Nate about the tail; he'd heard it had unusual properties. Ivan led Kevin across the farmyard and pointed at the grass, to the exact place where July Montgomery had died.

"And you think he was murdered?" asked Kevin.

"No doubt," said Ivan. "It was a government job."

"Why would they want to do that?"

"He knew too much. My grandfather was good friends with him, and he knew everything July did. In fact, he's lucky he's still alive. They once unloaded a truck of concrete blocks together, took them off the flatbed, one in each hand."

"Who's your grandfather?"

"He's next to the fire pit talking to Wally. That's his big rig parked over there, the one with the cool chrome horns. Want to see my new video games?"

"Sure. Where are they?"

"Inside my dad's house. Come on."

Lester Mortal arrived with the Helms. As soon as he saw him, Wally came over to talk. But Lester had been living in relative seclusion for so long that being around this many people left him looking as if he were standing in the middle of the road and watching a bus speed toward him. "I'm sorry," he said, backing away from Wally. "Give me a little time to adjust."

"No problem," said Wally. "We'll talk later."

Bud Jenks arrived with his mother and three of his cousins. Blake handed them beers from the tub, and Dart set a tray of bite-size roll-ups before them.

Several carloads of Nate and Bee's relatives arrived and immediately made themselves at home, pulling off juicy pieces of pork and eating them without plates. They all knew that Nate and Bee had been spending a lot of time together, and they couldn't help but wonder about it.

"We spent a week together in Slippery Slopes," said Bee.

"You and Nate always liked each other," said Uncle Ray. "Everyone knew that."

"We thought we'd kept it a secret," said Nate.

They all laughed.

A silver Mercedes drove down the lane and parked in the farmyard. Frieda Rampton climbed out with her husband. She looked confused and a little awkward until Amy and Buck came over, handed them glasses of strawberry wine, and sampled the pastries they had brought from a shop on the west side of Madison. Frieda's husband said he'd heard about the new prison being built outside Words, and wondered why Buck's construction company had turned down the job.

"My father's still the head of the company and he was against it," said Buck.

"Which one's your father?"

"Over there next to the roasting pig, writing in his notebook."

Dart came over and asked Frieda if she wanted to slap her again.

"No," said Frieda, laughing. "But ask me later."

"Come on," said Dart, "let me introduce you to everyone."

A blue Mercury sedan pulled into the drive. Jack Station walked over and showed Buck and Wally a picture he'd cut out of a catalog—the kind of doors he wanted on his garage. Blake met him near the food tables, shook his hand, and handed him a glass of peach wine.

About midway through everyone's first plateful of food, a motorcycle came up the road and turned down the drive, the sun reflecting off the chrome. Skeeter Skelton climbed off and Blake went out to greet him. Skeeter was wearing full leathers, a red handkerchief around his head, and an expression of windswept indifference.

"Glad you came," said Blake. "Are we still taking that ride together next weekend?"

"You bet," said Skeeter. "Do you think we should borrow a couple leisure bikes for the ride—heavy ones with loud pipes and big cushioned seats?"

"Might be a good idea," said Blake. "Have you ever heard of sour beer?"

"Of course. Do you have some here?"

"About a case of it."

"What are we waiting for, then?" said Skeeter with a smile, taking off his leather jacket.

Two cars filled with people from the church arrived next. All the women were in dresses, the men in suits or sweater vests. The new pastor introduced himself to everyone in a baritone voice, careful to make sustained eye contact.

As Nate poured another bag of ice into the beer tub, he saw something out of the corner of his eye beyond the farmhouse. When he looked up, the Wild Boy was in the hayfield at the top of the hill, watching.

Sitting at one of the tables, Bee noticed Nate's sudden interest, followed his gaze, and saw the child herself.

Across from her, August turned to see what Bee was looking at. He climbed out of his folding chair and went over to Nate.

"Do you see him, August?" asked Nate.

"I see someone or something that appears to resemble him," said August.

"He probably smelled the food from several miles away. I know wolves can do that. Let's take something up to him. Do you think he'll accept it?"

"Perhaps a bowl of fruit, nuts, and raw vegetables," suggested August. "He doesn't eat meat."

"I'll put one together," said Nate. "You take it up. I know he trusts you."

"How do you know that, Mr. Bookchester?"

"Your friend Ivan told Blake, Blake told my cousin Bee, and Bee told me."

August looked up the hill again. Then he saw Lester Mortal staring at him from the end table, a patient yet serious look on his face.

Winnie watched her son from another table. She saw the old veteran looking at August. When Lester noticed Winnie looking at him, he looked away.

Several minutes later, August took a basket of food up the hill. The child came over and they both ate a piece of fruit. August set the basket on the ground and sat beside it.

Winnie watched the other child sit next to him.

Then both children jumped up. A thin hand pushed against August's chest, knocking him off-balance. August tried to push back, but the other child was quicker and leaped back. August ran after him and the boy dashed through the alfalfa. They were both laughing, but there was something in the tone of the other child's laughter—even from this distance— that worried Winnie.

She went over to sit next to Lester Mortal, who was also watching the children while keeping a safe distance from the other guests.

"I think there's something you haven't told me yet about that child of yours," said Winnie.

"What makes you think so?" asked Lester, leaning away from her slightly.

"A friendship seems to be forming."

"Is there a problem with that?" asked Lester.

"There may be. August tends to become very involved."

"August never told me about that problem," said Lester, staring up the hill. "He's talked about a lot of things he's concerned about, Reverend Helm, but never that. He's worried about the future of bats, I know, and and the moral decline of this country. He's talked about his concerns for his friend Ivan and the health of Kevin Roebuck, and at one time he was afraid demons were immigrating into the earth and turning it into a new level of hell."

"I never heard that one," said Winnie.

"After his bat came back he never mentioned it again. He's also talked about his concerns for your own health and happiness, Reverend Helm, but he's never once mentioned wanting to be less involved."

"Call me Winnie, Lester."

"That child in the hayfield has been visiting your house for over a year, watching August. They like each other."

"I know, I know. But school is starting next week and I think it would be better for everyone concerned if, well, if August's time were devoted elsewhere."

"So you'd like for them to see less of each other?"

"I think that would be a good idea."

"It won't be nearly as easy as you think, Winnie."

"Why not?"

"For one thing, she's a girl."

"I knew it," said Winnie, gripping the table with both hands and breathing carefully. "I knew it—or at least part of me knew it. It's her laugh and the way she moves. I knew it. How old is she?"

"I don't know for sure, maybe a year older than August."

"You've made sure she looks like a boy—her hair and her clothes. You've encouraged people to think she's a boy."

"I hoped August would be less interested in her—that everyone would be less interested. I imagined that most people might tolerate a wild boy, but a wild girl, well, you know—"

"Just the idea of her would drive some folks over the edge," said Winnie, methodically tearing off small irregular pieces of the wrapping paper that covered the tabletop.

"Right," said Lester. "They'd never leave her alone."

"And apparently she didn't want to stay alone," said Winnie, looking up the hill at the two young people in the alfalfa.

"I guess not," said Lester.

Winnie put her elbows on the table and wrapped her face in her hands. "I wasn't prepared for this."

"I know," said Lester. "Me neither."

"She's a lovely creature, though," said Winnie, looking up the hill again. "I've always thought that, even when I believed she was a boy. You call her JW—what does it stand for?"

"A nickname. It stands for Jewelweed."

Skeeter went over to his motorcycle and turned the radio to a music station. At first everyone just sat there listening, but after a short while Frieda got up from the table and began dancing, her limbs moving in an entirely uninhibited way. Dart set down the tray of watermelon wedges she was carrying from the house and joined her. Then Buck joined them, and the sight of someone so big trying to dance lowered the inhibitions of those still sitting. Soon most of the guests were dancing in the driveway, including Violet Brasso.

"I didn't think this was going to be so much fun," said Frieda to Dart.

"Why not?" asked Dart.

"I didn't think I was in the right mood."

"Are you now?"

"It's the strawberry wine. Where did you get it? Is this your place?"

"In a way," said Dart. "I married into the rent."

"It's shabby, but it has potential."

"I know. Someday it's going to be really nice."

"Are you still working for Amy?"

"I'll be working for Amy when she's as old as her grandmother Flo."

"Why?"

"That's just the way it is."

Blake went over to his father's truck, found the same music station, and turned the volume up. The additional sound enlivened the dancers, and they were soon joined by several more from the tables. Ivan and Kevin came out of the house, looking for something to drink. August came down from the hayfield to get a plate of desserts. Bee walked over and poured punch into the boys' glasses.

Blake climbed down from the cab and watched the people gathered in his farmyard, thinking how nice it would be if Spinoza could join them. Blake imagined him taking off his jacket, drinking a glass of wine with Nate, sharing a piece of pie with Wally, talking with Flo, and dancing with Violet, Frieda, and Dart. And as he imagined this impossible scene, Blake found himself inside a moment of clarity. Time collapsed and all of his anxieties about the future fell away. The margins of his private life expanded to include everyone in the farmyard, and he understood that everything he could ever hope to accomplish was already contained within them. They held the limits of his freedom as well as his freedom itself. Their peace was the only kind he would ever know, and it would be enough.

Jacob walked over and stood next to him. Together they leaned against the Kenworth.

"Buck says the addition to the shop can be completed before winter, and as soon as it's done your father wants us to rebuild his diesel. Work is coming in faster than we can keep up with."

"No kidding," said Blake.

"Lester wants to hire August and Ivan to help him plant melons next spring, Jack Station wants us to put some solar panels on the roof of his new garage, and there are plans for a new prison a few miles from here."

"I heard," said Blake.

Jacob turned away. For a moment he seemed lost, wandering through the forest of some unbounded thought, staring at the piece of ground in front of the corncrib. A tiny cloud drifted aimlessly across the pale blue sky.

"Things are changing around here," he said, rubbing the back of his neck. "And with Winifred giving up preaching, I'd just like to know what's going to happen next."

"Everything that can," said Blake.

The gradual emergence of *Jewelweed*, from the bits and pieces of past events, imagined scenes, notes on the backs of envelopes, overheard conversations, dreams, and the shadow cast by fleeting premonitions, was greatly assisted by the help of many.

Edna, my wife, believed in the possibilities of a novel from the first glimmer of a story; her unflagging assurances and assistance, combined with her inspired understanding of the psychological layers behind scenes I was trying to depict, made the completion of the book possible. I am also deeply thankful for the generous encouragement and support from the John Guggenheim Foundation, whose fellowship created the much-needed space-time for the research and writing. My agent, Lois Wallace, offered welcome enthusiasm for the magical elements of the story, and Daniel Slager, my editor at Milkweed Editions, left his invaluable stamp on the text through intuitions into characters, pacing, and phrasing. Special thanks to my longtime friend James Noland, whose insights into the work of William Blake, Marcel Proust, and others led to the refinement and clarification of time-honored themes. I am also indebted to Edward Schultz for accompanying me on many difficult afternoon journeys through ideas too wide to go around and too tall to jump over.

Many others were instrumental in grounding the narrative within the real world, critiquing early drafts, offering information and recommendations, and sharing from the deep well of their own experience. Thank you, Mike Austin, Ben Barnhart, Andre Bernard, Calvin Clarke, Kate Fitzgerald, Joanne Greenberg, Darrel Hanold, Will Kilkeary, Charlie Knower, Jim and Leslie Kolkmeier, Kevin Larimer, Olive Anne Miller, Fred Milverstedt, Linda Murkin, Jan Netolicky, Paul and Karla Niederdecker, Emily Rhodes, Luther Rhodes, Alexandra Rhodes-Stanton, Paul Schaefer, Zach Schaefer, Lindel Settle, Robert Smith, Ron Stoltz, Peggy Swan, Ron Troxel, and Jim Vriesacker.

As a young man, **David Rhodes** worked in fields, hospitals, and factories across Iowa. After receiving an MFA from the Iowa Writers' Workshop, he published three acclaimed novels: *The Last Fair Deal Going Down* (1972), *The Easter House* (1974), and *Rock Island Line* (1975). In 1976, a motorcycle accident left him partially paralyzed. In 2008, Rhodes returned to the literary scene with *Driftless,* a novel that was hailed as "the best work of fiction to come out of the Midwest in many years" (Alan Cheuse). Following the publication of *Driftless,* Rhodes was awarded a Guggenheim Fellowship in 2010, to support the writing of *Jewelweed.* He lives with his wife, Edna, in Wisconsin.